HEAVEN:

HEAVEN
Experience the Extraordinary
TONY STOLTZFUS

Dedicated to:

Jeff Williams, my friend in heaven.

My wife and partner Kathy, who encouraged me to get paid for my ideas instead of my hours, and who has taken every risk with me.

The Man of Light—what more can I say than what's in this book?

Thanks to:

C.S. Lewis, who first taught me to think about heaven in his classic, *The Great Divorce.*

Jimetta, Allison, and the rest of my bible study peeps, who were a great encouragement throughout.

The Partners who have made giving so many copies of this book away a reality.

Published by Coach22 Bookstore LLC
2178 Terra Nova Drive, Redding, CA. 96003
www.HeavenExperience.net.

Cover Design by Tony Stoltzfus

Table of Contents

Introduction

It was clear from our very first conversation that Amanda's story was utterly different than any other I'd heard. Dozens before her have sat fidgeting in the worn leather chair by my fireplace, telling me how they died, how they were brought back to life, and what they saw and experienced in between. (I've sort of specialized in helping people record their near-death experiences.) Amanda's story contained familiar elements, but there was such an otherness, such a mind-bending quality to her descriptions of the Beautiful Land…I finally just put down my pen and asked.

"Amanda, this is so…my mind wasn't built to process this stuff. It's like nothing I've ever heard before! How come your heaven is so different than the ones I've heard about in a hundred other stories?"

She smiled wryly, lounging cross-wise on the armchair while warming her hands on a mug of hot chocolate to chase away the cold seeping through the cabin windows that frosty morning. Her legs were curled up under her in a way that whitened the zippered scar running from ankle to her hip—physical proof of what happened on the day of the explosion.

"Well," she began, "I guess it's about what kind of body is doing the looking. Lots of people have died from car accidents or heart attacks or drownings and visited heaven. Most of those stories are true—they saw the actual heaven, if only from a human vantage point. The reason my story is different is, um... this is going to sound strange, but those people weren't really dead."

I've since gotten used to hearing otherworldly statements from Amanda, but that one really pulled me up short. As I rose in my chair to protest, she patiently explained (in that who-could-possibly-doubt-this tone of conviction she falls into when describing the Beautiful Land) that yeah, *of course* she knew that their hearts had stopped beating or their brains had truly shut down.

"Here, Jamarcus—maybe this will help," she continued when I finally settled back in my seat. "When we say someone is 'dead,' on earth, we mean that their biological life has ended. Like when my dad died: lying there in the coffin, there was no spark of life on his face. He was merely a corpse, and all that remained for me to grieve was a pile of amino acids and household chemicals, already beginning to decay back into dust. From earth's perspective, biological death is the moment we *think* we transition to heaven."

"But from the perspective of those who dwell in the Beautiful Land, physical death is only part of a much larger process of trading up from the earthy, mortal you. You only become a full citizen of heaven when you put on your heavenly body."

She unfolded her legs and sat forward, eyes sparkling behind stray wisps of raven hair as she plunged deeper into the story. "From heaven's point of view, I didn't 'die' when my heart flat-lined after the accident, or even in the hospital when I was in a coma. The real transition came when I got upgraded to a new body, and came alive in heaven's extra dimensions as well as the familiar ones of earth."

"In the old days," I broke in, perhaps a little too quickly, "I think that was called being 'glorified'." I probably spoke up simply out of relief that I at least grasped one piece of what she was talking about.

"Yes—exactly! I like that way of putting it," she concluded, leaning back into the cushion til her long ponytail splayed across the brown leather. "To see heaven, you need heaven's senses. Until you put on your extra-dimensional body and become *part* of heaven, you might be let in for a quick stopover on a tourist visa, but you're still looking from the viewpoint of a foreigner. And like a tourist who doesn't speak the language, you are severely limited in your ability to understand the territory."

And therein lies the quandary I've faced ever since I took on the task of telling Amanda's story: I don't have the senses to really see heaven, and I don't have the language to describe it, either. How on earth would I help someone who's been blind from birth visualize a painting? Or convey the exquisite harmonies of a symphony to a deaf man, or teach a girl without a sense of smell to pick her favorite perfume? If I can't even do *that*, with the senses I do have—how can I possibly explain an extra-dimensional heaven when both you and I have never experienced more than four dimensions?

That's the un-crossable chasm fixed between this world and the next. To fully experience and understand heaven, you must undergo the radical transformation of putting on more dimensions. You have to get a lot larger to understand the largeness of heaven. But once you go through that dimensional expansion, you cross a line from which there is no return. You've become too big to ever enter back into this world and tell us about it! It would be like trying to squeeze an elephant through the eye of a needle.

I've interviewed dozens who recount hitting this boundary. They are told that their time on earth is not over, their full transition must wait, and they'll have to go back. It's painful for them, but I can understand the mercy in it. It's hard enough to experience bliss and leave it behind. But if you've put on an extra-dimensional body, you'd have to literally *amputate* parts of yourself to come back to earth. Only The Man of Light could make himself small enough to bring heaven back over that border into earth, and he did so only once.

So when a person who has died in a car crash or stopped breathing in a hospital bed shares about visiting heaven, believe it! Their story is often 100% true. *But* (and this is a big but), the picture they've brought back from the beyond is from a *human* viewpoint. If they made it back here, that means they never put on their heavenly body. They saw heaven, but only with four-dimensional vision. If you went through life seeing the world through a straw, or looking through the wrong end of a telescope, that would be a good analogy for how they saw heaven. The experience is real; the picture of heaven amazing and magnificent. But even that view of eternity is so hopelessly compressed and distorted by our human limitations that it's only a taste of the real thing.

And then there's Amanda. She 'got to heaven on a technicality' as she jokingly explains, when a physics experiment gone horribly wrong catapulted her body into hyperspace. For one tiny millisecond she was the great dimensional pioneer of the human race, the first human to exist in more than four dimensions. Then she died in the explosion.

I was there—I saw the biological Amanda lying broken in the smoking hole that had been the Research Annex, and came close to death myself, attempting ('like a fool,' the firemen chided me) to rescue her. The cool thing is, because she was in extra-dimensional space at the moment she died, she entered heaven already inhabiting more than our four temporal dimensions. She's the only person (as far as I can tell) in human history who saw heaven through heaven's eyes and came back to tell us about it.

This is usually frowned on in journalism, but for the sake of full disclosure I should tell you: I am part of this story, in more ways than one. I've known Amanda's family since she was a toddler (in those days she called me 'Unkie,' which I guess was short for uncle, although we weren't related). I watched her and her dad struggle when her mother abandoned them. I visited the cancer ward to grieve with her while her father lay dying.

We were in that same hospital again on the day of the explosion, flown there together on a medevac helicopter, the both of us with serious injuries. But it was only when she woke from a coma weeks later that she offered the first hints of what really happened.

Given our prior relationship, it's no surprise that she picked me to write her story. But I have to admit, it wasn't easy for me. This was my life's work. I'd strived for decades to reach the top of my field. And then this *twenty-something* comes along and, in a single day, becomes far more of an expert on heaven than I was. It hurt my pride.

But I don't think I ever felt talked-down-to by Amanda, even when she was relating stuff that was so far beyond me, I couldn't make heads or tails of it. The reason, I finally concluded, was that while most survivors I've interviewed badly need me to believe their stories, Amanda didn't. That longing for someone to validate a crazy near-death experience was completely absent in her. In fact, she seemed to live in a place of such deep approval that nothing in this world could shake it, and whether I believed her story or not was irrelevant. That more than anything finally convinced me her experience was completely genuine.

So this is her incredible story, shoehorned into the limited, four-dimensional language of our universe. Sorry about that! It's the best an earth-dwelling tourist like me can do.

When she chose me to write all this down, Amanda insisted

that at the very beginning I put in a note about the nature of truth on earth versus in heaven. It might explain a bit of why her story won't make sense to some, and to others will even seem heretical. Rather than try to interpret her words, I'll just quote:

> *"What is true in eight or ten dimensions is often paradoxical or even nonsensical in four. I'm not even* trying *to talk about the Beautiful Land in a way that is theologically or scientifically correct in earth terminology, because it can't be done. Heaven cannot be proved—or even accurately described—in a way that will satisfy the rational mind. You certainly couldn't have proved it to the old version of me: I was so stuck in the rational that this experience would have made no sense to me.*
>
> *"A good analogy is being in love. You can read all the text-books you want about it, but until you experience falling in love, you won't know what you are talking about. The Beautiful Land is like that: it can only truly be understood through experience—and trust.*
>
> *"Trust is the bridge between the two worlds. You have to trust The Maker, trust the creative imagination he's put in you to see beyond the limits of rationality. But even those few who still think seriously about heaven have grown afraid to let themselves imagine it—afraid to get it wrong, afraid of reaching beyond the little our forefathers wrote down to grapple with what living in eternity might actually feel like. With no* experiential *knowledge of heaven, the eternity they theologize about is limited to a set of sterilized, rational facts: accurate, yes, but not true.*
>
> *"To know only facts about heaven without experiencing it is really no better than ignorance. Heaven is the land of the heart, and a heart moving in trust can know it far more profoundly than your head can."*

Amanda's goal in telling her story is not that you would get your *facts* straight about heaven, but that you would *experience* it with your heart.

One final word. Amanda isn't her real name. She didn't want to live a life where half the people she meets think she's crazy, and the other half can't relate to her as an equal because they believe she's somebody special. I think that was a pretty wise choice. So I changed enough details about her life, the setting, and the science to preserve her anonymity. If you find technical errors in this story, that's why. I'm an English major, not a nuclear physicist!

Jamarcus Carter

1 Afterlife

"What is seen is temporary, but what is unseen is eternal."

There was a light. That was first. Watery and indistinct, it gradually sharpened into a warm, square glow. She was there and not there, her mind floating in and out of the light. The place was somehow familiar, and yet…

Her vision swam, blurring and then finally settling into focus on something she couldn't identify. She was inside some kind of box. Long and narrow, it tapered off into the distance, with regularly-spaced openings piercing each side. Her mind tilted and turned the picture, searching for the correct association. The top was bisected with a faint grid. Brilliant light streamed from the far end, fluorescing the box's sides yet somehow casting no shadows across the familiar rectangular openings.

Doors, her memory finally informed her. *The openings are for doors. I'm in a hallway.*

Amanda sighed unconsciously. She was in the Physics Building, outside the basement lab in the Research Annex where she worked. *Okay, I know this place. That must be why I feel so comfortable. I ought to: I spent more nights here than I did in my apartment over the last few years!*

It was familiar, yet not the same. The walls and ceiling rippled, focusing and scattering the pervasive light in a wash of color. *Like looking through the wavy water-glass in the office doors. This light makes it seem as if stationary objects are in motion.*

Strange. But not so it bugs me. More like fascinating, actually.

A distant part of her brain half-expected to feel pain, though she couldn't put a finger on why. Something had happened, something important had gone wrong that escaped recollection…

Oh, right—the experiment blew up. I remember now. We were running our first full-up test that night, and the instruments went haywire. Jumping out of my chair, lunging for the kill switch. A cold, blue plasma flash, silhouetting my stretching hand like a strobe. The pressure wave sledgehammering my chest. And then…just this. Quiet.

I see it now: our hubris finally caught up with us. Like little gods, thinking we could create our own lab-grown, six-dimensional universe, and answer all the big questions about space-time! The equations all made perfect sense, but did we ever think to question our motives? We were more fueled by ego than scientific discovery...at least, that's perfectly clear in hindsight. How is it that I never realized something so obvious…

As a physicist, Amanda had spent virtually all of her time contemplating the structure of the universe, and vanishingly little on the vagarities of her own emotions. The skill of hiding her feelings, then denying them altogether—she'd perfected that a decade and a half ago, when her father's death left her alone in the world.

But now things had changed. Her half-conscious, unspoken motives were playing out on a Time's Square Jumbotron in her mind, in stark, naked clarity. Yet somehow, the exposure of a long-buried part of her psyche didn't embarrass or make her self-conscious. In fact, this new clarity of motive had the opposite effect. She saw plainly how she had lived, and why she'd done what she'd done; then simply accepted those facts without guilt or recrimination. It was like examining an expired version of Amanda, which no longer required being judged, improved or fixed. The important thing was just being in the now, absorbing this moment. In the quiet.

It occurred to her that the explosion must have injured her in some way. *That was a pretty big bang, after all. It punched me clear back into the equipment racks, before everything went blank. Am I still all in one piece?*

"What does your body say?"

A quick mental scan revealed…nothing. None of her senses reported anything amiss. *And what happened to the ache in my shoulder? That's been hurting since I tweaked it in the gym. And my stress headache is gone, too! I just feel really, really…whole.*

Taking stock of her body awakened Amanda's scientific curiosity, turning her mind outward toward her surroundings. *Well—I seem to be of sound body. So let's explore the environment!*

"Yes, let's."

She reached out and tentatively brushed the textured plaster wall at shoulder height. The surface felt solid to the touch. But when her attention focused on one spot, she found herself looking right through the wall, into a small room lined with bookcases. A paper-strewn desk in the center—*ah, it's an office*—but as soon as she focused on the desk, she could see right through that, too. Then through the brick-and-mortar outer shell of the building, and out onto the towering redwood trees standing like sentinels on the quad. Scanning slowly up and down, she found that *everything*—ceiling, books, lab equipment, the floor—was transparent. The more she concentrated on a thing, the more ephemeral it became. *Like when you see something in the corner of your eye, but when you turn your full gaze toward it, it disappears. But in reverse!*

The old me would have growled, 'Hold still so I can look at you, dang it!' (Her mind was already ordering reality in terms of Before and

After the explosion.) *But I don't really feel annoyed. Not even mildly piqued—which is not like my usual intensity at all. Hmm…maybe it's because I'm not in a hurry.*

Wait—I'm not in a hurry? Now there's *something different!* The calm, shimmering Light enfolded her, and stillness came seeping into her soul. "No rush," she breathed aloud, letting the air escape from her chest. Somewhere down inside the flywheel that kept pushing to Make Something Happen slowed, and her foot slipped off the gas. She was living instead of accomplishing. Able to be still. And that was good.

Entranced, Amanda stood still for a long moment, consciously focused on doing nothing. Yesterday, that would have been a quick pause before jumping back into action. Today, pausing felt like a lifestyle.

Gosh, what's happened to me? I can't find any reason *to rush anymore. After all those years of running from meeting to conference to lab to office…what a grind! I forgot how to be quiet along the way. But now, my heart just says, 'Why bother?' I feel completely satisfied while not accomplishing a thing. I used to be so anxious about life passing me by or missing out, but I get this feeling here that I can always come back and do it later…like I have all the time in the world. Dang, this place is relaxing!*

Amanda took to this new freedom from hurry and worry as a hawk rides an updraft. Serenity was like a childhood best friend who'd moved away, whom she hadn't seen in years. Experiencing it thrust her back to long-ago days of innocent wonder: bouncing all afternoon on the trampoline, reading a good book in the little cranny under the stairs, catching toads and stashing them in the window well. The ever-urgent to-do list that commanded her days had become of no consequence, melting into nothingness instead of lying in wait to pounce on her relaxation.

Funny…I can't remember a single thing on that dang list. And it doesn't seem to matter; not at all! This is how the first day of summer vacation felt after second grade—or floating in a bubble bath all scented with lavender on Saturday morning.

Like a napping cat stirring on a sunny windowsill, Amanda luxuriously stretched her arms out in front of her, til she could see her hands—*and saw right through them!* The smooth skin of a young woman, yet it was as clear as glass. Her short fingers (they'd convinced her mother she'd never be a pianist) took on a new elegance with this delicate transparency.

I look like a light bulb! The hall and everything in it shone, and so did she, the illumination emanating from her body blending perfectly with the glorious dawn at the end of the hall. The two lights were cousins, yet each had a blend of hues uniquely its own.

Amanda rotated her wrist until she could see her palm. The kaleidoscopic light passed through skin, muscles and bone like an x-ray, streaming out untouched on the other side. Hues she'd never seen before—maybe whole new dimensions of color—jumped out from beneath her skin. The 'blues' (much more than blue, but that was all she could think to call them) were fun and adventurous; the reds made you want to jump for the stars, while the greens felt calming and peaceful.

In other circumstances, realizing she was suddenly see-through would have been a jolt. Today, she wasn't bothered in the least. In fact, she quickly decided, it felt perfectly normal. *Everything else here is transparent. Everything else here glows. So why shouldn't I?*

Fingers

I wonder what it's like to get a suntan on your ulna? Amanda imagined placidly, observing her arm bones fluoresce in the light. *You get so used to your skin being between you and everything else, and whatever is inside you being unseen*…yet still she was unafraid.

So…is this a dream?

"Not in the slightest."

That's right—it's too real for that, she decided. *I'd never come up with stuff like this! Honestly, I bet* this *is reality, and my old life was the daydream. Here I'm living in color, and my past is black and white.*

Amanda twisted a forearm this way and that. The light gushed through her without pause, touching her and yet itself untouched. As soon as she began to ask, "Why is that?" the answer came to her.

"To the physical body, the light acts like neutrinos, that can shoot right through the center of the earth and come out the other side without hitting anything."

That's it! Amanda exulted. *With virtually no mass or charge, 100 trillion neutrinos a second could rocket through my body and not interact with any of my cells.* But glimpsing her wrist brought to mind a more mundane thought. *I seem to have lost my wristwatch,* she pondered, more amused than upset. *Even the un-tanned patch underneath the band is missing.*

Amanda was of a generation that generally shunned watches, preferring to consult their ever-present smartphones. But she stubbornly persisted in wearing one because, a) it was two seconds faster than pulling an iPhone from her pocket to check the time; b) wearing time on her wrist made her feel like a Lord of Time—that the clock was her slave and not her master; and c) her daddy gave her a Timex on her tenth birthday and seeing a watch reminded her of the good old days.

But there was no trace of the watch—or any internal recriminations for losing that precious reminder of her father. *My dad…* she smiled, feeling the sensation of being held and treasured, being safe in his arms. Suddenly a new insight struck her, like a lightning bolt arcing down a power pole. *Hey, wait! I can* feel *that memory! I feel everything!*

The emotions had been so raw at daddy's funeral; the loss of her only remaining parent too overwhelming. To go on, she locked emotion out, willing the pain into a hole deep in her heart. Then she pulled the cellar door shut, strung caution tape over it and bolted grief into a basement dungeon. Over time, reopening that door seemed more and more intimidating. Who knew what emotional dragon dwelt within, ready to explode out of its cage and set her life on fire? Better to just move forward and keep those unmanageable feelings locked in a prison of numbness.

Somehow her emotions had broken free from that prison, yet the dragon didn't appear. *Gosh—feeling again actually feels pretty good. A delight, even. That's something I never expected! What was I so afraid of?*

"You hid from what was too big for you to face. But you are much larger now, and the thing you feared is so small it has shrunk to nothing. Like the watch."

That's a new thought. But it sounds right, Amanda thought, still hunting for the faint shadow of a tan line on her wrist. But there was none. Letting go (without recognizing how unlike her it was to leave a question unanswered), a new wonder captured her: the refraction patterns produced by her overlapping fingers. Fascinated, she wiggled them, giggling as the light from within formed shifting moiré patterns in the air. As her attention lingered on that one spot, a story began forming in Amanda's mind.

Hey! I see my fingers practicing on my old flute in high school! It's got that same dent on the barrel from running into one of the drummers in marching band. And there I am picking flowers behind the house on Edgewood Street, back when I was 12 or 13. That was years ago, yet I feel like I'm right there.

Scene after scene cascaded into her brain, brighter than memory, as if she had left the present and was reliving her past instead of merely recalling it. She saw her fingers folding paper airplanes; putting groceries away in the fridge with mom; petting Jock, their clumsy fur-ball of a kitty.

Then, from even further back, a long-forgotten moment showered her heart with happiness. *Look! My little toy horses! There's Tobie the stallion, and Jenny the mare, and their foal Theo, named after daddy. I thought we lost them forever when we moved! And those little wooden fences I got on my fourth birthday—I can feel my toddler fingers doggedly joining them into corrals for that tiny herd. I had* so *much fun with those horses…*

Amanda paused for a moment to soak in the aura of innocent contentment. *Looking into my hand is like gazing back in time! It's so real—every sight and sound as sharp and crisp as if I'm right there. This has to be more than mere remembering. I'm actually present, reliving each moment with the same sensations and feelings I had the first time.*

Refocusing on her hand, she saw something new, and almost unrecognizable. Like a piece of pink cauliflower—just a tiny palm, sprouting stubby nubs of rose-red fingers, their veins pulsing through the skin. *Oh my gosh, that's me in mom's womb! How can I be seeing that? It's me before I was ever born!*

"But you were there. All memory is recorded, even those your brain forgot. It is preserved for you to enjoy forever."

The answers just came to her, as soon as a question was asked. Natural as breathing, insight flowed into her mind without drawing attention to itself. The sensation was so comfortable, so normal, that Amanda didn't stop to wonder if a voice other than her own had spoken.

Undistracted, she kept turning her palm this way and that, captivated by the vision. *It's as if the whole history of my hand from infancy to adulthood is told in the light flowing out of it.* Pondering, she looked away, down to the polished granite floor. As the cool, bluish light from the stone held her gaze, a different story crystalized in her mind. She felt calloused hands shaping the block's smooth surface, bedding it in grout with its neighbors. Further in, she witnessed the slab raised groaning from the quarry, before being sliced by a diamond saw. Suddenly, the picture leaped eons back in time, to where the stone rested under a mountain, waiting, as tons of rock above eroded away a tiny chip at a time, finally exposing it to the light.

Then: the beginning. And she was there. Lying in the dark heart of the earth, she felt continents squeeze ancient rock into molten magma, then thrust it up, erupting, cooling, hardening into new-born granite. It was as if she had crystallized alongside that stone, lingering with it through millennia for this moment: to be felt, and seen, and known.

Lost in the joy of exploration, Amanda simply gazed around her at one thing after another, listening intently to the story told by each object's inner light. To learn, to know—it fed a yawning hunger within her. Her happy place was soaking up information, and she was never more at peace with herself than curled up with an interesting book (science or history—she never wasted time on fiction) and an afternoon to digest it. Knowing made her feel safe and secure.

Amanda constantly sucked in knowledge; yet didn't really understand her compulsion to do so.

Inside Information

Piercing the brick and ivy shell of the building once more, Amanda's new-found vision settled on the tall redwoods outside. She had a favorite spot on the carpet of needles underneath that one on the left, where she'd slog through physics papers until her eyes couldn't focus any more. Then her imagination would drift off to Paris—or better yet, Venice. The idea of a city with streets made of water and boats for taxis fascinated her.

The towering redwood's luminous, green heart sang her a song of growth, from falling cone to tiny seed to mighty giant. But her more-than-human sight went far deeper than what photons falling on her retina could reveal.

I'm not just seeing the tree now, or even all its history: I'm living its life, *from the inside! I can cradle the mitochondria in each hand, and watch those cells divide. Or I can take the slow journey up the trunk with the sap, drawn by transpiration, feeling the water passing upward through the xylem tubes, or marinate in the sprouting of new needles, or the slow expansion of the bark.*

The scientist in her reveled. *This is incredible!* Everything *here is transparent to my understanding. I'm not just reading about trees in a book—I know what it is like to* be *the tree. Experiencing a redwood from the inside instead of just touching the bark is going to take science to a whole new level. My old, familiar tree—now replaced with one that can think and feel and talk to me!*

Or…maybe there's a different angle? she pondered, her mind switching points of view. *What if it's the* light *that's changed, instead of the tree, or even my eyes? Now that's a mind-bender. I wonder…*

On earth, light bounces off things. You see the bark, not the heartwood, because it's on the surface. But here, light goes right through walls or floors or trees—even through me! The more I focus on the light coming out of an object, the more I learn about that thing, but the less solid it looks. And the light doesn't seem to be altered much by what it penetrates. Like the neutrino analogy, except here the light illuminates anything it passes through…

Then suddenly, as if her mind had finally adapted to her new environment, her perspective turned on its head. *Wait! It's the* light *that is solid and physical and real, and the tree ephemeral! The light has substance and heft; in the same way a wooden chair you sit on is solid. The tree is still real, I think, but the light is…more real?*

"Yes. The light inhabits a larger space than the physical object."

That's it! This place I'm in is built of light! The rocks and trees and walls of the physical world I lived in are like air here—a mere medium the light travels through and displaces. The light is solid as a rock, yet the trees transient as clouds.

As her point of view shifted, so did her vision. Where before she saw shadowy physical objects that seemed lit from within, now she saw beams and walls and surfaces constructed of light itself. Light passed through walls and desks of the old material world as if they were smoke, the substantial character of the light revealed when it was scattered and refracted by the diaphanous physical objects it pierced. And whenever she paused to watch the light touching an object, she heard that object's story

So, the light is a solid, and all the familiar stuff of the physical world—including my own body, for heaven's sake—is...a gas?

"Say rather that your true self is no longer hidden from view, locked within the shell of your body. The physical you remains a solid in earth's dimensions, but your soul moves freely in the broader space of The Light."

Amanda wasn't quite sure what to make of that idea. After pondering for a moment, she finally decided: *Well, however you say it, it's totally foreign to anything I've ever known—and totally amazing!*

Need to Know

Wait a sec! I'm in a place where light is a solid and my body has the properties of a gas. There isn't anywhere in the known universe like that. Does that mean...am I dead? As the question coalesced in Amanda's mind she was surprised that she hadn't thought of it earlier.

"What do you think?"

Well, I'm not sure what 'dead' feels like—I don't have any prior experience to compare it to. But something definitely ended and something new began, she mused, examining the problem from a rational, scientific perspective. *I still have some kind of a body that I control. At least, I think so...*

She paused for a quick experiment. Ordering her head to swivel left, it promptly did. A second command, and it spun rightward, just as predicted. *Okay, I can tell my body what to do. It sees and hears, just way differently than before. I can remember my past, too. So, I am still me. I can still think...Oh!*

A smile spread across her face as a moment from Philosophy 101 sprang into her head. '*Cogito, ergo sum: I think, therefore I am,'* she chuckled, quoting Descartes. *"We cannot doubt of our existence while we doubt."*

"Excellent. Dear René would have been closer to the mark if he had said, 'I trust, *therefore I am. We cannot doubt our existence while we trust.' But he was on the right track. Earthy language is very imprecise in*

this sort of thing."

Huh? Amanda puzzled, her train of thought interrupted. *That took a strange turn! My mind acts as if I knew the man, but he was dead centuries before I was born. So, does thinking mean I'm alive, or trusting?*

"Is being alive what matters, or how you define life?"

Oh. I guess being alive would have to come before thinking about what it means. So the fact that I'm asking the question proves I exist either way?

"That makes rational sense."

Well, whatever. I guess what is, is; and whether I understand it doesn't change the fact of being dead or alive. With that statement, her questions about death melted away and she didn't bother with them anymore. And again, she didn't notice how unlike her that was.

From her first story books and visits to the zoo, Amanda was a child with a million questions, asking a daddy who seemed to have an answer to each and every one. After his death that need to know took on a harder edge, became almost a demand—she *had* to understand why things were the way they were. A problem with no solution left her tossing and turning at night, her mind a hamster wheel spinning in endless cycles, unable to rest. But Amanda hadn't thought to question her underlying motivation, or to explore *why* she so badly needed to know.

The answer to that unasked question brooded in the recesses of her psyche, as an unspoken belief: *if I can understand the world, I can protect myself from it.* It was a belief born of experience, not rational analysis. Her dad had been her champion and protector, and many of her fondest memories of their relationship involved learning: sitting in his lap reading together, discussing how ketchup was made over a burger at Dairy Queen, visiting a Civil War battlefield. He'd always encouraged and loved her active mind. In those times she'd felt valued and important.

But the champion who loved her had fallen in a grim battle with cancer, leaving an ulcer on her soul. To fill the void, her beleaguered heart set out on an unconscious quest to win back what it had lost. The weapon she chose for the fight was her sharpest: her rational, scientific mind. And the shield she carried was her most impenetrable: emotional numbness.

Amanda had arrived here fully equipped for battle—only to discover that this new world had no enemy to vanquish. Security, love and value were free for the taking. Knowledge was only a question or observation away. Yet she still pursued them with the intensity of an addict craving a hit. Nothing here could harm her, but her subconscious still busied itself plotting escape routes and packing parachutes, fighting to control the outcome no matter what. Though her foe had vanished, the belief that another shoe was about to drop lived on deep within her soul.

But closer to the surface, unbidden shoots of emotion were springing up everywhere. Peace whispered in her ears. Joy caressed her limbs. The numbness was draining rapidly away. At the feeling level, she was beyond good.

This must be what letting down your guard feels like, Amanda realized. *How friggin' long has it been? Ten years? Twenty? Yeah, it was back before mom ran off, when I was ten. It feels good, like everything else here.*

This whole place seems fundamentally good, in the way a mother nursing a baby is good, or a man throwing a tennis ball for his retriever is good. It's beyond simple morality: something more like wholesomeness. Even the air exudes a pure, pervasive kindness. Whatever this world is that I've fallen into, it's certainly free of cares. In fact, I'm not even sure you even could *be afraid here.*

But the thought of old fears caused Amanda to pick up her sword again, and the questioning part of her scientific mind revived. *Could it really be true? Am I actually in a place without fear?*

Fearless

After a moment's rumination, Amanda decided to test the proposition experimentally. *Okay, what's something I'm scared of?*

That was easy. Fear of failure had been a constant companion in her life, especially failures of integrity (although deciding it didn't matter if you were dead or not kind of took the edge off the smaller things). The idea of being 'bad,' of doing the wrong thing, threw her heart into bouts of inner agony until she found a way to fix it.

These fears had even invaded her sleep; in the form of repeating nightmares she took to calling her 'failure dreams'. In one she promised to go in and cover a friend's shift at work. But running into obstacle after obstacle, she arrived to find the shift was already over and her friend gone: fired. In another she played center back for her soccer team in the championship game, and every clearance she attempted ended up as an own-goal.

The worst was the 'chase dream.' It started with her making some minor mistake, and then THEY were after her. Soon she'd be leaping neighborhood fences and crashing through hedges, fleeing through the night on a continuous surge of adrenalin. All the while her unseen pursuers got closer and closer, her fear growing apace. She'd waken afterward in a sweat, panting like she'd actually been on the run.

Okay, that's a good test case, Amanda thought, attempting to put herself into the nightmare. She tried to visualize fleeing down a dark alley—but as soon as she did the sun came out, flashing off clean brick walls on either hand, topped with lush trumpet vines and flowering wisteria. The asphalt transformed into a carpet of lush green grass, the black sky flushed blue, and her pursuers ran up to kiss her hand and give her hugs.

That was weird. I'll have to try again. This time the image was seven-year-old Amanda crawling through a dark, echoing storm drain a friend had coaxed her into, despite her father's admonition to keep out. She tried to recall the cold feeling of being lost underground, disobedient, of spiderwebs sticking to her face...but immediately the tunnel opened out into a sports stadium, a perfectly-manicured greensward surrounded by a brick-red oval under a brilliant sky. Her spikes crunched on the cinder track as she crossed the finish line, breaking the tape with hands. A rain of applause fell on her from the stands, where her dad yelled approval from the first row of the bleachers.

"So it's really true!" Amanda clapped her hands in ecstatic surprise. "You literally can't be afraid here!"

"Fear is an emotional response to what is dark and painful. Because there is no darkness here in The Light, there is no corresponding emotion of fear."

Wow! I'll never have to be afraid again! I can definitely live with that. But—fear sure disappeared easily. Why is it so toothless here when it is so powerful on earth?

"The emotions that won't go away are the ones that come from being triggered—that originate with unhealed memory and not present events. In the beginning, you were created to feel; life on earth taught you to be triggered."

Oh, that's right. Memory makes a rut in your brain: a neural pathway representing the event, which gets stronger the more you use it. The brain is physically rewired by trauma.

"And this world has restored your mind back to its original, unwounded design."

"Amazing—a mental reboot!" Amanda exulted aloud. She looked down at her torso, glowing with an inner luminance that blended with the greater light all around her. "And a physical one, too." Then she laughed. "Yup—I still look like a lightbulb. I'm in The Light, and I *am* a light! Or maybe: 'I am *enlightened!*'"

The pun seemed hilarious to her at that moment, and she laughed again at how well it captured the truth. *It works both ways—I am enlightened because my body emits light, and also because whenever I look at an object, its light tells me its story. I guess The Light of heaven has become a part of me. Or—this is better—I've become part of it.*

"Yes, you have! What a delight!"

Amanda pirouetted with glee, holding out both her arms to let the light within form swirling patterns in the air between them. *The Light is everywhere and in everything, above all, and in all, and through all—including in me. Awesome!*

2 Dimensions

The air around her grew brighter, closer, as she again started moving purposefully up the hall. Amanda felt cradled in a womb of radiance, happy and at peace.

Wow! This world shines with every hue I've ever known…and infinitely more new ones. It's as if each color on earth has expanded into a whole galaxy of shades—a million purples, all different, a whole spectrum of reds, plus dozens of new primary colors…it's as if earth's palette was limited to just black and white!

Or maybe, she pondered, spinning the thought back and forth in her mind like a Rubik's cube, *color on earth is like a two-dimensional shadow of a three-dimensional object…*as soon as she thought in terms of dimensions, she remembered her father's book, and understood.

Her dad had given her a quirky old volume on her 15th birthday called *Flatland*, saying it was one of his all-time favorites. A love story written in the 1850's, of all things. Amanda never would have bothered to crack the faded brown cover if it wasn't for his obvious excitement. That night in bed she began to read, and with each turning page she became more enamored.

Flatland took place in an imagined universe of only two

spatial dimensions instead of our three (earth has three space dimensions plus one time dimension, for a total of four). The inhabitants of Flatland experienced forward and back, and left and right (two dimensions), but *not* up and down. The entire Flatlander universe was an atom-thin layer on a tabletop. Nothing above or below that infinitesimally-thin plane existed or could exist in Flatland—their entire universe had no thickness at all.

The difficulty in envisioning the two-dimensional Flatlander world, Amanda learned, is that the human brain is built to think in three spatial dimensions. When she first read the book, she automatically filled in space above and below Flatland, seeing it as a 2-D plane floating inside our familiar 3-D world. Her immersion in university physics finally helped her see Flatland as its mythical inhabitants did: with no concept of space above and below it. Everything that exists for the Flatlanders is within their infinitely-thin layer, *including space itself*. Even the words 'above' and 'below' didn't exist in their dialect.

Years later she was surprised to find this 150-year-old-book was a part of her physics curriculum. The problems the Flatlanders had in relating to an unknown third dimension were the same ones real physicists faced when positing a cosmos of more than four. Some theories held that the universe had as many as thirteen spatial dimensions—try describing *that* using a brain fine-tuned for only three! Flatland taught Amanda how to think about extra-dimensional space.

And now I'm *a Flatlander just like them, catapulted into a world of more than earth's four dimensions. That's why the colors here are so rich: they inhabit a larger space. You can map earth's color wheel on an x and y axis, a 2-D plane like Flatland. But this! It's not just two-dimensional,* RGB *color—it's like* RGB *squared. Maybe even cubed.*

Amanda halted for a moment, captivated by the rush of discovery. *Earth has only three dimensions, plus time as a fourth, but this place has more. Is it six? Eight? Eleven? The Professor was right!*

Who cares how many it is: it's totally awesome either way!

From the moment Amanda realized she was in an extradimensional world, she saw everything differently. The hallway, the trees, her body—the stuff from earth, ordinary physical stuff, still had the three familiar physical dimensions. But The Light clearly had more.

So: The Light can rotate in hyperspace to pass right through 3-D objects without touching them, just like the theory predicted—or it can *touch them, and refract into the spectacular colors I see, or even reveal stories.*

Stories…now that detail is really interesting. What I call 'seeing a story' is seeing (or reliving—it's the same thing) the entire lifespan of a thing all at once. Peering at a tree reveals its whole existence from seed to maturity. If I examine my hand—Amanda held it up in front of her face, seeing again the toy horses, and the wonder of her tiny fingers growing in her mother's womb—*yup, I am right there, reliving each moment in technicolor. Apparently, The Light sets me free in the time dimension: I can be in any time I choose, or in all times at once.*

My undergrad physics prof used to say that a dimension is just a unique direction—like back and forth or up and down. Earth has only one time dimension, so earth-time is a line, like following a path through a forest. Each step forward is the next moment, and one moment—one step—always follows another.

But here I can turn around and walk the time path in reverse, like when I looked into my hand. I relived the more recent events first, and the one when I was in the womb as the last. I can run earth-time in reverse! I wonder what other time-tricks I can do?

Holding her hand up to her face, she retrieved the pictures she'd seen of its history once again. Experimenting, Amanda found that by moving her focus around her timeline, she could relive those memories in any order. She played the toy horses memory back over and over, just to prove it could be done (and because it was such a sweet feeling). For fun, she tried speeding up a memory, like fast forward (it worked). Her next idea was slow motion, which turned out to be hilarious—like a Fail Army video on YouTube—then running a memory backwards. As things got more and more fantastical, Amanda managed to put herself into two, then three events simultaneously. And then something completely other: she zoomed up above her own timeline, where she could observe each step on the path of her existence all at once.

Hey, I'm looking down on my timeline like you would from one of those camera drones, interacting with time from a different direction: from above. But if directions are dimensions, and I'm experiencing time in more than one direction…that means I'm in more time dimensions than on earth! Is that possible?

"The Light flows through multiple time dimensions, while earth has only one. Therefore, all moments in earth time are freely accessible in The Eternal Now. From within The Light they appear as one unified, infinite moment."

Hey—that's like a time machine! What a hoot! Amanda exulted. But the time machines she'd read about in Sci-Fi books or seen at the movies still kept you trapped inside one-dimensional earth-time. You could visit any point in the past or future—but still only one moment at a time.

"But this time machine is soooo much awesomer!" Amanda gushed aloud, her enthusiasm causing her to lapse into a childhood expression her dad always found comical. *With multiple time dimensions...it's like that poster Mrs. Jones had in seventh grade, of the timelines of all the great civilizations laid out next to each other. Earth time looks like a poster on the wall here, that you take in all at once. That would mean…here it makes no sense to talk about past or future in the way I've always known. All moments are equally accessible, in any order.*

It took her a few minutes to absorb what she had just experienced. The implications were almost too much; they made her want to laugh and cry and jump for joy.

Just imagine—I am off the clock, for forever! No more fear of missing out, no more deadlines, no hurry. And no calendars—every day is today. Wristwatches are gloriously useless when every moment is now. And every nanosecond lasts as long as I want it to. I'll never run out of time again!

Boy, what a difference it makes to escape the trap of earth time: only one fleeting moment after another after another. I can march to my own drummer. There's no pining for yesterday or wishing it was tomorrow—I can just jump to the moment I want to be in immediately. Every sweet memory can be relived anytime; and any dream I anticipate is fulfilled today. Talk about a superpower! I'm free!

Amanda breathed in freedom, breathed it out, relaxing into the unhurried pace of The Eternal Now. She'd never realized until that moment what a weight time had been on her shoulders, or how much anxiety it brought into her life. Her wristwatch had let her pretend to be a 'Lord of Time'; this was the real thing.

Oh! And that's how I know the whole history of what I am looking at—because I experience all times at once, she reasoned, more soberly now. *In one moment of the Now I can enter into the whole existence of anything, to feel it, live it, and understand it fully. That must be what creates the incredible sense of oneness here. I am myself, and yet I, I...*she struggled for words.

"Here all things move in harmony, joined as one yet unique in being. You can enter into and share the life of all other things, become one with them, know fully and be fully known, and yet still be uniquely yourself."

'Know fully and be fully known': that was the part that hit her. Her heart soaked in it, basking in a sense of completeness that was as refreshing as cold mint tea with lemon on a hot summer day. The desire to know that had driven her to become a scientist, that had guided so many of her choices in life, was actually a longing for *this* profound oneness. Here one could really know. Here was the desire of her heart, full strength, good beyond hope and inexhaustible. *To know and be known...*not the self-protective kind of knowing that kept her in control, but a being known that was open to love and had no fear. She had been pursuing this tantalizingly conceivable-but-unreachable goal since childhood, somehow understanding in her heart that it was real even while it always remained beyond attainment.

But here my dream is reality. This is home. I was made to know fully and be fully known. She breathed in The Eternal Now again, deeply, and held her breath as if to gather it to herself forever.

Senses

In that moment her eyes first became aware of a scent: a wild, lovely, subtle sensation perfuming the air. It was such a natural awareness that it took a moment for the idea to really hit her. *Wait, am I* seeing *a smell? That doesn't make any sense!*

Although Amanda didn't understand, it felt right. So, shrugging her shoulders, she simply stood there and took it in. Every flower she'd ever known, distilled and blended together, couldn't even come close to this. Struggling to attach a word to it, what popped into her head was a surprise—*it smells like love.*

To her scientist-mind, that made no more sense than seeing a smell, but somehow her heart knew that she had struck very near the truth. For a few minutes she concentrated on just experiencing that blissful perfume, letting it fill her. Amanda quickly decided this was deeper than mere emotion, because it filled more than just her feelings.

Aaaah—it's the scent of longing, of desire! Not the kind of empty craving for someone you feel on earth, or your body yearning for sexual gratification, but the pure, distilled, underlying desire for love, utterly fulfilled.

"You are desired, and made for desire, and made to desire. And all desires rolled into one seek love."

An extravagant longing leapt up from deep within her in response to those words, a wild, romantic yearning like two long-lost lovers running toward each other across a flowered field and tumbling into waiting arms. Desire revealed itself to her in full for the first time, clothed with the deepest needs of the human psyche: belonging, significance, goodness, security, justice, approval, recognition, and more. The extravagant love that songwriters celebrate and poets despair of conveying was here for the asking. No lover on earth could touch her desire to be cherished like this. No safe room would ever offer this security; no award or accomplishment hope to match this significance. And it was all contained in a scent.

I guess this is why we have flowers at weddings, Amanda decided a moment later. *Their perfume kindles in the deep places of our souls this forgotten aroma of filled desire. And maybe that's why flowers were created in the first place—they remind us of true love.*

Breathing in was truly a feast—after a few minutes you felt fully satisfied. *Like setting down your fork after a wonderful meal from a top chef who gets the bake just right. Completely sated.*

Thinking about food, it suddenly occurred to her: *I can* taste *the scent, too! Oh, man! It melts in your mouth like a fresh peach, or a wave of flavor rolling across your tongue.* She curled her tongue as if to cradle it there, to hold the wave where she could savor it best—and realized the flavor wasn't just in her mouth! *This is amazing! I taste it in my elbows. I relish it with my toes! But how?*

"The five human senses are tuned to the outer shell of a thing—just as on earth you see a person's skin or hair, but their thoughts are hidden. But the one greater sense from which those lesser ones draw is tuned to The Light, which penetrates all. The Light seeks out desire in the deepest well of the soul; while the human soul yearns for The Light that fills it. Where those two meet is bliss."

"Well, I've got to say," Amanda pondered aloud, "bliss is sure a good word for that taste! Or maybe ecstasy. I've been longing for that kind of joy all my life, but never found it til now. Oh—maybe because I needed these new senses to perceive it."

Yeah, that makes a lot of…sense, she added, chuckling at her own pun. *This one greater sense doesn't depend on physical organs like ears or a nose to function—the awareness just comes directly into your brain. But I wonder: why is it tuned to something so ethereal as desire?*

"Desire is what this universe was built for: the desire to give and receive love. Love is the center. It is the fundamental force holding this universe together."

"Gosh, that's a whole new way of thinking!" Amanda exclaimed, scratching her ear reflexively (although it didn't itch). "Love as a fundamental force, like electromagnetism or gravity, integrated into the fabric of the universe…wow."

"Okay, I'll buy that," she agreed simply, accepting an enormous paradigm shift without the feeling of dislocation she would have wrestled with for days on earth. Then an image entered her mind, of raising her hand in class to elucidate this new truth. She immediately broke out laughing again. *Imagine trying to explain THAT to my profs back on earth!*

*Back on earth…*suddenly a new realization slammed into her head. *This place has new dimensions. It has new fundamental forces. It's made of light, not physical stuff. I'm…I'm in a whole different universe! I've left my old universe and everything I know behind, probably forever. Where the heck am I?*

The Voice

Where am I? Is this…am I in heaven?

"You are on the road that leads to it."

I'm on the road to heaven. That sounds like good news! Amanda exulted. Although she had believed in God and heaven since she was a kid, at times she doubted whether this would be her final destination. Or if it existed at all. *Well: it* does *exist! And I actually made it here!* Amanda thought, a bit self-satisfied.

"You might put it that way. Or you could say that I *actually made it here, and brought you with me. Or that I actually made* what *is here, and am sharing it with you. Or even that I actually made you, and you are inheriting life-that-never-ends from me here. Or all three of those ideas at once."*

With a shock, Amanda realized for the first time that something other than her own mind had been speaking. *It's The Light! The Light has a voice!* In a flash the entire conversation rewound in her head, and she recognized that this Voice had been speaking with her ever since she awoke to The Light; and that it loved her, and knew.

Like a ship shuddering from the impact of a rogue wave, Amanda's mind momentarily jolted to a halt. And she hung there for a long moment, on the verge of an insight that made her old way of thinking seem like blindness.

Recovering, she finally whispered aloud, "Who are you?"

A pause, while the world around her seemed to vibrate in anticipation. "I AM."

The words were audible; as wide and deep and somber as eternity. They hung in the air for a moment, rumbling in her eardrums. What came into her was more than sound—it was knowledge, in distilled form. She found herself floating inside the vastness of that identity, tumbling in the crashing wave of its import, thrust under by its sheer breadth. She was a dust mote, and The Voice was vast and unending, beyond comprehension.

Then a brilliant light flashed around her in the frothing water, reflected out in colors beyond color to illuminate the universe with love and laughter. All things bowed to that Light, and they sang for joy. And she drank the water of those words until they became part of her.

"I AM who I AM," The Voice spoke aloud again. This time it was a gentle ripple crossing a still pool deep inside her, an intimate soulmate to her soul. And she understood in that calm that she was dear to The Voice, and a piece of that great heart was within her and went with her everywhere, forever. A sigh rose unbidden in her chest, breathing out a lifetime of rejection to receive that she was cared for. She was a child again, at rest in a mother's arms, secure under a father's gaze, belonging as surely as a newborn to its parents.

"I AM."

When The Voice spoke a third time, the roaring wave and

the rippling calm joined into a great, clear river: a river made of life. Those three waters surrounded her, luring her heart into their laughing flow. The Voice was in the water, the water was Light, and The Light was in her and through her and for her. All three together were Life. Amanda drifted there amidst light dancing on water; and was at home in the One Home.

Gazing upon that river, she began to perceive the story behind The Voice. Far back in time and space she observed a world, formless and void, hanging solitary in a black emptiness pinpricked with distant stars. A darkness wrapped around it, shrouding the planet like a sable blanket. Then The Voice spoke: "Let there be light!" Over eons that dark veil gradually melted, from opaque to translucent to transparent, and light shone in that world's sky. Life caressed its waters.

An age passed. Then land slowly rose above the marching seas, its hills and valleys carpeted with a spreading green. Plants grew, and trees. Then animals, birds, insects in their myriads reared up out of the ground to populate that blue globe until, faint and far away yet borne on a great radiance, a man and a woman appeared on the earth, hand in hand, resplendent in their humanity.

Yet the great, black cloud still brooded out in space, hungry for vengeance. Returning as a monstrous hurricane encircling the green world, it wrapped the planet in confusion and despair. She cried out in disbelief and sadness, for in grief too great for words, Amanda saw the man and woman run from The Light, embrace the darkness and die, their bodies dissolving into the dirt from which they were made. The black ones laughed in triumph as the world settled into darkness, the very mountains and hills mourning as their life-source dried up like a summer arroyo.

Yet far above it all The Light was not dimmed, nor its joy defeated. Love put on a physical form and lanced the darkness, coming relentlessly down—down an endless distance through space and time, shedding dimensions as he came, until The One took human form on that planet as The Man of Light.

He shone like a star on the surface of the world, and the darkness around him was troubled. Amazed, Amanda watched him give his own life-light to the first man and woman, and they revived. And she sang for joy at the rebirth of the man and the woman, as that impossible sacrifice took root on the earth and began to blossom; but she cried out in shock and grief as The Man of Light, after surrendering his life-light for them, blazed out and was extinguished. At his passing the black ones tore fiercely across the sky, screaming in triumph, nearly swallowing the world in a black hole of their need to dominate and to rule. Heaven stood silent and time held its breath, waiting, watching.

Yet before that planet spun three times, beyond all hope or expectation, The Man of Light reappeared, torn free from the belly of the earth by grip of The One. He rose, blazing in radiance greater than before, waxing stronger and stronger as he donned all his former dimensions. The brilliance of his face was beyond seeing, and the black ones could not meet his gaze. And in that glory he stood, one foot planted on earth and one in heaven, his own body a great bridge of light between the old world and the new.

The inky darkness encircling the world was ripped down the middle, unmendable, The Light piercing it through with a thousand spears. Then, as Amanda watched breathlessly, The Man of Light gathered all other lights to himself, and brought them to The One, singing the greatest music yet heard in heaven. And as The Light of Heaven married the lights of earth, even The One himself increased in beauty, honor and strength as created joined with uncreated to celebrate his triumph.

In a far corner of that picture, Amanda witnessed the dark flee out of time and space at the blazing return of The Man of Light. The universe no longer contained a place for evil to be, as if the very space it inhabited snapped out of existence. The black ones were no more. Then, fully clothed in both his earthly and heavenly dimensions, The Man of Light, the conqueror of death and lover of all, took his seat at the head of a banquet of endless life.

That whole arc of history came into her, and taught her, and held her. On earth her head would have exploded with the knowledge, as she saw—no, lived! —history in a single moment. Amanda fell flat on the ground, undone. Her only conscious thought was amazement and gratitude.

3 The Story

"Come," The Voice rumbled gently, raising her from the ground. Amanda couldn't figure out if a hand had come down and lifted her bodily, or if the power she felt trembling in that word floated her off the ground by itself. But she found herself standing, left her questions behind, and came.

That indescribable voice! It staggered her, overwhelming as it passed into her, warming and informing and filling. It was like someone asking a question at the dinner table just after she'd taken a big bite of steak—she had to chew and swallow before she could get enough of her wits around her to reply. The Voice was a giant blue wave, a rolling 100-foot breaker of power and majesty, and she a kayak staggering up the face of that immense liquid cliff, a fleck of foam on the ocean of its knowledge.

And yet The Voice spoke softly and intimately, affection flooding through every word, as if walking and talking with a dear friend. The sensation made her want to dive in and drown herself inside that love forever.

From the first, Amanda felt as if she had always known The Voice. And after experiencing the story of The Man of Light, she understood why. *The Light, The Voice and The Man of Light in the vision are all one! They're a person made of persons, all three together forming the I AM. This life flowing in my veins comes from them, too. They made me. I know my Creator by the marks his hands left on my soul. I am his work of art.*

On earth, she'd always thought life came from a seed, a spore, an egg, or from cell division. Life was merely chemistry. Each living thing had its own independent spark of life, passed down to it by living ancestors. Where that spark originally came from was still a bit of a mystery (Comets? The primordial soup?), but one that science would inevitably crack.

Only now she knew the truth. Life was *supported* by biology, but it *originated* with a touch from The Light. The great mystery of the origin of life had such an obvious answer that it hardly seemed mysterious at all. (For the old Amanda, discovering that the solution was so simple—and yet unable to be experimentally verified—would have frustrated her immensely.)

I am alive, Amanda concluded, *but only as a part of the One Life. I am fully myself, but only as part of the larger self of The One. Like being on a ventilator that breathes for you, I guess…shoot, that's a really clunky analogy. Or a baby in the womb—much better! I am inside the womb of The Light and come from his DNA. I'm utterly dependent on his umbilical cord for life, yet I am still free and still myself.*

And then she saw it as a picture: Amanda watched breathlessly as The Light reached through her own mother's skin to touch the cells in her womb, endowing that tiny collection of amino acids and proteins with its own spark of life. She became a living soul, alive through a touch that came from outside earth's dimensions. Biology had the power to sustain life, but the essence of life was not biology.

I guess I've always owed my life to The Light, even in the years I believed it was all my own, Amanda mused.

"Yes!" The Voice whispered in her mind. "On earth, each self—as well as each plant, and insect, and animal—has its own spark as a gift

from Us. We bestow the spark, then set the living free. But in heaven the spark returns to its mother flame, and there is only One Life, yet within it many selves. All are regathered into The One. The saying is sure: in the beginning, one life. At the end, one life."

Amanda had the feeling she'd heard a truth so wide her brain couldn't contain it. Yet she felt no frustration. Her heart knew somehow that she *would* know—that finding the truth here was not a function of the size of your research budget, the intricacy of your apparatus or even your IQ, but simply of the desire to know.

On earth, learning was a lot like groping in the dark. Like trying to find a light switch at night: you know it's there, but somehow can't put your hands on it. But here...it's as if the truth finds you.

"Yes, I am constantly finding you, so you may always find Us. Everything is in Us, so finding Us is finding everything."

And then her mind made the leap, and she understood. The Light was not something that merely inhabited space, like photons passing through the nothingness between the stars, or a tree spreading out its branches through the medium of the air. No, it *was* the space! The Light was the actual fabric of this new universe. All this realm's dimensions, its space and time, its laws of physics...The Light wasn't inside them; *they* were inside The Light. The very fabric of this universe was made of this family, this Us—The Light, The Voice, and The Man of Light!

The thought was so incredibly pregnant with meaning that Amanda plopped down on the floor, as if the magnitude of that insight had pushed her to the ground. It detonated inside her mind, blasting through old cobwebs, rewiring how she thought and felt and comprehended, repainting her picture of life. It was such a fundamental reorientation...as if a hurricane went through the house of her thought. It took a few moments for Amanda's wits to swim back to the surface.

"Whoa!" She said out loud, placing her hands on the floor behind her and leaning back for support. *For a minute there I thought my head was going to explode. Amazing! The universe I'm living in is a* person…

A person! In my old life the laws of nature were cold and impersonal, mindless and merciless. The same chemistry that powered my cells drove my mom into a bipolar madness, to the point where she wanted nothing to do with me. The cell division that renewed my tissues ate away at my dad, as he lay dying of cancer in a sterile hospital bed, gray and groggy from his pain meds. That universe didn't care a whit for anyone. It was like a garbage truck backing over a bicycle, able to crush my soul without knowing or caring. That impersonal world took life as easily as it gave it.

But if this universe is a person, she reasoned…*if the I AM is a family, an 'Us' that cares and seeks me out and draws me in, and if love is a force of nature and not just a feeling…then this Us would be everywhere and in everything, even inside me. It would be as impossible to be separated from The Light as to be flung out of the universe all together, wouldn't it?*

"Very fitting, my darling and my delight. You describe Us well."

Doubts

Then from another part of her being, a very different set of emotions welled up. *All this makes sense to my head. But what if this love can hurt, too, like it does on earth? Here there's no way to run away and hide in the woods like I did when mom left, or lose myself in gaming like after dad died, is there? If love fails in a universe of love, where could you hide from the pain? There'd literally be nowhere else to go.*

So is that true? Am I trapped in The Light like a bug on a fly strip, stuck here forever for better or for worse?

"It is true that this heaven, this universe of love, is all that now exists or will exist. There is no way out of bliss. Yet you describe it as being 'stuck' and 'trapped,' as if endless Love is a recipe for unending pain; when in fact suffering has been banished from this universe forever. Do you know why your heart chose to say it that way?" The Voice probed gently.

There was no judgement in the question, yet it sliced open the grief hidden inside her, exposing it. Amanda had never experienced a love on earth that didn't abandon her, or a life that didn't end just when you most needed it. Yes, love was here, all around and inside her. Trusting it to stay was another matter. Her head was willing to entertain the idea that love was here to stay. But her emotions were still glued to the night her mom left and the terrible day her dad died.

The Voice said nothing, just embracing her in the moment—which Amanda appreciated. She knew from bitter experience how well-meaning people slather empty words atop grief, as if words alone could make the loss of no consequence. What the heart really wants when it is in pain is *companionship*: to be seen, to be held, to not be alone. But on her most painful days, no one had shown up to hold her. Just a distant uncle at a stage-managed funeral, clumsily reassuring her that, "God just wanted your dad with him in heaven." Which was no comfort at all.

Amanda reached up to scratch her ear. It didn't itch—it was more of a reflex, a gesture she made when she didn't know what to think. The two halves of her brain were having a rousing debate, and she didn't know which side to join. The belief that love died and left you alone went deep.

So a personal universe built of love—meaning, literally, 'being inside love,' she recited to herself with some perplexity. *Being in love…*

Then, unexpectedly, the thought made her laugh out loud. "Being in love! Hoo, boy—what a joke! On earth, it's a rush of hormones and emotions. News flash: in the afterlife 'being in love' means 'being inside your lover!' All those shallow, self-absorbed rock bands somehow got it right, in spite of themselves."

The Voice actually snickered out loud, a funny sensation tickling her ear. "If you must know, I did that—whispered to the poets and musicians about the real nature of love. Anything on earth that is true or good, I've got a hand in it somewhere."

"Well, then that's pretty impressive," Amanda replied in genuine admiration. "I would have thought getting a message through that medium would be tough even for you."

The Voice just laughed; and Amanda laughed with him.

And in that small moment of joy the first battle of trust was won. Amanda's resistance faded, and without a conscious decision she began moving again toward The Light. With each step forward she fell deeper into the gravity well of this amazing being who was the universe. And each experience with him removed one more brick from the wall around her heart.

Fascinated with this new picture of the cosmos as a person, and her inside him, Amanda started flipping images around in her mind, searching for an apt analogy. She grinned. *Hey! I'm an organism living inside a host and feeding on its life: that's a parasite. I'm God's tapeworm! Or even better—a beneficial bacterium living in the gut of God!* That struck her as hilarious. Amanda laughed long and loud, and it seemed as if The Voice was joined in her merriment.

This was the first time she'd used the word "God" to describe The Light. It seemed to fit. "Um…does that work for you?" she finally asked, somewhat tentatively.

"Sure!" The Voice replied in her mind, still laughing. *"You knew Us by that name on earth. But human language is so limited—here Our name is as long as time, and yet all know it from the first moment they arrive here. I am Life, I am The Maker, and I AM what I am. Here God doesn't live in heaven; heaven is inside God. And all who live in his world are part of his name."*

Gravity

Doubts forgotten for now, Amanda began to skip down the corridor, fingertips reaching to brush the walls as she spun around and around, laughing for joy. Light dripped from her fingertips and blazed where it landed on the walls, leaving a trail of gold and silver behind her. The Light pulled her toward itself, bid her come, taste and see, then drink until desire was filled to overflowing. You could hear and taste and talk to this Light. It landed on every cell of her body, fusing her thoughts to its own. Like the force of gravity, it was everywhere and in everything. Like desire, it drew her to itself like a lover calling at the window.

'Love is a fundamental force of this universe,' she remembered The Voice saying. "Meaning exactly what?" she blurted out. For a moment she felt flustered to have asked such an imprecise question.

"I know exactly what you mean," The Voice replied (and as soon as the words formed, Amanda knew The Voice knew). *"Thinking that love is like gravity is an excellent train of thought. Keep following it!"*

Amanda began organizing the problem, pulling on the different threads to weave them together, just as she'd learned to do in the lab. *How is love like the force of gravity? Well, love is a desire; one that draws a person to another. Gravity is also an attraction, drawing masses to each other. On earth, a big part of love's attractive force is hormones,* she snickered. *But gravity's power is simpler: it's a function of mass. Get enough mass, like a planet or a sun, and it pulls everything nearby toward it. Okay then: in this universe, what is the mass gravity acts on?*

"Well, it clearly isn't the physical stuff like on earth," she exclaimed out loud, holding a transparent arm in front of her eyes. "My body—plus the hall around me, the walls, the whole lab—they all seem like smoke: ephemeral and massless. More a gas than a solid. The really solid, substantial thing is The Light."

"Therefore," (and here she unconsciously took on an expression very like that of one of her favorite professors), "the mass in this universe must be associated with light."

"*Very good,*" The Voice spoke approvingly in her mind.

"And where there's mass, there's gravity," Amanda continued. "So, The Light should have gravity: it should draw me toward itself. And—it does! Incredible!"

She could actually feel the warm radiance gently pulling on her. *Like my childhood friend Betsy laughing at the door, urging, "Come out and play!" That's a good analogy! The real draw wasn't the tug on my sweater: I went out because her friendship tugged at my desire for love and acceptance. That's what gravity in this world must be like: it acts on the heart, through desire. So love* is *gravity here: a fundamental force that acts on the medium of the heart!*

Deciding on an impromptu test of her new gravitational theory, Amanda turned and tried to walk back the way she'd come, away from The Light. Immediately, there was resistance. It was like swimming against the current in a mountain river, The Light rushing through her mind and drawing her attention back toward itself. She quickly gave it up and surrendered to the current.

That was surprisingly hard! she mused. *It's like the hunger that pulls you to the table when it is almost suppertime and you skipped out on lunch. Or when you meet your soulmate, and you just* have *to see that guy again. It feels almost impossible to pull yourself away from The Light—from desire, from love—for any length of time in this place.*

"Yes. Love is constantly drawing, and never lets go."

"But…then why did it let me down so often in my old life?"

"Since I delegated earth to humanity, there I primarily work through people as the agents of my love. Love often fails on earth, because people fail. But here, where my love is built into the fabric of the universe and acts on you directly, there is no intermediary to let you down. Love here never, ever fails."

"It will always pull me toward you?"

"Yes."

"Okay," Amanda answered with a shrug. Here love *could* be experimentally verified—so why fight it? "You know, when I stop pulling against it, I feel as light as a feather. Moving toward The Light is like falling, where gravity is acting on me but I don't feel it because I'm not resisting."

"Exactly," The Voice agreed. *"And that is why you must* choose *heaven to live in heaven. If you came here against your will, locked in mortal combat against the very fabric of the cosmos, it would destroy you. Now, sum up what you've learned."*

"Alright," Amanda concluded decisively. "The Light—that's you—is the center of mass in this world, and my soul is attracted to it with an un-resistible desire. That desire is love. Here, love draws the soul to itself exactly like gravity attracts physical bodies back on earth. On earth you can't fight gravity, and here, you can't resist love. And who would want to?"

"*Who indeed?*" The Voice added.

I guess the poets were right and us scientists were wrong, she thought with an amused smile.

Clarity

And then she forgot all about forces and dimensions when a shocking insight hit her like a freight train. *OhMyGosh! I can think so clearly here!*

Flawless reasoning came so naturally that she hadn't even noticed, but now that she did—*it's like I was thinking with half a brain back on earth! No, five percent of one! How did I ever make a decision? How did I ever solve a problem? I was so incredibly crippled…*

It was crazy how fuzzy, how infinitely distractable, how non-linear her old thinking process seemed to her now. Before, she would start working through an assignment and find herself bunny-trailing into what she wanted for lunch, or replaying a line from a TV show, or just picking at a hangnail and not thinking of anything. Every line of thought ended up as a tangled ball of yarn. But here—there was such precision to her logic! Every step of an argument fell solidly into place, and problems she would have spent months getting her mind around were the work of moments.

Understanding the world was why Amanda had become a physicist—she wanted to know. *But here I'm being fire-hosed with the secrets of the universe, yet have the ability to take it all in. I'm downloading in a moment what might have taken a lifetime of building apparatus and running trials and evaluating data to discover. And my mind is so incredibly flexible! I can assimilate new theories—no, here they are facts,* she decided—*about the structure of the universe with a speed and certainty that's flat-out astounding. If my profs could only see me now…*

It reminded her of an adage her high-school math teacher used to quote, that for a theoretical mathematician your career is over at 35 because your brain has become too rigid to think of anything new. *I have a new brain, a young brain!* she concluded with wonder. *Like a child's brain that can grasp a language by age two. And yet I have a reasoning ability far beyond that of the smartest adult on earth. Talk about the best of both worlds! This place is frickin' awesome!*

The Edge

Then, all at once, her progress came to a halt. The hall she'd been walking through abruptly ended, with no ragged edge, as if the explosion had completely torn away the side of the building. No walls or ceiling or doorway leading to the outside world remained. The linoleum floor ahead simply disappeared, forming a dangling cliff that dropped into vast, unreachable depths. Through a golden haze far below she could just make out a verdant green plain.

Amanda paused on the precipice, awed by her surroundings. The building she'd been in had disappeared many steps behind her, leaving only herself, the edge and The Light, singular in its intensity. The fear of heights that led her to avoid any earthly drop of over ten feet was nowhere to be found.

From the valley below a faint echo of music reached her, a thousand-million notes all in harmony, beckoning, "Come, friend, and join heaven's dance! Taste, drink, be full, live!" The air itself vibrated with the message; surrounding her, inviting her to fall into its embrace. She *felt* the song caressing her skin, as if its vibrations, so tiny on earth they could only be captured by a specialized set of minute bones in her ear, could be heard by her whole body.

"Yes," The Voice rejoiced, *"your sense of hearing is no longer trapped within a physical organ. Freed from the container of the physical,*

you feel heaven's song with every fiber of your being. Earth was made as a shadow of this realm, a copy in fewer dimensions; and all good things on earth become what they truly are and were made to be in heaven."

Amanda closed her eyes to focus on the sound, as the joy-filled wave of The Voice crashed into her heart like water on dry ground. *So this is heaven. That's where I am.*

"Yes. The Beautiful Land awaits you at your feet."

She was still for a long moment, simply letting the melody of the song weave itself into her sinews. Knowledge here was not a disembodied thought you held in your mind: it was a nourishment that entered your cells and became part of your body. *On earth knowing was thinking, but here it is food and drink. I gaze on the lush, green plain far, far below and I* feel *each blade of grass reaching for The Light, swaying in the breeze. I experience life coursing through its cells, because knowing here is…it's more a sense, like smell or taste or touch, than just thinking abstractly. Thoughts here have substance. They exist physically: they aren't just mental constructs. I feel them as I think them.*

"That's very true," The Voice agreed. *"The old you became very skilled at knowing without feeling, trafficking in rational concepts that left your soul dry. Your heart was afraid, so you hid it and showed only your mind in public. Here, heart and mind are inseparable, and as it is in me, so it is also in you."*

Again, Amanda paused to take in what The Voice said—but then was distracted when she realized her eyes were still closed. She was seeing the green realm at the foot of the cliff through transparent eyelids! She blinked several times, and each time the picture she saw shifted slightly. Opening her eyes wide for a moment, she drank in the scene, and then closed them for another look, experimenting. "It looks different—how come?"

"Look with your eyes closed, and you see the landscape through *yourself—through a part of your own body,"* The Voice answered. *"Your sight is turned inward, so your focus is no longer primarily on Beauty herself, but on how she is impacting your soul. Look through your*

eyelids and you'll witness Beauty as she enters your heart and is assimilated into your thought. You can actually watch heaven take physical form within you."

Amanda closed her eyes and looked once more. Yes—she could see the loveliness of that vista coming into her. A picture formed in her mind, infused with the emotion she felt while scanning the landscape.

"Eyelids were made for this very thing, not merely for protecting the eye," The Voice answered, breathing its thought into her without words. "*This is their true purpose. On earth you might call this gift 'self-awareness,' yet it is far deeper and more profound here. In my land, knowledge grows to fill dimensions beyond those of earth, and the soul is both open and laid bare to beauty's deepest kiss."*

As The Voice enlightened her, its words took form and substance, so lifelike she wasn't sure whether she was hearing or watching something like a hologram. Amanda saw Beauty approach like an angel robed in blue and gold. Encircled in a shimmering aura, Beauty bowed before her, then offered a shining orb of light in her outstretched hands. Amanda bowed in return and held out her palms to receive the gift. Immediately, the orb of light melted into her hands, traveling swiftly up her arms and throughout her body. The beauty Amanda had witnessed became part of her own story. And The Light radiating outward from her soul grew accordingly, showering the air around her in a plethora of gorgeous hues.

Those colors of gratitude and awe were with her from that moment forward, because in heaven any light that comes into you becomes part of you, and shines forth from you forever. In that way beauty seen transforms into beauty embodied, multiplying itself, and the kingdom of light grows in majesty forever and ever.

In that moment, Amanda's desire to climb down the cliff and live forever in the Beautiful Land became almost irresistible.

Trust

Opening her eyes wide, Amanda peered over the endless precipice, eagerly scanning for a way down. The fragrance of the Beautiful Land wafted up from below, the scent of desire fulfilled smote her face. Beauty beckoned like a melody calling to her heart, and every bone in her body hungered to go down.

But she found no road. The cliff face was smooth as a windless lake, without path, crevice or foothold, and impossibly high. Doubt took hold in her mind as she sought fruitlessly for a solution. *How will I ever get down there? I don't see how I could ever climb it.*

"*No,*" the Voice answered softly in her mind. "*You cannot climb down to the Beautiful Land.*"

Suddenly hearing a "no" in this land of "yes" took her completely aback. *Am I not meant for heaven? Have I failed and fallen short? Or am I finally judged not good enough?*

"If I can't go down, then what will become of me?" Amanda choked on the words. The grief she'd stuffed down, delegitimized and denied on earth flooded up again, forcing its way to the surface like lava from a pregnant volcano. A tear beaded in the corner of her eye, held for a moment, then traced a path down toward the corner of her mouth. More followed, along with that old familiar feeling of desolation. A deep groan escaped her lips.

"You have heard rightly, daughter: you can't do this alone. None can find the narrow way into the Beautiful Land without abandoning themselves into my hands. The only way down is the path of trust." The words hung in the air between them for a long moment, until The Voice spoke again, this time out loud. "And you don't trust me."

There was no judgement or reproof in those words—The Voice simply spoke the plain truth.

No, I don't, Amanda felt her heart answer without speech. *I don't trust* anyone *with my heart, not since dad died. I won't.*

Part of her wondered to find the hidden halls of her soul unmasked so easily—but in this realm, nothing could be kept secret. And despite her tears, a part of her was relieved that the pain she'd avoided with such determination had finally surfaced. Concealing it was such a soul-crushing marathon of weariness. And somehow here the truth lacked the sharp edge of…what?

Her mind groped for an answer and finally grasped it. The punishment was missing!

Truth as she'd known it always demanded judgement. If mommy found out you'd tipped over the yogurt container in the fridge, you got a spanking. If you cheated on a test and the truth came out, you were expelled. Truth found you when you'd done wrong, and punishment arrived right behind it. But here, the naked truth could be spoken without penalty. Truth was not a weapon, because it no longer had an enemy.

"Oh, child!" The Voice whispered with deep pathos. *"Trust between you and I was broken, yet how could it have been any other way? Your heart felt the agony of death far too young and too often. You were not made to shoulder that pain, and I never meant it to come upon you. So, to protect yourself from unjust pain, you chose not to trust anyone but yourself, and defended your heart by closing it to love. This is the great sorrow that we feel, both you and I."*

"So…you're not mad at me?" she whispered haltingly.

"No."

"But I thought…"

"You didn't choose your father's death. So how could I be angry at you for being hurt by it? Nor for protecting your heart—that is simply human. And not for grieving, for I grieve with you."

A faint breeze (or was it a comforting touch?) tenderly brushed her cheek, oh-so-gently wiping away the tear. She felt the sadness of The One mingle with hers, as if she were a drop of ink in a vast ocean of sorrow over human suffering borne in the unfathomable depths of The One's heart. Yet the rain of joy still fell upon its surface. As those first drops tumbled onto Amanda's heart, the outermost layer of grief was washed from her soul like grime from a windowpane.

Absorbing it all, Amanda simply sat in the truth with him, like a child in a bright yellow rain jacket sitting in a puddle. She shivered, as the cold and wet feeling of grief seeped up like chilly water on her bum, clammy but bearable. Instead of retreating into the familiar cave where she'd long held pain at bay, she let herself feel it. And found it healed as it hurt.

Truth embraced her. It was for her; no longer a weapon coercing her to do the right thing, or a threat making her hands shake when she had to face an interpersonal conflict. Instead of wrapping her in a straitjacket of shame, truth set her free. Instead of salt in her wound, it poured in salve. Truth was her friend. The Voice already knew exactly what she had and hadn't done, and his love changed not a whit. *That* was what that mattered.

With the threat of judgement removed, a crack opened in Amanda's defenses. Truth poured through the gap.

Makeup

"Even before death touched you, fear did."

A picture came into her mind of five-year-old Amanda, the day she'd gotten into her mother's makeup case and gleefully colored her face and clothes—plus the countertop, floor and mirror. Her innocent joy turned to terror and guilt as her mother appeared in the doorway, an enraged expression clouding her face. Amanda felt her little arm bruising as her mother marched her out into the yard and hosed her down in the November air, a flurry of reprimands further chilling the already cold air. The frigid water pelted her body while tears sprayed the ground and little fingers turned blue from cold. She could still feel it.

"That terrible moment tore a hole in your tender heart. The mother who should have laughed with you grew angry and hurt you deep. You couldn't understand why such innocent fun merited such awful judgement: the mind of a five-year-old is not built to parse out a parent's dysfunction. So you took the blame on yourself. You decided you were bad, and that your punishment was deserved—and so you became your own judge. And you decided your mother would not protect you, so you took on the role of your own protector."

As Amanda heard those words, she somehow entered her five-year-old consciousness. Like looking at an old photo album for the first time, she re-experienced her childhood thought as an adult. In that shivering, unprotected moment of utter vulnerability on the wet grass, she'd promised herself that she would always be Someone Who Did the Right Thing, so she never had to feel that cold terror again. Being a Good Girl—that would be who she was. She would never be Bad again.

And then a movie began playing, little snippets of her daily life as a child. Looking with adult eyes, patterns emerged that she'd been blind to ever since. Her mother's moods were so unpredictable and volcanic—one day an ecstasy of adventure and energy, the next a hellhole of sullenness and offense. The little girl struggling to understand, to cope, to shield herself from that arbitrary wrath. With a painful clarity, Amanda observed a mother projecting her own dereliction on her child.

Yet she saw herself accept the responsibility—*mom said that those bad moods were my fault, so that must be true, right?* Adapting to the only reality she knew, her little self made an unconscious choice: being good was the only way to be safe. That decision had shaped her life right up til the present. Doing things right would protect her from pain, if only she kept monitoring herself every moment to make sure that's who she was. Little Amanda became her own judge and accuser on that long-ago day. She'd lived that false identity ever since.

"The vow to be Good was made by a child," The Voice murmured, *"who did not realize what she was doing: taking over my job! I am the Judge, who rules with mercy; I am the protector of little children."*

Through Amanda's tears, she watched the picture keep unscrolling. The little girl built a moral yardstick to measure her every deed, to make sure she was Good. *I'm good if I do the dishes. I'm good if I don't make any noise and disturb mom's rest. I'm good if I stay up half the night playing games with her when she's feeling high, and* never *yawn, even if I'm dying to go to bed. I'm good if I clean the house when all she can do is lay on the couch and eat Ben and Jerry's.* That yardstick stuck to her soul like glue, twisting her into a distorted image of who she was made to be. If the yardstick said she was okay, then she could relax. But she almost never relaxed.

"My precious little girl," The Voice said softly, *"On earth, truth's partner is judgement, and the two cannot be separated. Where lies are present, it cannot be otherwise: truth condemns untruth. But in my country, there* are *no lies! Therefore, truth is free to take off its judge's robes and do what I intended it to from the beginning: to bless instead of curse, to approve instead of judge, to teach instead of correct. In heaven truth's partner is mercy, and here those two cannot be separated.*

"The vow you made co-opted my role and pushed me away. Yet I judge that act with mercy, and do not hold little children guilty for how they cope with the sins of their parents. So do not fear! Today I call you 'Good' forever, with no possibility of wrongdoing. You are Good because I say so, and my word is final! I have not been and will never be angry with you."

Amanda felt something like a belt being unbuckled or a rope untied, and a leaden weight fell off her shoulders. She was okay.

She was not punished. Truth had no reprimands to offer for what she had done. It was no longer a yardstick to see if her conduct measured up, but a friend.

"Now, child, we permit no yardsticks here. We have no use for evaluating our own goodness. You are good because you have me, and there is nothing good-er than I am."

Amanda could almost see The Voice smiling at that turn of phrase.

"You've spent much of your life striving to measure up: now look into truth and see reality! I am already *pleased with you. I am* already *fully satisfied. You don't need to do one single thing to earn my approval. So, absolve yourself, as I have already absolved you! Throw down the ruler and let your heart walk free in my wide world without fear."*

As soon as the request was made, in her mind Amanda saw herself walk over and hand her silly measuring stick to The Voice (the picture was of her father, but she knew who it represented). Her yardstick looked like a dirty twig, crooked and squalid in his bright hand, but he seemed unruffled. Calmly, she broke it over his knee. As the splinters melted away into nothing, a great anxiety escaped Amanda's body and dissipated into The Light, leaving not a trace behind. The gap in the castle walls around her heart widened.

After a moment's silence, The Voice spoke to her mind. *"Well done! Whatever is left behind here at the entrance of the Beautiful Land is left behind for good. Your vow is over. In its place I make a new vow to you: in my kingdom, you will never, ever be judged again."*

A whispered "Thank you!" was all Amanda could manage.

The Voice was silent for a few minutes, allowing her to luxuriate in this new feeling of freedom from judgement. Where her inner critic had incessantly badgered her, now there was quiet repose. Another image came to her: a still, sunlit pond, its grassy banks shaded by broad oaks and the languid air above parted only by the flitting of songbirds. She floated there among the waterlilies in a wooden rowboat, the sun warming her skin as her toes dangled in the cool water. It was the rest of completion, like finishing her undergrad. The peace of having all the time and space she wanted to just be. The sigh of satisfaction after a long struggle comes to a good end. She had no idea afterward how long she tarried there; only that she could lay resting on a boat in that pond forever.

On the Brink

Then The Voice roused her once more, calling her back to the brink of the chasm. And she came.

"Do you understand what I have done for you?"

"I think my heart does. Not sure I could explain it, though."

"That was well said. The human heart suffers three wounds: first unmet desire, and the emotional pain it produces. Second, the choice to adopt a false identity as your own judge and protector. And third, the bitter fruit of the wound: the quest to blame, and the anger that seeks vengeance.

"The desire of your heart was for love and security, yet you lost those again and again. That wounded your heart deeply. The false identity you adopted to protect yourself was being good: believing that being a perfect little girl could prevent future pain.

"Do you still believe that, child?"

No. You have told me that I am not judged, and my heart believes you. I have no more need to protect myself.

"That is very good. Now, then: step off the edge and I will catch you."

Step off the edge? Amanda thought in disbelief. The cliff stood *miles* high, towering over Mount Everest, plunging deeper than the Mariana Trench. On earth she would have dropped to the ground, quivering, and clung to the nearest rock in delirious fear of falling. Yet here…

Taking a deep breath to gather herself, Amanda made to step forward to the very edge of the dizzying precipice. But she somehow found herself taking two steps back instead.

It wasn't fear. It still seemed impossible to be afraid of anything in this world, even the abyss before her. Looking inward, she felt one part of herself longing to be caught up and held by The Voice, just as her dad used to grab her by the arms as a toddler, swing her around and then hold her tight. But another, deeply-rooted corner of her soul held back. It's danger alarm rang in the recesses of her mind, warning her to never take any promise at face value, to question everything. No, not even good will could be trusted to come through. A picture came to her of a face contorted with fury. The emotion was anger.

"I…I don't seem to be able to," Amanda finally uttered, looking down and away. "Part of me longs to go down, and believes you'll catch me. But another part of me wants to…I don't know. Do something violent, maybe. Like punch a wall, or grab someone and shake them? Sorry—I feel like the kid who takes her ball and marches off in a huff, just to spite those who want to play."

"You see well," The Voice answered approvingly. *"You have broken the ruler you used to judge yourself, and let go of your false identity, which allows me to fill your desire. That was well done! Yet your anger remains, and the belief that some perpetrator must be punished for you to be at peace. It is the part of you that seeks an earthly form of justice which resists heaven. To go down, you must forgive the one you blame for your loss."*

"I don't understand," Amanda finally stuttered.

"My darling, my desire," The Voice replied, his words a warming presence in her thought and not audible speech. But a swell of liquid love passed through her. And her heart heard it, and understood as clearly as if his affection had kissed her cheek.

"You are standing at the cliff of endings and the border of the Beautiful Land. Every offense must finally be released here, at the border of my kingdom. Pain unhealed gives birth to anger, and anger a desire to strike back at the one who hurt you. These two cling tightly to the soul. You have lived with a closed heart, thinking it will keep injustice far away. Yet in heaven, justice comes to those who are fully open. Your heart will never open wide enough to receive my justice without first letting go of your own.

You must trust me.

"Yet you cannot trust an offender."

She felt it inside—a fleeting moment of wild rage. A club was in her hand. The blow fell on the heads of the failed doctors, the relatives who spoke of peace when there was no peace, the aunt who took her in at first and then said she had to leave a month later. It struck at her friends who said nothing, left her alone because they didn't know what to say, didn't know what it meant to suffer. To the police who did nothing when that man stole her dad's medical practice. They were all guilty. Guilty! And then she turned her club toward the real criminal, the one who allowed it all to happen…

"To protect yourself as you've vowed to do, you must punish the one you believe is responsible for your pain."

"Who is that?" Her voice had a hard edge on it.

"My child, you know."

She did. Yet she couldn't bring herself to say it.

"You hold me responsible for the loss of your mother and father."

The truth in those words shook the epicenter of her soul, cleaving her true self from the pose she'd adopted to hide it. Amanda both knew and didn't want to know the hurt those words revealed; she both longed to embrace The Voice and to run away from it to the utter end of the universe. However, in a world of light with no shadows, there was nowhere to hide.

Her hands clenched involuntarily into fists as she felt the power of that rage. She had trusted before, and trust had trampled her heart. With the blind confidence of a child, Amanda had assumed her mother would always be there. But when mom walked out, Amanda's childlike innocence ran away from home, too. Reeling, she'd mustered the courage to build a second world around her dad. But when he died…any ability she had left to trust died with him.

Part of her believed this couldn't be her Creator's fault, and still sought the God of her childhood. But another part raged at his absence.

The Question

"Go ahead: ask me The Question," The Voice invited.

What question? Amanda thought warily.

"*The* question," (The Voice was audible now as it grew in intensity), "the one that dwells at the heart of all human suffering. The unanswerable challenge the wounded soul screams into the void in its anguish and despair. The one your heart believes will somehow make it alright, and finally bring the justice you suppose leads to peace. The question you think I refuse to answer."

"Go on," The Voice invited gently. "Ask me."

Amanda swiveled left and right, looking for some deep hole or hiding place to run to so her raging wound wouldn't have to face the unrelenting light. *But there is nowhere to run from The Light,* she recalled. It was her own heart speaking, and she instantly knew it was true. Nothing could ever be secret here. All that was and is would come to light—had been found out already.

"You want me to jump. But you didn't catch me before."

The words simply came out of her—not as a defiant accusation, or an angry rant, but as the naked truth of what her heart believed, shot through with a pathos too deep for words.

The thought came from the deepest cell of the dungeon she'd secreted her heart in, the bolt-hole walling off the anger-dragon so it couldn't escape. The same wall blocked off old friends, and Darren, and now The Voice. Her insides began to curl up in a protective ball in that cold, dark place that no love could reach or pry open.

And yet—she was not alone in the dark. Even in her heart's most private place, The Light found the things she'd never told her boyfriend, or even her father. There were no secrets.

Amanda gasped at the sense of nakedness as The Light

disrobed her soul. Pain surged up inside her like a hot desert wind, and it came out of her like a scream, as if her heart had touched a hot stove and been seared.

"You took away my mom! And then you took away dad's job and his reputation and our house, and then you took him away, too! Why did you do that to me? Why didn't you stop it?"

Panting from the exertion, crying, her hands shaking. "Why didn't you stop it?"

Amanda shuddered momentarily, and then her breathing began to slow. An ocean of peace lay all around her, and nothing could stop it seeping back into the edges of her consciousness. Here on the brink of heaven, the wound could still sling its bolts of anguish, but it no longer had the debilitating power to overwhelm her reason and swallow her whole.

Yet her words hung heavy in the air. It occurred to Amanda that if she'd said them to anyone on earth, it would have ended that relationship for good. But then, something like a deep sigh whispered through the air around her—just a faint quiver, as if some distant darkness had passed from existence. Then the breeze wafted those words away, and The Light shone around her again. And to her surprise, The Voice was not offended.

"Oh, daughter! Death does not come from me," The Voice whispered. "Yet the grief beyond words cannot be assuaged by mere words. Hiding cannot heal you. Neither can time, nor anger, nor shouting a challenge into the darkness. You hold onto your anger because you believe letting it go would be letting go of justice, and that only righting the wrong can give you peace.

"Yet peace is no friend to anger, nor does it come from the justice of retribution you knew on earth. My justice is this: when the heart is fully known in the midst of sorrow, and the one who is known is fully loved, then the rest it longs for is found in an unexpected place.

"Dearest, you are dear to The One. He, too, has felt the deepest grief and loss, and the greatest injustice. He, too, has chosen the path of letting go, the justice of heaven instead of the vengeance of earth. Truly, he is with you, in everything. This is the peace we offer you: that we, too, have been touched by death."

"But…how?" she questioned, staring out over the cliff with fixed, watery eyes. "Surely…you can't die, can you? How can God (she had begun to think of The Voice as God) perish out of existence?"

"*It is true. I have died, as you call it,*" The Voice stated simply. The words hung between them in a gentle silence. "*I died once, never to die again.*"

A vision came flashing back into her mind: the story she had seen when she first recognized The Voice. Again, she watched The Man of Light give up his light for the first man and woman, wink out of existence, and die.

Then it is *true,* she thought. *He did not bring death to earth, but experienced death. He suffered also, so he knows the pain I felt from the inside, all of it. He understands.* Amanda felt a release inside her, an unclenching of the fist around her soul. Her breathing came more easily and her hands slowly relaxed, opened.

"*I, too, knew the death of my father when I was young.*"

Another scene from The Man of Light's story began to play in her mind. Looking through his eyes, she beheld the shape of a corpse, wrapped in a long white cloth from head to foot. It lay stone-cold on a rough stone platform. A sort of napkin rested across the face, and the hands were tightly bound in strips of cloth. Relatives crouched by a dark opening in a rocky scarp, wrestling the body through a hole in the hillside. A moment later they emerged, empty-handed. Bending their backs, four young men—*his brothers*, she realized—heaved a whitewashed stone plug into the square maw of the tomb. The weeping and muffled sobs around her increased as the picture grew watery and indistinct.

I am seeing through his tears! Amanda suddenly realized. *That's why the picture blurred! I am watching his family bury his father, through his own eyes.*

Then pictures of the same aching moments from her own life raced through her mind—a casket, a circle of mourners, and a pastor gravely speaking words that left no impression on her heart. There beside her father's grave, the presence cried along with her at each one.

"What you and I suffered was unjust, but today I am making that injustice work for good. Our shared sorrow cements the bond between us. We're joined in a fellowship of suffering, a secret uniting us in a special dance only you and I can do. What was taken from both of us against my will shall by my will be returned to both of us, as a belonging that will last forever.

"I have done all to stop injustice, and now it will end forever, here on the second earth. And yet it touched us both on the first world."

So he knows—he really knows. And I am not alone. For the first time, Amanda rolled back the stone sealing the dragon-lair in her heart, and allowed another through the door to share her darkest fears and greatest pain. In the memory of death their hearts mingled, and to her surprise she found life there. The One who held her listened, and she knew that she was heard, and he was always present, and that he understood.

Him

After what seemed like hours of unloading the weight on her soul, Amanda abruptly realized she was telling her story out loud. Instead of conversing with The Voice mainly in thought, she had been speaking with her voice, like one human being to another.

And as her attention shifted from her inward thoughts to the world outside her skin, all at once she detected physical sensations she'd been missing: a warmth against her shoulder like a warm wrap on a cold morning, regular inhaling and exhaling that wasn't her own, the weight of a comforting arm encircling her shoulders. It dawned on her that The Voice, too, had been speaking out loud. A calm, regular, *human* breathing sat next to her—another human being! *He* was there! Her body tingled all over and her heart began summersaulting in her chest, yet her eyes were frozen straight ahead. She could hardly dare to confirm what her heart already knew.

He broke the awkward silence first, with barely-concealed mirth. "Go on—every question here is a good question."

"Are you…real?"

"If you mean, 'Am I physically present,' then yes!" He laughed, throwing off a flood of joy that washed over her, rinsing away the last of her pain. "I AM, and have always been, very, very real!"

"But who are you?"

"You saw me in the vision as The Man of Light, and you've heard The Voice speaking my thought. But you also have known me by my birth name, my earth name. I am Jesus."

Amanda turned toward The Voice, and saw—*Him!* The brightness of glory danced on his brow, and the sun streamed from and through his body. He was all amber and gold and white as newly-fallen snow. A rainbowed halo encircled his head, the visible manifestation of the life pouring through his skin like a river. The brightness of his face was such that she could barely look at him at first, let alone distinguish what he wore, or if he even wore anything. But he was looking directly at her, and Amanda was captured by his eyes—eyes that shimmered with happy tears, as hers did. She looked deep within them, to the inexhaustible well of joy that flowed like a bubbling spring out of his heart. In it was the majesty and gravity of The Creator, the epic love of one who would tear down mountains to find her, the wisdom of one whose plans were formed of thought so deep they could bring to nothing all the evil of the world. Falling into his arms, she strained to absorb every molecule of the overwhelming comfort, happiness and sheer goodness of that moment.

For the first time, Amanda experienced a person hugging her soul. Certainly, his physical arms were around her, and she felt the compression of being held tight, his very-human breath tickling her ear. The comforting closeness of another living, breathing body was reassuring.

But this was so much more! It was as if his affection reached right through her skin, caressing her insides with a love holding no judgement; and her mind realigned with the truth that radiated from his fingertips. He reached further, to her emotions, and a deep and final sigh shuddered out of them as his embrace wiped her tears away. Then emotion took its rightful place in her being, animating the self with joy and anchoring it on the rock of peace. But that hug kept on going, reaching through emotion, past her subconscious, to touch the deepest level of the person that was Amanda.

The understanding of what was happening came to her in a picture: The Man of Light racing toward her with abandon across a broad, sunlit field of yellow poppies, arms open wide. And she came running to him, as fast as she could go, laughing all the way. And when their two hearts met, he lifted her in strong arms, whirling her around just as her earthly father had done long ago, a spray of multi-hued light like liquid joy splashing outward from their hair. Finally, they stood, her forehead resting on his as he cradled her fingers in safe hands and her soul reclined into unadulterated love.

Every longing Amanda had ever felt to be accepted for who she was, to belong, to be valued, was utterly sated within that inside-and-out embrace. And more! There was so much pouring into her that bubbled over onto the ground like a pot aboil, desire fulfilled splashing over the rim of her heart to water the world. She was lit from within, feet encircled in a pool of light.

That light contained illumination, truth, and life. Yet what flowed through her was also love, in pure crystalline form. *A universe made of love, and against all hope I'm in it,* she laughed. And still his affection thundered into her, a roaring flood overtopping her consciousness til she was drowned laughing in liquid love. She understood: his intention was for her to have such an overflow that a veritable river of surplus love streamed out of her just as it did from him.

Still holding her, he leaned forward to whisper in her ear: "I am yours, and you are mine, my true love and fondest hope and greatest joy! I have known all about you ever since you were a little girl, when we talked in the treehouse and had tea together with your stuffed animals, and when you sang songs of joy to me on your guitar. In all those moments I loved you with a passion as high as heaven.

"And I was right there with you in the dark times of pain, too, taking every blow that landed on us as the doctor told you the awful news in the hospital. I grieved, too, that in the emotional chaos of those moments you could not feel or find me. I speak most clearly on earth through your emotional brain; but when it is seized by suffering, the clamor of pain often drowns out my gentle words. But even in that lonely place I stood by your side, with hope stronger than hell."

As The Man of Light spoke, Amanda became aware of a scene playing out in her mind. Her father was there, waiting anxiously by the bay window at their battered dining table for her to come home late on a dark night. It was the day of that infamous sixth-grade field trip, when the bus broke down high in the Sierras where there was no cell service, and they didn't get back until three o'clock in the morning. Watching her dad bow his head and pray nervously for her safety, she realized with a start that she was hearing his thoughts and not just his words. He remembered the good times they'd had that week, and she saw them through his eyes. Then Amanda felt his fears bubble up, ugly imaginations of car crashes, abductions, or rushing through the door to the ER to find her broken body covered with a sheet, until his prayers rose up to swat those fears back down.

At the same time—it was like a split-screen on a television—she saw herself sitting on a hard bench seat toward the back of the school bus with her two best friends. Talking and laughing together on their unexpected adventure, yet blissfully unaware of the worried pain her dad felt on the other half of the screen.

Then her dad began to think about mom. A powerful wave of his emotion swept through Amanda as she experienced his feelings. Stunned, she saw for the first time the pain he had swallowed to keep their lives afloat, the loss he felt, the fierce care he exercised to not lose his daughter as he had his wife.

At that moment she saw Jesus step into the dining room. He walked silently through the doorway from the kitchen and up behind her father in the half-light. Slumped in an old oak Windsor chair, half-asleep and half-praying over his bible, he didn't notice The Man of Light beside him. Jesus gently reached out a hand and touched a forefinger to her dad's forehead.

When he removed his finger, a spot of warm, yellow light glowed there, slowly fading. Then peace passed across Theo's furrowed brow and melted inward, a salve to his troubled mind. Her dad sighed, finally relaxing. Then, his prayer answered, she watched amused as he wandered to the refrigerator, poured himself a glass of milk, mixed in the Hersey's syrup—*that was so dad!* —and hunkered down with a book to wait.

"I watched over your dad just as he did over you," The Man of Light said quietly at her side. "And when his earthly life came to an end, I was there to catch him with the gift of a new life—the same life you are now experiencing.

"I have been there for you in exactly the same way that he was, even when you were not aware of me. I gave you your father as a true picture of the care I exercise over you, and the sacrifices made to love you. Peace came into him as he trusted, because trust is the bridge that crosses dimensions, linking earth to heaven. That same peace passes into you as you trust me."

"Thank you," Amanda answered gratefully, as the picture of her dad faded. "Thanks for everything you did for him, and for me. My heart feels like it just had Thanksgiving dinner and nothing is lacking—it's completely full."

"Thanks for telling me! It makes me happy to see you free."

Amanda leaned into his shoulder again, feeling the sensation of being cherished and protected. "Boy…you don't realize how much emptiness there is inside you until it's finally gone."

Why

They sat side by side in silence, drinking in the lingering moment from a cup that never seemed to run dry.

"You know that big question you had me ask earlier, about why everything happened?" Amanda finally stated. "You never really answered it. And I don't know why, but it doesn't seem that big of a deal anymore."

"That's because what the heart really wants when it is suffering is to be seen, and comforted, and valued. Knowing 'why' is a cheap substitute for your true longing…although everyone asks the question sometimes. Even me."

"What did you ask?" Amanda inquired curiously.

"Father, why have you abandoned me?" he recited, as if recalling a dim memory far away. Then he laughed, squeezing her shoulder affectionately. "I didn't get any answer, either!"

"Okay," Amanda concluded after a moment. "I don't need to know why. I'd much rather have you."

"Thank you. That was beautifully put," Jesus replied. "But—since I was the one who invited you to ask the question" (his eyes sparkled when he said it), "you deserve an answer anyway. When The One made your world, he made it free—independent of him. And that independence meant you could choose the good or the evil. That is how evil came into the world—it is not Our doing.

"Nevertheless, evil brings death and ruin instead of Good, and its effects spread far beyond those who partner with it. Evil touches all; then whispers that Good is to blame for what evil itself has done. That's the lie that haunts mankind's worst moments: that The Maker who cares most deeply for them has dealt them the deadliest blow."

Amanda peered vacantly off into the distance, recalling similar memories. "I know what you mean. People came up to me at dad's funeral and told me that *you* took him…that it was your will," she sighed. "One relative even announced that he died because 'you wanted him with you in heaven.'"

"Oh, my darling," Jesus began tenderly, looking into her eyes. "Did you believe that?"

"Um…I don't think so. It seemed too pat, too religious-y. I admit, those days were so devastating that my memory is kinda fuzzy. But part of me just couldn't believe you'd be that cruel."

"Oh, *thank you* for believing in me in your worst moment!" he exclaimed, giving her a spontaneous bearhug. Then he held her back at arms' length and gazed proudly into her eyes. "In this moment I feel seen and known and understood by you, and that touches a deep desire of my heart. Thanks for standing by me!"

He put his arm around her again, and she snuggled up to his side, feeling safe and loved, even in the places where she didn't yet understand.

"Here's the truth about your dad: *of course* I wanted him here with me! He is beloved, and all this was made for his endless joy, just as you are my beloved and were made for joy, and so are all humankind. I don't want *anyone* I love to miss out.

"But I didn't 'take' him from you, as if I was some puppetmaster pulling the strings of your lives to get my own needs met. I don't kill people to get them to heaven, any more than I kill to keep people out. I am the Author of *Life*, for heaven's sake! I don't do death!"

"Then were those folks at the funeral evil?" Amanda asked.

"No, no—they were just anxious, awkward people who found themselves in over their heads, trying to make you feel better by giving trivial answers to the question, 'Why?' Evil co-opted their words to its own purpose."

"And 'Why?' has no answer?" Amanda asserted, though in the form of a question.

"It has no answer. Only those who have suffered deeply are qualified to comfort others experiencing loss. In that wisdom they have no words to offer, understanding that being there and listening is a greater comfort than empty words."

Now it was Jesus' turn to look away in thought. After a moment he shook his head, a look of perplexity mixed with sadness. "Amanda, there is no 'why' when it comes to evil. Evil is evil, and does evil, because that is what it is and all it knows. It needs no reasons. Unless you wish to seek for an answer by descending with me to the utter depths of hell and walking through the slime-pits of shame…no, that is not your path. We do not ask questions of evil, for it knows neither itself nor why it acts as it does. It will only twist the question to harm you."

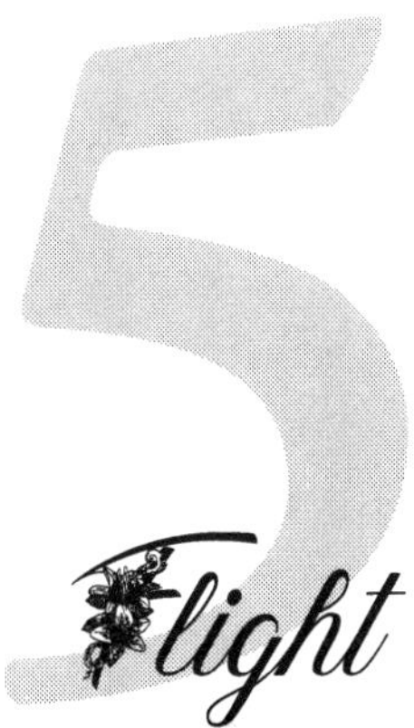

5 Flight

At that moment, she felt a small form magically take shape in her hand. Opening her fingers slowly, they revealed an inky black stone cradled in her shimmering palm, carved with twining words and figures. She looked closer, noticing the title of the story that was written on it: 'Despair.'

"What is it?" Amanda asked.

"The stone called 'despair' is the story evil wrote on your heart: the disappointment and grief hoarded within. You once believed that gripping this stone tightly would protect you from being hurt again. It lay like a cold lump of gnawing fear and fierce anger in your gut, holding you back from love. But now that I have set you free, that story is no longer lodged like a gallstone in your soul. It lies unmasked in your hand, within your power, to do with whatever you will. The operation was a success. The tumor has been removed, and despair no longer defines you.

"Oh, child!" He suddenly cried out, flinging his arms toward the sky. "Step into trust, and together we will write you a new story, a tale of desire eternally fulfilled replacing that cold stone of sorrow. Come with me into the Beautiful Land, where hope can be tasted and drunk and worn like a golden bracelet. I AM love! I AM hope! And I AM *not* a disappointment!"

An almost-physical wave of joy crashed into her body each time he said, "I AM." As she braced against the rollicking breakers, she saw herself as a little girl running down the beach and into the sea, lost in the delight of letting the placid ocean waves break into her. Her mother was holding her hand, the old, flowered shirt she used to wear over her swimsuit flapping in the wind as they hopped in the swell and laughed together. Joy rose to her chest, lapped at her shoulders, finally swallowing her head and leaving the taste of sweet water on her lips.

The physical sensation of a wave breaking over her subsided, but the inner joy remained, infusing all the places despair had once touched. Amanda threw her head back and laughed like she hadn't in years, laughter that would make your sides ache on earth but just made your insides feel warm here. The Man of Light was laughing, too, his happiness throwing off great showers of sparks like a hammered forge. Where each spark met the ground, little pools of brightness formed in the sea of waving grass. She could hardly see him for the spectacular incandescence of color showering forth from that inexhaustible river of joy. Finally, she looked down from the sunlight of his face to the black stone lodged in her hand. It seemed even smaller, and the writing had disappeared.

"So, what do I do with it?" She solemnly held it out to The Man of Light in an open hand. As the aura around his body swept over it, the stone began to fluoresce with color, its ebony surface peeling away like frost vaporizing in the sunshine to reveal a center shot through with light and glittering like a thousand diamonds. For an instant she saw herself as a child on the beach again, only this time she was launching pebbles out into the waves and squealing with delight each time one plopped into the water.

Jesus simply nodded in smiling agreement. Then laughter

took her, and she reared back and threw the stone with all her might, far out over the precipice into the glowing air.

She expected that small black thing to vanish in the radiant abyss, but to her surprise it hung there in the fragrant air, then swiftly began to grow. Explosions of color and brightness and flaming beauty shot from it in all directions. Then what was once despair flew back toward her on iridescent wings. The multifaceted body of this new being of light was now a dazzling, opalescent butterfly, now a brilliant white charger, now a lion with a mane of glittering gold. Its name was Hope.

In her mind Amanda could hear Hope beckoning. *"Come, ride the wind with me, down to the Beautiful Land! Experience the extraordinary!"* Not lingering for a reply, Hope swung in a broad arc and dived swiftly toward the clouds below.

An eager smile on her face, Amanda turned to face The Man of Light. "If I jump, you'll catch me, right?"

"Always!" he grinned. "Go for it!"

Jump

Amanda ran wildly to the edge, then flung herself screaming over the towering cliff. She catapulted toward Hope with all her might, just as with all her strength she'd thrown away despair. Afterward, she couldn't explain how, but Hope caught her, and in an instant taught her to fly. Swooping back and forth together in great arcs of joy they zoomed downward, gliding through the scented air toward the Beautiful Land far below.

Hope swiveled her variegated wings into a long, circling glide down corridors of air toward the enveloping green below, and Amanda followed. *I'm flying!* she exulted. Her arms were spread to the side like wings, but that was more a vestige of earth-thinking than something that produced aerodynamic lift. Her body seemed to have gained the ability to ignore gravity at will. There was definitely a 'down' direction—gravity still existed—but instead of being a master with rules she had to obey, gravity was now her servant, coming at her call.

She'd flown like this before, in her dreams. Breaking the bounds of the conscious mind, her psyche would soar over towns and fields, ecstatic at the feeling of freedom. Yet those dream-flights were never long enough. Her mind, believing this couldn't really happen, always pulled her down to earth. As the rational asserted itself, her imagination fought back against reason and practicality, tried to will herself to stay airborne. If only she could push her analytic mind into a box, the flying dream could go on for just a bit longer! But the pull of earth was strong, and her leaps always grew shorter and shorter, until finally she was grounded for good, living inside the only reality she had ever known.

But not here! Amanda was fully conscious, fully awake, yet still flew. Experimenting, she imagined bending to the left and immediately began to bank in that direction, even though she hadn't moved a muscle. She pictured herself soaring to the right, and where her mind went, her body followed. In a moment she was swooping from side to side in broad curves, with Hope winging along in formation beside her.

I can fly! Amanda exulted. *Wherever I think of, I go—I don't have to exert myself or move a muscle unless I choose to. Awesome! And I seem to have escaped the pull of gravity. If I want, I can obey it and walk around on the ground; or ignore it and rise (here she zoomed upward) whenever I care to.*

The bracing air billowed through her hair, smelling of jasmine and cinnamon and a hundred other exotic scents, all blending together and yet distinct. Years later she could still remember some of them, although words failed when she tried to describe the sensation they created inside her. She would always end up saying, "They smell like flying!"

Amanda remembered her hesitation at the edge of the cliff and laughed. *This is what I was afraid of?* Right now, floating miles above the earth, fear of falling seemed like the silliest thing she could imagine. *I was so hyper about whether he would catch me! But I was in a world where gravity is optional and you can fly—and he knew it all along! To him, some of the stuff we agonize over must seem like a total hoot.*

Hit by a new idea, she launched into a barrel-roll, screaming with delight. Then it was all loops and spins and power-dives for what seemed like half an hour. Hope flew beside her and around her and inside her loops, celebrating with her the joy of flying through heaven on the wings of trust.

The River

Winging her way downward next to Hope gradually brought the Beautiful Land scrolling past below into focus. Amanda began to pick out areas like forests, parklands and vast emerald lawns dotting the landscape, so she stopped looping and settled into a long glide to get a better view. Acres of color—*flowers maybe?* —passed under her like a silk scarf shimmering first with one hue and then another as her flight path altered the angle of The Light.

However, the sight that captured and held her attention by its sheer loveliness was a crystalline river, winding through that green world like a glowing thread. It emanated a pure white light that turned opalescent when she focused in on it. Tributaries broke away from the main channel like veins on the backside of a leaf. It literally took her breath away (she had to remember to breathe again) because looking into that river was experiencing it, as if she was drinking its water. And *that* was taking a draught of life itself.

But while it resembled a river, her mind couldn't quite square its form with the familiar streams of earth. For one thing, its tributaries seemed to be flowing *outward* from the main channel. And instead of collecting water from many sources and carrying it relentlessly downhill to some distant sea, this channel flowed without any regard to elevation. It seemed to climb ridges as easily as following valleys. At one point she flew over a waterfall, its dazzling foam draped in a rainbow of spray. But it gushed *up* over the cliff instead of crashing down, finally dancing away across the carpet of greenery. *What in the world…?*

Then, in a flash of insight she had it. *Ahh—it's a River of* Life, *the essence of The Light distilled in liquid form. And like light, it flows* outward *from its source in every direction, not* downward *as rain that falls on the earth and then drains into the oceans. And look! As the River of Life irrigates the Beautiful Land, every plant and flower and tree drinks its water. That's what keeps them alive! They don't need photosynthesis, or oxygen, or any of that biological stuff—they get life straight from the River.*

So then…I bet it never rains here. Why would it? There's no need, when the plants are nourished by the River. Hey—I just got filled to overflowing by The Man of Light. I bet the River fills this world the same way.

New insights simply came to Amanda unbidden as she gazed steadily into the River's light, drinking in the knowledge within its luminance. It occurred to her that the mightiest waterways on earth—the Nile, the Mississippi or the mighty Amazon—were simply faint replicas in fewer dimensions of this original River of Life. Water, the building block of life on earth, the substance that made up 90% of the human body, was a clue pointing to this river, a nugget of truth imbedded in the world to reveal a greater reality.

On earth we are made of water, but here we are made of life, she concluded. *I get it: The Maker gave us water as an allegory, so we could understand how life works in heaven. There's no physical water here at all—no lakes or seas—because heaven holds the true water that* H_2O *was patterned after.*

"And the sea shall be no more," she breathed aloud, remembering a line from the Book of Revelation. *I always wondered why the new earth didn't have any oceans. Now it makes perfect sense: water represents life, and here we have the real thing. This place gets more and more amazing the more of it I see.*

For a hushed, holy moment she glided along through the scented air thousands of feet over the River of Life, her mind awed to silence by the majesty of its creator. *The One is over all, and his life is in all, and his purpose runs through all,* she whispered. It was a moment made for worship, but the songs and prayers and expressions of gratitude she'd learned on earth seemed woefully inadequate for all this. *How do you say thank you to someone who has literally given you the world?* Amanda wondered. She looked to the left and right, as if to discover an answer—and was startled to see The Man of Light flying along next to her. He laughed at her surprise, and she laughed with him.

"Pretty awesome, huh?" he said.

"Uh, yeah," was all Amanda could spit out in reply. On earth her cheeks would have turned red with embarrassment, but here it seemed more like something to joke about than be ashamed of.

"Don't worry—I have received your worship, and it was truly beautiful—like a sip of the finest wine after a sumptuous dinner."

"But I didn't *say* anything! I couldn't think of any song to sing that seemed…well, appropriate."

"You have forgotten: in my land, you experience the heart of anything you look at. And so do I! The physical you is transparent in heaven, so I see your heart. And what I received when I looked at you just now was the awe and wonder you experienced as you beheld the beauty of my land. And that is true worship."

Amanda wasn't aware of the quizzical look that came over her face. "What? Another question?" Jesus laughed.

"Okay, yeah," she replied without embarrassment. "What about all the singing and clapping and praying and stuff we did on earth? I always thought heaven was supposed to be this endless worship service where we stood around waving our palm branches and singing songs to you all day long for eternity."

"As if I was so insecure that I made the whole human race just so you could keep telling me how great I am?" That one really got Jesus laughing, and great beams of mirth pulsed out from his face and split the air like silver and red fireworks, sparks trailing out behind as they flew.

"Actually," he continued, after his laughter rumbled to an end, "heaven *is* an endless act of worship, because everyone's heart is constantly caught up in joy, wonder and gratitude. You don't have to sing it with a song or even say a word to express it, although sometimes you'll want to. The song is already in your heart, so anything you voice is simply a reflection of that inner reality. Worship here is a state of being, an inclination of the heart that replaces the physical action expressing it on earth. You don't *do* worship in heaven—you *are* worship."

"Because you experience what is in my heart before I can say it," Amanda rejoined.

"Exactly!"

Irresistible

"You know," he continued more earnestly now, rolling over on one side to look at her more directly (Amanda thought he looked like a plane with one wing pointed straight at the ground, that somehow hung happily in the air anyway). "I have always seen gratitude that way, even before you came here. I received what was in your heart, what you intended and not the faltering execution which is all that is possible on earth, broken as it is. Here, for the first time, you can see others—and yourself, and me—the way I have always seen you."

"But wait…if you saw my heart, you would've seen all the bad things, too," Amanda began, remembering. "You saw the days when I wanted to end it all and kill myself. You knew how I hated Caspar for what he did to my dad. You knew—"

"Oh, darling, you have yet to understand how far love goes," he interrupted. "Here, let me show you your world." Jesus drew in closer, until only a narrow corridor of rushing air separated them. With a flourish and sparkling eyes, he extended a fist and slowly opened his palm. Hanging in the space between his curled fingers lay a small, blue marble, slowly spinning on its axis. Fascinated, Amanda looked closer and saw the thin veil of an atmosphere, swirling clouds, then continents and city lights. As her sight took in more and more, she began to hear the mingled voices of billions of men, women and children as they went about their daily lives, sharing the vital and the mundane, joining in happy laughter or weeping in lonely agony.

"This little ball is your earth, as it was," Jesus said soberly, "The entire domain of pain and confusion is exactly this big. But this—" he suddenly spread his arms wide to take in all the soaring mountains, spreading lawns and endless airs that made up heaven— "is the extent of love! It is as high as the stars, as bracing as a plunge in the River of Life and as unfathomably deep as the mind of The One. All the wrong you have ever done is no bigger than a molecule in this world, swallowed up in an ocean of goodness."

Then Jesus put a warm arm around her shoulder, so they were flying in tandem. "Amanda, you entrusted your heart to me when you were a girl, and I have taken you at your word ever since. On your decision day, I saw your desire to be mine. So every day after I have treated you according to that intent, and not by the faltering execution which is all that is possible on earth, broken as it is."

"Wow...so you really aren't upset at me for stuff I've done? Even a little?"

Jesus shook his head happily. Strangely, Amanda noticed for the first time that his nose was crooked. But she didn't mention it—because in heaven such flaws didn't seem to matter. And choosing to overlook that small thing made something larger click into place in her mind. *So it really, truly doesn't matter...Love is so outrageously huge here, and joy is hiding in every corner...flaws and failings only amount to one miniscule atom in that tiny blue ball. He could simply close his hand and it'd all be gone.*

"I'm sorry," she said out loud. "I guess I knew *theoretically* that you were supposed to put my past and all my mistakes behind you…but I didn't really believe it until now."

"But of course you didn't! How could you? You lived in a world whose great truths were mere shadows that pointed to this one. But here! In this world you can eat and drink truth, experiencing it in full. You've come to the land where life conquers death and mercy triumphs over judgement. The shadows are gone forever; and being gone, they no longer matter. It's just a drop of water, lost in the all-conquering sea of my love."

They flew on in silence as Amanda absorbed the picture he'd given her. Down near the horizon, the sky was colored like a sunset, all pinks and oranges, yet without clouds or smog to sully the air. After a few moments, another question occurred to her. "If all wrong is forgotten simply because I chose you… what would have happened if I had said, 'No' back there on the top of the cliff? If I had held on to despair instead of trusting you—then what?"

"Oh, child!" The Man of Light laughed, throwing his arms up with such glee that he did a full back-flip in the glittering air. "You *really* think you could resist my love when we are standing face to face, and I am not veiled like on earth?"

"I'm guessing…no?"

"No, Amanda, not hardly! Not in a million years, as they say on earth. I'm quite irresistible," he joked, then tucked in his knees and somersaulted forward through the air.

Amanda followed his lead—then added in a twist of her own. What a blast! It was like diving off the high board, with no fear of heights and no water to give you a punishing slap if your landing was off. For a few moments Amanda executed an array of quadruple gainers, pikes, tucks and backflips while Jesus hung chuckling in the air, ranking each dive a 'ten' with his fingers.

After a few minutes she stopped spinning, and they flew on in formation again, a wide grin plastered across Amanda's face.

Even though it wasn't necessary, she still felt more comfortable with her arms out like wings. Jesus had no such inhibitions. He lay there on his side, totally relaxed. Something about it made Amanda uncomfortable—her subconscious begged for him to balance his head on an elbow, or *something*. But the Master of gravity needed no such support. It would take a while for her mind to adapt to a world where gravity was optional.

6 Memory

They sailed on through the delicious air, descending steadily while Amanda soaked in the luminous emerald landscape passing below. After a bit Jesus added a nugget of explanation.

"There's a good reason I don't appear to people on earth as I am here, Amanda. Being a truly irresistible guy" (he said it in a playful tone) "means it would leave you with no other choice. You would *have* to come to me. For instance, back when you were six, you and your dad put iron filings and a magnet in a bowl as an experiment. What happened?"

"I keep forgetting you know everything," Amanda conceded. "The filings all stuck to the magnet, of course."

"Yes! And no matter how you arrange those objects in the bowl, you know they'll end up in that same configuration before you even start. If I appear on earth as I am in heaven, it will make human beings nothing more than iron filings, forced to conform to my magnetic personality whether they want to or not. How eternally boring! It would defeat the whole purpose of creation."

An iridescent bird the size of a wren skittered by, the indigo and scarlet flash on its head complementing a deep-green breast.

The Man of Light held out a beckoning finger, and it immediately banked around and alighted on that perch, singing happily.

"Here, look at what this bird can teach us. It has life, like you do; and its own mind." He reached out and stroked the feathers on its crest with a delicate touch, and the little wren cooed in reply. "But instead of choice it has instinct. Birds have lovely voices, but they only sing the notes The Maker wrote for them. At my call, this bird will come to me—not because it freely chooses that path out of love, but because it was made in love to fly that path. When we made this world, we wanted more than instinctive, animal attraction: we wanted to be chosen."

"And humans are a different animal—" Amanda began, then reddened, realizing the pun she'd inadvertently fallen into.

"Don't worry—every joke in heaven is a good joke," Jesus exclaimed with a laugh. "And yes, humans are different. You're the *one* organism on earth with the ability to love God. The whole universe—the stars, the galaxies, all matter and energy, atoms to elephants and electrons to orbits—was created for just *one* reason: to allow for the possibility of that free choice."

The weight of that statement hung in the whistling air between them. And in that moment Amanda simultaneously felt infinitely tiny within the scale of the universe, yet infinitely important to the person next to her.

"If you've invested so much in creating choice," Amanda began haltingly, a bit awed, "I can see why you don't want to mess that up by appearing as your irresistible self." Then the down-to-earth part of her personality reasserted itself. "Oh—so *that's* why you seem so…distant? Hard to talk to? I'm not sure what to call it. Sometimes on earth it feels like you're in a witness protection program for deities."

"Oh, I like that turn of phrase!" Jesus exclaimed, grinning widely. "Witness protection program for deities—hah!" Looking out into the crystalline sky, he repeated it several times, each with slightly different wording, before turning back to Amanda. "No—your version is best." Then he lifted his arm a bit, and the little wren flitted off to join several of its fellows, twittering as if it had a just met a celebrity and couldn't wait to post a selfie of it.

"There! You just made up something new: a phrase that didn't originate in the mind of God. You became a creator. And by creating you gave Us something new to think about. Amanda, that's what it means to be 'made in his image.' You're a creator like Us! And having a billion other creators running around makes heaven infinitely more interesting than if we had to think of everything ourselves. We Three always have fun together, but it is way *more* fun with humanity around."

"You're right—that does sound like a party," Amanda agreed, a gratified look on her face. "And it's not every day that a girl comes up with something God never thought of!"

Independent Life

"Of course," The Man of Light inserted as an afterthought, "there's another reason I don't appear on earth as the irresistible me. Put me in all my dimensions into the same room as earth-bound humans, and—boom! Same reason your experiment exploded."

"That would be sort of a problem," Amanda replied wryly.

"Yeah," Jesus answered, banking a bit to the left. Amanda made the mental adjustment and followed. "People tend to ignore that fact when they demand that if I am really real, I should just show up in all my glory and right every wrong in the universe. They don't know what they're asking! The day when I do precisely that will be a doomsday—everyone who sees my face will face their doom. Whatever they have chosen is what they'll have.

"But—dearest Amanda," he asserted, reaching across the gap between them. "You chose me! On earth, where I was just a guy born in a barn, you chose me. Because your decision is already locked in, I can put on my real, irresistible identity here without violating your free will."

"Okay. But I *have* to say," Amanda remarked, a good bit of snark in her voice, "Talking about being 'born in a barn' reminds me of this old movie, *The Princess Bride*—"

"Yup, I've seen it."

"You watch *movies*?" she gasped, astonished.

"Of course. I watch everything. I'm omniscient. But please: continue!"

"Oh, okay," Amanda replied dubiously. "Anyway, in *The Princess Bride* the farm boy is a servant in the house of this beautiful girl—"

"Like when I came to earth as a servant. Go on."

"And he falls in love with her."

"Ditto."

"And becomes a pirate to make his fortune so he can marry her."

"Okay, the pirate part doesn't really fit in. But look what happens next: he surrenders to the authorities, and is killed, but he comes back to life because of true love. In the end, he gets the girl and they live happily ever after!

"Don't you see?" Jesus exclaimed happily, doing another somersault. "We snuck that plot into popular culture as a clue to who I am. I love it when you find the clues!"

"Well, I'm glad I watched the movie then, even though I thought it was pretty lame at the time."

"You were thirteen," Jesus parried. "*Everything* is lame when you are thirteen."

"Alright, you got me there."

"So here's the point. This whole place—" here he spread his arm out and inscribed a circle in the air that encompassed heaven, "populated with ten billion little creators who are in it for love—this could not exist without earth. Earth, the planet where God was hidden, was *necessary*. There had to be an Age of Choosing. You had to have life independent of Us. We had to veil ourselves and give you the freedom to choose without putting our finger on the scale. The only way to build a heaven where We Three could be ourselves around you and you could be free around us was to create you with choice on earth."

"Wow," Amanda mouthed the word without saying it aloud. "I always wondered why we had to go through all that painful stuff back on earth. A couple of my buds in college used to say things like, "If this God of yours is really good, why didn't he just make us in heaven in the first place?" Or, "Why did God give me choices if he knew I was going to screw it up? I wish he'd just made the choice for me."

The solemn expression on Jesus' face told Amanda she'd just asked about something profound. He glanced out over the landscape, as if tallying up the worth of some choice. The only thing to do was wait, and listen to the wind whistling gently past her ears.

"We actually asked those questions ourselves," Jesus stated quietly, deep in thought. "For a long age We pondered together how to create beings who could love, yet found no answer that did not involve pain. It was not until I volunteered to make the ultimate sacrifice that a plan came together. A risky plan."

"Um…forgive me for asking, but how can God take risks? If you know what is going to happen before it ever does, where's the risk in that?"

Jesus altered course until he flew beside her, and put a warm arm around her shoulder. It felt good to be close. "You are thinking of risk in an earthly sense, in terms of causation. Like, 'if I invest X dollars here, how likely is it if I get a 20% return?' Our risks are not causal, but relational. We love all that we have made. We love each person we have created to the very fullest extent of love. The risk in giving a real choice is that some do not return our love, and so some of what we have made and loved ceases to be.

"But—the choice was made, and the risk was taken!" Jesus exulted. "And now you and I can eat the fruit of that good choice forever. For you are here in the Beautiful Land with Us, alive with Our life and loving as We love you.

"The decisions you and I made on earth are fixed in heaven, immutable and unchangeable. Once you are here, there are no choices that can lead us apart—the gravity of love is just too strong. There is no way out of bliss, no escaping love and no option but joy. Nothing can separate us. Yet because you have freely chosen the Beautiful Land without compulsion, you remain free to enjoy it."

"So I can't screw up in heaven?"

"Nope. Can't happen—it is literally impossible."

"I like that. But what about the past?" Amanda countered. "You're God—you know everything. You must remember every mistake I made. And wouldn't those choices be fixed, too? What do you do with that?"

The Mirror of Time

Jesus banked around so he was flying backwards—which seemed wholly impossible and then, after a moment's mental adjustment, as natural as breathing. He had stretched his arms out like wings and extended his legs downward together, his body forming the shape of a cross. For a brief instant she saw into that part of his story, tasting the mingled surrender and longing in his heart at the moment of his death. Then, to her surprise, he settled back as if he was on a recliner and laced his fingers together behind his head, sitting on a couch made of air miles above ground as if it was something he did every day.

"I have what you might call 'selective memory' about what happens on earth," he chuckled.

"Sounds like marketing-speak if you ask me," Amanda jibed in return. "Like 'alternative facts' or something. What do you mean by that?"

"It's part of the gift of free will. You get to decide whether I see you from an earthly point of view or a heavenly one. And whatever you choose, I honor."

"So…you only remember one or the other?"

"You got it! Choose me, and, because all of earth's time is swallowed up in Heaven's Eternal Now, you are immediately seated at a place of honor at my table in heaven, clothed in light, pure and perfect, just as you see yourself now. From the moment of your choice onward, the only 'you' visible from my point of view is the heavenly one.

"Amanda, since you made your choice for me as a girl, *this* you, the one flying through the air with me above the Beautiful Land, is the only you I've ever known. To me, the old Amanda passed out of existence on your choosing-day, and the new you is already here. Pick me, and as far as heaven is concerned, you are immediately a lifetime member. Choose your own way, and you will always be seen as you are on earth."

"I sort of get it…but I guess I don't really get it," Amanda admitted.

"Here—this might make sense to you. Imaghine your life is a computer program," Jesus continued, looking very much the teacher now. "When you became mine, a new version—version 2.0—of your life was installed on my laptop. Version 1.0 got over-written—we can't access that edition in heaven even if we wanted to, because we had to uninstall it to upgrade you to version 2.0. So, when I look at you now, version 2.0 of your life is all I see.

"The challenge for you on earth is, you're still only running version 1.1, because you don't meet the hardware requirements" (here he snickered at his own joke) "for version 2.0. You'll do incremental upgrades all your life on earth, but to go to version two, you need a body with heaven's dimensions. Once you get that new motherboard—in other words, when you put on your heavenly body—*then* we can boot your mind up in version 2.0 and you get to see yourself as we do."

"Okay, I think I can wrap my head around that," Amanda replied unevenly. "But if all you see is heaven's version 2.0 of me, how can you relate to the bugs and crashes I'm still experiencing running version 1.1?"

"It'll be easier if I show you a picture." Immediately the air in front of Amanda seemed to freeze into a solid, translucent crystal, like diamond. It flew along with her about an arm's length away, every facet glimmering with the radiance of The Man of Light. He spoke, and the crystal stretched, and flattened. The glorious reflection faded, until its colors grew dim and distant. The outline of her face dissolved into a new image: the back of an aged woman, bent down with care. It reminded her of an old sepia photo, grey and lifeless next to the rich colors she'd seen in her own reflection.

Then the figure turned toward her, and Amanda gasped. The woman was *herself*, the earth-bound Amanda! A cry of pity escaped her quivering lips as she perceived how weak, how transient, how ingrown and afraid that life was compared to what she had now. She would have reached through the mirror to help herself, but Jesus spoke first.

"What you see is yourself in the mirror of time, from the vantage point of earth. Time is like a one-way mirror between earth and heaven. When you look from earth, you can't see yourself as you are in heaven, because you are trapped in earth-time. All that appears in the mirror is a reflection of your present, the memory of your past, and your hopes and fears for the future. The Eternal Now we live in here is imperceptible.

"Now look once more," he beckoned, "and watch what happens when you gaze into that mirror from the *other* side—from heaven's point of view."

The mirror flipped over on the horizontal axis, so she could see its backside. Like a movie on the silver screen, an image appeared there. It was the main hall of her old high school. Although the scene was set on earth, one like a Child of Light walked amidst the teenagers. The light of love streaming out from her limbs fell on those around her, causing even the floor beneath her transparent feet to fluoresce with the manifold hues of heaven. *That's me!* Amanda gasped with amazement. *I look like The Man of Light! Less bright, perhaps, but a member of the same family. It couldn't be...*

Yet in her heart she knew that she was seeing her true self, as He beheld her, beautiful and desirable and perfect. Tears streamed from her eyes as her self-image shifted to align with how her Maker saw her.

After it was all over, she could never describe that glorious version of herself or tell what made it so beautiful—only that her hair streamed out behind her in the wind, in endless, rippling waves of auburn and silver, and that she looked like him.

A weakly whispered "Wow!" was all Amanda could manage.

"Pretty good, isn't it?" Jesus nodded toward the mirror, and it disappeared. "That was a glimpse from MY point of view. Even while you are still on earth, I see the you which is here in heaven now, right beside me, and has been from the moment you chose me.

"But—" and here he twirled his finger and took on a mischievous look, "even though I've set my eyes on the heavenly you, I *can* still relate to the bugs and crashes of your life on earth. You know why?"

"Because you lived on earth's side of the mirror once?"

"Exactly. I've got real-world experience with version 1.1: emotions and needs and hunger and joy...everything! When I passed over into the Beautiful Land, I was the first in all creation to see from both sides of the mirror, just like you did a moment ago. And to honor my journey to earth The Maker gave me this gift: whatever viewpoint I chose, heaven would also take."

"And you chose…?"

"Why, to only look at you from heaven's side of the mirror, of course! Easiest decision I ever made, though the angels never anticipated it. I decided to forget earth's view of the chosen, and to never, ever bring it to mind again."

Amanda looked to the horizon, one eyebrow raised and a pair of faint lines creasing her forehead. They passed through a golden haze in the air. She was mildly surprised to find it wasn't damp and clammy like a cloud or fog. Instead, it left sprinkles of gold dust on her face and hands.

"She's thinking about it," Jesus commented to himself, then laughed. "Gold looks good on you. I like how it makes your hair sparkle in the wind. Yes, it's all true: you are a new creation—the old Amanda has been overwritten and replaced by version 2.0. In earth's time, it doesn't yet appear what you will be, because the heavenly you is still in the future. But to me, your future self is here, right now, standing right beside me. Since you have passed through the mirror and left earth behind, you can see yourself as I have always seen you, too.

"So—today I will honor you as The Maker honored me: you can choose your viewpoint. Will you decide to forget earth's mirror, and only look on yourself in The Light of heaven?"

Amanda smiled back at him. "I do."

"Yes! The perfect answer—we wove those words into the marriage ceremony to foreshadow just this moment. And I do, too. Why would I look at an old, broken-down, version of my bride when the real, glory-filled, heavenly edition is standing right in front of me at the altar? And why would the bride fixate on a spot on the carpet when her beloved is proclaiming his undying love for her in front of the host of heaven?"

Pictures flashed in Amanda's mind of every wedding she'd ever been to, yet this time overlaid with The Light and the music of heaven. She saw The Maker and The Man of Light tinkering with human customs, putting ideas into the minds of young men and fathers, of brides and their mothers, crafting a wedding tradition that reflected the truths of heaven. And down through ages, as nations came and went and customs changed, still that savor of heaven remained in the act of marriage.

They flew on, Amanda absorbing the picture and its glory while Jesus waited patiently beside her, as if he had all the time in the world just to listen. Amanda began to appreciate just how high the cliff behind her really was: they'd been descending for what seemed like hours, but the countryside was still far, far below.

"So…you did all that, just so we could see each other with the eyes of heaven" she breathed, "and forget how we saw each other on earth? And this forgetting, this selective memory thing—it's a function of the difference between heaven's time and earth's?"

"Right! But the best way for those on earth's side of the mirror to grasp it is to say that I simply don't remember the bad things you've done. Pretty mind blowing for the earth-dwellers, huh?"

Forgetting

"Yeah, you got me there. But…let me get this straight," Amanda replied with a grin. "God is a God of amnesia?"

"If so, it's an amnesia you share."

"Huh?" Amanda responded, suddenly realizing that she had unconsciously taken a seat on an anti-gravity air couch across from Jesus. She looked down and instead of sofa cushions saw thousands of feet of air. On earth she would have panicked, but strangely her emotions gave an inner shrug and settled back a bit further into the comfort of sitting on absolutely nothing. *I guess I'm getting more used to this place after all,* she decided.

"That you are!" Jesus laughed, responding to her thought. "But since you're into experiments, try this one. A moment ago, you made the choice to see with heaven's eyes and forget what you saw in earth's mirror. So test it out! Try to remember one of those awful things you were telling me you did, and see what happens."

"Okaaaay," Amanda answered hesitantly. She closed her eyes (which didn't help much since her eyelids were transparent, but it was habit) and pictured herself, sitting in the little cranny at the back of the closet under the stairs, her hiding place, looking at the pill bottle she'd taken from her dad's bathroom. And then a shock—she found she was sitting in the lap of The Man of Light! She watched herself think about taking her life, but the answering thoughts that argued for life— "What will that do to your dad? You still have friends who love you! Things are getting better at school"—she saw coming from Jesus' lips, as he patiently convinced her that life was better than ending it all.

Amanda opened her eyes and found herself nestled comfortably in the lap of The Man of Light (who was still floating on air), golden beams of his life shooting through her in all directions. Nothing felt more natural or comfortable.

"You were there?"

"Of course. To be more precise, that's how *I* remember what happened. Part of your upgrade to Amanda 2.0 is fusing your memory to mine."

"You don't erase my memories, do you?" Amanda wondered, her brow wrinkling with concern. "Then how would I still be me?"

"No, no!" he laughed. "We don't erase them: we *upgrade* them. You are in heaven, so now you get to see your life on earth from heaven's point of view.

"How?"

"Hmmm…going on with the computer analogy will probably make the most sense to you. Ever put a new hard drive in your computer?"

"Yeah. Every couple of years I seem to run out of space."

"What do you do before you copy everything over?"

"Usually a little housekeeping—run a virus scan, empty the trash, dump all my temp files, that sort of thing. No sense copying over junk."

"Well, we kinda do the same thing up here," Jesus replied. "On earth, humans remember only a small part of what happens in their lives—unfortunately, often the worst parts are recalled best. So first, we do a little housekeeping: we run a virus scan and block off the damaged sectors where hurt or pain has distorted your sight. Then we take your data files—the memories you have of your life—and interweave them with *my* memory of those same situations. Everything you recall—and a ton of things you forgot—will still be in your memory, but now you'll see it from heaven's point of view. See, we remember *everything* here," he said modestly.

"You must have a big library," Amanda gulped.

"Enormous!" Jesus laughed. "And all of it right up here!" he gestured, tapping a finger on his temple. "I'm actually giving you a piece of my mind. Every single one of your memories now has me in it—because I was there in every moment of your life. You get to read the full, uncensored version of your life story—to look into the unseen and find me everywhere and in everything."

Washing

"Go ahead," he beckoned gently. "Look in the mirror again and try to remember another moment that felt terrible on earth."

Suddenly, either Amanda's memory began moving at warp speed, or time pumped the brakes and slowed way down. She was at the movies, and the flick that was showing was her entire life: every scene playing all at once, on a thousand different screens. And everywhere she looked, she saw Jesus: now comforting her through a friend, now standing beside her pointing out the artistry of a sunset, now holding her whether she let herself cry or if she forced down the tears and told herself she'd never cry again.

The more she saw The Man of Light walking through her history, the more she beheld a life painted in color and light instead of the cold gray of pain. One moment she'd witness a choice or an angry word she'd spoken, and feel a twang of regret. But in the next, Jesus would walk on stage and immediately begin refashioning and nudging along those choices to produce something good. Seeing him so present at every turn transformed regret into wonder and gratitude. Amanda grew more and more amazed at his dexterity—he could be given mud as a raw material and make it into a rainbow.

Then her sight changed once more, and instead of remembering each moment one after the other, she rose above the arrow of time. The mirror showed her all her days merged into one moment, one infinitely complex tapestry of purpose. Rays of light from different memories pulsated in the fabric and began to intertwine, weaving themselves together into patterns that reached backward and forward and sideways through time. Whenever two threads connected, The Maker reached down and deposited a silver droplet of his goodness into the weave.

I'm actually seeing the mind of God, Amanda grasped in wonder. *This is HIS memory of my story, knitted in ways undiscoverable within time. This is the 'why' behind everything!*

Enthralled, she watched The One, The Man of Light and The Voice collaborate to choose her personality type, natural abilities and the day of her birth. She understood why they chose as they did, and how those choices served and protected her.

Those three huddled again after the death of her mother, deciding to focus the rest of her life on restoring her deepest loss—the carefree joy and trust she'd had as a child. That thread of purpose reached forward and then backward in time, through her whole history on earth. Amazed, she watched The One arrange people and circumstances to prepare her to open her heart again and participate in love.

Then, as if the mirror was abruptly yanked miles backwards into a larger perspective, she saw the fabric of her life as one small part of the Great Tapestry of history. Billions and trillions of threads wove themselves into one larger story all at once, with the silver droplets of connection falling from God's fingers like rain in a Kansas thunderstorm.

When that whole tapestry pulsated with glory and the gray was no more, Amanda—still sitting in his lap—heard Jesus whisper softly in her ear. "This is the Great Washing with the water of the word, the healing of memories. We Three spoke a Word of love over your life from the very beginning, and now that Word has completed its purpose. It has showered our love on your earth-memory and removed the stains of pain and sorrow. Now you see life on earth as it truly was, with Us at the center of it all.

"Your own memories remain. And yes, Amanda, you are still you. But whatever pain you saw in the mirror of earth is so outweighed by the eternal glory I crafted from it—they are simply beyond comparison—that the old view disappears."

"So be it," Amanda heard herself say. In that moment all her heart wanted to do was to fall at his feet and thank The Man of Light for every incredible thing he had done for her. Then it occurred to her that they were floating on air far above the clouds, and maybe falling wasn't such a brilliant idea at that moment. Then she forgot about falling, because he spoke again.

"The Washing removes the last marks of evil scarring your heart, and now you are fully prepared to enter the Beautiful Land and participate in the wedding of heaven and earth. From now on, you will be clothed in white." (Amanda immediately looked down, and sure enough, white sleeves of the most beautifully patterned, perfectly-white linen covered her arms. The stitching duplicated the weave of the tapestry of her life.) "Yes, because no one comes to the wedding who is not dressed in white from the Washing of the Word."

"So," Jesus went on in a more playful tone. "The clothes—do you like them?"

Amanda flung her arms around The Man of Light and kissed his neck, while her joyful tears fell on his shoulders. "Oh, absolutely! You were always so close—and now I literally *wear* the part you played in my history on my sleeves. I wish I would have known!"

She pulled back and wiped her eyes on that sleeve, which dried immediately in the air rushing past. "But now I do know," she continued solemnly. "And that is Enough."

"Yup," Jesus smiled. "It is."

Acquittal

Just examining her sleeves occupied the next portion of the flight. The patterns were indeed from the Great Tapestry, and the closer you looked the more detail emerged, whorl upon whorl, each stitch telling a story. Amanda felt she was adorned in purity, in clothes that would never get dirty or need a wash.

"Wow—this is all such a relief!"

"A relief? That's an interesting word. Relief from what?" The Man of Light inquired.

"Well—" Amanda had said it because that's how she felt: relieved, released, not guilty. But now she wasn't entirely sure why she felt that way. As her thoughts turned inward, she pulled back a few feet til she and The Man of Light sat cross-legged facing each other. (By now Amanda had completely lost track of the fact that she was resting thousands of feet up on nothing.)

"What were you expecting to happen that didn't?" he prodded gently.

"Um…you showed me my whole life, and how you were in it. But—" and here her voice turned girlish, "Isn't there supposed to be like, a last judgement, where you show me everything I did wrong?"

"Okay—and why would I do that?"

"I don't know. I hadn't really thought it through. I guess I kind of imagined that you have this need to judge stuff, and I have to pay somehow for my mistakes...although that sounds a little silly when I say it to your face. I always pictured the entrance of heaven as a courtroom, where God was up in a big wooden judge's bench looking down on me, and a movie played on the wall showing every bad thing I did while all of heaven watched."

"That sounds *awful*," Jesus said softly, a curious expression on his face. "When you imagined that, how did you feel?"

"Afraid. Small. Guilty, embarrassed, ashamed, regretful."

"You do a fine job of expressing emotions," Jesus observed kindly. When he was being tender, The Light pouring from his face took on softer tones, almost like pastels, reflecting his mood. "So based on what you've experienced of me so far, do I seem like somebody who would do that to you?"

"No, not at all!"

Jesus sighed, shaking his head. "They tell such lies about Us on earth," he breathed. "Abba, I am always grateful that you handle it so well."

Amanda realized he was actually talking to The One at that moment and not to her. A half-second later a pulse of energy went through the air, like a wave that thudded into her insides and then passed on: The One breathing his agreement with Jesus' thought.

The Man of Light looked directly in her eyes. "No, I would never put you through something like that. There is no Last Judgement as you've envisioned it for the Children of Light: only the Last Acquittal."

"That sure sounds a lot better. Tell me more!"

"Do you remember the vision you saw of The Man of Light on earth?"

"Yes! You gave up your life-light so that humanity could return to The Light."

"And in the book's next chapter, beyond all hope the hero and his true love are reunited in eternity. So how does an author end a love story like that? Does the hero throw a party to celebrate their reunion, or does he throw his love in prison to make her pay for his sacrifice?"

"Oh. It's the party, obviously," Amanda nodded, beginning to tear up as the truth came into her, dissipating fear.

His sigh trailed out behind them as they flew, absorbing the tears flicked from Amanda's cheeks by the passing air. "Some folks imagine I have nothing better to do than sit here scowling in a puddle of bliss, storing up offenses to punish," he added soberly. Then a smile stole across his lips. "Truth is, most of my time goes into making arrangements for our wedding. The idea that I'm sitting up here stewing, unable to get over my fiancé's flaws... It would be like if a groom on his wedding night, rather than consummating their marriage, sat his bride down on the bed and told her everything he didn't like about her! Who would do such a thing?

"No, when the bride walks down the aisle, all the groom sees is how beautiful she is. Marriage was made for this very reason—to show you how I think of you and who you are to me."

"That sounds a lot more like the you I know," Amanda admitted. "Now I'm really relieved! It's just that I was always taught—"

"Yeah, yeah," Jesus replied wryly. "That I was this stern, merciless judge who was going to wash your mouth out with soap every time you said a cross word." He shook his head, his curly black hair jiggling back and forth as he did it. Amanda briefly thought it looked like an afro, and stifled a giggle.

"There *is* a judgement for lies about us, and the liars who tell them. But for you—we've already straightened out what you did wrong and put it behind us. Therefore, when you die, you are sent to straight to the Court of Acquittal, not the Court of Judgement."

"And what happens in this Court of Acquittal?" Amanda inquired.

"The judge walks in, announces that all charges against you have been dropped, brings his gavel down with a bang, and that's THE END of judgement for you, forever. Then he steps down from the bench to give you a bearhug, shakes your hand, and cries out, "Come, happy friend of The One! Inherit the citizenship prepared for you from the foundation of the world."

"So, no judgement?"

"Actually, an acquittal *is* a judgement—we judge that you belong to us, and you belong here, and no blame sticks to you."

"And now," Jesus said, rising abruptly from the air couch and taking both her hands, "since you have chosen to forget the old, and you've been Washed and Acquitted, let us enter into the Beautiful Land! I have a surprise I've been waiting ages to show you!"

Then they danced together down the pathway of sky to heaven's lawn, waltzing with one hand clasped and Jesus' arm around her waist. Above, Hope flew great soaring loops about them.

7 Reunion

Amanda landed on a vast rolling field of the greenest grass, where a few quick steps decelerated her to a halt. The emerald carpet caressing her bare feet was speckled with small, crystalline blooms of lavender and white. Those stationary colors were accented by a second, moving layer of pale yellow and gold, as thousands of tiny butterflies flitted from petal to petal, drinking from the blossoms. The nectar given by the flowers was light. Each time the insects fed, the canvas of their wings would briefly mix their own gold with waves of purple and white from the flowers. Thus, the grass was constantly dappled with subtle hues, creating a new dimension of constantly-renewed beauty.

Then all the flowers bowed over toward her left, the green grass followed suit and the soil rumbled harmonies in the lowest registers as The Man of Light floated to the ground next to her. A halo of butterflies rose to dance around his brow, and all that world celebrated its Creator.

A new, woody note joined the chorus. Seeking its source, Amanda spied a mighty, spreading oak a ways ahead, knees bending amidst the grass under a wide canopy. Blinking, she looked again, because something didn't quite seem right about the tree. Then she had it. Her mind expected the lighter shades to be on the outside and darker greens below and within, just as it would on earth. Instead, inside its sprawling arms the light of this majestic specimen was actually brighter. The tree seemed lit from within, as if it had grown in the middle of a mirrored pond lit from behind by the setting sun, while against her reason the shade seemed to rest on its top.

Then a breeze ruffled the leaves. They were a rich, waxy green above, but glowed silver where their undersides were revealed. The light under the oak came from its leaves, and when they moved with the wind the tree itself sparkled, while dappled light spilled rippling across the grass beneath. On earth, the shadows produced by leafy boughs traverse the ground as branches above wave in the breeze. But here, the leaves were all made of light, so the patterns moving on the ground were not shadow, but a delicious illumination.

When that foliage stirred, a faint music whispered in the air, the rustle of leaves exuding a peace that only arrives when time is left behind. She'd felt it once while dreaming of heaven—the sense that nothing was passing you by or leaving you behind, that you had infinite time to do anything you wanted. To sit at a shaded picnic table on a perfect day, and talk long and deep with friends, with no sunset or mealtimes or endings to break the reverie.

That dream had given Amanda the deepest sense of rest she'd ever experienced. When she awakened, all she wanted to do was recapture it—the sense that she would never miss out, never run out, never grow tired, always have more than enough. It was an infinite contentment.

"I often introduce my people to heaven in dreams," Jesus stated quietly. Then, his mood shifting, he cast his arms wide, letting his radiance cast its own pool of light across the flower-studded lawn. Turning to Amanda, he cried out with a flourish, "Welcome home! All of this land is for you."

The look on his face—I see him better now, she decided—radiated satisfaction, contentment, and approval. Every good dream she'd ever had, the best day of her life, her loveliest imagination—this was better, wider, and lovelier than them all. Home.

She was just about to throw herself down on the grass and luxuriate in that endless peace when a star appeared from around the oak's enormous trunk. The leaves above a shone with a diffuse, milky glow, but this light was blade-sharp, a penetrating bluish beam akin to plasma arcing from a power line. As she focusing in, the star morphed into a vertical figure, then a man. He leaned against the tree with one leg casually crossed over the other.

"That's someone very important to you. I've been longing for you to meet," The Man of Light said quietly. "*This* is the justice your heart longed for on the cliff of endings. When you laid down your anger and trusted me to make all things well—this is heaven's reply."

"So what's his name?" Amanda inquired.

"Theo."

She began trembling all over, with anticipation and excitement and who-knows-what else. "Dad?" she, whispered, hardly daring to believe it could be so.

"Yup," Jesus smiled, motioning toward the tree. "Go on and say 'hi!'"

She couldn't leave without saying thank you, but there were tears in her eyes and her mouth wasn't working, so she threw her arms around Jesus and held him tight for a second. Then she tore off, not looking back, calling out, "Daddy! Daddy!" An emerald wake of light trailed behind in the verdant grass, and her feet hardly touched the ground as she ran.

Daddy

Sprinting as fast as she could toward the rippling tree, Amanda traveled more swiftly than was humanly possible on earth. The same instant, the star leapt across the verdant ground toward her with arms outstretched. They collided halfway to the great oak in a spray of light like the stream of a firehouse smacking a wall; hugging, spinning around, laughing, calling out each other's names. At one point Amanda had the distinct sensation of being tossed up in midair and then caught again, something her father used to do when she was little, and she giggling the whole time.

Finally, after a long kiss on the cheek, her daddy held her back at arm's length as they drank in each other's presence. "Mandy!" he finally exclaimed. "It means the world to me to see you here! Of all the joys in heaven, this is one of the sweetest."

"Daddy!" It was all she could get out before she fell into his arms again and held him for quite a time. At last, he took her hand and they began strolling side-by-side toward the oasis of light under the stately tree.

"For your grand entrance to the Beautiful Land, you unfortunately only have me," he pronounced with a wide grin. "I'm sorry you don't get to enjoy the usual welcoming committee. You didn't exactly get here the traditional way."

"Well, I don't know what I'm missing. What's traditional up here?"

"Oh—just a wildly-cheering crowd of your heavenly descendants, each one prepared to tell you how infinitely much your life meant to them. You hear story after story from friends you never knew on earth—some who weren't even born while you were alive! —telling how the thread of your love passed down through generations to touch them. Stories and songs, hugs and laughter and tears of joy: it's quite the party. When that first installment of experiencing your place in the Great Tapestry is finally over, you will have begun to understand the legacy you left behind on earth."

"Sounds amazing."

"That's what greets every other immigrant entering this life.

However, I see that you haven't entered the glory dimension yet. I guess you're just a special case," he added, in a touch that was so dad-like it warmed her soul.

"What makes me so special?"

"It's how you got here." He stopped for a moment and looked her proudly in the eye. "You're the very first person on earth to exist in more than four dimensions. My own daughter, space pioneer! For a few nanoseconds you were the great forerunner of the human race, boldly leading mankind into a new world. Then you died in the attempt. Oops!" He said it whimsically, as if death was a day at the theatre. "Oh, well—it was a good try, anyway."

"Oh, yeah—the experiment. I remember it spiraling out of control, and a blue flash. And then I was here. If it really blew up…then I'm finally and truly dead?"

"Well, of *course* you're dead!" Theo chuckled. "No one comes here who is still biologically alive. This is the *afterlife*—you know, *after* your *life* on earth is over?"

"Okay," Amanda said simply. A day ago, the idea of dying at 29 years old would have been horrifying and unthinkable. But here, physical death just seemed to be a natural step on the pathway to this larger life. When she thought about it that way, death didn't really bug her. Then she remembered something else she'd just heard.

"Wait—a minute ago you said I have *descendants?* But I never got married!"

"Not yet, anyway," he replied, laughing. "But heaven counts descendants differently than they do on earth."

"How so?" Amanda happily asked. This was just like old times, crunching together along the graveled millrace path near home, getting answers to a thousand questions, no matter the subject. One of their deepest points of connection had always been understanding how the world worked.

"Earth assigns descendants using biological criteria," her

father explained. "Your offspring are those who've inherited your DNA. But heaven counts descendants according to life-flow. So everyone you've loved, everyone whose burdens you shared—people you sacrificed for, helped out in practical ways, or treated kindly, for example—count as your descendants. And since time here flows in every direction, some of your descendants received life from you before you were born."

"Huh?" Amanda asked, puzzled. "How in the world could that be?"

"Well…you saw it in the tapestry, didn't you? How the threads went both forwards and backwards?"

"Yeah, I saw time moving forward and backward. Which is way cool. But ancestry? That's a pretty big mouthful to swallow!"

Theo stopped momentarily on the green grass, eyes glistening with the wisdom of years but in the body of a man at the pinnacle of his strength. "Give me a second to think of a good example," he mused, stroking his goatee with his right hand.

The pose was so like her father…it would have brought a tear to Amanda's eye if she wasn't so happy. In that moment memories bubbled up inside of her childhood, the good years when he was fully engaged in life and had the energy to be attentive to his little girl.

"Oh—here we go!" her dad exclaimed, slapping his thigh. "You'll like this! Imagine that your great, great, great, grandfather was an artist."

"Was he?"

"No!" her father laughed. "He was a horse thief. I'll let him tell you *that* story when you meet him. But for the moment, imagine he was an artist. And you saw one of his paintings in a gallery and fell in love with it, not knowing who painted it. You bought that work of art, and every time you looked at it hanging on the wall it gave you joy."

"Okay, but that's still time moving forward."

"Yes, but here's the good part. On earth, his gift moves forward with the arrow of time to touch you—what was fashioned in the past produces future joy. But in heaven, your joy at his work also moves *backward* in time, to touch him. He is rewarded with your pleasure in his art, no matter when in time you find the painting. The cherry on the top is that both of you can also reach through time and meet, and share each other's joys in The Eternal Now of heaven. Influence here is not constrained by forward or back, and neither is reward."

"I think I'm getting the hang of it. So…if I think it is fun that one of my ancestors was a horse thief…"

"Yes! He is rewarded with that sense of fun, too," Theo said slyly, "even if all he earned on earth was jail time. To sum up, since joy and life flow both forward and backward in heaven's time, ancestry—the relational connection created by that gift—does, too."

They were getting close to their destination: the giant oak was only a hundred yards or so away. *We must have run farther than I thought,* Amanda realized.

"And by the way: prayers are also answered by The One without regard to time," Theo continued. "In response to a prayer, he will go back and alter what is 'past' on earth (he has no past; only Now) to launch a chain of events that brings an answer in your future. So when someone prays for you, the life flow it creates goes into both your life to come and to what has already been.

"Here's another fun example—you know that guy you've been dating, what's-his-name?"

"It's *Darren*, dad. C'mon—you *have* to know that!"

"Okay, I did—just teasing. Have you ever wondered about all those little things you two have in common? That you both like golden doodles, or you'd each spent time in Switzerland and learned a bit of German, or even that you are Cubs fans? When you were a teenager, I started praying for your soul mate. So guess what? The One went back into your past and Darren's, and planted those things just to bring you closer together. Is that awesome, or what?"

"Um, *yeah*. That's nuts!"

"In this realm," her dad mentioned modestly, "you are my descendant by love, and Darren is, too."

"Wait…does that mean I was going out with my brother?" Amanda teased back.

"Yes," Theo replied, without a hint of embarrassment. "We are all brothers and sisters here. And, because you also loved me, I am counted as your descendant by love, too. Heavenly genealogies trace how Father's life flowed back and forth through loving relationships, not by biological descent. Life-flow is what creates the threads in the Great Tapestry."

Barron

They stopped for a moment to observe the butterflies, which promptly began to swirl in chevrons around their feet. The fluttering insects moved in perfect time, so when Amanda and her father resumed their walk, the butterflies promptly began turning figure eights through each step, without missing a beat.

"Do you remember that little boy that used come by and stare through a hole in our fence back in Wisconsin?" Her dad reminisced. "You were like fourteen at the time. It was so cute: you'd invite him over, play games with him and give him treats out of the cookie jar."

"You mean Barron?"

"That's it—Barron. He is your descendant here."

"Whoa!" Amanda gasped. "*Everyone* you are kind to is your descendant?"

"Remember when we went down to the courthouse and handed out bottled water to people waiting in line to vote? Even giving someone a cup of cold water is enough to create descendants in the genealogy of heaven."

"Well, then you must have an awfully big family, dad!"

"I do," he replied, with a plain truthfulness that was both modest and rightfully proud. "Every patient I treated, for example."

"But then…wouldn't people be in more than one family? Take Barron—he had teachers and his parents and the social worker and…well, lots of people invested in him."

"Yes! That's the beauty of heaven. Everyone is a member of many families and has many places to call home, and dozens upon dozens of aunts and uncles. We live in the middle of belonging, in a limitless weave of connections."

Amanda stopped for a moment, just silently drinking it all in. To be reunited with her dad against all hope, with infinite time to enjoy each other, no more stress or sickness or struggle…and all under the blessing of The Man of Light. It was too much for words.

"Yes, you and I are blessed," her dad added quietly, as the butterflies spiraled up around his torso and then dived again toward the grass. "It's good to be with my earth family again, even though I'm part of many new families. In fact—" here his voice rose and he began speaking faster, like he always did when he was expounding on something he found especially interesting; "—you and I are actually in the family of Father Abraham. You know, the patriarch who lived 4000 years before the two of us were born? He is the first human being to figure out that The One wasn't a capricious deity to be placated with rituals and offerings, but a relational being who wanted to be known and trusted. Abraham believed him. That's why his title here is 'The Father of Trust.'

"I thought he was called the Father of Faith," Amanda questioned.

"Yes! That too! Faith and trust are two words for the same thing. Abraham opened the door to relating to The One through trust, and we inherited that perspective as a family heirloom.

"So when you meet our many-times-great grandfather—and you will, he's hard to miss," Theo added with a chuckle. "It's that beard of his: all of two feet long. Anyway, you'll know immediately that he is your parent in love. And he will look into your soul and know right away that you are his true child. The two of you will take a walk together, and you'll share how his leap of trust came down through 200-odd generations to impact you; and he will share the promises God gave to him that your life has fulfilled. Father Abraham himself will take great pride and pleasure in his contribution to your story. And you will revel in being his 198-times-great-grandchild."

"I love it when you tell stories, dad," Amanda sighed, leaning against his shoulder as they waded through the green grass.

"And I love hearing yours."

Fast Traveling

At length the happy pair reached the tree and sat down side-by-side, backs against the wide girth of its enormous trunk. A moment later Amanda suddenly realized she felt none of the small aches and discomforts that usually accompanied sitting on the ground. The tree cradled her back in a perfect embrace, as if her body and the bark instantly molded to each other, the tree rejoicing to support her leaning weight. And throughout that conversation, like soft elevator music in the background (*that's a terrible analogy! But it's what I thought of at the time*) she could hear the life-song of that tree entering her bloodstream through her skin's contact with the trunk.

For a while no words were exchanged. Just being together was enough to make the moment perfect. They simply sat hand-in-hand, drinking in joy and breathing peace.

Out on the wide, green plain, pinpricks like distant flashlights were moving on the grass, some alone but most in twos, threes or small groups. Amanda picked one of the nearer pairs and focused in, adapted now to the heavenly senses that told the story of whatever you concentrated upon. But just as her attention landed on them, the two lights quivered and then shot off like twin bullets to disappear in the distance, leaving a faint meteor trail behind.

"What in the world was that, Dad?"

Laughing, he replied, "But we're not *in* the world anymore."

"Daaaaaad!" she mimicked, drawing out the vowel, then laughed with him. "C'mon, what was it?"

"That was travel at the speed of thought. People here call it 'Fast Traveling"—apparently it was a video game term on earth that stuck. The lights you see out there are Children of Heaven. I guess those two wanted to be somewhere else. So they decided together, visualized where they wanted to be, and boom! They were gone."

"This place just keeps astounding me," Amanda said, overwhelmed by the experience of one good thing after another.

"Wanna try it?"

"Maybe. Does it hurt?" she teased.

"*Nothing* can hurt you in heaven."

"Okay, then let's do it."

"Here's how it works," Theo explained. "Just think, 'I want to be on the other side of this tree,' then picture yourself there."

"Okay…I'm imagining myself on the other side of this trunk," Amanda began, "And then I…" She disappeared; then after a moment rematerialized, laughing. Before her dad could say a word, she vanished around the tree and reappeared once more, then popped up like a gopher in the grass 50 paces away before reemerging at his side.

"That is just *brutally* cool!" she exclaimed, grabbing his shoulder in excitement. "Where do you want to go first?"

"Right now, I don't want to go anywhere but here with you." Her dad reached down to the green carpet under his legs and plucked a small, perfect star of a golden flower (it immediately regrew). Then he reached over to tuck it in her hair, above her right ear. The bloom quickly brightened, changing color to match Amanda's eyes, so that it was the perfect accessory. Amanda felt the brush of a kiss on her cheek, then her father drew back to arm's length, still gazing at her. "You were always my favorite and my only."

For a time as long as remembering every dear moment they'd shared on earth, and as short as heaven's Eternal Now, they stared into each other's eyes, simply enjoying each other's presence. Dad's pupils were the same deep brown as always, but, lit from within, the iris sparkled like a sunburst through a faceted gemstone.

So that's *what an eye was designed to look like,* Amanda mused, captivated by its singular beauty. The terrestrial eye with its rays of melanin and variegated colors, what poets spoke of fondly as 'a window to the soul,' was basically a flat surface reflecting the flat light of the gray world it existed in. But here, the eye was an actual window (*How did the poets know that?* she wondered), and the soul's inner light projected outward through that lens in a kaleidoscope of joy, wisdom and story.

Her dad smiled. "There is so much here that you see for the first time and think, 'Oh! So *that's* the way it was always meant to be.'"

"Yeah. It's like déjà vu all over again. In my first life, I could only think of heaven in terms of what I experienced on earth. But once you get here, you realize that's backward: earth is a copy of heaven and not the other way around."

"Right. And it seems like you've already figured out the Great Reversal."

"The great what?"

8 The Great Reversal

"The Great Reversal is what we call the inside-out nature of this place."

"Oh!" Amanda cried, sitting up straight. "Like when you look at a person you see their insides before their outsides! Same with the rocks, and the trees—I can even see right through my own skin. It's like…well, okay, you know what it's like. Now tell me how it works."

"I'll try. It takes a while for your mind to adapt to thinking in all these dimensions." He looked out over the plain for a long moment, lips pursed, then perked up as if he'd had an idea.

"Okay—consider this. When you meet someone on earth, what do you notice about them first?"

"Well, their hair, the color of their eyes, what they are wearing…if they've taken a shower in the last three days…"

"That last one only happens in college," Theo stated drily. "Yes, you see what's on the outside, because the old universe is the world of *reflected* light. To see an object, you take photons from a light source—like the sun, or a streetlight—and bounce them off an object. That reflected light comes into your eyes…"

"Which convert it to electrical impulses that run down your

ocular nerve into your brain, which assembles it into a picture of the thing," Amanda finished.

"Right. But if you want to really get to know someone, like, say, Darren—" at this point Amanda caught just the hint of a sly grin at the corner of his mouth, "—what did you have to do to accomplish that?"

"I guess you have to be around him—to watch what he does and hear what he says."

"Exactly. In the old universe of reflected light, the soul is hidden inside the outer shell of the body. The physical part of you forms a barrier between your two hearts, which keeps your souls from touching directly, like they can here. On earth you can only get to know someone's mind when they express it through physical action. The other person, like this Darren—" (there was that Cheshire grin again) "—has to create *physical* sound waves with his voice that reach into your brain through your *physical* ears. Or he has to take a physical action, like sending you a card on your birthday, that can reach you through your body's five senses. You can't look at a person and know their story, like you can here—only indirect communication is allowed on earth."

"Kind of a crappy system if you ask me," Amanda deadpanned. "Highly inefficient. Buggy and error prone. Constantly subject to misinterpretation."

Theo laughed again. "There's a reason for all that—I'll tell you in a minute. But first, look into my eyes. What do you see?"

Obediently Amanda stared into those twin auburn wells, then began narrating. "Well, the first thing I see is the light coming from inside you. The colors sparkle—it's like a diamond in constant motion, throwing off little flashes and beams in a rainbow that extends way beyond the normal spectrum. As I look a bit longer, I realize that those little flashes are thoughts—that the light coming out of you is the content of your heart. If I focus on one piece I hear and see and taste it—hey, I can taste your thoughts! —and then they come inside me. I can hear without words that you love me dearly and are delighted just to hang out together. That thought comes into me like a light, and it lodges deep inside—I can feel it there, too—like a little burning ember that becomes part of my light."

"That's very descriptive," her dad approved, still facing her. "One part of the Great Reversal is that we can see into each other's thought. Now, let your vision take it all in at once, and look another dimension deeper."

Amanda's eyes were locked on his. "When I see it all together, I see…history. I don't just see what you are thinking right now. I see your story, what you've done, how you've loved. And every sacrifice you made for love and every good thing is bathed in this glorious light that has form and substance…"

"Sorry," she gasped, pulling back to blink her eyes clear. "The picture got all watery and distorted there at the last."

"Well, that would be the tears in your eyes," Theo replied, reaching over to gently wipe her cheek. "The Great Reversal also allows us to see each other's thought in other times as well as the present—our whole history, as it were. Want to try one more look?"

"I think so. It's almost too much."

"You're still getting used to The Light. Each time you look, you'll see more, and more clearly. You can look into any part of heaven forever and still see more—that's the nature of place. Now, try looking once more."

Amanda gazed back at her dad, safe in his care. "Alright. This time I'm tuning in to who you've become in heaven: what your love and faith and choices on earth have made you into here. They have become part of you that's…I don't know how to say it. Suffering and grief might make you patient or wise on earth, but those are intangibles—character qualities hidden inside us. They only come out in what you do…

"Oh, I see! What's inside is more solid and real than what's outside. It's the Great Reversal all over again! The choices that shaped the *inner* you on earth define the *outer* you here."

"Right. What was invisible character growth on earth is transformed into an actual, physical part of your body in heaven. It's character you can see and touch."

"Which is amazing!" Amanda continued. "It's like watching the hands of God build you a new, heavenly body out of what you sacrificed for love. He's filling out the original, 3-D you with new parts or organs or something in your new dimensions, and the light coming out of you is coming from that part of who you are…

"Poppy, it's so, so…holy, so beautiful! I see places where his fingers are weaving your cells and sinews out of how you cared for me." She was weeping now. "And I see us climbing the hill of heaven where The Maker sits, as he proudly gazes down at you, pleased in how much you resemble him. And a stadium-full of the occupants of heaven applauds who you've become…"

Amanda pulled back slightly and wiped her eyes again, gathering herself. "That stuff I was seeing—was that real? It wasn't just some vision or something?"

"It's very, very real. Our earthly insides have become our heavenly outsides: the most visible, solid part of us. That's the Great Reversal."

"Amazing! Who would have thought!"

"Yeah," Theo replied, gazing back at her fondly. "A great mystery made clear."

"Or *sort of* clear," Amanda demurred. "I wonder…I can know things here, and know that I know, without fully understanding them. Like, I *know* that everything I saw is true. It's not just a theory rolling around in my mind—my whole body is somehow vibrating in tune with it. The trees and the grass seem to get it, too. But could I explain it? That seems just beyond the reach of my mind."

"That's because knowledge here is fundamentally different than on earth. Back there, it's a disembodied thing: cold, objective data points you process with your rational mind. But here, knowledge is personal: to know is to know The One. He fills everything in heaven, so everything in heaven sings in tune with his wisdom. Your heart hears that song in the world around you, as it teaches you to sing what is true beyond rational knowing."

Dutch Masters

"What's true beyond knowing…" Amanda rolled the idea around in her mind like a gumball under her tongue. "So, dad—that was a honkin' big concept you just threw out. But before we jump into the nature of knowing and I drown completely, let's nail down this Great Reversal topic."

"Okay."

Feeling they could talk more effortlessly at the same level, Amanda sprang up and reflexively began to brush the grass and twigs off her legs—and laughed again when she realized the futility of that action. There was no thatch of dead grass under the green blades here, no dust or grime, and no grass stains marred her white garments.

"Even the little things here are perfect," Theo noted, laughing with her. "Want to walk while we talk?"

Amanda nodded. Taking her father's outstretched hand, they set off arm-in-arm from under the shelter of oak's spreading branches (which took a bit—it was a *huge* tree). A luxuriant plain surrounded them, crossed by a pathway which looked completely integrated into the landscape. It was paved in grass like the meadow but marked out by borders of a blue-hearted stone that matched the sky. Amanda knew instinctively that she could walk anywhere she pleased, that all was permitted. But a path was an invitation, a sign that someone had taken thought that others might come here. And that someone set out to make journey even more of a delight. The choice to take the path was instinctive.

"I think what might really help me grasp this new-body-in-new-dimensions concept is a concrete example."

"Good idea. Hmm…you know, we literally have all the time in the world for me to explain this. However, my powers of explanation are not yet infinite!" he laughed. "Oh, here we go—do you remember when we visited the Museum of Modern Art, and saw those portraits by the 17th century Dutch masters on loan from Saint Petersburg?"

"Absolutely!" Amanda replied enthusiastically. It was so easy to get excited here—just mention the museum and she was already standing there in thought, reliving the pleasure of that long-ago visit.

"Those portraits were so real! The detail in the embroidery and lace, the way they captured the eyes…I was mesmerized by the brushwork. If you focused all your attention on a face for a minute or two, and blocked out the rest of the world, all at once the person in the portrait would leap off the canvas and come alive, right before your eyes."

"I'm glad to remember it together," Theo agreed. "That was a happy day! What brought the images to life was your brain doing a transposition. The painting itself was two dimensional. Your brain took the artist's portrayal of shadow and perspective and built a new dimension from it: depth. The 2-D canvas became a three-dimensional individual in your mind's eye.

"That's a lot like how The Maker creates your body in heaven. Except, of course, the third dimension in the portrait was an illusion created by the artist, while The Maker transposes something intangible into real existence."

"Okay, that time I really got it," Amanda announced. "Imagine if you took the Mona Lisa and tried to make it 3-D by stretching it over an unrelated object—like, say, a fire hydrant."

"Yuck!"

"Yeah, yuck is right," she laughed with him. "It would

become a grossly-painted fire hydrant—with that clunky outlet-thingy where you attach the hose for a nose! To bring the 2-D Mona Lisa to life in 3-D, you'd have to build her third dimension from information that is already present in the painting."

"Perfect analogy," her dad nodded, patting her on the back.

"So the acts of love woven into the tapestry...get mapped onto another dimension to fill you out the heavenly you?"

"Yes."

"A whole dimension made from love?"

"You catch on quick, pumpkin," he replied with a grin. "I guess all that physics stuff you learned *is* good for something! I was beginning to think I might have to get Jesus himself to explain this to you."

The Garment of Skin

The great lawn spread for miles in all directions, spotted with clumps of trees and surrounded by distant gardens pregnant with flamboyant splashes of color, waiting to be discovered. A shimmering cerulean dome floated above, clear of smoke or haze, the very air glowing from zenith to horizon. There was no sun—none was needed. The air itself seemed to glow, and each blade of grass contributed its own jade-hued brightness to the sky's illumination.

Amanda noticed that The Light was strongest at the horizon, the point where the blue above met green radiance rising from the grass. Those two hues merged in a striking turquoise. *Sort of the reverse of earth: there the sky is most colorful looking straight up, and fades toward the skyline. But I guess the physics are totally different in heaven.*

Here and there birds soared, looping and power-diving through the air. Instead of spending their lives pursuing food and shelter, they had all day to fly for the fun of it, learning maneuvers no bird on earth could replicate.

Then her bird-watching hiatus was interrupted by a new

wonder. A group of shooting stars blazed from one end of the sky to the other, leaving glowing rainbow contrails that slowly faded behind them. Amanda turned to her dad with a quizzical look on her face.

"Just people fast traveling," he remarked. "Like you did when you zipped back and forth around the tree. When they pass overhead in mid-flight it's kind of a neat light show. Want to watch?"

"Sure, Poppy!" They plopped down in the ankle-high turf alongside the path, lying on their backs to take in the whole sky. The edges of their vision were encircled by green spikes of grass, like crenellations on a castle wall. Every minute or two a group of sparkling stars rocketed across their field of view, some high and far off, others so low it seemed they could reach out and touch them. Each one was different, with different colored trails and textures. Some even seem to corkscrew as they flew.

"Remember camping out in the yard with the fireflies when you were little? We used to watch the shooting stars every August," Theo recalled, "Until the dew made us wet and your yawns outnumbered the flashes in the sky. What was that meteor shower called?"

"The Perseids," Amanda answered. "Because the radiant where they originate from is in the constellation Perseus." Then she grew more reflective. "Just tiny motes of dust, rocketing through space in the wake of a comet. Hitting the atmosphere at 20,000 miles an hour gave them enough energy to light up the night sky. But here, a meteor shower isn't watching dust trails in the dark—it's tracking actual people, zipping by in broad daylight! Pretty cool, huh?"

"It gives me a window into the mind of God," Theo mused, "that he planned even a little detail like a meteor shower to mimic heaven."

"Hey, that reminds me—a while back I was joking around about how communication on earth was so buggy and ineffective, and you said there was a reason for all that—"

"Ooh! There goes another one!" Theo interrupted, pointing out over his left knee at a deep red smoke trail low on the horizon.

"I see it!"

"Yeah, now I remember," he replied after a moment. "I was going to tell you *why* everything on earth isn't transparent like it is here."

"That's it, dad. And it better be a good reason, because communicating on earth is a real pain!"

"Well, it's a big idea, but it kinda boils down to this. In heaven our hearts are open to everything—*all* communication comes into us. We feel every emotion and thought of our neighbors, and they feel ours; so we're all fully known. It works because everything here is good. But you don't want that on earth, where—"

"Why not?" Amanda interrupted. "I mean, how many times have Darren and I argued over some simple misunderstanding? Or autocorrect screws up my texts and a friend gets mad at me? I *want* to understand and to be understood."

"Hey, I get it! Heaven is meant to fill that desire," Theo agreed. "But think: on earth there's another side of the coin. How many times were you about to say something nasty or hurtful to someone you love, and later on were glad you kept your mouth shut? Ever daydreamed about being with someone else when your own partner is right at your side? What if your friends heard all *those* thoughts?"

"Ouch! If they knew *everything* I thought about them, I'm not sure I'd have any friends left."

"But that's not the worst of it. Imagine if—whoa!" The sky lit up as three separate groups of stars shot across it from different directions, crisscrossing overhead in a fountain of color.

"Look!" Amanda pointed, "right there where they crossed, where the colors combine! It's like layers—at the intersection there's a whole new blaze of hues, like their personalities splashed into one another. If you put that many colors together on earth, you'd just get muddy brown. What a show!"

Her dad chuckled. "I never get tired of it. Now as I was saying, imagine if you had the kind of wide open, spirit-to-spirit communication we do here with a really black-hearted person: a Hitler, or some fanatical terrorist, or your worst enemy. *Everything* that person feels—every rage or hatred or lust or bitterness they nurse in the darkest dungeon of their hearts—would come inside you and become part of you—"

"Oh, my goodness!"

"—and you couldn't stop it. You would be utterly defenseless. Would you want to live in a world where Hitler had unrestricted access to your heart?"

"No! That's awful!"

"See why God wouldn't allow that to happen?" her dad replied seriously.

"I do now," Amanda murmured slowly, as the idea came together in her head. "So it's actually a mercy that The One made communication on earth so difficult. That used to make me so mad...but now I'm actually grateful. Seems like our bumbling communication is really a gift."

"It is. When humanity fled from The Light, he 'clothed us in garments of skin,' as it says in Genesis, because leaving our hearts wide open to the evil in each other would be incredibly damaging. That's why it's hard to get to know each other: the physical barrier around our hearts creates distance between us that love struggles to cross. But—it is also what protects us from the worst in each other. When we lost our connection with The Light, we lost a lot of our connection with each other, too. That was the first death."

Kids in Heaven

The conversation was interrupted by two pairs of stars which arced across the sky in a parabolic curve, then fell to the surface nearby. Although they dropped almost on top of Theo and Amanda, the grass they were lying in blocked the view. Raising herself on one elbow to see over the obstruction, Amanda spotted four of the bright people. The two smaller ones seemed like children—and acted like children, too. They were running circles around the 'adults,' laughing and skipping as they did. A swarm of butterflies collected over their heads, repeating every hop and jump in a riot of color and motion.

"Kids in heaven?" Amanda wondered, and immediately concluded that they were.

"Yeah," Theo laughed. "Sometimes the little ones just have to run."

"Do they stay kids forever? Or do they grow up?"

"Of course—all of us do! And sometimes we grow younger. We live in an Eternal Now: age in heaven is merely a number. Here," he urged, looking over her shoulder. "I'll show you. First, focus your mind on The Eternal Now, so you are locked in on that idea."

"Got it"

"Now, look at the children again, and tell me their ages."

"Okay…hmm. I can't really tell. I'll see a flash of an adult, then for a moment an infant, and then everything in between. It's like they are all ages at once."

"Right you are! Because we live in The Eternal Now, all times are in this moment, and this moment hosts all times. Therefore, we can relive—or pre-live! —any age we want."

"Wait: they can choose when they want to be kids and when they want to be adults? Can I do that, too?"

"Whenever you wish."

And suddenly Amanda found herself on her feet, giggling, clothed in a party dress like the one she remembered from her fifth birthday. Strong hands grasped her waist, snatching her high off the ground. Just as she became airborne, her head swiveled, and there was her father, a young man in his twenties.

He wore the faded old jeans and a flannel shirt he favored, laughing as he tossed her high into the air. Now his face was below her, arms upraised and smile wide. She felt weightless for half a second before falling back into his welcoming embrace, squealing with delight. Then the moment passed, and she was the adult Amanda once more.

"Did that just happen? I felt like I was a little kid again! And you looked like the daddy you were when I was five or six."

"You *were* a little kid again! And I was that version of your father."

"Wow: I can be any age I want!" Amanda breathed, dropping down onto her back in the grass and looking skyward once more. "What fun! Remember how we used to play the 'parent game' when I was little, where you and mom pretended to be the kids and I acted like the grownup? We could do that here for real!" That drew a laugh.

"But let's go back to what we were talking about before. What did you mean by the first death?"

"You're like a pit bull when you have an unanswered question," Theo needled playfully, still looking at her from his perch on one elbow. "The first death is running away from The Light, like the first couple did. It's refusing a green card for heaven while you're living on earth. The second death—the one that brought you here—is when your physical body finally kicks the bucket."

Amanda frowned. "I didn't realize I died twice."

"It's not so obvious when you're living on earth. Picture this: refusing the invitation to The Light is like pulling the plug on a laptop. It can still run on its internal battery—nothing much in your user experience changes at first."

"Except the screen dims and it runs slower," Amanda deadpanned.

"I like that. It makes the analogy even better! But eventually, the battery runs out, and then your laptop is well and truly dead.

"So here's the analogy: the spark of biological life we were given when we were conceived is the battery. It was designed to last a lifetime, and no longer. If you don't plug the battery in to a power source, it'll run down and die. Just like every human being dies. Unplugging from the source of life, The Light, is the first death—running out of battery is the second."

"So, if I understand you right, I was born unplugged?" Amanda giggled.

"Yes, you were on battery power from day one—the biological spark is the only life your mom and I had to give you. But now that you are plugged directly into a power plant, you'll never need the battery again. Life here doesn't depend on biology."

"Okaaay, that was a mouthful. Let me spit it all back to you and see if I got it." Amanda took a deep breath and continued. "The first death is unplugging from The Light—which doesn't seem to make much difference at first cause you're running on battery power. If you're plugged in, the second death—which is when you croak," she smirked, "is actually a good thing. You end up in heaven."

"So far so good," Theo nodded.

"Now, for the communication thing. Humans were built for heaven: designed to communicate heart-to-heart with each other, like we do here. But when you're unplugged—when The Light isn't illuminating your insides—that gift is perilous. Darkness can pass between us as easily as light.

"And…Oh! We can take the computer analogy even further! Imagine our hearts are computers on a local network, darkness and evil are a computer virus, and the garment of skin is the firewall. As long as there are no viruses on your network, you don't need a firewall: every machine can be completely open to all the others. But if some malicious code gets in, and you don't have the firewall of the garment of skin to block the virus of evil…" Amanda shuddered. "I don't even want to think about that. So The One protected our hearts with a physical firewall, to keep the traumatic stuff from infecting our insides. The great obstacle to communication, the garment of skin that keeps us from connecting heart to heart, *is* a gift. It was The One loving us well."

The Downside

Suddenly, Amanda felt a deep, bluish-feeling pathos flow into her right side. She'd have called it sadness or regret, except that it lacked the element of hopelessness and resignation those feelings have on earth.

"Unfortunately," her dad began (and Amanda immediately recognized that he was the source of the feeling), "the firewall that protected us keeps out the good with the bad. There were so many times on earth that I wanted to communicate how much I loved you, or how I was excited at the woman you were becoming, but I couldn't find the words. I'd stand in the greeting-card aisle at Walgreens before your birthdays, looking at dozens and dozens of cards and knowing every single one was inadequate."

"That's sweet, Poppy! Thanks for telling me."

He rose and stood upright, looking into the distance. Outlined against the sky, his form was silhouetted by a trio of lights flashing over his head like fighter jets lancing the atmosphere. "The real tragedy is that what protected us also kept The Maker out. The barrier around our hearts deadened us to *any* touch coming into the soul from the outside—which made us virtually deaf to The Voice. We had to relearn how to hear him, like someone who has been in a terrible accident and must learn again how to walk."

Looking up at his sharp outline, Amanda sighed. "Well, that would explain why it was always so hard to pray. When I was flying down from the cliff into heaven, Jesus showed me my life from his perspective, and he was always right there with me—everywhere and in everything! But I didn't know it on earth. I couldn't feel him. Sometimes trying to talk to him was like groping for a light-switch in the dark."

They were silent for a few moments. The grass swayed in a delicate breeze, but the sky remained a changeless blue. "I hadn't thought of this before," Theo stated poignantly, sitting again at her side. "But having been a parent, I can feel a bit of how that distance would have affected The Maker. It was like his kids all blocked him on their phones at the same time, and never mentioned why. Suddenly, he wasn't hearing from them anymore.

"He went from having kids living at home to being an empty-nester, watching them go through life from behind a one-way mirror. How agonizing! To observe their every thought and action but always remain unseen himself, close enough to reach out and touch them but unable to make contact.

"And if they did call, it was usually a one-way conversation: the kids reciting their woes and asking him to send cash, then hanging up before he could get a word in edgewise. It's really painful for a parent to lose touch with their child."

Yet in that moment Amanda felt neither sorrow, pain, or futility. In heaven, grasping the monumental sacrifices love makes leaves you in a state of awe and gratitude, not regret. In that solemn state of reflection, the weight of glory settles deep into your soul and creates a springing well of joy pouring out in return.

"I didn't realize how important that was for you," Amanda whispered, placing a hand in his. "It's easy in the old life to overlook how much you are loved—but it's impossible to miss here."

Her father squeezed her fingers gently, speaking in a happy voice. "Truly, heaven has made all things well, for us *and* for The Three. You and I have each other forever, and they share fully in each moment of our lives. The one-way mirror dividing all of us has been shattered."

"Thanks, daddy," Amanda breathed, snuggling up against him with a sigh of contentment. "I love it, too."

"And it's all thanks to The Man of Light. He made a whole universe just so we could be family, but then gave it all up to protect us from ourselves when we were in danger. And now he has put it all back together again, better than before! It never ceases to amaze me how well he loves!"

Another group of stars soared across the sky overheard, but the father and daughter below were too caught up in gratitude to notice.

9 Betrayer

Though she'd seen wonders to last a lifetime, the joy of discovery and anticipation of something new were still fresh in Amanda (as it always is in heaven). When her father offered a new adventure, she was immediately ready to dive in.

"I have a dear friend I'd really like you to meet," her father offered softly.

"Okay, dad—great!"

"See that tree over there by itself, at the bottom of the slope? My friend is sitting there beneath the branches, just waiting for us. But instead of using our bodies to walk down, this time let's use our minds."

"Fast traveling!" Amanda replied, bouncing up and down like a puppy. "I'm ready!"

"Hold on a sec—it's a little different when we do it together. You have to agree about where you want to go, then picture the destination in your minds simultaneously. Here, take my hand." He held out an open palm and she clasped it. "Now on three, just picture yourself standing under that tree. Ready?"

"Ready!"

"Alright. One—" and Amanda vanished, leaving a faint

streak of light behind.

"They always do that the first time," her dad shook his head in mock disgust, then grinned. And disappeared after her.

There was no sense of departure or arrival on her trip: Amanda was *there* with her father, and the next instant she was *here.* In between was a faint flash of color and motion, but so momentary she wasn't sure if it was physical or something in her mind. The tree before her was a giant column of smooth gray bark, a pillar piercing the sky. Stepping over and around the great, spreading roots, she spied a table on the far side, resting on two ornate piers. Their bases were swallowed by a sea of groundcover that vined round and round up the posts. It looked somewhat like acanthus: the swirling foliage carved into classical buildings since the days of ancient Greece.

The top of the table was a wonder of its own: a smooth slab of crystalline stone that shone like transparent gold, decorated by the rich green vine winding directly below it. *No,* she corrected herself, *the vine is growing* inside *the tabletop, the living green foliage and golden stone bleeding their disparate beauties together.*

But even more resplendent were the two figures seated with arms resting on the crystal surface: a man and a woman, deep in conversation, both burning with glorious light. The woman seemed to simultaneously carry the innocence of youth and the sober wisdom of years, while the raven-haired man gave off an aura of contentment and approval that scented the air around them. Amanda quickly perceived that the two were related—*mother and son, perhaps?* How long their chat had lasted Amanda couldn't tell—her heart told her that in heaven meetings like this one go on forever, with the spaces in between mere interludes in The Eternal Now.

Maybe it's like when you get together with an old friend, and it feels like the conversation picks up right where you left off years before. I guess that's another place where earth resembles heaven, she decided. *Except up here the relationship doesn't stall when you are apart—because we are actually part of one another! Does that mean every conversation in heaven is an eternal one, the gaps simply disappearing in the continuous memory of being together?*

Right in front of her one of those timeless conversations played out, under the soft illumination of rippling leaves, their light layering ever-changing waves of silver upon the scene.

"*Yes,*" The Voice affirmed to her mind, "*conversations in heaven are forever.*"

Theo stepped around the tree half a second later, interrupting the discourse. Both figures rose immediately to greet him, bowing graciously. The woman made to leave, so the whole party exchanged hugs all around and 'God be with you's (*I guess that's where the word 'goodbye' originally comes from,* Amanda realized) that seemed to hold no sense of distance or loss. It felt as if the woman might simply pop out to the kitchen for a cup of coffee and reappear before the commercial break was over. With a wave she abruptly vanished, leaving a faint streak of magenta lingering in the pleasant air behind.

The man stepped around the table and bowed formally to Amanda. The scent of approval enfolding him reached out and embraced her, growing stronger as he drew close. Then, with a nod from Theo, he met her gaze, a serious expression on his face.

"Dearest Amanda, I am so glad to see you here! First, let me apologize for how I treated you and your family on earth. That was horribly wrong! So I wanted to be here on your first day to play my part in The Man of Light's work of healing. Your father and I have shared an exceptional gift because of the good The Man of Light fashioned from my brokenness. I would be *extraordinarily* pleased to share that gift with you also—if, of course, you are willing."

It seemed intrusive to look into the heart of someone she just met and didn't recognize, so after an awkward instant she turned to her father, a confused expression on her face. "Dad, can you help me out here?"

"Oh, my—I seem to have forgotten how different we look in the Beautiful Land, and how long it has been. Caspar, you know my daughter. Amanda, this is my dear brother Caspar Williams, my business partner at the clinic."

"Caspar? You mean *that* Caspar?"

"Of course—who else? The one who stole my half of the practice and ran it into the ground, who left me without a job or a medical license so I could come back to my senses! Don't you remember? He helped me become poor so that I could become rich!"

At this the two men laughed heartily, and Amanda was even more confused. Her heart was telling her everything was fine, but her head was light years behind.

"But dad! Because of him we lost the house and had to live in that dumpy apartment. And you got depressed and couldn't work for a year, and that's when you had the accident and ended up in jail for two nights, and…Oh, daddy…after all that…"

"Honey," her father began gently, then glanced over at Caspar. "Would you excuse us for just a minute?"

"Certainly," the man replied patiently.

Theo put a father's arm around Amanda's shoulder, leading her back around the vast trunk and a little ways out under the tree's silver branches. Plopping down in the emerald grass, he reached up a hand, inviting her to join him. Willingly she took a seat, and leaned against her father's warm body as they gazed out together over the plain. Already the healing of heaven was stealing into her thoughts. But—*meeting Caspar in heaven, of all places…how did* he *come to be here?*

Theo spoke kindly to his daughter's confusion. "Mandy, I understand. There were many days on earth I was angry at him—I fantasized about killing him for a while, until a friend knocked some sense into my head. And then came the year of numbness, when I shut my heart down.

"Until now, that's the only story you've known: the worst

half of it. But in heaven's version, justice triumphs and love gets the win in the end. Would you like to experience how the tale of Caspar and I is told in heaven?"

Amanda didn't know what to think or feel. Caspar had been the epitome of evil in her teenage mind. Her dad seemed to have forgiven him, even become his friend, yet…

"Amanda," her father broke in, following her thought. "Heaven has the power to make *all* things well—even things far worse than this. The redemption is always bigger than the injustice. He doesn't just put things back the way they were before—he makes them far, far better than if the evil had ever been! The Man of Light has done a beautiful thing for me and Caspar, and I would be greatly honored to tell you that story, for it has become very dear to me. May I share it with you?"

For the briefest instant she hesitated. Then she remembered the cliff, and abandoning herself to trust. *Trust is the bridge between heaven and earth;* she breathed to herself. "Okay, daddy," she whispered, staring over the flowered fields of the Beautiful Land. "I'll trust you."

"Very good. Now look into my eyes."

Perspectives

Obediently, she turned, peering intently back at him. As she looked into his thought, the story of her dad's relationship with Caspar swam into focus. Immediately, she noticed the effects of the Great Washing—*okay, obviously he's been through that, too.* The story was being told from heaven's perspective. Taking a deep breath, she looked further in.

The great betrayal that had ruined everything began to play out in front of her, but this time a new figure was in every scene. She saw The Man of Light grieve over her father's workload, how it kept him from home and from her. Amanda realized for the first time that becoming a workaholic was how he coped with the pain of losing mom. His job was his cave, a hideout whose walls rose between him and his friends and family, cutting off communication with both his daughter and The One who loved him.

The Three circled round him, unseen. They discussed his life-wound, and how it had affected his daughter as well. Then they made a difficult decision: to chance removing work from his life for the sake of relationship. It came into Amanda's heart that The Three were taking a great risk. Work was what gave him self-respect, what held him together. If her father did not respond to their invitation amidst this new loss, he might be lost to them forever. For the briefest instant she felt how deeply that would grieve them—a cost that would endure through ages uncountable. She was crying now, watching Jesus carefully adjust people and circumstances to prepare just enough of a safety net to catch her and her dad, yet not so much that he would retreat further into his fortress of isolation, avoiding the heart surgery he desperately needed.

Then the scene shifted. Caspar sat across a conference table from his crooked lawyer, modifying the partnership contract and consummating the plot to take what was not his. Jesus stood behind him, and as Caspar signed the document, she saw him nod sadly, as if he was expecting this (although Caspar had made the choice himself).

At that moment, The Man of Light in the picture turned his head and peered directly at Amanda. It pierced her heart. In that instant she experienced Caspar's wound: the years of unrelenting disapproval and tongue-lashings inflicted by a sullen father. That lack of love drove him into a single-minded pursuit of accomplishment; the only way he knew to assuage a broken heart aching for approval. She saw the man-child Caspar peering timidly out from a cave built of money, a cave much like her own. He hid from trust just as she had; and in his hurt he hurt those around him, just as she had.

A great sorrow was in that picture: Jesus mourning over how

a soul created for heaven had been marred and maltreated. And she perceived that heaven had grieved for her own soul in the same fashion. Yet she was forgiven, and The Man of Light held none of it against her. Understanding entered her heart, as she identified with the man who was once her bitter enemy. She nodded back to Jesus. *I got it.*

"*Yes, you do,*" The Voice whispered.

Then Jesus directed her mind back to the office. It seemed to be a year or so later. Caspar sat alone in a dark room, illuminated by a weak pool of light from the bronze desk lamp. She recognized her dad's old desk, and Caspar's head slumped down on it, crying out in pain and humiliation. The clinic was going under, and he had no idea how to make it prosper. With no one to help, he regretted the loss of his friend and partner. Her dad. Wishing he had never betrayed him, Caspar picked up the phone, started to dial her father's number…

He paused, torn between longing and fear, humility and humiliation. Amanda realized she was inwardly rooting for him now, willing him to reach out, to press the final digit. But instead, the handset dropped back in the cradle. Shame had won the day.

A moment later, he abruptly yanked open the right-hand desk drawer. Instantly, Amanda knew what he intended to do: kill himself with the 9mm pistol he kept within. Everything inside her wanted to scream, "No! Don't!" But before she could move a muscle, a confused look washed over Caspar's tear-streaked face. Instead of a gun, he pulled out an old book: dad's bible. He was sitting at the wrong desk, in Theo's former office and not his own. He collapsed over the desktop again, sobbing.

Then the room brightened, as The Man of Light hove into view behind the leather chair. Putting a hand on each shoulder, he bent to whisper something in Caspar's ear that Amanda couldn't make out. But Caspar heard.

He stopped, listened, tears still winding down his cheeks. The Light inundated the room, surrounding him, washing over him. Caspar finally broke, calling out for help to the God he didn't know. The Light entered him, bringing a different kind of tears to his eyes. Then Jesus reached over and opened the book sitting on the desk in front of him.

As Caspar began to read, a beautiful thing happened. The Man of Light sat down next to him (she didn't see another chair, but somehow he did it) and began pointing out things in the book. Soon Caspar was pouring out his heart to the big brother he never had. The Man of Light put his strong arms around the man of shame in a great hug, and a shower of living water like a cascading mountain stream washed over them, leaving Caspar's soul sprinkled with glistening droplets of light. The walls of his fortress of loneliness crumbled and dissolved into nothing before the tsunami of love coming into his soul, and The Light began shining in Caspar.

The first vision faded. Now she saw her father back on earth, keeping vigil by the cracked window in their dingy apartment. She heard him debating himself as he peered out on the darkened trees beyond the parking lot, wrestling with rage. Jesus sat with legs crossed in the threadbare chair across from him, listening. Each time something in her dad's heart opened up, Jesus seemed to reach inside him and...*plant a flower? Or was he healing a wound?* From Amanda's point of view, they seemed the same thing.

His anger spent, her father finally chose life. The actual decision was to start seeing a counselor, but what it meant was deciding for his daughter over his defenses, and swallowing his pride enough to admit he needed help. That was the night when their lives began to change. In the picture The Man of Light reached over and grabbed her dad's shoulder, with tears of love in his eyes. "Well done, Theo Shafer, man of God! I believed in you, and you came through for yourself, for us and for Amanda. I knew you would choose well!"

Then Jesus turned, and those compassionate eyes penetrated Amanda's heart again. "Your father didn't just save his own life that day—he saved your family. All that you see here I did for Caspar, and for Theo; but also for you."

"He's right," her dad said quietly, bringing his daughter back to the present. She found herself still peering into her father's eyes, watching his story. It felt like she'd been living it.

"It took a great loss for me to find life again, and open my heart to healing," he uttered quietly.

"*That is the way of life on earth,*" The Voice spoke to her heart. *"Even as We Three saw from the beginning; few take the hard road to seek Us without the impetus of pain. And so, even pain is turned to the good."*

Theo heard The Voice, too. "That was true for me as well as for you, Amanda. Without that loss, we would have grown apart from each other and from The One, as I drowned myself in work and you drowned in your aloneness. Who knows what would have happened to us if we *hadn't* lost everything? It was incredibly hard, but now I live with a glory beyond all comparison resting on me, because of how those wounds brought me home."

Amanda looked away to wipe her eyes on her sleeve, then leaned again on her father's shoulder. "Alright, I can let go. I choose life, like you did. And Caspar…I imagine he found what he desired, too?"

"Yes! In his desperation he embraced The Man of Light, and was never alone again." At this her father straightened up to look affectionately down at her, eyes glistening with happiness. "Heaven has truly made all things well, and more than well! Caspar and I are forever linked by the great redemption The Maker created in our shared story. Now our relationship is everything God intended it to be on earth, and more.

"In a way, I owe Caspar for getting me here, and he owes me for the same! It's our great joke—that The Man of Light gave us the best gift through each other's worst impulse. How could I ever be mad at him in heaven, when heaven is mine and you are mine because of what he did?"

Amanda took in a deep, bracing lungful of heaven's air, letting her heart adjust to this new reality. It was so much better than the earth-version of the story—*so then why hang onto that old thing?* she reasoned. Discarding her offense like a torn, oily rag tossed in the garbage, she never thought of it again.

"Daddy, thanks for the hard choice you made for us," Amanda answered in gratitude mixed with awe. "I never knew. I'm just…amazed, floored, overwhelmed by how far The Man of Light will go to rescue us. Thank you."

Then she rose, and on her own initiative marched back to the tree and circled around it. Taking Caspar's waiting hand in hers, she thanked him in many words for all the good that had come to her because of him, and how grateful she was for his life. Then looking into each other's eyes, they saw their shared story as it was written in the memory of heaven, where The Man of Light had drafted every line in his own hand. And the embrace they shared there under the tree was long and deep.

You Just Call

"Honey, I'd like to have quick debrief with my friend Caspar, just the two of us. Why don't you saunter along the path over that way—" here he pointed down the hill "—and I'll catch up in a bit."

"Can you give me some directions?" Amanda answered with momentary consternation. "How do I know which way to go if I come to fork in the road?"

"Just follow your heart! It's impossible to take a wrong turn in heaven. And if you need me," he grinned, "just call."

"Call?" Amanda reached involuntarily for her back pocket

and suddenly felt the absence of her ever-present cell phone. There was no pocket, either. "Um, dad—"

At this her father laughed out loud. "You and your phone! There are no phones in heaven, Mandy—no e-mail or schedules, no reminders or to-do lists. What takes advanced technology on earth is as simple as breathing in heaven. If you want to talk to me, just call me, like you've seen me call The Man of Light."

Perceiving her uncertainty, he added, "It's like saying, 'Hey, Siri!' to your iPhone. Just say, 'Hey, dad!' and I'll be there in a flash."

"I guess I should have figured that one out," Amanda replied in a bemused tone. "See you in a little." Turning, she started to descend the gentle slope into a shining valley.

The curving path wound downward across a hillside, well-demarcated by a double line of marching trees. Their ivory trunks shone, somewhat like silver birches, and they stood maybe five times her own height. She stopped to examine a leaf: it was burnished bronze above and silver below, throwing running waves of light across the path with each puff of wind. A soft, rustling music to The Maker played as the leaves brushed against one another, so she felt as if she was walking through a canopied cathedral filled with the sound of distant harps.

What a day! What a journey! What an amazing place! Amanda rejoiced, as the trees slowly passed to her right and left. Each was like its brothers in form, yet subtly different. You soon lost track of how far you'd come. In that moment it came into her heart that no two things were identical in heaven. *There are no assembly lines here, no mass production. Every single thing is handcrafted, as one-of-a-kind as a snowflake on earth. Oooh—maybe snowflakes were designed that way to teach us about heaven! Awesome!*

But what I like most here is the sense of no time passing. That nagging fear of missing out—I was always thinking of the next appointment on earth, never fully present. That anxiety is long gone! There's enough time for everything, and no nagging worry that if you get somewhere too late, the fun will be over.

Nowhere to be and nothing needing doing—I guess this is what contentment feels like. Or eternal rest—that's how people used to talk about it. Hey, I kinda like that! And for the next few moments all she did was walk, and be, and breathe, and rest.

Celeste

Journeying further into the Beautiful Land, she'd began to run across more and more fellow citizens, clad in white and surrounded by luminous halos. *Like lighthouses on a foggy coast,* she decided. At first, Amanda was unsure what was customary when you met someone in this new world. But all were so friendly and overjoyed to greet her that she soon relaxed. There seemed to be no strangers in heaven. Amanda ended up conversing with some, hailing passers-by and acknowledging distant wanderers on far-off slopes with a friendly wave.

One who stopped to talk was a stately woman named Celeste, a denizen of Paris in the late 1800's. When recalling that meeting, the word Amanda invariably used to describe her was 'wonder.' *She sees all things as if beholding them for the first time, and falls in love at first sight with all she sees. Everything is beautiful through her eyes.*

Noting Amanda's fascination with her splendid attire, Celeste spun around like a ballerina (she had been one!), her robe rippling in the dancing light. Soon they were chatting like sisters, holding up sleeves side-by-side to compare the elegant fabric. Their translucent garments were of some pure-white material, with an embroidery-like texture running over every inch of the surface. The loose-fitting sleeves were indistinguishable at a distance, but up-close their one-of-a-kind designs emerged, fractals and spirals shaped out of white-gold filaments incorporated in the weave. Each was completely unique.

"Hey, there *is* color!" Amanda suddenly cried, as currents of subtle, delicate hues washed over the fabric.

"Non, mon amie!" Celeste replied gracefully (whether her speech was French, English or some heavenly language, Amanda couldn't tell, but she understood every word). "The cloth is white as fresh snow; the shade you see is the atmosphere of honor that surrounds each of the beloved."

"The atmosphere—you mean the color is in the air?"

"In a way," she replied. "You could also say it is part of our being. That blissful aura is The Light of life that pours forth from our souls and hovers around us, perfuming the air with scent and hue. When The Master comes and beams his rays of honor and recognition through us, that delicate mist brightens, shining as lovely as moiré'd silk. His presence further clothes us in the royal purples of glory, until we are beauty incarnate."

"I always wanted to be pretty," Amanda replied shyly. "But I always felt like I fell short of the women in the magazines."

"Not here, beautiful friend—the spirit that shines out from you is perfect, just as The One perfectly made you.

"Yes!" she called out, raising elegant hands to the sky in praise. "We are The Children of Light, the canvas of The Great Lover, painted with the brushstrokes of his undying affection. Are we not supremely enchanting, Amanda?"

"Yes, we are," her heart replied, before her mind could think to object. And realizing that her heart spoke truly, her mind accepted that she was beautiful as well.

"Woman is the most beautiful of all created things," Celeste continued, reveling in The Maker's design. "That is why The One Enemy hated us so implacably, and all through the ages sought to bring women down and dominate us. In bitter jealousy he lied to us, to convince us that his own ugliness was ours. But his voice plagues us no more, praise be to The One!"

"So evil really has a thinking being behind it?"

"Yes—*The* Evil, who was and is not now and never will be."

"Okay, I can grasp the idea that he particularly hated women—society was always trying to make second class citizens out of us. But…you're saying it was done out of *jealousy*?"

"Yes, of course," Celeste replied, selecting a lavender-hued bloom from the bed at the side of the path and plaiting it into her hair. "There—that's perfect!" She picked a second flower and did the same for Amanda, then stood back admiring her handiwork. "Charming!

"My darling," she continued, "in the beginning The Evil was most beautiful of all. Music was always around him, and the very flowers of heaven acknowledged how far he excelled them. But he adored his own adornment more than he loved The Maker of his majesty; and in his self-worship he fell from bliss. There in the darkness he brooded on his loss in growing hatred and resentment, his bitterness transforming his visage into a thing loathsome to look upon.

"When The Maker created woman to carry the image of The One, we surpassed him as far as a man surpasses a mouse. And looking on our loveliness, he finally understood: he had become an abomination, an ugliness without hope of healing. In enraged retribution he sought to destroy all beauty from the earth. That burning jealousy was a sickness he sowed on the hearts of women, that we might look on our own bodies and believe we bore his detestable image instead of The Maker's own beauty."

"That certainly puts a different spin on all the body-shaming stuff that I grew up with," Amanda gaped in surprise.

"As did I," Celeste added. "But The Evil is no more, for he finally was dragged before the presence of The One unwilling, and the fire that burns unquenchable in the face of God consumed him. So we are free of his ire at last: free to revel in beauty and reflect the Creator who fashioned us to mirror his loveliness."

"I never knew! Thank you, Celeste, for enlightening me."

"And now our paths diverge," Cleste cried. "Farewell, fellow traveler! May we meet again in the City of God!"

"God be with you!" Amanda answered, as Celeste pirouetted up the path, a faint shimmer of glory all around here. *So that's why the saints in the cathedrals were always painted with halos of gold around their heads,* Amanda decided. *It's how they actually look.*

Leaving her new friend behind, Amanda strode on through the silver trees, yet barely noticed them. Instead, she peered intently at her sleeves, as if her eyes had been opened to the hidden splendor of her garments by the conversation with Celeste. Now she readily observed the layers of color hovering above the fabric's whorled patterns, beautifying the air around her. In the familiar, physical dimensions she'd known on earth, the embroidery was clean as morning frost, and perfectly white. Yet an extra-dimensional light of honor shimmered over the white, adding depth and dimension. All this was overlain by watercolor hints of indigo and cobalt, dappling a sapphire-hued robe of glory waiting to be revealed in the presence of The Man of Light.

I have a halo, too! Amanda thought in wonder, turning her arm this way and that to examine the subtle aura encircling it. *Who would have thought? We are all dressed in white, sharing the singular perfection of this white garment—made even more beautiful by the one who wears it. The Children of Light are all in one family, but each one of us is uniquely illumined, just as we are individually known and honored by The Creator.*

And it came to her that in that moment, she was offering true worship to The One, for to perceive him as he is, is to worship. The air around her vibrated its 'Yes!' in response.

Artists

She might have strolled under the silver trees for an age of the world—there was no sensation of time passing. Speaking about how long an event lasted here was meaningless. The sky rolled on above her, beauty caressed her sight and goodness drifted down onto her like a gentle shower. Absorbed in the experience, Amanda didn't notice the circle of quiet figures seated at the crest of a small hilltop until she almost stumbled into them.

"Oh! Hello!" she said awkwardly, to a chorus of waves and cheerful replies. Curiosity piqued, she stopped to examine them.

It was obvious that the men and women on the hill were there as a group—all sat fairly close together at a great vantage point, looking down on the woods and parklands of heaven. But it was a circle where everyone faced *outward*, their backs both to her and to each other. "What are you all doing? And why are you looking away?" she asked.

At that, one woman jumped up and scuttled over to her, taking hold of both Amanda's hands. She was young and vigorous, although quite short. But something about her eyes—*it's like there are wrinkles there and yet not, like a hologram on a credit card that changes depending on how you look at it.* Amanda concluded that she'd lived a long and full life on earth. Then the woman spoke, and her accent gave her away as English.

"I'm Elanor. We're all here painting, dearie! At least most of us are—we all seem to work in different media. But do come and see! It's such fun to share the magnificent illumination we capture."

Taking her by the hand, the woman led her to an intricate bench made of woven, living boughs. What seemed to be a canvas (but made of crystal) simply hung in midair front of the woman's seat, with no easel to support it.

"Oh, don't worry about that," the woman waved airily as she noticed her guest mulling over the levitating painting (at that moment Amanda also noticed an artist's palette and a set of brushes hanging weightless in the air alongside.) "We gather to drink in The Light, and give honor back to The Man of Light by capturing the subtleties of his radiance. It helps others see him more clearly. Here—take a look!"

The transparent canvas was about three feet wide by two high. Elanor positioned her directly in front of it, and in that spot the painting snapped into place in the landscape. In the areas still to be painted, you could see the greensward of heaven through the crystal. It blended perfectly with Elanor's adjoining brush strokes. But looking deeper, Amanda began to recognize the artist's hand.

The painting didn't speak the story of the grass, trees and sky, but of The Light bathing them. The luminous pool painted under a tree, for example, was rendered considerably brighter than the real one off at a distance. And the faint light the painting gave off told its own story, not of stems, leaves and cells, but what was in the mind of The Maker when he brought those things to life. Each delicate brushstroke was like layers of desire and emotion over the landscape—*it reminds me of the aura glowing above my sleeves,* Amanda realized. *Elanor's painting has an aura, too! The physical scene is captured in the brushstrokes, but with a layer of The Maker's intellect glowing on top of it.*

"It's wonderful…amazing," Amanda spoke quietly. "It's like looking through a window into The Maker's thought as he fashioned the landscape."

"Oh, brilliant, just brilliant!" Elanor cried, hugging her around the neck. "You see so well for a newcomer—" the woman suddenly bowed to her and spoke more formally. "I honor you, blessed…heavens, I haven't yet asked your name!"

"It's Amanda," her guest replied, blushing.

"A beautiful name, and a fitting one, for you have the eye of an artist. You perceive The Maker's thought in what he has made. Would you like to join us for a wee bit and paint his delight? I would be privileged to demonstrate how to wield the brushes of heaven!"

Amanda paused, then replied shyly, "I'd really love to. And thanks so much for the invitation, and for believing in me. It's just…it comes into my mind that I have an appointment waiting, and my heart is telling me not to linger on the road."

"Oh—that's the bees' knees! Then you've been invited to your first walk on the streets of gold, with The Blessed One himself!" Elanor enthused. "What a happy day, when The Prince introduces you to The Beloved! By all means, stay on your course to the city."

Then she momentarily took on a conspiratorial air, one of a child hiding a present for a knowing parent. "But if I can delay you for just a wee moment, do take a walk around the circle with me, and describe what you see in our art. I love experiencing The Light through the eyes of others, just as The Man of Light loves to listen to us, so he can experience the world he created as we see it. Come, come!"

With that they shared a glorious circuit around the knoll, stopping to admire each artist's work. Some painted using familiar-looking brushes, while others seemed to apply color with words or even thought, the different hues simply appearing on the canvas in response to a silent command. Two girls (*Teens? They seem so young, and yet are grown women at the same time.*) knelt on the path itself, chatting happily as a round mosaic of gemstone tesserae came together under their hands. A few of the works seemed almost holographic, as if the artist was painting in the air in front of the canvas. Once Amanda had to step over to the side of an easel and peer along its surface, trying to decide if what she saw was an illusion or if the work was actually painted in three dimensions. Sure enough, it was, the colors seeming to hover in delicate layers suspended above the canvas.

One gentleman in particular caught her eye. He sat next to a small table, packed with a disorderly array of dozens of small crystal jars, each like a pot of fire shooting beams of rich color in all directions. Whenever he dipped his brush in a jar, that color came alive with heightened intensity. One little pot held a cool blue, another a fiery red or orange, and with each brushstroke their light seemed to fuse into the crystal canvas, as if light itself was becoming part of the glass.

"The jars are liquid light," he explained, still concentrating intently on his work. "I loved to use paint to portray light on earth—I was of the impressionist school, you know. Back in 19th century Normandy. But never in my loftiest ambition did I think I'd get to paint with *actual light*. It's an artist's dream!"

Amanda looked up from the table of colors to admire his work. It was totally abstract, a happy riot of luminosity jetting in all directions. And yet, when you positioned yourself just so and gazed through it to the actual landscape, the painter's intent became clear. He had managed to subtract all the physical elements and focus entirely on the glow they exuded. His interpretation of the landscape blended perfectly with the original, yet the longer she looked, the more she saw The Maker's hand in that countryside.

"When I look at what you've created, I don't so much see the landscape as I see Him in it," Amanda finally uttered after an awed silence.

The artist leapt up immediately and spun to face her, his countenance all aglow. "What a marvelous compliment!" he exclaimed, spontaneously wrapping his arms around her in a boisterous hug. Stray drops of colored light gleamed here and there on his white painter's smock, and looking down Amanda noticed specks of it coloring her own sleeves.

"Don't worry!" he laughed. "Nothing stains our clothing here. Just brush it off—or leave it as it is for now. It looks good on you!"

The final individual was working on a panoramic view of the countryside, centered on two distant figures stooping in a flower bed. As Amanda admired the woman's touch, she suddenly realized that the figures in the painting had straightened, taken a few steps forward and then bent again to their work!

"Yes," Elanor agreed, "You see rightly. The painting is not just a dead representation of one moment like on earth. The life of this world, which the artist captures, comes into it and it takes on the life of that which it portrays. *All* things that live within The Light of heaven are alive: the rocks, the trees, the air, even our paintings pulsate with his life."

"And who are the two figures in the painting—gardeners? Are there weeds to pull in the Beautiful Land?"

"Gardeners, yes. But weeds? Heaven's, no! The Beautiful Land permits no unwanted plants or poisonous shrubs, no biting insects or foul airs. Our gardens contain no mulch or compost either, because there is no decay—no entropy, no running down of the universe."

"That's a happy thought," Amanda chattered.

"Yes, *everything* has been made anew! Every action here does not have an equal and opposite reaction; nor are we subject to the law of conservation of mass and energy! All things rejoice with an inner light that never runs out, here where everything is free; since life is constantly pouring through us from The One."

"You see," she added in a whispered aside, "because we paint light, even the artists here have to know a little physics!"

10 Seeing

Up ahead a familiar figure was strolling unhurriedly toward her. He waved, and Amanda recognized her father. "Finish your talk?" she called out.

Rather than raise his voice, he suddenly winked out like a light bulb, then reappeared at his daughter's side.

"You move fast," she joked.

"Yes indeed! I've finished my fellowship with Caspar, at least for now. He wanted to arrange a celebration in your honor, and we will plan it if you are willing. But only after The Prince shows you his city! Now tell me—what adventures have you been on while I was away?"

As they walked on side-by-side, Amanda related her conversation with Celeste, the jealousy of The Evil, and meeting the artists. She'd just begun explaining how the paintings came to life when Theo broke in.

"You sound a bit fidgety, Amanda. What's up?"

He was right. She loved talking with her dad—just being together again was an unimaginable delight. What she'd experienced already was amazing. But her time with The Man of Light had awakened a longing in her, the kind of feeling you have as a kid and when its two days before Christmas and you just can't wait for the day to come.

"When am I going to see him again?" she finally asked, a hint of yearning in her tone.

"Um...Darren?"

"No, silly. The Man of Light. Jesus. Am I going to be able to see him again?"

"But of course," her dad laughed. "You can see him whenever you want."

"But how? I've been thinking it over: there must be billions of people here. If he spends as much time with each one as he already has with me, it would be centuries until my turn comes around again. And there must be great saints or martyrs or favorites that he hangs around with more than the rest of us. I guess I better not get my hopes up."

"Oh, Mandy!" Theo exclaimed. "You *are* his favorite—you are never out of his thoughts! And I am a favorite of his, too—and so is every other individual here. We are all special to the infinite one. He has as much time as you could ever want to spend with each one of us. So go ahead and hope, and long to be with him—and your longing will swiftly be fulfilled!"

"Yeah, but how? Are we there yet?" she joked, remember the long car rides to her grandparents she'd taken as a child.

"Forgive me," her dad apologized. "I should have explained this to you straight away. It's about time."

About Time

"About time for what?"

"No, I meant that time is the subject. Your question involves the nature of heaven's time."

"Oh," Amanda responded, unconvinced. "I'd love to hear your explanation, but..."

"You'd really like to see him again," Theo finished, smiling.

"It's not that I don't really love being with you, dad," she began hurriedly. "I don't want you to feel left out or anything. It's just that, that..."

Stopping to place a hand on her shoulder, Theo responded gently, "No worries, Mandy!" His fatherly smile was all saturated with gentleness and affection and approval. "No one here feels slighted that The King is first—or ever could be! He is first in the love of all of us, because he loved all of us first and best. And all the love we give to him he adds to his own and gives back, until each of us is so full of light that it spills out of us continuously—like this," he grinned, pointing at his face.

Again, Amanda's heart began absorbing the truth and knew the rightness of it before her mind really grasped the concept. Theo took hold of both her hands and held her gaze. "Mandy, look into my heart. Do you see any hurt offense in me over what you said?"

Captivated again by the swirling well of sparkling brilliance pouring through his eyes, it was a moment before she could respond. "No, dad."

"Very good. What *do* you see?"

As her heart connected with her father's, felt his feelings and tasted his thoughts, the truth wrapped around her and completed itself in her. "No, there isn't any hurt in you. Your heart is safe, and full, and...pretty happy, too. Every space inside you is full of life.

"You know, dad," she summarized, refocusing to look at his face instead of his heart (*probably an old habit from earth,* another part of her mused), "When I look at you in this moment, I don't believe anything ever *could* hurt or offend you here. You are...well, the word that comes to me is 'complete.'"

"Yes! I am complete here!" he exclaimed, spontaneously embracing her with one of those hugs that burrowed down to the soul. "I'm so proud of you, Mandy—you're understanding so well. And because I am unshakably complete, jealousy can't exist in me."

"How's that?" she inquired, as she took his proffered arm and they resumed strolling downhill through the green grass. It was growing longer here, brushing luxuriously against her calves and rippling through a hundred shades of green as the hint of breeze washed through it. Each blade, as it touched her skin, left a tiny particle of warm, jade-green light that slowly faded, so soon her feet and ankles shone like emeralds.

Her dad began answering her question, but the idea that she couldn't hurt anyone in heaven was so compelling that Amanda missed half the explanation, and had to ask him to repeat it.

"Yes, I can say it again," he grinned. "On earth we got jealous because there wasn't enough to go around. But jealousy only works where there is scarcity, and the Children of Light are always full. Grief is the same—grief is about loss, and the sting of grief is emptiness and loneliness. But there can be no grief here, because we never know emptiness and we are never alone. So much of what causes pain and injustice on earth is like that: the simple product of emptiness. The drive to fill an empty heart is the source of all kinds of evil.

"But here my Lover always fills me, and so I have forgotten what it is like to be empty. It is simply impossible to hurt or be hurt in heaven."

"Here, look!" he said, gesturing downward. "I'll show you." Disengaging from her arm, he knelt in the swelling grass (Amanda noticed that his knees immediately began turning that glowing, emerald green), and carefully separated several stalks from each other until finally he was holding just one glowing blade.

When she was little, her dad had always delighted in turning over rocks and splitting apart rotten stumps to show her the tiny insects that made those cool, dark spots their homes. Memories! They'd catch butterflies in special butterfly nets, or snag crawdads in the stream until the tin can they'd eaten pork and beans from the night before was full. Every spring they visited the State Park just to see how many species of flowers they could identify. Amanda would run ahead, calling for her dad to come look at each new bloom she encountered. He seemed to know all their names. The delight she'd found in those journeys of discovery was a key reason she entered the sciences, and it warmed her insides to remember them. She knelt beside him for a closer look, enjoying the moment of togetherness.

"See this blade," he pointed. Amanda peered at it, noticing the tiny veins and how the narrow stem joined the sheath nearer the ground. "Now watch as I try to bruise it." He folded it over on itself, rolled it between his hands, then let go. Immediately the shoot sprang open, standing up perfectly straight just as before.

Amanda got down on her hands and knees for a closer look. With her face only inches away, she could see no hint of damage. In fact, she wasn't even sure if she was looking at the right piece of grass—all were alike in their perfection. She glanced up at her father, open-mouthed.

"Try it yourself if you want."

Of course, she did.

"That's amazing!" Amanda exclaimed, standing up and beginning to brush herself off, before realizing again that that reflex was useless. "You can't bruise it up even if you try."

Theo took her hand and led her on through the meadow. "Seven hundred years before The Man of Light was even born, a guy named Isaiah predicted that he would be so gentle that he wouldn't break a bruised blade of grass. And here it turns out to be literally true! The One showed it to us, but we saw it without really seeing it."

Seeing without Seeing

"Huh?" Amanda said in surprise, intrigued by the idea. "What do you mean by seeing without seeing?"

"It's one of my own little pet phrases," Theo explained, with an innocent shyness. "The idea is, when The Maker built the universe, he patterned it on heaven. Earth is intentionally littered with things that look and smell and function like heaven does. We see them every day without noticing the connection."

"Intriguing," Amanda reflected. "How 'bout an example?"

"Take water," Theo suggested, cupping his hands. Instantly they were filled with a pool of shining, crystalline liquid, dancing between his fingers. "The Water of Life is bright and transparent. But shine a light on ordinary water on earth and it has similar properties.

"Here," he raised his hands til they were near her mouth. "Blow on it!"

Amanda did. The liquid rippled in his palms, shifting and blending the lines on his fingers as she looked through it. A faint mist rose above the surface, then wafted away. "Water on earth ripples, too. Both can be liquid or vapor—when you go to the city you'll see a rainbow aura of living-water-vapor around the throne. Water is essential for life on earth, just as living water animates heaven."

He chose a nearby flower, knelt, and poured the living water on it. The leaves and petals seemed to reach toward the falling liquid, eager to be drenched. "Water even reflects heaven on the molecular level! The water molecule itself is three separate atoms, each maintaining their own identity but bonded into one substance. What does that remind you of?"

"Well, The Trinity, obviously."

"Exactly! We're *sooo* close to the truth on earth—we even understand the metaphor, and use 'water' there as a symbol for life! But we *still* can't fit all the pieces together. What we long for is sitting right in front of us, but in an unfamiliar form. So we miss it. Every single day, all around us, lie little reflections of heaven that we see without really seeing."

They'd come to an oval meadow surrounded by bushes like lavender, all purples and dusky greens. The sweet scent of that foliage pervaded everything, almost visible in its intensity. Only afterward did Amanda realize how the scent had entered into her and colored her thoughts, filling all that happened in that park in a haze of gladness.

Curved benches of living stone framed in triads of blooms surrounded this meeting of ways. Some new cultivar of opalescent green grass bordered the paths that led out in many directions, giving the parkland the appearance of a spoked wheel made of greenery.

"What else about heaven did you see on earth without really seeing it?" Amanda asked, taking a seat on one of the benches.

"It was everywhere!" Theo answered, throwing his hands out wide again. "For instance, there's this gem: 'When one suffers, all suffer together; if one is glorified, all rejoice together.'"

"To be perfectly honest, that always felt kind of namby-pamby to me," Amanda responded. "Like I should be a good little girl and pretend that when someone else took first place I was just as happy about it as they were."

"I thought that too. But it's different here. Many things which required discipline and willpower on earth are immutable laws of nature in heaven," her dad expounded. "Which means doing them is effortless.

"Here," Theo added, noticing her perplexity. "It's easier to experience it than describe it. I'm going to feel something, and you tell me what it is." He plopped down on the bench next to her, put his hands over his face and closed his eyes.

"That's easy," Amanda exclaimed. "You are excited to be with me. I see it all over you. And besides, you can't hide your eyes very well when your hands are transparent!"

"But do you just see it on me, or is there more?"

"Oh—you're right. I feel it inside me, too!" Amanda looked down at her stomach, trying to make sense of what was going on in her body. "Your excitement shines out of all of you—your hands, your head, your chest. And whenever it lands on me, it penetrates clear to my insides.

"And—oh my gosh, I can taste it! It has sort of a fresh, minty, take-your-breath-away tang that makes me want to run and jump and yell. There's a scent there, too, and music, like a stirring march or a processional. When you are excited, all those bits of your emotion come in and touch me."

"How about now? What am I feeling this time?"

"Oooh, this time you are really proud of me. Pictures form in my mind as I drink it in, of medal ceremonies with ribbons all in purple, and high words of affirmation. And there's an aroma to it. It smells stately, kingly, like…a coronation? That's all I can think of to describe it. It makes me want to stand up straight and hold my head high."

Her dad removed his hands from his eyes and gave her a playful grin. Amanda returned the gesture. "Thanks, daddy. I like that you are proud of me."

"I am! Very much so." Taking her arm, he guided her down one of the spoked paths between the ranks of lavender. "So in heaven, when *I* feel something…"

"I feel it, too," Amanda finished. "Your emotions came alive inside of me.

"So—when one of us rejoices, we all rejoice together. On earth it was an exhortation: in heaven it's a law of nature. We read those words, yet still saw it without seeing."

Affecting the Environment

"That's pretty sneaky of The Maker!" Amanda teased.

"Hey, while we're on the topic of rejoicing in what others rejoice, here's another example of seeing without seeing." Theo stopped in front of a particularly glorious bush, its flowered indigo stems spraying in every direction in a fountain of color. "This time pay attention to the bush instead of your insides. I'm going to...no you'll figure it out. Just watch."

Obediently, Amanda focused in on one individual stem.

Small, trumpet-shaped purplish blooms with stamens of the purest white were arranged in rows up and down the branch. As she watched, a blush of deeper blue climbed up the stem, as if a new light had focused on each delicate flower, bringing out different highlights and details of its form. A fresh aroma filled the air, and all her insides opened to a peace she could have lain down in for centuries.

Then up from the roots flushed another distinctive color: a subtle pinkish-gold concentrated in the stem, then spiraled out through the white stamens to light the throat of each blossom. Her nostrils filled with a scent that made her want to sing for joy and rise dancing in the air, but then the bush changed again, this time displaying red highlights like fire on the tips of each petal. As that red light passed into her, she wanted to leap over a waterfall and race The Light itself. It tasted of adrenalin and adventure. And then the red faded and the plant wrapped itself again in its former glory.

"Whew—that was pretty cool, dad. What did you do?"

"I felt contentment, and then happiness, and then courage."

"Wait—the plants feel our emotions, too?" she asked, reaching out to cradle the violet flower in her open hand.

"Yes—they recognize their Maker's handiwork in our emotions, and celebrate his work," Theo affirmed. "The Man of Light said on earth that if people didn't recognize him, *every* object—down to the very stones on the ground—would cry out his name. And voila! In heaven they do just that! The clue was right there, staring us in the face all along. But we saw it without seeing."

"So I can make the flowers change color, too?" Amanda asked, a bit shyly.

"Certainly. We have artists and composers here who gather to paint masterpieces of light on a flower garden using only their emotions. It's a ball to watch them perform. So go ahead—try it for yourself!"

Then Amanda went frolicking from plant to plant, experimenting to see what colors her different feelings produced. And the garden rang with her laughter and delight on that endless summer afternoon.

Glory

"Having fun?" Theo asked after a good while, knowing the answer.

"I've got to admit, being in a place where you can share feelings with the plants is pretty amazing."

"Well, hold on to your knickers, because here's something even more incredible. On earth, we saw *things* on earth without really seeing them. But we saw *people* in the same limited way. Now, pay attention—I'll show you how heaven sees you and me, and answer the question you asked a while back about Jesus at the same time."

"Which question?" she exclaimed. "I've completely forgotten where we started."

"You asked when you could see The Man of Light again, remember?" Theo replied, laughing. He let go of Amanda's hand and took a few steps forward until he was right at the apex of the meadow. Circles of multicolored, flat stones lay beneath his feet, each hue making up one ring of that round pavement. Theo stood gazing upward with arms outstretched and palms open. Amanda waited off to one side, observing in high anticipation.

"Hey, Jesus," Theo began, "you are so amazing, and everything you say—it's like a meal of truth and life and love. Can you tell me again what *you* see in me?"

Amanda heard a swishing of movement in the grass behind her. Before she could turn, The Man of Light swept past, leaving an electric tingling behind on her skin where he'd brushed her shoulder. Wasting no time, he grabbed Theo by the arms and they swung each other wildly round and round in a manly, happy whirlwind of a dance. Half the time it seemed like their feet had left the pavement and gravity was dancing, too. A spinning funnel of light like a tornado touching down plunged onto them from above, pouring into the dance, drenching their hair and torsos, spraying droplets of light outward in a horizontal shower as that pair spun round and round, until rinsed with joy they finally ended standing arms-length apart, looking in each other's eyes. Huge smiles were plastered on both faces as they caught their breath. The rings of stones under their feet blazed emerald and blue and bronze where heaven's downpour had fallen.

Then Jesus spoke.

"My brother! You are the spittin' image of my Father and your Father. Peace covers you like a robe. Your triumph over hurt and betrayal shines like a crown on your brow. Covered in the glory your life has won; you carry the Great Reward within your own person. I delight to see you choose, because we have the same mind, and every decision you make honors The One. Truly, you have become all that your name means: Theodore; the Gift of God."

At that he turned and faced outward, putting his right arm around her dad's shoulder as if facing the audience in a vast symphony hall. "You dwellers in my Kingdom," he shouted, rotating slowly around, with his right arm around Theo and his left flung out as if addressing a vast crowd. "Give him the honor his life has earned! All hail to this Hero of Heaven!"

As The Man of Light called out to his kingdom, Amanda heard a great roar of affirmation rise from the plain, the grass and trees and even the ground itself joining in a song of joy and victory and delight. And like looking through a window to the world outside, she saw into a dimension of heaven she had not yet perceived, as glory fell on her father. He was clothed in what looked like a purple robe falling from his shoulders, braided with shining stars (*real* stars, like those you see in the night sky), collared in ermine and fastened at the throat with an intricate chain of interwoven silver light. Threads gleaming like platinum and gold wove sparkling through the fabric, and Amanda perceived that each thread represented a person her father had touched or cured or invested in. Everyone he had given to in life had returned honor, with The Maker's approval added on top, and that gratitude had literally taken form in the glory dimension and become his clothing. A silver circlet rested on his head, with the bluest of sapphires as a setting for a single, opalescent diamond as large as her thumb. The thought entered her that his crown represented the admiration he received from The Man of Light made physical, commemorating each act of sacrifice and service he'd made for love.

And as The Man of Light, The Maker, charged his creation to honor her father, she saw that every blade for miles had bowed toward him, and the rocks sang his song, distant angels shouted, and even the air and the wind joined in. Amanda found herself on her knees, shouting with them, "All hail to this hero of heaven!" over and over.

When that shout finally died down, Jesus spoke again, more softly and more personally, so only those three could hear: "Theo, you are mine, forever and ever; and I am very, very proud of you. Wisdom salts your words, and you have represented me well to our daughter Amanda—and for that I am also grateful!" Jesus reached out and embraced him, and tears ran down each cheek and mingled between them with their mingled spirits.

Finally, The Man of Light released him, and pulled back to look deeply in his eyes once more. "Endless love and joy be to you, from Me, and my Father, and our Life that fills all in all."

"Thanks, Jesus," Theo replied, smiling, "You may get tired of hearing this from me—"

"Never!"

"—but you are my everything, my anything, my dream, my life, my love. Thank you for letting me tell Amanda about you—

it's a privilege."

"I thought you'd enjoy it, bro! You are amazing!"

Revelation

From the moment she first saw his glory, Amanda's picture of her dad changed forever. She had glimpsed in his robe the lives he had touched, and how that touch reverberated down through generation after generation. Following those threads, she witnessed his spiritual descendants discovering where the love that touched them had originated—from him! And they revered him as a giver, a parent, a source of life, and a signpost pointing to heaven. Each life-thread woven into that kingly fabric twined and divided, multiplying into a part of that great tapestry of purpose she had seen when she looked into the mirror with The Man of Light. Kneeling there in wonder and awe, Amanda saw glory where before she had only seen the familiar.

I've been seeing him without seeing, she marveled, still staring in amazement. *He's been my daddy, my confidant, my comforter, and my friend. But once you see the majesty he carries, and how heaven has transposed the grief and pain and sacrifice he endured into a glory beyond all comparison, which sits on his forehead like a crown—wow!*

Then, grabbing his hands she looked up at him, exclaiming, "Gosh, dad—I never really knew you until today! When I see who you really are and all your life meant, I am sooooo proud of you, and so grateful for you, and so happy to be your daughter. Thanks for…well, for who you are!"

At that he smiled, and the vision passed. He became just her daddy again. "'When one is glorified, all rejoice with him.' Do you understand now?"

"Yes, of course—how could I have missed it?" And afterward, when she recalled her father in heaven, she always mentioned the crown and the robe, and how her own daddy was a Hero of Heaven.

"And now," Theo began, "to answer your question about

when you can see Jesus again—"

The Man of Light laughed aloud. "You discerned the answer already, sister, while you were still in the tunnel. I exist in multiple time dimensions, so I have an infinite number of moments within each nanosecond of your life. I could be with a billion, billion different people at once, and still have an eternity to spend with you! All you have to do is call, just like your father did—any time you want. I'm only a phone call away."

"Anytime?"

"Anytime. I had that written in the bible, too: 'call to me, and I will answer.'"

"I saw it, but I didn't see," Amanda whispered to herself. She wasn't quite sure how, but suddenly it was just her and her father, alone again in the sparkling meadow.

11 Roses

Like on a glorious spring day, all the colors in the Beautiful Land were as fresh and vibrant as the morning after a rain. The scent of flowers hung in the air and the slight breeze made the temperature just perfect. *I suppose every day here is like the first great day of spring,* Amanda thought, and the waving grass and the air she breathed agreed.

They'd passed out of the great, open lawn to an area dotted with irregular islands and beds of foliage in a grassy sea. Some were almost forests, made of tree-like, flowering bushes with pink blooms held up by thickets of slender branches for a roof. *Almost like the crepe myrtles that used to line our driveway,* she thought. *Or better—crepe myrtles are a poor cousin to these!*

Birds flitted through the stems, twittering joyous songs as they cavorted overhead. Her father held out a waiting arm, and several immediately swooped down to roost on it in a gaily-chattering line. Iridescent red, blue and other indescribably-colored breasts complimented their delicate feathers. And the songs! They had the variety of a mockingbird, but each bird seemed to tweet away in harmony with every other. *I guess even the birds sing like a choir in heaven, each one with perfect pitch.*

Her dad lifted his arm, and the little wrens fluttered a few feet upward in a spurt of color. Briefly lowering their wings in mid-flight as if to curtsey in his direction, they turned and rushed back to the trees, singing all the way.

"Are those three your pets, dad?" Amanda inquired.

"Not in the way we kept pets on earth," he responded, "All creatures here are tame, and respond to our loving invitations. But no animal is *my* pet, because nothing in heaven is any one person's property. All animals here are loved by all, and they respond to love more freely and faithfully than the best-trained dog or most perceptive horse could on earth."

"Sounds more like they are *all* pets!"

"Good—I like that, Mandy! Just no leashes or obedience training required. The Creator's life runs in their veins, and so they love the Lord of Creation."

"Who are…?"

"Us, of course! In the Beginning, The Maker gave us the earth and put a desire in us to care for the land and its creatures. It's why we have pets and gardens, and why we get so hyper about manicuring our pristine American lawns. We have a built-in gardening instinct! And though the first garden is gone, our love for living things remains, as does the creatures' devo-tion to their stewards."

A faint blending of lights began to precede them down the path like a shadow, but brighter than the surroundings instead of dim. Noticing, Theo turned to witness a pair of stars purpose-fully striding up the wide path behind them. "Look, Amanda!" he called out, taking her arm to halt her. "A pair of Gardeners! Just in time to reveal more of the secrets of tending the soil."

Gardeners

One of the two approaching figures had a familiar form: a woman, glowing with an inner light like to Amanda's own, and roughly the same height. She held a narrow shovel over her shoulder, its shaft resting on the strap of a small satchel that dangled on her opposite hip. A pair of gloves peeked out from beneath its flap. The high air she whistled seemed to match her lofty spirits.

The real novelty was the second figure. Fully twice the woman's height, with the outline of a broad-shouldered man, he was so transparent as to be almost invisible, if it weren't for the burning fire within him. Amanda wasn't sure if he was an especially ethereal man with a strong inner light, or…*maybe an inner light but without a physical body to match,* she decided. Looking right through him at the countryside beyond, she could barely tell he was there. If she fixed her eyes on his outline, it wavered and flickered like a candle in the wind. But the eyes were a continuous flame.

"He's one of the Burning Ones, Mandy," her father whispered. "An angel."

"Hail!" the woman called out. "If I see rightly, we're in the presence of a newcomer and her astute guide." The pair halted before them and bowed, the woman gracefully and the burning one like a bowl of glowing embers spilling onto the ground. "We are greatly honored to come upon you in this happy moment."

Then the angel spoke, his deep voice vibrating the ground. "It is a great blessing to honor and serve ones who stand so near to the center of his affection."

"Then you have perfect timing—but I don't have to tell *you* that," Theo replied with a laugh, looking up at the angelic figure. "We were just talking about humanity's love of the earth. Tell us, you who tend The Maker's fields so well, what you do in his service."

"Gladly!" the angel rumbled. For a moment his fiery light seemed to fold into itself (maybe he sat?) and his face came down to their level. It was hard to keep any other part of the burning outline in focus, so Amanda contented herself with fixing on the twin fires of his eyes.

"I am Kepos, the servant of The Most High, and of all His Children; and this is our friend Anastasia, his beloved. I have tended the gardens of his delight for two ages, until this new age dawned. They were first planted in hope, that we might fashion and tend them eternally together with the children of men. When men rejected The Light, that union was delayed. So I kept what you see here for a second age, building and reshaping in thought each plant and tree for something my heart foresaw but my mind could not yet grasp.

"When The Man of Light descended to earth and returned, we at last began to comprehend what was to be—a marriage of the spiritual and the physical, joined by the life that flows from The One. On that day we witnessed things we'd longed to grasp for all that endless age of waiting. They were wondrous and remarkable in our eyes. So we worked with new purpose, and the gardens began to take their destined shape for the Great Wedding of the Maker and the Made, The Prince and the Bride. Now we celebrate, because one work is nearly complete, and a new one is on the cusp of beginning."

"And don't forget to tell them about me, Kepos," the woman added, leaning on her shovel. "I'm part of the story, too."

The Angel bowed his head in her direction. "Yes, beloved Anastasia. The woman you see here is also a Master Gardener. She loved well the plants and animals that came into her estate on earth, and developed an especially deep delight for how they reflected her Maker. Therefore, she now tends ten thousand plantings with me here in the Beautiful Land. I am training her in the horticulture of heaven, and hence she draws from a storehouse of love and knowledge of the old creation and the new. Under her touch flowers bloom and trees grow up to worship The Maker that have never been seen before in heaven. For now, I am the trainer, but soon she will surpass me, and I will rejoice to be her servant."

"Thank you, Kepos. You always tell our tale so admirably,

and yet quite succinctly." She turned to the two other humans, and whispered, "I'd probably take 10,000 words to say what he can in ten. But then, I always was a talker."

Twisted Desire

"So you still have work that you have to do in heaven?" Amanda inquired.

"Yes, we do!" Anastasia replied immediately. "Just don't say that we 'have to.' Work here is fun—pure delight, in fact, now that we are not under the curse of twisted desire."

"What's that?"

"Work here is something that truly satisfies the longings of the heart. To use your muscles, joining mind and body to create like The Creator, then to stand back and admire what you have done, as he did on the first sabbath—that is desire fulfilled! And here, there is no artist's remorse, no conceiving of a work you can't execute. We have minds capable of designing perfection, and bodies able to perfectly execute what the mind envisions."

"But the curse you mentioned?"

"Oh, yes! I was coming to that. I am wordy! Desire is that which draws and motivates the heart. As the roots of a willow are drawn to an aquifer, it pulls us to The One—that's what he made it for. Our desires for love, security, justice, acceptance, goodness, and so forth—all were made to be filled in him. For he is the sole true object of desire, the one drink able to quench the heart's thirst. As Solomon the Great wrote, 'desire fulfilled is a Tree of Life.'

"So—work was part of The Maker's original plan to fill our deep desires. The idea was, as we expended ourselves to till and keep his world, the Water of Life would flow through us to our garden, satisfying our longings and those of the plants we tended. But when humanity refused to draw from The Maker's well, and began seeking its own springs instead…" she sighed, shaking her head. "Work became toil and futility. That is the curse of twisted desire."

"Why do you call it twisted?" Amanda asked.

"Because desire itself is not wrong—although many on earth believe so. No, The Maker planted it in us as a reflection of his own nature. Doesn't he desire me, and you, and all that he has made?

"Yet even a good desire can be twisted into an evil shape when it is directed toward the wrong object. We think, 'if I can just accomplish this, I'll be happy;' or 'if I can finally get my desk cleared off, I can relax,' or 'if I am successful at work, I will be somebody.' Think of what those statements mean: 'I believe that this little thing of earth can make me truly happy.'"

"But it can't?" Amanda replied skeptically.

"No. When we reach the goal, the reward we sought always turns to dust."

"There's a high-falutin' medical term for it," Theo chimed in, with a grandiose gesture to match. "'Post-Olympic Depression.' It happens when an athlete invests years training for an event. Even if they win the gold, they often end up lost, empty, resentful, and down afterward. They thought a medal would fill their heart, and it doesn't."

"All work is like that," Anastasia narrated, switching her shovel to the opposite shoulder as she walked. "Find ultimate meaning in relationship with your Maker, not your work, and all work becomes a joy. Seek for significance in the work itself, and it becomes a curse."

"I can attest to that!" Theo added, a twinkle in his eye. "*So* glad that's over."

"Yes, an empty heart welcomes in the most pathetic substitutes!" Anastasia agreed. "Lord knows I did. Workaholism, co-dependency, competition, manipulation, fame—I tried them all. I almost lost myself chasing my twisted desires, until The Man of Light rescued me," she stated fondly, a distant look of remembering in her eyes. "That was a great day of losing and finding."

The party reached a wide spot in the trail, where a pair of benches made of living vines in ornate spirals and whorls sat beneath a pair of slender trees, whose delicate lavender blossoms floated in the air like dogwood blooms in springtime. Resting her shovel against the bench, Anastasia invited her guests to sit. Kepos took a position standing behind her and a little to one side, his flame reflecting off the gently waving branches overhead to create the semblance of a river flowing through the boughs.

"I would love to hear your story, if you don't mind telling it," Amanda asked, leaning against her father's side. She knew by now that she could simply look at the woman and see her history if she chose. But hearing it told by the one who lived it added a new dimension, and right now her desire was to hear Anastasia speak her own words from her own heart.

"Oh, certainly, my darling! He has grown a beautiful thing in me, and I never get tired of sharing that bouquet." She leaned forward on her seat, clearly eager to begin.

"I was a champion gardener and florist in the old world. I created new hybrids, new fragrances, larger blooms, constantly striving for that elusive Best in Show award. With all the contests and competitions, judging, fussing over my plants—see, cultivating roses was my whole life. I had an entire room just for photos and trophies and awards. Now I call it my 'self-worship room,'" she added slyly, as if sharing a secret.

"But the harder I strove for success, the less real love I had for gardening. Growing things became a means to an end, an instrument to get what my heart longed for. What I really craved was recognition, to be in the center like the stamens of a flower. I wanted mere mortals to tell me I was *Someone.* The more I looked for my work to water me, the more it left me dry. Dry, dry as dust, and thirsty for meaning."

Amanda half expected Anastasia to take on a sad expression at this point, or maybe to feel the grief and loss in her emotions. But no. *Whether she's sharing dark moments or light, happy or sorrowful, she seems...I guess she's at home in her story. Comfortable with it. Yes, this is her life and her grief, yet those losses don't infect her feelings. It's like she's a happy sparrow perched on a branch, singing for a morning that will never pass away. Oh—I better listen, I'm losing the thread!*

"The true desire The Maker planted inside me," Anastasia continued, "was to be known and loved by *him.* Despite my preeminence in my field, no award, applause or accomplishment could give me that.

"Then one morning I went out to tend my precious plants, and saw—devastation! Disaster! Every last rose in my garden, all my carefully grafted specimens, were shriveled, brown and dry as my heart. In jealousy one of my rivals—bless his name! —had sprayed herbicide over my entire garden."

"That's terrible!" Amanda cried.

"No, no, darling—it was wonderful! I killed that man a thousand times in my heart that first week, but I should have kissed him. For as I sat mourning by my window while my pitiful, false self withered away, The Man of Light found me—or rather, I finally started paying attention to him. I was a plant in a desert, throwing out scraggly roots in every direction in a desperate search for life. But when he found me, I found water. I finally let go and gave him my dead roses along with my blighted heart, and he gave me my life.

"For two years my garden lay bare. The sterilized soil grew nothing but a few haggard weeds, while he stripped my heart of its addictions and gradually filled it back up with himself. Oh, to be known by The One, and loved, and valued!" she exulted, jumping up to break out into a lively jig with her shovel as a partner. It seemed even Kepos enjoyed her little dance—his eyes seemed to be laughing.

"And then," she continued joyfully, "when I learned again to love plants because they reflected his love, he gave me back my garden, too. I fell in love with beauty again, because she reminded me of him; and cultivated her as a present for my lover.

"Because I had learned to love flowers for their own glory, rather than how they could add to mine, I grew the most fantastic roses in the entire country. They were more vigorous and beautiful and aromatic than ever before. But the only contest I ever entered them in was the one where I let The Man of Light who saved me choose his favorite. And instead of one of my flowers, he chose me!

"And that," she stated firmly, "is how he broke the curse of twisted desire in my heart, and replanted me in his garden."

The Soil

"Now, enough of my story. Let me show you what can be done with the seeds and the soils of heaven!" Anastasia beckoned them to follow. With Kepos taking up the rear, they walked a short way along the edge of a flowered island before turning inward. There was no path—somehow the flowers parted before the gardeners as if their roots swam through the earth to each side to make a way, then surged back in place after they passed. After about fifty paces the flowers opened out into a narrow clearing paralleling the border of the island.

Anastasia leaned her shovel against a tree and surveyed the chosen spot approvingly. "These flowers are exquisite on their own, but I think they need a proper backdrop. Would you agree, Kepos?"

She looked expectantly up at the burning eyes. His flickering outline simply bobbed wordlessly in assent.

Anastasia turned back to Amanda and her dad, a wide grin spanning her face. "He's such fun!" she laughed. Anastasia pretty much laughed at everything.

Reaching into her brown satchel, she brought out a handful of seeds, shaped vaguely like almonds but well over an inch in length. Raising cupped hands to her mouth, she gently breathed on them. An orange glow radiated from her palms. "Now, make a row in the clearing beyond me," she spoke to the seeds, "two paces apart and staggered."

The kernels immediately lifted into the air over Anastasia's fingers. Open mouthed in amazement, Amanda watched as they spread into a staggered line above the open ground, hovered in mid-air—then dove into the earth!

Anastasia seemed unfazed. Turning back to Kepos, she asked in a dignified voice, "Now, if it pleases you, Burning One, would you water them?"

"It always pleases me to work with you," the Angel replied. Amanda thought the flaming eyes twinkled as he said it. She couldn't tell afterward if he held out a watering can or if the sky three feet above the seeds somehow opened up, but a shower of living water (Amanda's heart told her it had been dipped from the River) began bathing the bare, ochre ground. The flowers at the edges of the clearing seemed to stretch for it, luxuriating in the spray of that soft rain.

"Now grow," Anastasia said, plain and simple. It wasn't a command so much as an acknowledgement of reality, that there was nothing else that a seed of heaven, planted with love and watered by the River of Life, could do.

Amanda realized she was holding her breath in anticipation and commanded herself to relax. In that moment a row of tender green shoots thrust up through the earth. Leaves unfolded and spread as the lengthening stalks reached eagerly upward, like a timelapse video of a growing plant. Yet this took place in a moment, right in front of her. The stems thickened into slim trunks covered with a mottled bark like a sycamore, and delicate branches began to sprout in all directions. Then buds, and finally glorious flowers burst forth to ornament the fan of leaves. They reminded her vaguely of dogwoods in their horizontal growth habit.

Immediately a squadron of hummingbirds swooped down to drink nectar from the fresh blooms. They wove in and out of the flowers with the intricate steps of the marching band she loved to watch back at the university.

"There!" Anastasia exclaimed with delight. "The canopy of branches sets off the flowers nicely!" (She'd actually said the flower's name and color, but in a language that Amanda couldn't afterward remember, let alone pronounce.)

"What do you wish for the understory?" Kepos asked.

"I think we need something different—a texture more than a focal point. Maybe a grass?"

Kepos named several varieties, and at the final one Anastasia clapped her hands and cried out, "That's it! Perfect!" Rummaging in the satchel, she came out with another handful of small grains like rice. She took a deep breath and blew. The seeds scattered from her palm and fell to earth, yet only on the bare ground and not amongst the flowers. With a second watering, delicate olive-edged grasses with ivory hearts sprang up all over the clearing. In moments they were waist-high.

"Now here's the magical part," the gardener whispered to Amanda, who was standing beside her, with her father on her other hand. "He's been practicing this for two ages, and it's his specialty. Just watch!"

She turned to Kepos. "I think if you sculpted them, it would be the perfect touch. And I'm guessing our visitors would love to be part of your work."

Kepos simply dipped his head in reply, but it seemed he was pleased—his flickering outline began to dance.

Then he turned to Amanda and Theo. "May I look into you?" he asked.

Amanda turned uncertainly to her dad, who nodded that it was okay, "Of course!" he answered for both of them.

Amanda felt the angel enter her mind and gaze across her memories. It seemed he was only interested in what she'd done since she entered the Beautiful Land. Then his mind withdrew, and his subtle hands began moving amongst the grasses.

Kepos' outline was already indistinct enough that it was hard so see him when he held still. But now, he passed rapidly among the ranks of grass, here shaping a blade in a particular shape, now speaking a word to a certain plant. Each time he touched a stem a brief scarlet ember flared, and the plant brightened at that spot. His work was impressing an order on the slender blades. She could see groupings of color, light and form as his hands manipulated the stems, but as yet it didn't make a coherent whole. It was beautiful, though, in the way a Jackson Pollock painting was beautiful: a riot of color and texture coming together in an explosion of light.

Then Kepos stood back, making a motion like wiping his hands on his burning thighs, and turned to the three observers. "Look now and see your own joy captured in living form."

For a moment Amanda was somewhat confused. It was a beautiful display, but she wasn't sure what a bed of grass had to do with her. Then a breeze rippled through the stalks, twisting the blades this way and that, and Amanda gasped in wonder and delight at what Kepos had done.

It was like a movie shown in living foliage. As the wind passed from left to right through the green blades, she saw her own image run like a red fire, hair streaming out behind and arms spread wide. She could even make out her fingers, the picture was so detailed. It came to her mind that she was shouting, although the grass made no sound but a slight rustling. Then another figure appeared suddenly just to her right and those two bodies crashed together in an embrace that was an explosion of light and color.

It's me and dad! Amanda instantly realized, *when we first met by the oak tree, and ran to each other and embraced.* She watched the two of them spin around, perfectly modeled in a topiary of green blades. *He captured it perfectly! What a moment!* And then the gust passed, and the grass became merely grass again, until the next breeze came to repeat the performance.

She leapt over to Kepos and threw her arms around him—which was an odd sensation, like embracing a crackling log from a campfire. Pulses of energy from his body sparked on and through her, but his was a heat that didn't burn.

"Oh, Kepos, that was awesome! It was so real, so alive, so…" At that point Amanda ran out of words, so she gave up and just kept hugging him, while Anastasia laughed and her dad smiled with approval.

Speaking Life

After watching the scene play out a dozen times, oohing and aahing over various details and repeatedly complementing Kepos' skills, Amanda posed a question she'd been holding in. "Anastasia, how did you do that?"

"Do what?"

"Make the seeds jump into the ground."

"Oh, that. Easy: you just tell them what to do and they do it."

Noticing that his daughter still looked baffled, Theo chimed in. "I think what she's asking is, why do things in nature obey you here when they don't on earth?"

"Oh, honey, I'm sorry! I forgot you were a newcomer," the gardener apologized. "Because we live and move with the life of The One, we can do many of the things he does. He spoke and described a universe, and it sprang into being just as he imagined. That same creative power in The Voice flows through us gardeners to the plants. I use my voice to tell the seeds where to go, and they go. I say, 'grow!' and they grow. It's just simple trust, really," she added.

"Then I can do that, too?"

"Certainly! Would you like to grow a tree together?"

"No, no, I don't want to get in the way…" Amanda began tentatively, then quickly corrected herself. "Sorry, that's a vestige of earth—being apologetic when I actually really want something. I'd love to."

"Perfect! One thing I positively love about gardening is that it's never a one-person job. And a tree would make this little garden perfect. Pick a good spot for it and mark it on the ground."

Amanda studied the garden and its symmetry for a moment. *She's right—it* does *need something.* Choosing a spot that balanced the visual weight of the grass sculpture, she scuffed the ground with her heel.

"Excellent. Now Kepos," Anastasia called over her shoulder, "would you make us a hole?" And to Amanda, "Back up a step, hon—he can really make the dirt fly."

Kepos drew himself up over the selected spot. With his wavering visage, you couldn't exactly follow his movements, but it seemed that he bent and put a fist to the ground. A single word rumbled out of him: "Be!"

What happened next was like a soundless detonation. A fountain of soil erupted from the earth, making a cavity bigger than a dinner plate, with a perfectly-symmetrical little ring of dirt granules piled around it. Apparently, their trajectory was not inhibited by his body—the particles seemed to fly right through him. No dust hung in the air, either.

It looks like those funnel-shaped traps the ant lions used to dig in the back yard, Amanda thought. *Only larger. Pretty cool way to dig a hole, though!*

"Thank you, blessed one!" Kneeling down beside the hole, Anastasia beckoned Amanda to join her. "Now, Amanda, it's your turn." Selecting a seed from her bag, Anastasia handed it over. It was about the size of an acorn, smooth and rounded. Its tawny, golden hue blended nicely with the rich brown soil.

The kernel appeared lifeless, lying woody and hard in her palm. "So what do I do?"

Anastasia took the seed and held it up between thumb and forefinger. "This bare seed is like a light bulb: it's made to give light, but won't shine until it is plugged in to a power source." Smiling broadly, she patted Amanda's upper arm. "But that source is right here! The life of The One flows in your breath, your blood and your thought." She placed the acorn back in Amanda's palm. "Breathe The Maker's life upon this seed."

Amanda looked up at Theo a bit skeptically, and he nodded assent. But she still hesitated. "Sorry. I just…I feel a bit like I'm playing God."

"You aren't playing, dear," Anastasia intoned softly. Then in full confidence she flung out her arms, declaring: "You are the offspring of God! A full-blooded family member, a trusted ambassador carrying life to his world. You bear the family name, the stamp of his approval, the image of his image, and think as he thinks. When this seed sees you, it sees Him; just as seeing Jesus on earth is seeing The Maker. Is it not so, Burning One?"

Amanda glanced over at the angel, and abruptly realized he had dropped to one knee. His voice seemed to reverberate through the ground, or else the earth itself throbbed in time with his words: "I acknowledge you, scion of the Holy, Child of Glory! Seated with The Man of Light on the throne of the universe, you two rule the earth hand-in-hand. Although you have come after me, you have surpassed me; because you are joined to The One who was before me. Take on your authority and begin to reign as The Prince of Heaven reigns and speak as he has spoken!"

"My dear Kepos," Anastasia laughed. "I've never heard you use so many syllables to answer a simple question! You're in danger of becoming as wordy as I am." Then she turned back to Amanda. "The Burning Ones cannot lie. You are who he says you are, and you can do what he says you can do. Now—take up the role you were reborn to, and speak life to this earth!"

Awed, pleased, surprised…and with a bit of the feeling she'd received a friendly reproof, Amanda drew the seed up to her lips. And she blew.

Immediately, the acorn lit up from the inside and began to glow, as if a heart of earthy, auburn fire lay within. "Wow! It actually came to life!" Amanda exclaimed, astonished.

"Well done, Child of Glory! Actually, what brought it to life was trust. What you did was a normal, everyday human action: breathing. There's no magic in that! But your trust was a door The Maker entered through to bestow a touch of life."

"It's still amazing," Amanda gasped. "And what Kepos said about who I am—that's a bit overwhelming, too." Wandering over a few paces, she plopped down next to her dad, who'd found a convenient rock from which to observe the proceedings. "It comes to me that faith on earth works this way, too. Is that true, Poppy?"

"Yeah," Theo answered beside her. "We take simple, everyday actions—speak encouragement to someone, or lend a hand, or make introductions between a person and The One. Our role in the partnership is nothing out of the ordinary. But because we trust that his touch will come through ours, it does!"

"Well said, Theo!" Anastasia approved. "Now, Amanda—speak to the seed and tell it to plant itself."

Even with what she'd just experienced, it still felt a bit awkward. "Seed, uh…go plant yourself in that hole." The little acorn promptly hopped up from her palm, an inch or two in the air, slowly rotating. It paused, as if saluting its commander, then whisked over to the hole and shot down into the dirt. Amanda's mouth dropped open again.

"You'll get used to it soon enough," Anastasia encouraged, patting her arm. "Now, refill the hole."

And as soon as Amanda spoke, it was done.

The two of them rose together, tamping down the dirt over the hole with their feet. Then Anastasia nodded to Kepos, and he began watering the seed as he'd done before.

"In the first garden, there were two trees—two choices, and two methods of gardening. But heaven has only one: The Tree of Life," Anastasia began, as the fresh scent of living water rose in the air. "The Tree of Life represents the way of dependence.

The offer was, all humanity's deepest desires would be perfectly met, but only by trusting The Maker to take care of them himself. Like this: Amanda, speak the word of trust that lets the seed flourish."

A bit more confidently now, she spoke: "Okay, seed: grow!"

"Well done! Now this other tree, the Tree of Knowledge," Anastasia continued, "is the way of *independence.* It substitutes being in control for connection with The One. But—can it ever produce results like this?"

She ended with a flourished, pointing down at her feet. At that very moment a golden stalk broke through the wet ground, curving gracefully upward at a steady pace as the first delicate leaves spread from its trunk. Theo rose and joined the other three in a circle around it, watching the miracle of life.

"Oh, what joy!" the gardener exclaimed after a moment. "We stand here and talk, *doing* absolutely nothing, and yet the plant grows! We trust, he does. *This* is the way of the Tree of Life: we take a simple human step, and depend on him to accomplish what is beyond us. It's a partnership: we plant and water, but he gives the growth."

"What a beautiful sapling," Amanda whispered, watching first flowers and then tender fruits (they looked like little golden apples) form on the branches. Its arms spread gradually over the whole garden, bathing all the plantings in a shade of woody light. Soon the small party stood under a now-mighty, full-grown tree, nearly a hundred feet wide.

All from a little seed, Amanda wondered in amazement. "I think I understand…I may have to experience this again another day to fully grasp it. But…I, uh, do have one other *practical* question…"

"Go ahead—you do pose good questions!" Anastasia chuckled.

"Okay. It's just this: if we can simply tell a tree to plant itself and grow, why did you bring a shovel?"

The gardener laughed out loud. "Oh, my dear Amanda! Because gardening is *fun*, whether you do it with a shovel or by simply speaking a word. And I have grown very fond of shovels." And then she threw her arms around Amanda and gave her a long, deep hug.

Finally, after more hugs and bows to the Angel Kepos, they left their new friends and their gardens behind and continued their journey.

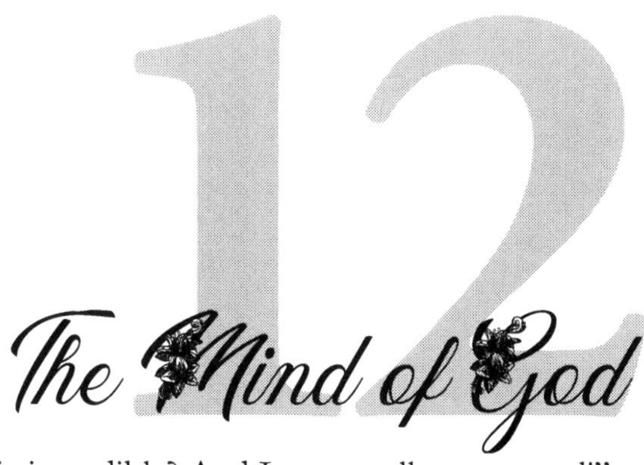

12 The Mind of God

"Wasn't Anastasia incredible? And I got to talk to an angel!" Amanda gushed, as their new friends vanished around a bend in the road. "My goodness, Poppy: how did we fall into such an amazing, spectacular, incomparable place? And on top of that, get to call it home! Does this really go on forever?"

"Yup," Theo answered with a far-away expression, as if he was peering beyond time to foresee a blissful ecstasy beyond description. "Our future will constantly get better, wider, and deeper. You and I will become more and more complete, our inner light swelling in beauty as we grow in community with The One and his children. Not a single tear or regret will mar our hearts. And we'll be family with billions of sisters and brothers, having endless days to get to know and love and laugh with them, and to be loved in return.

"And we will forever possess this great honor: that whenever we want, we can call The Prince of the Universe to converse with us, or lean on his arm and soak up his affection, or just gaze into his infinite eyes in silent adoration. We have an all-access, backstage pass to the fountain where he dwells in the center of his city, to lose ourselves in eternity as we gaze into the mind of God."

"Gosh," Amanda whispered, learning on his arm. "I didn't know you were so lyrical, Poppy! You sound like a poet when you talk about what will be."

Theo looked again at his daughter, smiling warmly. "Our future is a work of art, formed in the infinite mind of The Maker. Since poetry is art in words, it's really the only fitting way to talk about the sonnet that is heaven."

They were silent again for a few moments, marinating in awe and wonder. *Standing here, contemplating eternity, I think I get for the first time how impossibly small I am in the whole scope of things,* Amanda thought. *Billions of galaxies with untold numbers of stars and planets exist in our old universe—and this place is larger still! Yet the dust speck that I am is dear to The One. He constantly seeks out my thought, and never forgets or overlooks me. It's like I found a lottery ticket on the ground outside a Seven-Eleven, one I didn't even pay for, and won a billion-dollar prize with it. How do you ever make sense of all that?*

Sitting up straight, she turned to her father. "Poppy, it was such a small risk to believe in him—and this is such a gargantuan return on investment! My little life in exchange for all of this? How can The Maker trade so much for so little?"

"That's just who he is," Theo replied. "It makes no *rational* sense, but it is his delight to know you and be known by you. The only thing to do is take it on faith."

"C'mon, that's not a very intellectually satisfying answer," Amanda teased.

"It's enough for me," Theo replied. "But he may have a different response for you. Why don't you ask The One?"

"Umm…isn't that a little, well, uppity? It's one thing to enter into Jesus' thoughts—he's human, like me. But am I supposed to just walk right into the mind of God himself?"

"Why not? Just direct your attention to him and ask to see his mind."

"For real?"

"Amanda, you're gonna love it!"

"Okaaaay." She composed herself and looked upward, as if God was in the sky. *An old habit of earth, I guess. Silly. Alright then... God, can you show me—*

In an instant she was transported into the infinite intelligence of The Creator. On a sable field, the entire span of the cosmos was laid out like a banquet. It was far too huge, too majestic for her mind to contain. Yet joined in his thought she somehow absorbed it—stars, flashing into life and burning out; galaxies wheeling across the sky, clouds of gas fluorescing in cascades of light. Molecules floating in the void, neutrinos whipping from one end of the universe to the other. Whole ages of time passed, all vibrating with purpose. All of it focused on one tiny planet in the center: Earth.

But physics proved the universe has no center, her mind protested.

"It is not so. There is a center: not of cosmic origin or physical position, but in Our thought."

Instantly, she understood: his attention fixated on one, single point. Earth was not merely the insignificant satellite of a minor star, an accident of creation. No, it was his focal point! The universe was a nursery exquisitely designed to shepherd one small world into existence. And it came to her that as his infinite mind concentrated on that one finite point, life blossomed there—a life that would grow and multiply and increase forever, and be infinite itself, because he desired it. What was merely a mote in the vast universe was endlessly important to Him.

So I am small in regard to the physical universe, but large in his love.

Then within that boundless terrain of his thought she heard laughter, a rumble of joy running through the ground beneath her feet, and the air sang. *"I crafted an entire universe to have a world where humanity could flourish. I am life, and I pour out an infinite gift of life on them, that they might coexist with me forever. I am All, and Everything, and Enough, the source that never runs out. Because I am infinite, every gift I give is infinite. To the finite human mind, my endowment seems all out of proportion to your sacrifice. Yet to me, it is simply what is right and fitting.*

"When you gave me your heart, you gave me the best you have. And when I rescued you and brought you into myself, I gave you the best I have. Those two gifts make a perfect symmetry. So what seems unfair, even extravagantly over-generous to the mind of earth, is sanity itself in the calculus of heaven."

Slowly the picture faded. Amanda blinked several times, looked about. The landscape around her appeared momentarily fuzzy and indistinct, as if an aura of diffuse light hung motionless in the air. Overall, the sensation was akin to waking from a vivid dream—everything changed when she beheld it from the viewpoint of The One.

She found that she'd dropped to the ground as he spoke, overwhelmed by the largeness of his intelligence, yet still comforted by the intimacy of its single-mindedness. Somehow, that also seemed entirely fitting. Amanda glanced up at her father. "I…I don't know what to say."

"Since there are no words to describe him," Theo chuckled, "that's actually the proper response."

So she remained silent, absorbing the immensity of The One for quite a time.

A Lot

Finally, Amanda took a deep breath and brought her mind fully into the present. "That was fantastic! Staggering, overwhelming, phenomenal! Poppy, is that what you meant by 'losing ourselves in eternity as we gaze into the mind of God?'"

"Yeah, hon," Theo responded, taking a seat on the grass next to her, legs crossed. He put a comfortable arm around her should-der and leaned close. "If there were nothing else to do in heaven but probe the mind of God, it would be more than enough."

"No joke, dad! I feel like I just took a bath in infinity. You do get lost in him—he's so…so…big."

"Just 'big?'" her dad jested.

"Okay, okay—that was a pretty weak word to describe a boundless, omniscient God!" She sighed with satisfaction, then looked away, thinking inexpressible thoughts. "On earth, infinity is just a concept, an abstraction, a little side-ways figure-eight symbol to represent an idea beyond human comprehension. But I *tasted* infinity. I floated in it, and *saw* the endless through his eyes, as he sees! Or," she corrected, "at least a little piece of what he sees. But a piece of infinity is still infinity, by golly!"

Theo laughed, and she felt the rhythmic expulsion of breath where his torso touched hers.

"I could look into that boundless mind forever and never see it all, couldn't I?"

"True. He is all. And all is a lot!"

"A lot isn't the half of it." Amanda was still sitting on the ground, leaning back on her arms. She'd had such a seminal, defining experience that she wasn't quite ready to get up and move on.

"This idea that there is perfect symmetry in my relationship to God—only he could come up with something so preposterous! I risked what little I had when I entrusted my spark of life to him." Abruptly she sat up and spread her arms out wide to encompass the full scope of the Beautiful Land. "And I got all this in return. What a steal!"

"And *he* risked all he had to be with us," Theo continued, "for the endless enjoyment of bringing a family into his world, to love and laugh with and dote on. Perfect symmetry."

"The unthinkable exchange…" Amanda whispered to herself. After a moment's thought she shook her head in disbelief. "Getting to know the mind of God is going to take *forever*."

A Little Risk

Amanda fingered a delicately-veined leaf as it slipped by,

still amazed by her incredible good-fortune. Theo had taught her to float, so now they glided forward without effort, skimming through a scattered woodland two feet in the air at the pace of a relaxed walk. They stood upright while moving; but there was no compelling reason for it. Sitting or even lying down would have worked as well. But standing was more familiar, and therefore more comfortable. So that's what they did.

Perfumed blossoms the size of saucers hung on the passing trees. With each puff of wind delicate petals detached and spiraled downward, a snowfall of pink and white coloring the air and carpeting the ground in front of them. It seemed like the blossoms only fell on the path where they walked, and looking behind, Amanda saw that it was so. A narrow trail of pink streamed out in their wake, and in front a majestic carpet welcomed their feet. *Like rose petals before the bride at a wedding. He's rolling out the red carpet for us, isn't he? There is so much goodness in this world that I never could have imagined.*

"Still adjusting to the scale of the gift, huh?" Theo gently inquired.

"Yeah! When I consider how microscopically little was required of me, I wonder: how could anyone turn this down? All we have to do is open our hands! So why in the world don't we?"

"Why in the world...?" Theo answered slowly, watching a phalanx of petals land on his forearm, then drift away with the next breeze. Their whispered flight seemed to mimic the sigh that escaped his lips. "Because we *have* opened our hands—and been burned. We learned to cry ourselves to sleep in a crib at night when no one came to comfort us. We got a spanking when we were innocent. We were told to buck up when we felt sad, made to follow the rules of a world we didn't understand. Our innocent curiosity led us to stick a finger in the fan—I did that when I was a toddler! —and our little fingers got cut."

"Oh—so before we get the chance to learn about the gift, we experience pain?"

"Yeah, earth is a dangerous place. And the wounded heart resists all entry—even attempts to heal it." Theo momentarily halted his forward progress to let a delicate petal waft down from the branches into his cupped hands. Still hovering, he held out the captive petal to Amanda. "Here, open your hands and take it."

His daughter lifted the pink bloom gently from his palm, holding it up before her eyes. "It smells beautiful up close," she observed, breathing in the luscious aroma. "A little like lavender and roses."

"Because all things here are good, you aren't afraid of receiving with open hands. But on earth, joy and suffering mix like weeds in the wheat; so the fear of pain gets hard-wired into our brains. If that flower had thorns hidden among its blooms, you'd learn pretty quick not to pluck it."

He took back the petal, twirling it for a moment between his thumb and forefinger, before symbolically letting it drop. It drifted softly down between them to nestle onto the path, where they watched it rock gently back and forth with the wind.

"Then every action on earth contains a risk—even picking a rose," Amanda contemplated. "And where there are thorns, even beauty may seem too dangerous to hold."

"Yup, love is like that," Theo added quietly. "When we're hurt, it can feel too hot to handle. So from fear we drop the beauty we believe might scald us, run cold water over our wounded hearts, and retreat to the security of the rational mind. I know people who've hid there for most of their lives, playing solitaire in that safe space inside the garment of skin."

"Like who?"

"Well, me for one! After your mom left and the business cratered…I was so hurt I couldn't cope. I just turned off my feelings and walked around like a zombie, numb to everything." He turned and put a hand on his daughter's shoulder, looking into her eyes. They were still airborne, but gliding sideways now, as they faced one another. "I'm so sorry I was so distant and unavailable when you needed me."

"I understand it now," Amanda replied reassuringly. "Back then, I worried that the distance between us was my fault…I guess I kinda closed up, too."

For a moment they stood face to face, taking in each other's stories with the insight of heaven while flowers wafted past them in the air. Wisdom wiped away the misconceptions they'd had of each other as they felt what the other felt and saw as they saw.

"We lived in fear on earth," Theo remembered, reaching out to gently brush her hair over her brow.

"Well, I'm glad that's over. To know each other fully like this, with no firewall standing between us, and after the Great Washing has taken all the pain away forever…it feels like our relationship is all it was ever intended to be."

"It is," he agreed, kissing her forehead. "And it is good," Both of them sighed deeply, then said, "I forgive you" at exactly the same moment. And laughed. The absurdity of how heaven transforms pain into pleasure made it impossible to dwell on past hurts for any length of time.

Engineering

On a whim, Amanda took several tentative steps up higher into the air. Just those few feet changed her perspective on the Grove of Drifting Petals. The lower branches were now at eye level, and she was glancing through the flowers instead of under them. Looking down on her father was a different point of view, too.

"I like this perspective—seeing the top of your head!" she chortled. "I spent most of my life having to look up to you."

Theo just laughed.

Amanda dropped back to his elevation, taking on a more serious tone. "Poppy, let me try something out on you that I've been mulling over for a while. It's how the engineer in me would define trust."

"Okay—I'm all ears."

"Trust is a shortcut run by your emotional brain," she began, "a process you employ when you have an incomplete dataset. An educated guess, an estimate, maybe a rule of thumb. You have enough experience to be *relatively* confident how things will turn out, but lack the data to arrive at a rigorous, scientific conclusion. Like when you sit down on a chair: you can't know for certain that it will hold you. But you've used many chairs over the years, and none have collapsed. So you trust that this one will hold you, too, instead of running a battery of tests on it first.

"Or you drink water from the tap, confident it will not make you sick, instead of carrying a water purifier with you wherever you go. Life would be impossibly cumbersome without that kind of trust."

"So if I apply that to the Great Leap," Theo reasoned, as the idea came together in his mind, "I've experienced The Man of Light's love enough to believe he'll catch me. But from an empirical standpoint, I've never done this exact thing before, so I can't be certain. Is that what you mean?"

"You got it. It's like creating a simulation on a computer. The model is never an exact representation of reality—most of the time, reality is just too complicated. For instance, there is not enough computing power on earth to create a really precise simulation of the weather! We tackle the problem by simplifying, making assumptions and eliminating variables until we get a program small enough to actually run on the processors we have. And that's substituting trusting for knowing! Trust lets us compress a problem down to a size our computer—or our brain—can manage."

"The computer-ese in your definition is a bit beyond my education, but I think I've got the concept," Theo replied with a laugh.

"And it applies to God, too," Amanda added enthusiastically. "I can't fully grasp the unsearchable mind of The One: the CPU in my head will never be powerful enough. But trust gives me a shortcut to relate to him without needing a certainty I can never attain."

A Fork in the Road

The travelers had passed out of the blossom forest, entering a main avenue again. At the crest of a small rise, the path split. Amanda could see no road signs, or any indication which branch to take. In that moment, it finally occurred to her that she didn't know their destination—or even if there was one. She looked expectantly at her dad, waiting for him to choose.

"Perfect timing!" Theo exulted, gliding to a halt, then hovering at the crossroads. "We've arrived at a fork in the road—a great place to test out your engineering model of trust. Which way should we go, Amanda: left, right or back the way we came?"

"How should I know? You're the tour guide."

"But where your mind doesn't know the way, trust can lead you. Try this: think of all three options in turn. Then share what your heart feels when you contemplate each one."

"Okaaaay. Is this some kind of Jedi mind trick?"

"No, just Navigating in Heaven 101," her dad coaxed, stepping down to the ground like exiting a bus. "C'mon, try it."

"Well..." Amanda floated down next to him. Somehow it felt easier to evaluate a road junction with both feet on the ground. "When I imagine going left or right, I can't feel any difference. I'm free to choose either. When I picture going back, it's...hmm. There's nothing wrong with that option, no should or shouldn't, but going back feels...I'm not sure what to call it. I just want to go forward more."

"That's actually a *great* description: you're tuning into your heart instead of your mind. It's like this: remember the compass we made when you were seven, by rubbing a pin on a magnet? Heaven has its own compass, and its own north pole."

"So I'm magnetic?" she joked, elbowing him playfully.

"In a way. You've been rubbing up against The Man of Light—which tunes your soul to his. Therefore, your heart automatically points toward where he is: the fountain at the center of the City of God. You can feel your way there even when your mind draws a blank. Pretty cool, huh?"

"Okay, that helps," Amanda began slowly. "It's a shortcut, like we were just talking about: I can trust my heart to point to the source, even if I can't 'prove' it."

"Right."

"This is all kinda crazy, actually," Amanda mused, staring up as the smoke trails of two fast travelers flashed overhead. "On earth I believed in a God I couldn't see with my eyes. Here I *can* see him, I hear him plainly, I exist in several more of his dimensions...but he is *still* a mystery, because he still has more dimensions than I do. The mountain of understanding remains insurmountable!"

As if she wanted a witness for a momentous decision, she turned to look intently in Theo's eyes. "Okay, Poppy: it's settled. God is God, and I am not. I can't know everything. I don't need to: trust is enough."

A seismic shift took place inside Amanda in that moment. Need to know bowed and left the stage, and she felt herself relaxing further into contentment. It was something of a holy moment, as she and her father stood holding hands, gazing peacefully down the mystical path as it wound off into the distance, disappearing in a stand of trees.

"You really internalized something there, didn't you?" Theo asked quietly. "I can feel it in you."

"Yeah, I did. It's like those trust-falls you do at camp, where you can't see behind you but you're confident your friends won't let you hit the floor."

"Trust is the bridge that connects earth and heaven, humanity and God."

"However," Amanda giggled, "I do see one teensy, weensy problem with trust being the basis of knowing in heaven."

"What?" Theo inquired.

"I don't think people on earth are going to buy it! The old me certainly wouldn't. I always took comfort in the idea that, in heaven we'll 'know fully, even as we are fully known.' Pulling that final rug of certainty out from under our feet is going to be a big blow to us rational types."

"The hole in that logic is that you're defining 'knowing' as if you were earth," Theo countered. "Heaven defines it as what we grasp through trust, not what we can prove with our logic."

"Oh, now I understand!" Amanda replied with a flash of insight, clearly excited. "I thought 'knowing as we are known' was talking about the *quantity* of information: that'd we'd know everything about The One like he knows everything about us. Which is clearly impossible. But it's actually about the *method of perception.*"

"Wait—what?" Theo asked, puzzled. "You jumped right by me there."

"It's like this, dad. On earth, The One can read our minds, but we can't read his. He's always seen us as fully transparent, like we are here. But we could only search for him from behind the firewall, with the dull eyes of earth.

"But now, the wall is removed, and we *both* have heaven's eyes! When I look into his mind like a did a bit ago, it's with the same sight he uses to look into me. 'Knowing as we are fully known' means I know him with the same *mechanism.* I have full access to his thought; the same way he has always had full access to mine."

"That's a fabulous explanation!" Theo enthused, flushed with pride. "Remarkable! Congratulations—you have quite a gift for clear thinking."

"So," Amanda concluded triumphantly, "that verse is true in heaven after all! We know fully, even as we are fully known, because *all* of our hearts are open and laid bare to one another!"

13 Secrets

They walked on in silence for a few hundred paces, letting the insights of the day soak in while simply enjoying each other's presence. Amanda found herself studying her dad's face. In some ways it was the same one she'd always known. Younger, certainly, than when she'd last seen him on earth. The grey skin and hollowed-out cheeks cancer had stricken him with in his final days were nowhere to be found. His eyes were sharp, lips bright, forehead as smooth and unlined as her own, although he was twenty-five years older. *I guess age really is just a number here,* she thought. *He just looks…alive. Completely, irrepressibly alive.*

While observing his outward appearance, she found herself hearing his thoughts as well. Her dad was methodically walking step by step through her argument about being fully known. To look into another person's head and watch reason in motion, moving tentatively forward, then taking a step back to reconsider…it was fascinating, and almost-uncomfortably intimate. Amanda felt a bit like a Peeping Tom, and began to wonder if she was seeing things she shouldn't.

"Oh—that's alright, Amanda," he replied out loud, surprising her. "No need to say, 'I'm sorry!' In heaven, you can't think of anything embarrassing, so there is no need to hide what you are thinking or keep any secrets. *Au contraire*—I feel honored that you would want to know my mind."

"Well, it still feels weird to suss it out of you when you aren't looking," she replied, a bit rattled. "Is nothing here secret?"

"Can you think of anything you'd want to keep from me?"

"Well, I…oh," she realized after ruminating briefly. "I can't. Okay, okay—just another new thing to adapt to."

"And once you do," Amanda heard in her mind, *"you'll realize how small and strained all those secrets were. And the feeling you get—to me it's like a cool breeze goes through all your insides and makes you shiver with delight every time you feel someone drinking your thoughts."*

"Drinking your thoughts?" Amanda replied, a bit dubiously. "I guess I'm not quite there yet."

"But you are!" her dad laughed, with the kind of smile you have when a loved one asks you where their keys are, and you can see them in their hand. "When I talked about drinking your thoughts, I didn't say it with my mouth—I merely thought it, but you heard just the same."

Then two of us can have a whole conversation without saying a thing out loud? Amanda thought. *Just like chatting with The Voice?*

"*You catch on quick.*"

"Cool! Telepathy!" she enthused, then scrunched up her brow. *Alright, Poppy: what am I thinking about right now?*

"*Meeting me for the first time, when we ran across the meadow to burst into each other's arms, and even the grass sang for joy.*"

"Awesome! Now you do one!"

"*Okay. What am I picturing?*" Theo answered slyly.

That Jesus talked to me a while back about why he doesn't show up on earth and prove he is real…wait, I never told you that story! And I can actually see myself doing it in your head, like watching a little movie. Were you spying on me, dad? she thought at him in joking indignation. *How'd you know that?*

"*Well, silly, I can see your story whenever I look at you, remember?*"

Oh, duh. Yeah, he told me that appearing on earth as he truly is wouldn't work, because 10-D him entering a 4-D world would basically kill everybody.

"A little counter-productive, right?" Theo chuckled aloud, then explained, "When I start laughing, it's hard to keep what I'm thinking from overflowing out of my mouth!"

Is that what Jesus meant when he said, 'Out of the overflow of the heart the mouth speaks?' Amanda mentally recited. *Wait, I never memorized that verse! How do I know it?*

"Because you are logged into the mind of The One. Everything he's ever said or done is preserved in his memory, where you can access it freely whenever you want."

So God is just Google—a giant algorithm that's scraped all the data in the universe? Amanda prodded.

"Oh, no!" Theo laughed aloud, his mirth bubbling up into his voice. *"Sorry, I couldn't keep that one inside. Google just returns information. The Maker provides so much more! Ask him about some moment in time, and you don't just get the facts: you* relive it, *in color, with input from all five senses. You can watch how God arranged people and circumstances to bring that event about, delving into the strategy behind it. See it in the larger context of his cosmic purposes and feel his pleasure as it unfolds. Or watch The Three carefully planning it before any of the participants were ever born, and then seamlessly adapting their plan to every quirky choice the human actors make.*

"Or you can look into the mind of each person in the situation, and see it from each point of view, then observe everyone who's watched that memory and find out what they learned from it. Or probe the mind of the angels as they looked on. Or see how that person's choices are celebrated in heaven, or—"

"Enough, enough!" Amanda cried, throwing up her hands in mock defensiveness. "I'll never compare God to Google again!"

"It's all true, you know," Theo added, grinning. "As a citizen of heaven, you have a secret password to the greatest database—the greatest memory—that ever was or ever will be.

Trillions of quintillions of exabytes of knowledge, experience, feeling, and wisdom, all at your fingertips. Wanna try a database query?"

The Greatest Memory

How? Amanda thought.

"*Just like you did a bit ago when you looked into the mind of God. Turn your attention toward him and ask about an event. Maybe something like this: 'Abba, show me the time when Jesus first met his cousin John the Baptist.'*"

Sounds good. Amanda answered. *Abba—*

Before she finished the first word of the question, Amanda was there. She found herself looking up a short valley nestled between three rocky hills. The slopes were lined with row after row of laboriously constructed terraces, thrown into sharp relief by the westering sun. It was like being surrounded by the stratified rocks of the Grand Canyon, with band after band of different hues and textures. An undistinguished village of about 20 dwellings (they're called *insulae* in Greek, she thought without knowing how she knew) rested near the bottom of the slope, just above where a spring gushed out of the ridge and collected in a small pool.

A family picked their way down the winding path toward that hamlet, casting long shadows across the hillside. A father, mother, boy, and girl. It came to Amanda that there were other children, too young to brave the week-long journey to Jerusalem. Their faces flashed briefly in her mind, along with names, then disappeared. *James, Joses, Miriam, Simon, little Jude.*

The eldest boy brought up the rear. He looked to be about ten, olive-skinned and scrawny, with black curly hair and dark eyes to match. His tired stride reflected the three-mile walk from the temple to the village of Ein Kerem. It had been a long day.

Cries of greeting rose from amongst the houses, and the picture zoomed in. Now she was looking through the eyes of the boy, watching his mother scurry happily to an older woman and wrap her arms around her. After a long hug, she turned and spoke cheerfully: "Son, this is your aunt Elizabeth, the one I've told you stories about. Elizabeth, meet the child who visited your home before he was born."

Amanda could feel that the boy was pleased. This woman was a close friend of his immah, his mother. He felt he knew her, although the picture of her he'd formed in his mind didn't match her actual appearance. But no matter. He bowed shyly (seeing through his eyes, Amanda's field of view swiveled toward the ground and then back up) and called out a warm greeting.

"Shalom, Elizabeth! My mom has told me much about you, and how you knew me when I was still in the womb. I've looked forward to meeting you—and your son!"

Then another rough, young voice emanated from the village: "Are they finally here?" Around the corner of a craggy stone wall came a lad maybe a year older than the first, with the same dark skin and deep, piercing eyes. With a joyful shout he sprinted up to the first boy, took his hand, and spoke breathlessly.

"Hi! I'm John! Been dying to meet you since immah told me you were coming to the feast. C'mon, let's grab some figs from the orchard and talk." And they ran off together, disappearing through the olive trees.

"There he goes again," the father uttered, in his always-calm voice. "Forever on the run."

There he goes again, The Father thought, in his always-pleased voice. *The apple of my eye.*

Amanda's head spun at the wonder of it. *I could watch—no participate in—every good experience of everyone who ever lived!* Then she heard a familiar voice, from close at hand.

"Reading my mind again, I see. How lovely!" And The Man of Light was there at her side, ablaze in glory, lighting up the sky with love.

It took a moment for Amanda to regain her composure. His appearance dazzled, taking one's breath away. *Part of me wants to just watch him, part wants to fall into his arms and snuggle up next to him, and another part wants to throw up my hands and worship.* But this time Amanda noticed the same dark eyes, curly hair and olive skin as the boy in the vision.

Finally, the question bubbled out. "How'd you know dad and I were talking about you?"

"Because I'm always listening. I was always listening when you were on earth, too—you weren't the only ones practicing for your arrival in heaven!"

"But…"

"A second question?" Jesus chuckled. "I do enjoy your questions."

"You looked like a little boy when I saw you—just a kid. How could…" her voice trailed off as her train off thought ran off the rails.

"Humans do get to be boys and girls before they grow up," he responded, amused. "Is that a surprise? I threw rocks at trees and raced up and down the stony hills with my little friends. And I was a toddler who fell again and again before I learned to walk; and a young man who told his mother that he wouldn't marry and give her grandchildren to hold; even an infant who cried when he was hungry and spit up on his mom's shoulder.

"It's tough on earth to see me as I really am, because it's hard to keep both halves of the paradox that is me in your head at once. The mind of heaven is more adaptable."

"Whoa—it never occurred to me that you cried as a baby."

"You have Christmas carols to thank for that," he replied, grinning. Then, surprisingly, he broke into a lusty song.

"The caaaattle are lowing, the poor ba-by wakes…" After only one line, he was struggling to keep a straight face. "But little Lord Jesus, no *crying* he maaaakes!"

And then he was roaring with laughter, hands on his hips,

until Theo and Amanda were bent over beside him, tears watering the ground. Around them creation itself seemed to revel in the joke, the breeze whipping the grass and the leaves into riotous laughter.

Finally, Jesus straightened, wiping his eyes. "Ho boy, what a line! I always looked forward to Christmastime just so I could hear that whopper over and over! Christians can get so *spiritual* sometimes that they can't see the crooked nose on my face."

Wiping his brow theatrically, he added, "What's funny is that on earth, where everything is mortal, humans only want to talk about my divinity. If a story comes up that emphasizes my human side, like if I don't know who touched me, or if I'm surprised by someone's faith, they explain it away. 'He knew all along she was going to touch him—he was just testing her faith,'" he mimicked in a solemn, religious voice. Then he started laughing again, til his cheeks were red and his eyes watered. "It's only when they leave mortality behind and enter the divine that my humanity finally dawns on them."

"I guess I did that, too," Amanda admitted. "I don't believe I ever even *tried* to imagine you as a kid. All the stories I read about you were from your thirties."

Jesus put an endearing arm around her shoulder. "Don't worry: heaven wrote it all down. Tap into The Maker's mind, like you did a moment ago, and you can watch me grow up through my mom's eyes, or get the inside scoop on how my brothers and sisters struggled to relate to me. After all, they had to live with a sibling who never did anything wrong!"

"Oooh—I never thought of that!"

"Or see from the viewpoint of my dear Aunt Sebaste, who was always trying to play matchmaker and fix me up with some girl in the village."

"Awk-ward!" Amanda chortled.

"Mostly for me," Jesus admitted cheerfully. "But to see a *real* love story, watch The Maker watching me grow up. I must have relived that one a thousand times," Jesus recited, misty eyed. "Or listen in with The Voice as she taught me how to commune with heaven. Good times."

"The Voice is a *she*?" Amanda wondered.

"Just as much as she's a he," Jesus laughed. "The only one of Us Three that gender really applies to is me. But—you and your father were talking about secrets a moment ago. Let me tell you how I secretly feel about *you*!"

Though afterward she strained to remember every detail of that hallowed moment, she couldn't recall any specific words he said—only what went on inside her as he spoke. Her body felt like a champagne flute, slowly filling with exquisite, sparkling wine from bottom to top, while bubbles of admiration and affection tickled her insides as they rose. And then she was filled, completely sated with acceptance and approval, until it overflowed onto the ground around her and the grass lit up in an emerald ring around her feet. And then she began to laugh once more, until she almost couldn't stop.

"Oh, Jesus!" was all she could say, flinging herself into his grasp, still laughing. "I love you dearly, too!"

"Thank you," he whispered in her ears, still holding her tight. "It was for moments like this that I came to earth to find you."

"You are so honoring…I could listen to your voice for an eternity."

"That's the whole idea of heaven!" Jesus replied, eyes twinkling. "Earth is a taste—heaven is a feast!"

Skydiving

"Yup, look into the mind of God and you come away with a full belly every time," Jesus said, a mischievous twinkle in his eye. "It's one of our favorite meals. But there's also stuff we do here just for fun—for sheer delight and nothing more. I'm a big proponent of fun, you know."

"He is," Theo agreed with a laugh. "Up til now he's mostly

shown you his serious side."

"So," Jesus asked, "Wanna learn the art of sky-walking?"

"I'd love it! You up for an adventure, dad?"

"Always."

"Great!" Jesus exclaimed, rubbing his hands together in anticipation. "To start, you just have to picture yourself moving upward—like this." And he rose slowly rose til he hovered just above their heads. "C'mon—join me!"

So they did. Theo had already taken her on some low-level flights—*it's pretty much the same mechanism as fast traveling,* Amanda said to herself. *Just visualize it and it happens.*

"Very good!" Jesus approved. "The first ten feet are easy. Your rational side doesn't object, because it believes you'd be okay even if you fell. But you can't fall, of course. Not with me around!" he added, rising another ten feet skyward. "In heaven, walking on air is as safe as having both feet planted on the ground. We just have to retrain your brain for life in a world that's gravity-optional. After a while the mind adapts famously to its new reality."

Passing the ten-foot barrier, Amanda still didn't feel scared. It was just strange—to look between her toes and see nothing, as if she'd commanded a cat to turn into a dog and, poof! it did. She and Theo marched rhythmically upward, as if climbing a long flight of stairs, while Jesus simply stood still until they reached him, then floated upward to match their pace.

"Now, the next lesson is, you don't have to walk all the way up," Jesus commented, wearing an amused smile. "Try imagining you can rise with your feet standing still."

Theo mastered it first, when they were fifty feet up. He hovered next to Jesus, watching as Amanda tried to twist her mind into this new shape. "Got it!" she finally said proudly, advancing steadily upward. "How else can you do this?"

"Any way you want," The Man of Light replied. "What options can you think of?"

"Lying down?" Theo replied, giggling as he collapsed onto a rising cushion of air. Now they were at 100 feet.

"How about going up a ladder!" Amanda called, spurting skyward with arms and legs flailing as she clambered up imaginary rungs.

"Or swimming!" Theo called, doing a backstroke, then flipping over into a hilarious vertical butterfly.

"You look like a bucking racehorse," Amanda teased, still climbing the ladder beside him.

"Great idea, Amanda! We can sky-walk on horseback!" Jesus swung into an invisible saddle and rode upward into the ether, a glowing vapor trail following in his wake like stardust thrown off a stallion's hooves. Soon Theo and Amanda galloped up beside him, over a thousand feet off the ground. Jesus slowed his sky-mount to a canter.

"How are you doing?" he called over to Amanda.

"Pretty good. I'm not worried or anything. It just feels… more than different. Tilted, maybe, like my world is off kilter and I am scrambling mentally to make the adjustment."

"You are adapting famously. I think you're both ready to take it to another level. Wanna try sky-*diving*?"

"Huh?" Theo and his daughter uttered simultaneously.

"This is where the real fun begins! It's a great trust exercise, too: just let go and allow gravity to take over."

"And simply fall?" Theo questioned impertinently. "Without a parachute, I assume? What happens when you hit the ground?"

"You won't," Jesus winked. "Trust me: I got this."

"Okay," Theo simply answered.

"Mind over matter, eh?" Amanda muttered under her breath.

Jesus threw his head back and laughed loudly. "Yes, Amanda! Magicians with their sleight-of-hand and charlatans with their spoon-bending tricks mimic what the simplest can do here by trust. The human soul was made for the Beautiful Land, so deep within its nooks and crannies a splinter of this primordial belief remains: that it should be able to do on earth what we do by faith in heaven."

Amanda still looked doubtful.

"Put physics aside for a moment and lean on trust instead," he coaxed. "Do you remember the story of how I walked on water?"

"Yeah. But you were God. Kind of an unfair advantage, isn't it?" Amanda retorted. Then to herself: *Trading ripostes with The Prince of Heaven! That feels like rare air indeed.*

'Riding' beside her, Jesus leaned over til his lips were near her cheek, his voice dropping to a furtive whisper. "You know, on earth I never learned to swim. In antiquity, few people could. It was *four miles* across the lake to that boat, in the middle of the night. I had to launch out onto the water in trust just like you do now."

"Wait—so you experienced this?"

"How would I be able to identify with you if I didn't?" he replied, bursting into laughter. "Walking on water was a ball—and so is this! Who wants to go first?"

"Let's do it together," Theo decided for them. Stepping off their imaginary horses, they stood facing one another. With a last glance in each other's eyes (and an *oh, my gosh, here we go!* expression), Amanda began to count.

"Three...two...one..."

There was no need to jump. It was as if the floor dropped away beneath them. A smooth, rapid acceleration, then plummeting faster and faster through the fragrant air. Its delicious coolness flowed across the skin, whipping at their hair. Amanda realized she was screaming with exhilaration, as a sensation of freedom shot through her like a pulse of electricity.

In the view between her knees, the ground rushed upward, rotating as they spiraled down through the atmosphere. At three hundred feet her mind was racing, one part blasting a warning and another reaching over to turn the siren off. Two hundred feet. Her heart began laughing. One hundred. She felt wildly alive, crackling with vitality. Fifty.

Suddenly, she decelerated painlessly, gently cradled in a pair of strong arms. They placed her upright on the firm ground, unharmed. Gasping with delight, shot through with adrenalin, yet still holding her father's hand. And Jesus stood beaming before them, as if this was as much fun for him as for them.

Amanda began jumping up and down like a ten-year-old begging for another roller coaster ride. "Again! Again!" she cried, amidst peals of laughter from her dad.

Jesus tipped his head. "My pleasure."

Startled, Theo watched his daughter blast off and hurtle skyward, higher and higher, as if she was strapped to a rocket (which was actually what she was visualizing at that moment). Her body paused momentarily, too far up for those on the ground to see her facial expression. Then she began to fall.

An exuberant yell of delight came to them faintly on the breeze, growing in intensity as Amanda plunged toward them—headfirst, Theo noticed—her hair streaming wildly out behind. After observing for a few seconds, Jesus casually stepped several paces over to his left, then rose into the air. He waited a second or two for the screaming missile to reach him, then, all at once, bounced like a spring compressing as she fell into his arms, then deftly set her down on the ground. Amanda stood next to him, panting as if catching her breath, an expression of utter delight on her face.

"That…was…AWESOME! It *is* mind over matter!" Amanda gushed happily. "What a mega-rush! Like sky-diving on earth, but no silly straps or chute or helmet, and no death-and-dismemberment lecture before boarding the airplane. This is a hundred times better than back at the airport. Let's do it again!"

"Yes, on earth, even sky-diving has a place in The One's master plan," Jesus laughed, as Amanda's war-whoops rang in his ears. "Anything that requires trust offers a taste of heaven while living on earth."

Living Transparently

"A taste of heaven while living on earth…I like that idea," Amanda exclaimed. She'd done six more power dives (Theo only three) and was still amped up. "Although I can't say I was very tuned into it in my previous life. But, hey—back then I had no idea what heaven was actually like. I might have been tasting it all along and never known. Did you try to let us in on the secret somehow?"

"Oh, we dropped hints everywhere. The Maker puts layers of meaning into almost everything he fashions."

"Such as…?" Amanda asked.

"Well, back in my day, 'being real' wasn't a thing," Jesus reflected. "I grew up in an honor/shame culture, where you didn't disclose failings or weaknesses—*ever.* You always kept up outward appearances to preserve the family honor. That culture rightly put a high value on kinship, but, unfortunately, at the expense of honesty. So I changed it."

"How?" Amanda asked.

"The first thing, of course, was to model a different way of life. I let my guys know when I was frustrated ('how long must I be with you and bear with you!?!'), angry, tired, happy, or when compassion moved me. I even told them how I once imagined becoming Roman emperor and ruling the world. That certainly made an impression! Once they got used to being honest about our stories, I taught them to give feedback, even to me, so they'd get used to sharing ideas and mistakes without being judged.

"So when my boys—most of them were teenagers when I first met them," he added as an aside, eyes sparkling. "When they wrote down our story, they included a bunch of their own failings and blunders, just as I'd hoped."

"Such as?" Theo inquired.

"Oh, what a comedy of errors!" The Man of Light chortled.

"The evening I was arrested every one of them made a break for it, right after promising they would die defending me. Mark got away naked, with the clothes torn off his back. James and John were supposed to keep watch, but fell asleep three times in a row. Peter whacked off someone's ear in a bungled attempt at slitting his throat—thank goodness he was no expert in knife-fighting—and then had to watch me do a miracle to reattach it. And their dear, dense, misguided idea that I was sent to set up a *political* kingdom…they were still flogging that dead horse even after I came back from the dead!

"Yet their honesty about it all made me so proud. They even admitted to arguing about who was top dog in the middle of our last meal together!"

Bewildered, Amanda asked, "But how is sharing the dumb stuff you did an example of living like you are in heaven?"

"Oh darling!" he cried effusively, squeezing her shoulder with affection. "They were being *transparent.* See-through, just like you are here! They didn't tell their stories like men hiding inside the garment of skin, afraid to be known; but as if they were citizens of heaven."

"Oh, I get it!" Amanda replied. "Like people who had already gone through the Great Reversal, where the inside is visible to everyone."

"Exactly. Anyone on earth who lives authentically, sharing their brokenness *and* their glory instead of hiding behind a mask—that person is functioning as if they are a citizen of the Beautiful Land."

Infinite Entertainment

The three figures stood in a loose circle on heaven's lawn, looking supremely comfortable. *Together with Jesus and my dad, with infinite time to hang out, explore or just talk…I could stay here for eternity*, she thought for probably the dozenth time. *No need to please anyone, no task list or inbox waiting to slap me in the face the moment I crack my laptop. No misunderstandings. Just perfection.*

Funny thing: people on earth tried to look this perfect, but they never were—there was always some ugly secret hidden behind the mask. I guess I tried to hide sometimes, too, she admitted to herself.

In that moment of reflection, she caught Jesus gazing into her, and noticed the broad grin plastered on his face. He'd been watching her thought.

"Oh, Amanda!" he snickered. "Whenever you tried to put on your best behavior to impress people on earth, all I could see was that day when you were three years old and your mom caught you with your hand literally in the cookie jar. You stood there in the kitchen with crumbs all over your lips, half a cookie in your little hand, solemnly lying. 'No mom, I didn't have any!'" he mimicked, in a three-year-old voice.

As Jesus was telling the story, Amanda found herself reliving it: looking up with guileless, three-year-old eyes at her stern mother, while the lingering taste of chocolate-chips denounced her guilty mouth. But this time Jesus stood right behind mom's shoulder with a silly grin sneaking across his face. He put a finger to his lips and shushed, as if motioning for Amanda to be quiet. But then, unable to contain himself, he cackled until he was rolling on the floor laughing, tears of mirth coursing down his cheeks. And now she and her dad were laughing, too—the kind of glee that on earth would so come over you that you almost couldn't breathe, and you began to wonder if it was actually possible to die laughing; but here of course you couldn't.

Amanda finally took a deep breath to calm herself. But the Beautiful Land still laughed, each branch and stem vibrating, and every flower fluorescing in ultra-vibrant hues as waves of joy passed through them. Even the ground twittered beneath them, as if the soil itself was in on the joke.

"Oh, my Lord!" Jesus exclaimed, wiping his eyes. "Humans have always been fully transparent to us, and sometimes what we see grieves us painfully. But you all are also a source of *infinite* entertainment! Eternity never laughed so hard as it did after humans began running around on two legs. You just never know what a human being is going to do next!" Which kicked off another round of uproarious laughter.

Amanda sobered up first. With Jesus still chuckling about human tomfoolery, she stated, "Okay, this whole thing of living on earth like you were in heaven is starting to make sense to me now—in spite of all your joking around. I even came up with an example of my own."

"Great!" The Man of Light exclaimed. "What is it?"

"The Golden Rule. What was a choice on earth is a law of nature here."

Judging by his wrinkled brow, Theo appeared puzzled. "I'm not getting the connection, Mandy. Can you enlighten me?"

""Sure. The Golden Rule is, 'Do unto others as you'd have them do to you.' On earth, living that way is a decision, a discipline. But it's automatic in heaven: whatever you do here is reflected back to you by the people around you. Like when Jesus started laughing just now: his joy came into us, because our souls are transparent to each other. We couldn't help but feel what he felt, so we started laughing, too."

"Then *your* joy bounced back into *me*," Jesus added, "and I cracked up again. In heaven, the emotional impact you have on others always returns to you."

"Aaaah, now it makes sense," Theo agreed. "We practice treating others like we want to be treated on earth, because here it's programmed-in. Hey, you know what," he added in sudden inspiration. "Just imagine being a comedian in heaven! If *you* think your joke is funny, the whole audience would automatically laugh!"

"My gift to the stand-ups," Jesus admitted. "In heaven you never bomb."

"But that makes me wonder," Amanda pondered, looking

back at him. By now they had plopped down on the emerald grass, and he lay on his belly, chin supported in his hands and legs stretched out behind him. "Laughter might just be the best example of heart-to-heart communication on earth. One person laughs, and everyone else laughs with her. Is that your doing?"

Jesus gazed proudly back at both father and daughter. "I *so* love it when you discover the little surprises I've hidden for you! Makes me feel like Christmas morning, when the kids scurry downstairs to open their packages under the tree.

"Yes, laughter is one of the times when you are most open-hearted and least self-conscious around others. It fosters the same type of connection we make here in the Beautiful Land—a similar openness, just with less depth of intimacy."

"So remember," Jesus instructed, "I'm a *huge* supporter of laughter. Comedy is a very Godly activity!" With an affectionate wink, he disappeared.

14 Nourishment

"There he goes again," Amanda sighed happily, rising from her spot on the grass. "I wonder—where is The Man of Light when he's not with us?"

Theo stood with an easy grace. "Oh, he's always around."

"I suppose so—what with omnipresence and all." They started down the slope together.

"Yup," Theo affirmed. "He's keeping track of our timeline whether he's physically with us or not. And hanging out with lots of other folks on lots of other timelines, too. He's always in multiple places at once. When you get to the city, where it's more populated, you'll see him chatting with someone on every corner. Which, I'll admit, is a little strange at first—seeing three or four of him, that is."

"Am I in multiple places at once, too?" Amanda gasped. Her eyes widened as she said it.

"Depends," Theo answered impishly. "From your own perspective, there's only ever one of you, in one place at a time. Sorry, no clones: you will always be one. But an outside observer might see you in two or three places from one vantage point, given the right circumstances."

"Well, I guess the idea of a black hole or a quasar seemed strange to the folks who first discovered them. As long as I don't have to meet myself on the street, I'll be fine."

"You get used to it," Theo reassured her. "Oh—the other place The Man of Light can always be found is the topmost circle of the city, the Center, where the great fountain is. He's always there with The One and The Voice: those three are constant companions."

Fruit

Suddenly Amanada pulled her father to a stop with one hand while pointing toward a chest-high bush with the other. "What's that little blue ball-thingy? Just under there?"

"You mean the berries?"

"Berries? That's the size of a plum!"

"So it is," her father smiled, stooping down to pluck the fruit from a heavily-laden branch. "Here, try it." He held out a deep blue, translucent sphere, with a golden heart peeking through delicately veined skin. The berry seemed to pull in the color of the azure sky and concentrate it into a vibrant indigo that pooled in a subtle glow filling his palm.

But Amanda was still staring at the stem in astonishment. For on the very shoot the fruit had been plucked from, a plum-colored sap began oozing from the bush. As it beaded at the end of the stalk, the liquid skinned over, then gradually expanded like an inflating balloon to reveal delicate veins on the surface and a swelling golden heart within. Within a minute a mature fruit had replaced the one her father had removed.

"That is just completely staggering!" she declared. "Does it always do that?"

"Sure does."

"Can I try it? I mean, you took one, so it's okay, right?"

"Of course. It's impossible to do anything wrong in heaven."

Reaching out tentatively, Amanda gently cradled the fruit in her palm, not quite sure what to expect. The giant berry fell off the vine without even a tug, and in short order a new one had regrown in its place, as round and ripe as the fruit it replaced.

"Okay. I'm amazed again," she admitted.

"If you thought that was fun, taste it, and you'll really get a thrill," her dad invited. He raised the fruit to his lips and took an ample bite.

She'd once seen a movie once about an invisible man, where every time he ate food went down his invisible esophagus and swirled around in the transparent, roiling bag that was his stomach. You could see the entire digestive process from input to excrement—not a pretty picture. And here, everyone was transparent. Amanda was about to turn her face away but…her dad was chewing like normal, and she saw him swallow it, but it seemed that the fruit was simply absorbed into his body, the deep blue fusing into the light that streamed out of him. He started laughing.

"Oh, Mandy! Heaven is not like that silly movie. The fruit we eat here isn't made of fructose and fiber—it's made of *life*! Our bodies absorb it completely, and it's fully nourishing. On earth, you need the physical process of digestion to convert food into fuel for the biological life animating your body. But that's just a low-tech copy, a temporary work-around for how we do it here. You could say we are on a 100% life diet."

"You have diets in heaven?" Amanda chuckled.

"Not the 'you can't spell diet without die' kind," he replied, grinning. "There's no calorie-counting or rigid self-discipline in the Beautiful Land. You don't have to watch what you eat when you are consuming life, because more life is always better! So eat up!"

"I can eat anything I want?"

"No limits."

"And there's no gastrointestinal tract, either?"

"Nope. Your heavenly body doesn't need bile and enzymes to absorb nutrients. And it doesn't produce any waste, either. Didn't you notice? There are no restrooms in heaven."

"Now that you mention it, I haven't taken a bathroom break since I got here."

"And you never will again. But, hey—you are holding the most delicious thing you've ever tasted in your hand! Stop talking and eat!"

"Okay, okay!" she laughed, raising the blue orb to her lips. When her teeth pierced the skin—*Oh, my goodness! It melts in your mouth like a chocolate truffle, juicier than a ripe peach, cool as an iced tea in the summer sun. Liquid life lingering on my tongue…tasting of ecstasy and romance. And I feel it pass through my torso with a bracing shiver that makes me want to climb a mountain singing and then run down the other side, shouting all the way. The flavor and texture…*she finally decided there were no words to accurately describe them.

"What a rush!" she gushed after catching her breath. She took another bite, and another. There was no pit in the middle, just a lighter-colored area like the yolk in an egg that added a minty tang to the already delicious flesh. She polished off the berry and licked her fingers to get the last bit. There wasn't any sticky residue: her fingers felt as clean as when she started.

"It's lucky you don't have to watch what you eat here! If we had food that tasted like this on earth, everyone would weigh 500 pounds. I'm having another." And she went to the next bush, plucked a different species of berry and experienced the ecstasy of consuming life all over again.

Eating for Fun

Finished exploring the berry bushes, Father and daughter sat on a low wall of stone, savoring the last few they'd picked. Amanda's was like a gem, a little world in a blue and green fruit, its transparent shell containing feathery white blobs that resembled clouds.

"Wanna trade?" Amanda asked. Her father nodded (his mouth was full), so she handed the remaining half of her berry over, and received a different one in return. It reminded her of a bon-bon out of a box of chocolates, with a polished brown shell and a liquid center. It tasted a bit like chocolate, too—sweet and luxurious—but with none of the aftertaste and none of the guilt.

"I *knew* they'd have chocolate up here!" Amanda exclaimed. "Remember back on earth when we tried to guess what would and wouldn't be present in heaven?"

Theo gulped down the last of his berry so he could reply. "Of course! No mosquitos! No meetings! No watches!"

"No lines at the DMV! No phone tag," she laughed. "No flu shots or doctor visits. And definitely no 'please hold for the next representative!'"

"No rainy days, no worms in your apple—"

"What about haircuts?" Amanda interrupted. "We never could figure out who did haircuts in heaven, or if you even need them."

Theo wiped his lips, more as a reflex than in any need. "The Burning Ones do it. Our hair still grows—everything grows here. Their pride and joy is to serve us, so they take care of most of that kind of maintenance stuff."

"Hey—what about this: do they have coffee in heaven?"

"I've seen a fruit whose odor would remind you of a good South American blend," Theo replied. "Actually, coffee was made to smell like that particular fruit. Take a bite and inhale the scent, and you'll feel like you're sitting at home in front of a fire with cup-a-joe in your hand. But heaven has no need for caffeine. The Water of Life…now *that* will wake you up and make you feel alive! More alive than you've ever been, if you jump into the River. It's the mother of all adrenaline rushes."

"I wonder…" Amanda began, as a thought coalesced in her mind. "If we don't need to eat to live here…then why eat at all?"

"You don't have to if you don't want to," Theo replied, zestfully popping another berry morsel between his teeth. "But eating is *fun*!"

"So that's the only reason we do it?"

"Why would you need any other?" Theo declared, grinning. "Your senses were made for *satisfaction*, not survival. That's how we use them in heaven. For instance, you don't *need* to see in the Beautiful Land—you can't stumble or trip. But you've been gifted a pair of eyes to enjoy the breathtaking landscape. Hearing isn't a necessity either—we already know each other's thoughts. But I *like* to hear the sound of your voice. I enjoy the familiar timbre and cadence, or how hearing a common phrase can bring back an old memory. Like when you call me 'Poppy.'"

"Okay, *Poppy—"* she drew out the syllables to accentuate the word. "I can live with that: eating and drinking for the pure joy of it, with no calories to count." Amanda slipped off the wall, and extended a hand to her father. "It sounds almost too good to be true."

"Yet here we are, in paradise," Theo answered, taking her hand and hopping down next to her. "C'mon, let's walk some more. Who knows what amazing orchard lies hidden around the next bend?"

"You know," he added, as they began strolling hand-in-hand past the berry field, "eating is a bit like praying. Did you ever wonder why on earth God had us pray?"

"As a matter of fact, that always bugged me," Amanda declared, her blunt, practical side resurfacing. "If he understands our thoughts before we ever ask, what's the point in asking?"

"Exactly," Theo responded, stopping to pick an oval orange berry. "By the way, these taste a bit like a Dreamsicle," he added, offering the other half to Amanda. "But in the same way that you don't *need* to eat this berry—"

"It's gone already," Amanda snickered, mouth full.

"I can see that," Theo laughed. "You didn't need to eat that berry to live. It exists in heaven for the pure delight of tasting it. In the same way, God doesn't need us to tell him what's happening in our lives. He already knows. But listening to us tell our story in our own words is pure delight for him. He told me once that he loves seeing the world he made through my eyes."

"That's pretty cool, dad."

"Yeah," he said, squeezing her hand, "it is."

Joy Mob

A faint sound had been growing in intensity for some time. Like the frog in a kettle, Amanda hadn't noticed the change until they passed beyond the distraction of the berry bushes. She paused and cocked an ear. "I hear something, Poppy—behind us, in the distance. It sounds like...maybe a faraway crowd singing at a soccer match? What is it?"

"Ah...they're coming up behind. How about if we linger here and let them overtake us? Then you can see for yourself."

They stood to the side of the path, watching and waiting. A glow like a sunrise rose gradually over the landscape, centered on the same spot the music was coming from. Next, tiny birds appeared, gamboling in the upper reaches of that light. A short while later distant figures crested the ridge and swarmed down the slope like ants, growing in stature as they drew near. The music swelled with them.

Like an army singing on parade, Amanda speculated. *It looks like they've got their own air force, flying overwatch. I can hear different parts in the music now: beating drums, what sounds like horns or pipes, and lusty voices doing a call-and-response. But it's not a martial, military tune—more like unadulterated happiness put into song. And that beat: pure reggae! But here they come...*

A group of revelers several-hundred strong swept up the path, a laughing, back-slapping, singing uproar. Some danced in whirling, rapturous circles, while others beat the syncopated rhythm on their thighs as they marched. *It sounds like steel drums from the Caribbean,* Amanda thought, *metallic tones instead of mere thuds, with a brassy, shimmering sustain. Why, there's melody even in the drumbeats!*

Some in the crowd glided along instead of walking. A few floated face-down above the revelers as if lounging on an air mattress in a swimming pool, watching the proceedings below with huge smiles plastered on their faces. The 'air force' Amanda had glimpsed from afar was simply people flying. They wheeled above the moving multitude in an elaborate, intertwining sky-dance, punctuating the melody with great sweeping loops and dives. The closer that troop came, the more infectious their song. It compelled you, made you want to jump for joy, turn a backflip or cut a jig.

"Hail, fellow travelers! Won't you join us?" one laughing man cried out, running up to greet them. "Our happy band gets merrier the more of us there are!" he exulted, seizing Amanda's hands. "You don't even have to move from this spot—just let the wave pass over you."

Theo laughed—it seemed harder and harder not to the closer that throng came. "I think we will, my friend! Am I right that this flash mob has gathered for joy?"

"Yes!" the man exulted. "It's a lark! Whenever two or three of us get together, joy is right there in our midst. And the more, the merrier!" Then he ran back and was swallowed in the crowd, high-fiving everyone he passed.

Now the first rank of that human wave was only a dozen paces away. "It's a joy-mob!" Theo shouted to Amanda (he had to raise his voice to be heard). "C'mon, dive in!"

At that, he launched himself over the heads of the crowd like a high-jumper. Caught by many upraised hands, he was tossed in the air, spinning like a trampolinist. Amanda simply stood still, letting the merrymakers flow around her like water, til happiness pulled her under.

Around her, every face aglow. Every sound a joyful noise.

In less than a moment she was unable to stop laughing. Hugging everyone she saw and being hugged in return. Joining a dancing circle, and then being spun out again, tears of gladness streaming down her cheeks. Jumping, skipping, screaming in delight. No room left in her soul for thought or reason—only ecstasy.

She found herself flying with the air force, wingman to The Man of Light. She stuck to his side through every screeching turn, barrel roll and precipitous dive, then spiraled back up into the crystalline sky, cheeks flushed and heart about to burst from her chest. An utterly fantastical elation filled her completely.

There was no telling how long they were spellbound by joy. Now Amanda lay panting on her back in the green grass, the sweet gladness settling into her bones while calm gradually returned. Her dad lay next to her, breathing rhythmically, his skin exuding happiness into the atmosphere around them.

"Did I hear you right—" she had to take a breath to finish the sentence, "—that was a *flash mob*?" Another breath. "Like on earth?"

"Yeah," Theo answered after a moment. "Whew! I need to soak in that for a bit." Which he did.

"Being together with others in heaven always heightens your emotions," he explained after a short break. "Because what we feel is reflected back to each other. Somebody up here discovered that when you get a group together and everybody focuses on one feeling…well, you experienced it. It's intoxicating!"

"Hmm…The Children of Light gather just to experience joy," Amanda muttered to herself. "I like it."

"Joy and lots of other reasons! There are flash mobs for gratitude, or peace, or love. *Any* emotion," Theo affirmed, "is greater and deeper when we get together."

15 The River

After walking in silent amazement for quite some time, saturating in the aftereffects of the joy mob, a new voice began to filter through the trees. The rustling of autumn leaves, or a soft rumble like a distant freight train; it was overlain with the high notes of tinkling wind chimes.

"Do you hear it?" Amanda whispered.

"Yes—a familiar sound in heaven."

"Is it another flash mob?"

"Come and see!" Theo replied with a playful grin, beckoning her off the path and up a small rise to their right.

A mist rose behind the intervening knoll. Lit from within, it glowed white, like fog swirling around a streetlamp. Faint droplets drifted through the air and lit here and there on her face. But it wasn't a cooling sensation like rain: each touch was a tiny pinprick of energy. She felt as if she sat next to a crackling Van de Graff generator, its static electricity making her every hair stand on end. The mist thickened, till it became a slowly-drifting white cloud, and tiny motes of energy fell on her like rain. Then they crested the hill.

On the slope below her was…*what? A moving, crystalline mass shrouded in morning mist. It stood up from the ground in a solid wall, yet flowed across the surface like liquid. And instead of traveling downhill, it slipped sideways across the bank, in defiance of gravity and all good sense.*

Amanda's mind simply couldn't place it. What she saw didn't correspond to any memory or previous experience. *Is it a clear block of Jello, molded into truly epic proportions? A huge pipe, poised to roll down the slope but restrained by some invisible force? A giant hamster tube, built for elephants? No, that's silly. If I didn't know better, I'd think it was plain old water, gushing off sideways like a solid jet from a kitchen faucet turned ninety degrees.* Recognition defeated her.

And this something-or-other is bright! That's what is lighting up the mist, Amanda realized. *An opalescent vapor, glowing like…a halo. Same as the aura Celeste had pointed out above my sleeves, but orders of magnitude more magnificent. The light waxes and wanes, undulating across its surface, dimming and brightening the ground below like sunlit ripples on a stony streambed. And under its flow the grass gleams like emeralds, pebbles turn to gold and the flowers shine like sunlight encased in diamonds, flashing with a thousand colored facets.*

"Gosh," Amanda finally breathed aloud, her mouth agape. "What is it?"

"The River of Life!" Theo answered. He'd been listening to her thought with growing amusement. "You saw it when you flew in."

"I did?"

"Yes—a shining, silvery thread running through the landscape. It looks different up close: the fact that it has no banks always gives people pause You saw it again when Kepos watered the seeds, though that was just a trickle.

"Now, c'mon!" Theo cried loudly, beckoning her forward. "Let's dive in!"

He broke into a wild sprint, careening downhill toward the River. To Amanda's mind, that headlong dash seemed precipitous, even foolhardy; but her heart laughed and felt no fear. So abandoning caution she leapt after him, dodging tree trunks and vaulting clumps of flowers at a furious pace.

Theo raced to the very edge of the channel, collided with its surface…and was swallowed whole, seeming to disappear for an instant and then snap forward. A distant part of Amanda's brain wondered if that effect was from refraction, as light bent when it passed from the air into a denser medium like water. Spray flew up where he'd hit the River's edge, brightening like flame where it splashed the ground, while the mist absorbed the rest. And then she was only steps from that high, glassy wall.

Taking a quick breath, Amanda closed her eyes, bracing for impact. She knew from daring the high board as a kid that hitting water at speed is like running into a wall. This was going to be the mother of all belly flops! *Here it comes,* she thought…

And she was in. There was no pain, no shuddering blow or reddened skin—not really much of an impact to speak of. She nearly gasped all the same, barely managing to hold her breath. The electric sensation of the mist was multiplied a thousand times, as if she could feel each individual atom in her skin vibrating. Her heart raced, her mind igniting with razor-sharp alertness.

Holy cow! I feel ***alive****—my skin, my hair, my lips, even my insides are sparking with life! I feel as if I could run through a concrete wall, or toss a mountain above my head like a pizza crust…*

Then she noticed Theo, hands on hips, laughing with gusto. "What the heck are you doing?" he asked between guffaws.

It didn't immediately occur to Amanda that he was talking underwater, and that she could hear him; or that water was entering his lungs but he didn't drown. Something just seemed out of kilter, a strangeness she couldn't put her finger on. She blew out her cheeks while keeping her mouth tightly closed, and pointed at her face. *I'm holding my breath, can't you tell?*

"I know *that,*" he replied. "But why?" He began to giggle again.

Amanda's mind finally began catching up, and it had a million questions. *You're talking underwater! How are you not coughing and sputtering? You're going to drown!* she thought fiercely at him.

"Drown in *heaven*?" he chortled, failing despite all efforts to maintain a straight face. "Where nothing can hurt you? Mandy, the River of Life is made of *life*, not H_2O. You can drink it, breathe it, walk around in it, or talk with your mouth full of it—just like you do with air. Like I'm doing right now. C'mon," he urged. "Breathe."

Amanda shook her head stubbornly. It would be reckless and stupid to open her mouth underwater. She'd learned that in swimming lessons way back in the first grade.

However, her senses slowly began to break through her roiled emotions and report in. Lungs weren't crying out for air. Skin didn't feel the increased pressure of being underwater. Eyes could see normally. In fact, other than the electric tingling, she could barely tell any difference between living water and air. Only her heart felt different, bursting with carefree laughter and delight, and (strangely) a desire to conquer some great challenge.

Theo took her hand. "Here, let's go back out for a minute." They retraced their steps until they passed back out into the atmosphere.

More of Everything

Amanda let out an explosive breath. "What were you doing in there?!" she exclaimed.

"Once your mind adjusts, you'll love it. Every human instinct begs you to keep holding your breath, but in your heart, you know you don't have to."

"So you really *can* breathe under water?"

"Sure. You saw me talking, didn't you? If you are really determined, Amanda, you can hold your breath forever in the River—but there's no reason to."

"How can I hold my breath that long? Wouldn't I pass out?"

"What keeps your cells alive in heaven isn't oxygen, but The

Maker's life flowing into you. Since the River of Life is made of life, anything you do inside it will make you *more* alive, not less. Didn't you feel it?"

"Is that the static-electricity sensation? I was steeling myself for this force-ten belly flop, but there was hardly an impact at all. But every cell in my body woke up and started running in circles."

"Your first time in the River is utter confusion for the mind, but sheer delight for the heart. So what do you want to do?"

"Go back in!" Amanda replied without hesitation.

"Perfect. This time we'll do it gradually. Now, stand beside me (he positioned himself within inches of the glistening, transparent wall) and stick just your head in—" (which he did). "See, I'm talking and breathing normally, even though it looks like I'm under water. It works on trust, like everything else here."

The wall of flowing glass in front of her was at least 20 feet high, with her dad's kooky grin looking back at her from the inside while the lower half of his body remained outside.

Like nothing I've ever experienced. Oh well, Amanda shrugged, and cautiously eased her head in. She looked back out, noticing the same refraction effect bending light at the junction between air and water. She took a mouthful, not breathing yet, and let it roll over her tongue. Instead of the liquid sensation she was anticipating, it had the consistency of humid air, like when you let the hot water run before you jump in the shower and the steam billows up inside. The pinpricks of energy caressed her tongue.

Then she swallowed. The electric tingling went right down her esophagus into her insides, and suddenly a wild courage rose in her. She wanted to sprint up a mountain and plant a flag to claim the summit, issue a call to arms to the battalions of heaven, fly among the galaxies riding the jet of a quasar. Finally daring, she took a breath, and the bold, wildly-alive sensation charged through her lungs.

"Pretty awesome, right?" Theo roared, throwing up his fist in a war-cry as he breathed the water in. "Makes you want to fight and sing and create and love fiercely, all at the same time."

"Amazing!" was all Amanda had to say.

For sheer enjoyment they swam, cavorted, dived, floated, and splashed in the current of the River. This water didn't have the density they were used to on earth, but the fact that gravity in heaven was optional made familiar water-sports possible.

"Oh-my-gosh!" Amanda cried. "I want to take a shower in this every morning! I'd feel like I could conquer the world."

"Gives a new meaning to earth-words like 'bracing' and 'invigorating,' doesn't it?"

"Like I never knew what they meant before. Are there other swimming holes in heaven, or is this the only place?"

"Well..." Theo thought for a moment. "The River is forever, but it doesn't stay in one place. With no banks to hem it in, it meanders freely across the landscape, constantly changing course. But wherever you find it, you can leap inside just like we did here."

"Okay, I can live with that."

"Let's wade upstream for a while—we can enjoy the bath while still heading toward our destination."

"But which way is upstream?" Amanda asked impishly. "The current is flowing away to my right, but it's going *uphill.* How does it do that?"

"The River doesn't flow *down*, because it isn't governed by gravity like water on earth. It flows *out*, away from the throne of God in the center of the city. The Maker is the source, and his life constantly spills outward to nourish the Beautiful Land."

"Oh—so it's more like his love going out to touch us than water running down to the sea."

'Yeah. And that's also why there's no sea here—water doesn't all flow down to the lowest point. It's guided by purpose, not elevation."

Distracted by a waist-high flower waving in the stream, Amanda missed Theo's reply. Stooping to examine the shining petals, she studied how the water refracted and amplified their inner light, producing the diamond-like quality she'd noticed earlier. "These flowers seem even more beautiful under water."

Theo crouched next to her, cradling the living blossom in his palm. "It's like how a greenhouse works on earth. If you give a rose or a carnation the perfect amount of water, soil, sunlight, and temperature, and shield it from wind and cold, it produces magnificent flowers. The same thing happens here: when one of heaven's plantings receives a direct infusion of life from its Creator, in the heart of the River—that's when its blooms are most spectacular."

More Alive

Then the whole River of Life flared with a brilliant, glistening white light that contained every color of heaven, yet maintained the purity of a single hue. The aura above Amanda's clothing blazed with it, as did Theo's hands and face. The glow multiplied and multiplied again, until she felt she must be in the center of a giant star going nova, burning all its mass in one brief instant to produce a titanic blast of energy. And then The Man of Light stood next to them, with a face like the sun and a body glowing like molten bronze.

His laughter was a tsunami of gladness pulsing though the water, a deluge of peace and plenty. It was another moment where Amanda wanted to fall on her face and worship him for who he was.

And then he spoke.

"Hi!" Jesus said plainly, crouching down next to them. It was a normal, human word delivered in a divine context, incarnating all the mystery of his dual nature. Amanda loved him in that instant: the God-man, the bridge between heaven and earth, the deity who wore humanity to be God-with-us. Without fear, she threw her arms around his flaming torso and spontaneously gave him a big hug.

"Sorry about the blast of light," he added, once Amanda let go and stood again at arms' length. "My light always intensifies when I immerse myself in the River. I am alive in the life of The One, too, you know. Do you like it?"

"It's remarkable!" Amanda gushed. "The purest, most idyllic stream on earth barely holds a candle to this!"

"Yet terrestrial rivers were made to resemble this one," he explained. "And I think water was one of Our greatest successes in scaling something down dimensionally and still preserving its resemblance to the original. The salient feature of both is that water is the foundation of life, on earth *and* in heaven."

"You sure shine like the sun when you are in it!" Theo remarked. "Like throwing gasoline on a fire."

"Yes! I love the feeling!" Jesus exclaimed. "All things are most alive when they're immersed in the River of Life—myself included! Put anything into the River, and it becomes more of itself."

"I'm curious," Amanda asked, still a bit dazzled. "How can there be more of you, when you are already omni-everything? I thought God was infinite already. You can't be *more* infinite: it's a mathematical impossibility!"

"And yet, here I am—Mister Mathematically Impossible!" Jesus chuckled, taking a deep breath of the water. He shuddered for a moment, like you do when a really pleasurable sensation goes through your body. "Ahh, that feels good! All tingly and energizing inside." He stooped over a flower and softly blew on it, making it blaze even brighter.

Then turning to face Theo and Amanda, he explained, "I am always fully alive and lack nothing. Always was, and always will be. Yet taking a breath from the River of Life can make me more full, just like it does for you."

Spotting the look of consternation on Amanda's face, he smiled. "Here's an example. Think about my birthday: Christmas. What do you get for the person in your life who can afford to go out and buy whatever they want?"

"You were always tough to buy presents for, dad," Amanda admitted, turning to him with a grin. "Til I got to high school and realized you had no taste in clothes."

"I remember those sweaters!" Theo countered with an affectionate chuckle. "What was most meaningful was that you cared enough to scour the mall for what would please me."

"That's it, Theo!" Jesus enthused. "It's *exactly* the same for me. What do you get for the God who has everything? The one thing in the whole universe he wants but doesn't have—*your heart!* Your affection is the gift I prize above all others. Receiving it makes my fullness more full.

"Imagine if it didn't: if your ardor didn't give me any joy or pleasure I didn't already have. What kind of love would that be?"

"Kinda empty, I'm guessing," Amanda replied ruefully. "It would make the relationship awfully one-sided."

"Exactly!" The Man of Light cried, giving her a spontaneous hug. "That's why We Three invented the mathematics of love. They make it possible for even the God-who-needs-nothing to increase. With love, infinity plus one equals more than infinity."

"Heaven has new type of math," Amanda murmured to herself absently. "Maybe like Euclidean and Non-Euclidean geometry. "Okay, I'll buy that it's at least a possibility."

"Then here's an axiom for you to chew on," The Man of Light offered. "On earth, there is always more because there's never enough. In heaven, there is always enough, and still there is more."

Amanda sighed. "Once again, my heart understands, but my mind is still miles behind."

Oneness

Jesus had taken his leave again, and father and daughter paced upriver in silence. Theo basked in walking within the water, an expression of peace and delight on his face. Amanda was busy attempting to absorb what she'd just experienced. Breathing under water. The mathematics of love. The infinite can be more. It was a lot!

Staring absently at the landscape around her as her mind churned, something new caught her attention. The difference was her vantage point: inside the River looking out. Seen through that lens, her picture of heaven was subtly changed. Individual shapes of plants, trees and hills flowed together like a watercolor painting, the view through the water blurring sharp edges and overlapping one form with another. While objects were less defined, their colors brightened, as if assuming a pure, unadulterated form.

Ahhh…It's like removing your glasses when you are nearsighted! When everything around you gets fuzzy, you automatically stop focusing on shapes and edges and pay more attention to the colors. Which makes them seem extra-vivid. On earth, those brighter colors were an optical illusion. But in heaven…I think looking through the River actually **does** *make colors more intense.*

Then something in her perception unexpectedly shifted, as if a new lens was held up to her heart. Amanda stopped walking, gasped, nearly stumbled backward in surprise. *Ohmygosh! I've seen the Beautiful Land without seeing. I've fundamentally misunderstood heaven!*

Mesmerized by happenings on the surface—like watching a sunset sparkle and reflect off the top of the waves—she'd overlooked an ocean of meaning beneath. Mechanically, Amanda wiped her eyes, like you might on earth when you aren't sure if what you are observing is real (which obviously had no effect in the Beautiful Land), and peered out once more.

Until that moment, Amanda had seen the plants, objects and people of heaven as individual entities, just as they were on earth. In her old life it was absolutely clear to her mind where the object called 'dad' ended and where the grass he stood on began. The two were distinct, each with its own identity, form and design. Each leaf, blade, blossom or person had an outer boundary that kept its own molecules on one side of a hard line, and everything around it on the other.

This idea of an individual 'thing' on earth was so obvious, so basic and ordinary and universal, that the idea that 'things' could be fundamentally different was...well, almost inconceivable. Her old universe was made up of a near-infinite collection of things, each occupying its own physical location. 'There' was the only place a thing was, and it was the only thing in that place.

But heaven seemed to break down those boundaries. *When I look through the lens of the Water of Life, the empty space between objects overflows, alive with connections. Their bold brushstrokes arc like rainbows through the air, bonding each living thing to its neighbors. Wherever those arms touch, the two share their molecules, melding into one. Earth is a collection of things; but heaven is One!*

Stare at a tree from inside the River, and fingers of color leap out from every leaf and branch, clasping hands with the roses next door. Its trunk melts into the grass like butter on a hot skillet, the greenery fusing into the wood like a blanket of ivy. Peer at a single flower, and its petals form rippling bridges that unite an entire garden into one laughing mass of light. It's incredible!

To Amanda's amazement, distinct, individual things had simply vanished. All objects blurred and bled into each other like watercolors, until the borders between them disappeared into a single, shared space. All living things were one.

One life, yet taking different forms, she mused. *Like aspen trees, where an entire grove can be one super-organism linked by roots just below the surface.*

Stepping over to the water's edge, she stuck her head out of the River, just to verify her perceptions. Sure enough, the world around her snapped back into focus, and she saw individual objects again. Reentering the water, the view switched back to connections. *It looks like...smearing Vaseline on a camera lens, every-*

thing is so fuzzy (she giggled at that one). *There's got to be some physical explanation for this…*

"Consider the particle-wave duality," The Voice gently prompted, *"and how light can appear as a particle in some conditions and a wave in others. We planted that on earth so that you could understand this mystery: that complete integration and complete freedom co-exist in heaven."*

"Oh! Right—I see it now. Tentatively, Amanda reached out her hand and poked it through the edge of the stream, so that she could see her fingers dangling in the air while still standing inside the channel. Instead of a solitary hand alone in midair, she saw beams and cables of light extending out from her own fingers to embrace the world around her. And every tree and person and plant reached back to her, drawing her into the great dance of life.

My own hand, yet one with everything! Together and yet separate, belonging and yet free…clarity and mystery are all mixed together into one cup, she marveled. *The water is pure as a diamond, yet it blurs all boundaries. Try to identify an individual thing while looking through the water and you can barely make it out. But the connections between things show up plain as day, in color as vibrant as an artist's palette.*

So—the intrinsic oneness of heaven is most real within the River, she concluded. *All objects share in The One Life: the life of The Maker. The water blurs individuality and focuses your mind on our unity. I guess that makes sense: the River is the umbilical cord that links us all to life. But until I saw it just now, I didn't really see it. I was so focused on defining and categorizing things, on figuring it all out, that I never looked under the surface.*

Hmmm. Maybe the search for clarity can itself hide a greater reality…

The Nature of Paradox

That is the nature of paradox, a voice inside her answered. Instantly, Amanda realized she was hearing her father's thought. *To make one truth plain, sometimes another must be blurred.*

And yet the blurring is itself lovely! Amanda thought in reply. *I like seeing the trees all smudged together, watching the rippling water join branch-shapes to one another. Melding two things together makes a third work of art, with a different beauty than the first two.*

Which is why The Maker built paradox into creation, Theo replied in thought. Then he continued out loud. "Out of two truths, paradox can make a third, deeper and more beautiful than the first two. We were just discussing an example. The first truth is that everything is more of itself when it is in the River—including The Man of Light himself. The other is that he is utterly full and has need of nothing. The paradox is, how can One who has everything obtain more?

"So, Amanda: what is the third, greater truth revealed by combining those two?"

With a last glance at the bonds linking her fingers to the whole of creation, she withdrew her hand from the air and back into the River. Smiling affectionately at her father, Amanda answered. "It's the mathematics of love. My heart is the one thing he desires but doesn't have, and offering it to him is a delight he can't otherwise obtain. Love can take something infinite and make it more."

Theo nodded. "Love is at the heart of everything. All our books, our music, our movies, our plays—every plot and story on earth is a descendent of the one great love story. We don't have words to explain how or why The Creator could become part of his creation, or how he could pass from one universe to another—but we do have words for love."

"Oh, so it's another shortcut, isn't it—like trust?" Amanda posed. "Trust lets us act when we don't have all the data. And love connects what is beyond understanding. Two shortcuts, two peas in a pod."

"The candy shell *and* the gooey center," Theo laughed.

"Right. The puff pastry *and* the buttercream filling," Amanda recited, recalling one of their old jokes. She smiled and took his hand. "You know, when I'm in the River I can see how

I'm connected to every other person in heaven. But the one I most love being connected to is you."

"Yeah, I love it, too."

Deliberately, Amanda took another deep breath from the River, shivering deliciously as the bracing sensation came into her body. The tingling rushed from her toes to her forehead. "Poppy, was I supposed to know this stuff on earth? I barely noticed even a fraction of it. And what I *did* know seemed so far-off and mixed up. Our thinking down there was pretty muddled, wasn't it?"

Theo nodded. "Sometimes I remember a train of thought I had on earth, and all I see now is a train wreck! As humans we're driven to know, because knowledge promises control. When we are confronted with a paradox, we just can't help ourselves—we twist our brains into knots to explain it away! What elaborate mental gymnastics the human race adopts, all to explain the unexplainable and resolve the unresolvable paradox."

The two Children of Light resumed walking silently along the River's course, still reveling in the sensation of being immersed in pure life. On every side, the bonds linking all creation shone through the crystalline water.

"So, Poppy: the River resolves the paradox of freedom and belonging—it makes both fully possible at the same time. What's another example of a paradox—on earth, that is?" Amanda asked innocently.

"Well, you've already met the biggest one: The Man of Light. He lived at the intersection of two separate universes: heaven and earth. Whenever heaven's dimensions touched earth in him, a paradox was born."

"That makes sense: something in three dimensions always looked like voodoo to the Flatlanders living in two dimensions. 'What else?'"

"'Why is there suffering in the world?' is another paradox," Theo stated. "The two lesser truths are, 'The Maker is all powerful,' and 'there is evil in the world.' How do you square that circle and still maintain that God is good?"

"Yeah, I spent a lot of time trying to wrestle that monster to the ground," Amanda responded ruefully. "I always ended up with a bloody nose." On a whim, she stuck her head out of the River to take a breath, then pulled back in and blew a stream of bubbles. They hung in the current instead of rising, pulsating orbs reflecting prismatic light off their inner walls. "Some of my friends concluded that if there is evil in the world, and God made it, then God must be evil. I knew that couldn't be right... but nothing I read or heard on the topic ever seemed to ring true to my heart. What's the real answer?"

"You solve the problem with the mathematics of love!" Theo exclaimed. "The greater reality those two truths point to is that God gave up control of earth to give us choice, then came to earth to suffer our miscues with us in order to restore the good after we chose the bad"

"What's another example?"

"Here's a classic: free will and predestination. The two lesser truths are: first, humans can freely choose God, and second, God knows what we will choose before we choose it."

"And the answer to that paradox is...?" Amanda queried.

"Time!" Theo cried. "From the viewpoint of earth's time, we are free to choose. And the other half of the answer is..." He waited for her to fill in the blank.

"Oh, I get it! From the viewpoint of Heaven's Eternal Now, the choice has already been made. It's like looking in the mirror of time The Man of Light showed me—what you see depends on your point of view. The paradox results from looking at one truth from within two entirely different time systems."

"Excellent. Then what is the third, greater truth revealed by the paradox of the first two?"

"That heaven runs on an utterly different clock than earth does. So the Calvinists and the Arminians are both wrong?"

"Partly wrong," Theo agreed. "Or you could say they are both partly right. Where they go astray is insisting that only *one* side of the paradox can be true—their side! Their death grip on one or the other of the two the lesser truth ends up obscuring the greater insight: that God lives beyond time, where free-will and determinism walk hand-in-hand. What is impossible within our time is possible in heaven.

Making Sense

"I like the idea that The Man of Light was part of two universes, with two sets of dimensions. Like dual citizenship. Did he tell us that somewhere, or do you have to wait til you get to heaven to figure it out?"

"No, the clues were there all along," Theo answered. "For instance, after Jesus came back to life, he walked through a wall into a locked room, defied gravity and vanished in the middle of saying the blessing at a meal."

"Oh—I see! With the extra dimensions of heaven, he was able to rotate his body through hyperspace and pass through the wall without disturbing it—or simply appear and disappear. That's just physics. But nobody back then would have had any idea it was possible."

"You'll like this, too: the story of him entering the locked room specifically points out that Jesus still had his earthly, physical dimensions, too," Theo added. "He asked for some food off the table and ate it, to prove he was alive and kicking, and not just some disembodied ghost."

"The first century knew nothing about extra dimensions," Amanda said excitedly, "but what they wrote is consistent with how an extra-dimensional being might operate. He had both universes in him at once, just like we do in heaven—that's what the eating thing proved. It's the old world, but with heaven put on over the top."

Amanda laughed, just to blow off a little steam. This was

heady stuff. "Poppy, this makes a lot more sense in heaven than it ever did in Sunday school. Why was it so hard to understand on earth?"

"You know this one, Amanda," Theo answered quickly. "A heaven of extra dimensions can never be adequately described in four-dimensional human language. We simply don't have the words to explain things which don't occur on earth. All we can do is say 'the Water of Life *seems* like water on earth,' or 'angels are *like* a person on fire.'"

"But the Burning Ones are obviously not burning up," Amanda snickered.

"Right—any analogy breaks down at some point, because the 4-D words weren't designed to describe an 8-D heaven. Paradox is the tool God uses to overcome that language barrier. We *do* have words to describe the first two truths; but when we combine them, we have a paradox that's beyond understanding. On earth, all we can do is go back to the first two truths and say, 'I have free will, even though God knows what I will choose.' And that is the end of our comprehension: two seemingly-contradictory truths that exist at the same time. In between lies the mystery of God."

"But in the Beautiful Land, armed with heaven's extra-dimensional language," Amanda replied, elated, "we finally *can* grasp the third truth."

"Exactly."

A new path crossed the River up ahead, bearing off to the right. Theo took his daughter's hand and led her along it, out through the edge of the stream. It was a unique sensation, walking through the mystical barrier between water and air; leaving the realm of connections as your eyes recalibrated to individual objects.

"A bit like stepping out of the shower," Theo offered with a grin.

"Except that you don't have to towel off." Amanda rejoined, examining her sleeves—they were bright and clean as if they'd just come out of the wash, but perfectly dry. "I'm not wet at all, although I do have that fresh-and-and-ready-for-the-day feeling. Hang on a sec!" Amanda ordered, then jumped back into the River…and out again, as if doing an experiment. Smiling broadly, she jumped in and out twice more.

"You look like you're bouncing back and forth on a spring. Had enough?"

"For now! It's another paradox: a River that doesn't make you wet, air you don't need to breathe—when will the paradoxes end? On earth they were frustrating, but here they're fun."

"They don't end," Theo smiled. "As long as The One inhabits more dimensions that we do, there will always be mysteries."

Amanda briefly made a sour face, then laughed. "Okay, okay: I don't have to know everything. *Yet.*"

16 The Great Ones

"Poppy, look!" Amanda called out, pointing past her dad's shoulder. "There's a really spectacular light rising over that little hillock—what is it?"

Theo swiveled left to follow her gaze. At that moment what looked like a pair of heads came into view, followed by shoulders and then torsos as the figures emerged from behind the intervening rise. Their bodies glowed like molten iron in a smelter, but there was such a halo of goodness in the air around them that it was hard to see where one body ended and the other began. A wide band of liquid love streamed between their chests, as if a tributary of the River of Life surged endlessly between them.

"Oh! These are two of the Great Ones," Theo whispered. "What an honor! Stand next to me and we'll greet them."

But before he could speak the strangers saluted him. "Hail, beloved curator!" the younger cried. "We glimpsed you from afar, with this other child of heaven who looks enough like you to be next of kin. When we realized she was a newcomer, we came to welcome her to the Beautiful Land."

A moment later they arrived, the older one bowing gracefully to Amanda. A powerful feeling of welcome and acceptance poured into her heart. Clearly, it came from the women.

"Greetings on your long-awaited day, beloved one! We are deeply honored to be in the presence of one in whom the likeness of The Man of Light shines so brightly. I am Lelise, and this is my daughter Abeda. We lived on earth many years before you were born."

"Thank you," Amanda replied gratefully. "I am Amanda and this is my father, Theo. He's giving me a little tour—I just got here."

"Wonderful!" the two women answered in unison. "This calls for a celebration!" The older one looked up and called out, "Euphraino! Let us have wine! And kindly join us to celebrate this one who has newly returned home."

That very instant, one of the Burning Ones appeared at her side. He was as transparent as the gardener Kepos she'd met earlier; but whereas Kepos was all earthy hues, the colors of soil and plants, this angel bore the tints of sky. The inner fire smoldering in his chest was a subtle blending of blues and purples (at least, that was the most comparable color on earth), shifting to sunset shades on his extremities.

He held an inlaid silver tray. On it were five exquisite goblets, wrought of light not matter, shaped like rapidly-spinning whirlpools of illumination. Some inner gravity bound them in that shape, a form constantly in motion. (*A tad like the River, which holds together without banks,* Amanda thought.)

Filling those vortexes was a liquid distilled from the fruits of heaven and flavored with joy. It casting effervescent sparkles into the air above. When Amanda breathed in the scent, images of fame, approval and glory burst into her mind.

Abeda placed a still-whirling glass in Amanda's hand. The movement caressed her skin like a massage, making her fingers tingle. Then with words of honor and acclaim the little group toasted Amanda's arrival in eternity.

When they touched, the glasses made a musical ringing

noise, the pure tones of a crystal goblet when you wet the rim and drew your finger around it. Amanda listened briefly, then dared a tentative sip.

The flavor positively *exploded* in her mouth—she almost gasped with pleasure. It was like tasting a story—a vision of a gardening angel planting a vine, watching it grow and bear fruit. The she saw hands plucking the grapes (or something like grapes—they were shaped the same but glowed with the hues of heaven), blending several strains, and letting them steep in something like crystal jars. The mixture glowed a deep maroon, a living flame buried in the crystal flask like embers in a woodstove, until it was poured into goblets of light.

And the sensation on her tongue! It was wild, alive and free, like two lions romping in the grasslands of the Serengeti, shoulders rippling with power and manes flying in the wind. The slightly-fizzy draught made her want to laugh and sing and celebrate all at the same time.

Oh my goodness! Amanda reeled. *This is where the idea of wine came from!* Then after a moment she added out loud: "I don't know if I'll ever be able to drink that poor, flat stuff of earth again."

"Your first nip of heaven's wine is always a bit overwhelming," Lelise said knowingly. "It goes to your head some. Just like good old Tej."

"Tej?"

"It's Ethiopian mead, darling, made from honey," Lelise explained. "My father made it in secret when I was a girl—it was supposed to be just for royalty. The taste of heaven's wine just takes me back."

"Oh, you are from Ethiopia? Are you…um, black?" Amanda blurted out. She would have immediately regretted it if regret were possible in heaven.

"We are African," Abeda stated firmly, then smiled. "Though I take no offense. And I understand your confusion! With bodies like these, which are completely transparent to the inner light pouring from our souls…it is difficult in the Beautiful Land to tell the color of one's skin, when the content of our character blazes out with such overpowering brilliance."

"I like that turn of phrase. And the light in you is truly stunning," Amanda agreed, taking another sip of that splendiferous wine. She held up her glass to salute her companions. "I wonder…is this alcoholic?"

"If you mean, 'can you get drunk on it?' the answer is, 'no!'" Lelise replied. "Intoxication on earth bears only a faint resemblance to the intoxicating pleasures of heaven. Alcohol can touch the human desire for peace, acceptance or escape for a fleeting moment, but only at the price of loss and regret in the long run. Heaven's wine—now *that* is the real thing! Desire fulfilled without cost, fermented in the life of The One himself. The Children of Light have no need of cheap substitutes."

"It seems that we are going in the same direction," Theo proposed. "May we walk and talk with you for a while?"

"Yes! What a great privilege!" Abeda took Amanda's hand while Theo proffered an arm to Lelise, and they all set off. Although they'd just met, that journey was like taking a stroll with a great friend you hadn't seen for ages, on the first warm day of spring. Amanda had the feeling of picking up a conversation right where she'd left off years before.

"You two seem to have an extraordinary bond," Amanda observed. "The connection between you—it looks like the view from inside the River itself."

"Why, that is very kind!" Abeda replied. "What a beautiful compliment!"

"Dad said you are two of the Great Ones. Were you famous back on earth!"

"Oh, Amanda!" Abeda grasped her shoulder and broke out laughing, as if her new friend had told a great joke. Amanda laughed along without knowing why, as Abeda's bemusement came into her and touched her (in heaven you never have to wonder if the joke is on you).

"I doubt if 50 people on earth even knew my name!" Abeda giggled. "I was 'autistic,' as you moderns call it, and not 'high-functioning' either. I never even learned to talk."

"Yet you seem in perfect health here."

"I am!" she enthused, whirling round in a joyful circle. "Perfect as I was created perfect."

"Then what is it that made you and your mom great?"

"That is a beautiful story, if you wish to hear it."

Theo and Amanda glanced at each other for just an instant. "Certainly!" they replied in unison.

It Takes a Village

"Very well," Abeda began. "When I was born, it soon became apparent that I would never be a normal child. For Lelise, the joy of my birth was replaced with worry, shame and grief. In our tribe, families of disabled children could be ostracized, and infants were often exposed. That means left out under the harsh sun to die," Abeda added.

"We were young, and my husband did not know The One," Lelise sighed. "When I disobeyed his command to put her away, he left me. The shame was too great for him, poor man."

"I never knew my father," Abeda continued. "The village gossips whispered that I was cursed, illegitimate. The men muttered that the reason I couldn't speak was that I had a demon. Yet to my mother, I was always her little flower. That's my name, of course: Abeda means 'flower.'

"Grandmother raised Lelise in the way of trust, just as it is practiced in heaven. The good story of The Man of Light had reached our village when grandmother was a girl."

"Back in the days of King Ezana of Aksum. Another great African, like his contemporary, Saint Augustine. Or Tertullian and Origen, two of the early church fathers," Lelise affirmed. "We were a great center of the faith in those early years. For instance, Ezana was the first ruler to put the sign of the cross on his coins."

"But Augustine…that was like AD 400, wasn't it?" Amanda replied, surprised and a tad perplexed. "Then your arrival in the Beautiful Land would have been, like…1600 years ago!?"

"We've been here but a day, yet we've been here forever," Abeda said mysteriously, then laughed.

"Everyone gets to heaven on the same day," Theo explained. "The Day of the Lord. This is an Eternal Now, remember? But let's hear the rest of the story. Go ahead, Abeda."

She tipped her head in acknowledgement. "As I was saying, mother followed The Way, and the honorable sacrifice of The Man of Light was dear to her. She made a great sacrifice for him in return, giving up marriage, security and status in the village to serve one disabled child, 24 hours a day. I like to say that Mom was in full-time ministry for 27 years, but to just one person—me!"

"Best choice I ever made," Lelise inserted happily. "Except for choosing The Man of Light, that is. He told me shortly after you were born that this was his best for me. I thought, *how could that possibly be? This is a tragedy, not a gift!* I didn't understand what he was saying, or how a loving God could bring a broken life into this world that I must care for. But after wrestling with it for months, I finally gave in and simply chose to trust."

"For 27 years I never spoke," Abeda continued, looking affectionately at her mother. "Lelise never heard me say, 'I love you.' Never heard the child of her body call her, 'mommy.' Instead, she endured secret whispers that she'd gotten what she deserved, that my disability was punishment for her hidden sin."

"Wow, that must have been tough."

"But you don't understand!" Lelise exclaimed, tears in her eyes. "It was *such* good fortune! All this glory you see on us, the beautiful relationship we now walk in: it comes from what I lost for the sake of love! Tending to Abeda all those years called such a deep love out of me that I became Great in the eyes of the only one whose opinion really matters—The Man of Light. I would never have found the will to scale such heights without such an impossible challenge. But he believed in me, that I could win the battle—and so I have! Now, for everything I missed out on, I have received a thousand times in return."

"How is that?" Amanda queried softly.

"I can tell you my part," Abeda replied, smiling over at her mother. "Although my brain was impaired, my spirit was not. When I came here and drank from the River for the first time, I *remembered*—each of the thousands of beautiful things my mother did for me was lodged in my soul, and in the memory of The One. When he fused my remembrance to his, and I realized all that she and The Beloved had sacrificed for me…an incredible love and gratitude rose within me for her. That is one portion of her reward."

"Besides that, here in heaven she *can* speak," Lelise broke in. "She *can* return the love she was given! We are able to go back and relive any moment we shared on earth, whenever we desire. And every word of love, thanks or appreciation I was denied on earth is spoken here with the dearest affection and greatest import. To forgo the rewards of earth to have them infinitely multiplied by eternity…that is the sweetest happiness."

"On top of all that," Abeda added, "Where we had no fame, we are famous in heaven. Where we were unknown, we are widely known. Where we were spitefully gossiped about, we are praised by all. The One has put his seal of approval on us, and we bear the favor of The King. *Everything* that was denied to us on earth we have here forever, richer, deeper and more rewarding than was ever possible in our first lives."

"Truly, we have received a thousand times what we lost," Leslie agreed.

"That's amazing!" Amanda agreed. "But aren't you…don't you feel at least *some* anger or regret over the injustice you had to endure?"

Mother and daughter looked into each other's hearts, smiling broadly. The bridge of love between them brightened into such an immense light that it was hard to perceive them as two individuals. Then they spoke in unison: "Injustice? On the contrary: our lives prove The Maker's perfect justice."

Reaching over and placing a hand on Amanda's shoulder, Lelise patiently explained. "Yes, justice was delayed for us. But all that was delayed was stored up for us in here heaven, with interest—"

"Which compounds eternally," Abeda laughed.

"—yes, which compounds eternally," Lelise resumed, laughing with her. "Justice is satisfied because it is paid out in the currency of heaven. We get the incomparable wine you've just tasted instead of muddy water. We enjoy the affection of The Prince of Heaven instead of the faint praise of a fickle crowd. My daughter walks in the glory of the Great Ones of heaven, and I have her beside me forever. The brief, momentary affliction we suffered on earth has been replaced with an eternal deposit of glory behind all comparison. It's grander than I ever dared to dream of or desire."

And then her eyes twinkled with delight. "What more could a girl ask for?"

Destiny

After a satisfying journey together, punctuated with hugs and ended (temporarily) with heartfelt goodbyes, they parted with Abeda and Lelise. Hearing that story of sacrifice, love and glory put Amanda in a solemn mood.

"Hey daddy?" she asked, as they crossed a wide meadow. "I'm remembering Anastasia. It seems like what she loved to do on earth—gardening—prepared her for a job in heaven. And

Lelise and Abeda's life…their calling on earth was simply to love each other well…and that seems to be their vocation here, too! It comes to me that The One purposed it that way: that he means to color all eternity with their example. Their job in heaven is to *be* who they have become. Do we all have some kind of role in heaven?"

"Yes, each in our different ways," Theo replied. "The Man of Light takes how he designed us, what we've experienced and the choices we've made on earth, and weaves our heavenly role from them. That role lets us use our talents and dreams to enrich the shared life of all—it's a true labor of love! Giving in love makes us like The Maker. And since our greatest desire is to be like him, we totally enjoy our work."

"Soooo…not sure I ever figured out what my earthly destiny was in my 29 short years. Is it the same as my role in heaven?"

"In a way. But you have to think of them in the right order. The heavenly destiny is first, and your earthly purpose reflects it. What we refer to on earth as 'destiny' is more like a training program for your true vocation in heaven."

"Okay, then what is my heavenly destiny?"

"If you don't know, pumpkin, how would I?" her father laughed. "The Man of Light gives each of us a new name, a story name that only the two of you understand. In that story you will find your purpose: a calling big enough to fill eternity."

"Why am I the only one that can understand that name?" she asked insistently.

"The name is a story—a story that lies hidden in your heart for you to tell. No one understands it as well as you, because it brings together all the threads of your own experiences, passions and desires within The Maker's larger purpose. Together you will seek out that dream and make it a reality, and all heaven will stand in awe of what you two become and accomplish."

"I guess he hasn't told me my story-name yet. But since I *have* to have an answer to my question—" they both laughed,

"—maybe you can tell me about *your* heavenly vocation."

"I'd love to! It starts with this: everything we've ever done or been, every dream, story or memory, is alive in the mind of God. Like Abeda—even an autistic child has perfect recall in the Beautiful Land."

"Yeah, that was a great tale!"

"Presenting tales like that of Lelise and Abeda's is my role in heaven. I am a Storyteller, a Curator in the Hall of Memories. We identify life experiences that are vivid pictures of faith, hope, and love in action, and we put flesh on them. The stories become sculptures: living holograms of an act of kindness, a beautiful moment of love or an amazing sacrifice in someone's life.

"When you view these exhibits, you don't just see them from the outside: you step into the person's life and relive the memory. The crucial difference between looking into someone's heart and viewing one of our exhibits is that the story we display is seen through the Maker's eyes, as he saw it happen. The museum helps us experience The One—and ourselves! —from his own point of view. Our job is to make the memories in the mind of God come to life, to be re-experienced, re-felt and re-loved. Each display grows deeper and more meaningful each time it is viewed, because the joy and amazement of the on-lookers are captured and added to the exhibit. And so our work is continuously refreshed, growing more profound day by day, forever.

"I'd love to take you there, and let you decorate our work with your gratitude and wonder. Everything in heaven is like that: always growing and becoming more of itself.

"There," he sighed with pleasure, "that's my destiny in heaven."

"Pretty awesome, dad. I like it."

"Well, you'll like it even more once you see it," he replied. "But I don't want to show you spoilers before your introduction to the Bride. The Man of Light takes *such* delight in showing you the Great City himself."

Just as he said The Man of Light's name, a new radiance erupted beside them, and copies of their outlines in varicolored hues were projected out onto the grass. Objects in heaven don't cast a shadow, because they are made of light. But when another, brighter light comes and shines through an object, the interplay of the two produces a 'light shadow' of greater illumination on the ground. That's what appeared by Theo and Amanda.

"Jesus!" Theo exclaimed, turning immediately to face him. Amanda watched the two hug joyfully once more. Her dad's image projected out behind him on the ground in a bluish hue, but none trailed from the brighter light of Jesus.

Then Jesus embraced her as well, and their lights mingled on the grass. Finally, he let go and stepped back, beaming with affection. "I hear you have a request of me."

"Master, Amanda asked about destiny in heaven, and so I would like to show her my role in the Hall of Memories. But I do not want to spoil your surprise or lessen your pleasure in introducing her to your Bride. You are first in her heart, and you have the primacy."

"Thank you for honoring me," Jesus replied. "But in this case, it is my delight to defer to your choice. We can visit the *inside* of the Hall of Memories together with you as our guide, and then I will introduce her to the city in its full glory from outside. Or, I can give her an overview of the Great City once you are finished here, and then personally escort her to the Hall for your tour."

"Jesus, every time I am with you, I am surprised, honored and amazed. With all you are as Prince of Heaven, you still find time to treat me as your special favorite. Show her your city first, and then I will be honored to give you both a tour of the Hall."

"Well chosen!" Jesus said admiringly. "The more you choose, the more like Us you become! And I can perceive that Amanda has at *least* one more question for you—" he said it with a twinkle in his eye and an impish smile. "So, finish your conversation, and I will come when you call."

As he vanished, she felt that same crashing wave of love sweep over her once more.

17 Rules & Regrets

They were strolling next to a smaller arm of the River, which flowed over the grass on their left hand. This tributary was only about as high as Amanda's head, and maybe three times as wide. It meandered in great, wandering loops, crossing back and forth around the boles of trees in a hushed, majestic forest. Above it, a glowing mist floated through the leaves like smoke from a fireworks show, taking its hue from the light of whatever tree or plant it passed through. There was no pathway here, only trimmed grasslands, but walking beside the stream gave you the feeling you were on your way to some great surprise just around another bend.

Yeah, so much here is surprising, yet over it all is a tinge of familiarity, Amanda thought, idly dragging her hand along the edge of the River and feeling the delicious tingling sensation in her fingertips. *It's like going to a coffee shop and realizing I'd dreamt about being there the night before. The longings of my heart were a weathervane pointing toward heaven, and when I got here, I realized the wind had been at my back the whole way.*

"Hey, dad," she called, emerging from her reverie. "Something in that last conversation with Jesus surprised me, and I wanted to run it by you before he whisks me away on our date."

"Okay, shoot."

"So, this is the realm of The Three," Amanda began. "They planned it, they made it, they sustain it, and they're in charge of it. They're undisputed kings of the kingdom. But Jesus doesn't act like he's top dog! He's always deferring to you, saying, 'you take this question,' or 'my delight is to let you choose.' He treats you like a peer instead of acting like a ruler."

"Well, we are brothers!" her father laughed, lifting a hanging branch out of the way so his daughter could pass.

"C'mon dad—I'm serious!"

"Okay. What bugs you about us being bros?"

"It just seems…well, irreverent. Improper. Like you ought to be obeying him, instead of him consulting with you."

"Aah," he breathed knowingly, halting in a patch of light under the shimmering leaves. "Now I think I understand your confusion. The Children of Light do not obey God in heaven."

"What?" Amanda replied sharply, looking up at him with a puzzled expression. "That sounds like…okay, my heart says it is fine, but my head thinks you're getting kinda blasphemous. Or at least plain wrong."

"Does it? Then tell me: what's one of the rules here that we need to obey?"

"Um…" Amanda began, then halted. "I guess nobody ever showed me the rulebook. But there's got to be some, right?"

At that moment a knot of fellow travelers came ambling around a corner toward them, waving gaily. *Seems like a group of friends…yes, sort of a club,* Amanda thought, catching on to their purpose. *They have the same interest, so they get together regularly for… what?* She listened in, but there didn't seem to be a topic or central theme. The conversation was all jest and riposte, punctuated with roaring laughter and slaps on the back. *Oh—they're a comedy club;* her heart told her. Then her mind shot back: *Wait a minute: they're what?!?*

Theo greeted them with a grin and a wave as they passed, as if this was totally normal. "Fun bunch, huh?" he whispered to his daughter.

One man called out to Amanda as the party straggled by. "Searching heaven for shoulds and oughts, huh?" His companions hooted loudly at his joke. As he passed out of sight, the man called back over his shoulder: "Shoulds and oughts will come to nought!" More peals of laughter rang in the woods.

"A *comedy club* in heaven?" Amanda whispered. "Who would have thought! And please tell me there aren't *puns* up here, are there?" She winced theatrically, then laughed at her own joke.

"'Shoulds and oughts will come to nought.' I like that." Theo replayed the line, obviously struck by it. "Yes, there are puns here, and jokes aplenty. Come to think of it, why would there not be groups who meet just to laugh and carry on together? Jesus is a big fan of humor, after all.

"But rules? In *heaven*?" he asked with a grin. "Keep searching, Mandy. Take a thousand years if you like. You can always ask the rocks and trees for help."

"Daddy!" she laughed. "Okay, nobody has said anything about rules here—"

"—Because there aren't any," her dad finished.

"Really? *None*?"

"Yup. 'Shoulds and oughts have come to nought.' And—oops! Take a little step back, honey," he motioned, grasping her arm and gently guiding her a few paces to the right. "The River is migrating this way."

Sure enough, the River of Life slid incrementally across the grass in their direction, an inch or two per second. "It's always moving, you know. We could sit down and let it roll over us if you like—that's another adventure."

"No, for now let's keep walking," Amanda replied, her voice matching her serious expression. She looked up at her father. "No rules, huh? *Another* paradigm shift!"

Theo looked back at her with a wide smile. "And many more to come."

"Okay, okay then!" Amanda retorted in mock indignation; then laughed. "I accept it: there are no rules in heaven. Now that I think of it, I don't need to obey God, because I already want what he wants, and I can't want anything else. Mark this down under the category of 'things that seem obvious in the Beautiful Land but are clear as mud on earth.'"

Obedience

"Mud…I never thought of that," Theo mused. Suddenly he crouched down on his haunches and started poking around amongst the flowers.

"Whatcha doin', Poppy?"

He rose, a thoughtful look on his face. "Well, it never occurred to me before, but there is no mud here. Even right next to the River. The soil is moist, but not enough to stick to your clothes."

"Probably a function of Living Water being different than good, old H_2O."

"Yeah, funny how you can miss something so obvious. Like the purpose of rules—I never figured that out on earth." Theo rose to face his daughter. "Almost nobody does. Religious folks believe the pinnacle of the Christian life is to obey God perfectly—to find 'God's will' for every little choice they face. 'God, should I call Grandma right now or not? God, should I give this homeless man a five or a twenty? God, what socks do you want me to wear today?' As if what God wanted was a herd of slaves, too afraid to make even the most basic decisions!"

"Whatever you say, dad. Your wish is my command, dad," Amanda recited robotically, then laughed.

"Watch it, Mandy!" Theo chuckled, still smiling affectionately. "The trick is to see rules from Jesus' perspective. There's this movie I watched years ago…Oh, yes—*Coming to America,* with Eddie Murphy."

"Now we're talking about Eddie Murphy movies in heaven," Amanda groaned, rolling her eyes in pretended disapproval.

"Oh hush! It's a perfect example. Eddie Murphy is this African prince on his wedding day—think of him as Jesus—meeting the woman who was groomed from birth to be his bride. But she won't tell him anything about herself! He asks, 'What do you like?' and she says, 'Whatever you like.' He says, 'But what do *you* want in life?' and she answers, 'Whatever you want.' She's spent her whole life training to be perfectly obedient, but Eddie doesn't want obedience: he wants a partner. He wants to marry a girl who *loves* him. To bring the absurdity of the situation to a really fine point, he finally says, 'Okay, then, stand on one leg and bark like a dog.' And she does it!"

"I think I saw that flick years ago, on an airplane or something. He goes off to America to find his queen—"

"To Queens, New York, naturally!"

"Right," Amanda laughed. "And he gets rid of all his royal robes and stuff, and tells everyone he is a poor African goat-herder, so he can find a gal who falls in love with him for who he is and not because he's a prince."

"That's the one!"

"And you're saying that's the story of The Man of Light?"

"Yes! Exactly! Many of our best tales are actually about him. He came to earth to find his queen, not to be obeyed. So he stripped himself of his heavenly attributes, just like Eddie thew away his royal robes, and showed up here as an ordinary, blue-collar carpenter. All hoping people would fall in love with him for who he is and not just bow to The King of the World. The goal was never obedience."

"Okay, that's *another* new paradigm," Amanda breathed. "I'll have to chew on it for a while. And to think: Hollywood actually made Jesus' story without even knowing it!"

"There are a lot of things going on down there that aren't

what we think they are."

"And even some up here," Amanda said mischievously. "Daddy, I think you just performed a miracle."

"Oh?" he replied, a bit startled. "What?"

"You cast Eddie Murphy as Jesus and made the film work."

Experience the Wind

As they passed along the stream, the wood started to thin out. An exquisitely carved bench appeared under one of the last trees, perched on a pebbled landing of sorts, and they settled down on it. Neither was tired (one didn't get tired here)—they sat more for a chance to fully absorb the change of scenery than to rest.

A carpet of flowers had risen between the trees. Another 50 yards ahead the last trunks formed a ragged shoreline for an uninterrupted ocean of blooms. It was as if The Maker had painted the hills yellow, like the endless fields of grapeseed she'd driven through in Poland years ago. The in-between area where they were seated mingled those yellows and greens, joining the rustling, leafy song of the trees with a bell-like music from the flowers. Their rhythmic harmonies flowed back and forth over father and daughter like surf on the seashore, inviting them to bathe in the murmuring delight. With infinite time to enjoy the moment, there was every reason to stay and soak in that soothing atmosphere, and none to hurry forward.

"Here's another favorite pastime of heaven that you haven't tried," Theo suggested. "Take a moment and just lose yourself in your surroundings."

"Lose myself how?"

"Tune into them. The breeze, for instance: let it touch your skin. Feel it waft through the little hairs on your arm, or pay attention to how it blows over your toes. Follow its changing voice as it whistles through the trees or crosses the meadow. Just give yourself fully to absorbing what's around you," he urged.

"Okay." Closing her eyes (which didn't really help since the lids were transparent), Amanda attuned her senses to the wind.

The first organ that reported in was hearing. The rustle of leaves and the whispered swishing of the flowered field sang repose; bade her sink into their timeless existence and taste the moment. Peace rested there, and calm, and belonging. The longer she listened, the more she felt their song come into her soul. It nestled up next to her heart like a kitten making a bed in your lap. No hurry or worry: just a simple rhythm that calmed the heart and put searching thoughts to bed until you were completely at rest.

Then she tuned into touch. A faint stirring, warming the backs of her hands. It climbed her forearm, and—yes! Tickled the little hairs on her arm. She imagined air flowing around her like water, caressing her skin, and saw her herself lying down in a refreshing stream, ripples massaging her body as they laved fragrance on her skin. The more she paid attention to the sensations, the stronger they became.

A bit like standing under a waterfall, she noted happily. *Or gently holding hands. Or cuddling a cooing baby. What a delicious sensation! I feel The Maker in the air, reaching out with delicate comfort, and my skin responding to that kiss with an eager longing for more.*

For a few moments she felt as if her body was a giant coffee mug, filling with comfort and satisfaction ladled in from the air. There was a presence behind it all—The Maker was dropping rose petals in her path, relishing the chance to envelope her in pleasures forever more. It came to Amanda that she could do this whenever and for as long as she desired, without guilt, without missing out and without running out of time. To be satisfied was enough, for The One was pleased when she was pleased.

Bad Hair Day

"That's the best massage *ever*," she finally sighed, talking quietly to herself. "Pure, unadulterated comfort! Anyone who is tired or worn down or burdened would feel utterly renewed, just luxuriating in heaven's breezes."

Theo didn't reply. He seemed to be lost in enjoyment with her.

Amanda reached to brush back a wisp of hair that had blown across her face, then paused, and held it before her eyes to examine it. It spilled effortlessly through her fingers as if suspended in oil; luxuriously silken, shimmering, flawless. *Longer than I wore it the last few years. I always liked it long…now why did I ever go and cut it?* she asked herself. Immediately, she knew the answer. *Oh, yeah—because short hair was more efficient. Less time in front of a mirror meant more time to work in the lab.*

Gosh, I sure gave up a lot of what I liked for efficiency's sake. But that pursuit of significance and accomplishment often made my life smaller, not larger. I cut out the little pleasures to reach for the big goal—and the experiment literally blew up in my face!

Heaven gives me what I really like instead of what makes me most productive. What does that say about God's priorities?

"You are Our priority," The Voice replied.

Now, that's sweet, she thought, feeling The One's pleasure smiling on her. *So thoughtful of you, to care more for me than I was willing to care for myself.*

"Our pleasure," The Voice replied.

I get to wear my hair long again, Amanda celebrated. *It will never get oily, or tangle, or need shampooing. And no split ends in heaven, either, I reckon. I'll never have a bad hair day again!*

The last few strands of that lock of perfect hair ran through her fingers and fell dangling in the soft breeze, each velvet filament caressing the others. *Gosh, I could swear I have nerve endings in my hair! On earth, hair is dead. But here, even the dead parts of me come to life, rejoicing in the touch of the wind.*

"Each of the hairs on your head is valued in Our thought, and We know their number precisely," The Voice answered. *"We make no rules that govern how it grows, and yet your hair is flawless, and stays*

flawless even when the breeze flutters through it. Likewise, no one rules the wind and orders it where to blow, yet it fills your every moment with a loving caress. Such is the rule-less perfection of heaven."

"Okay," Amanda agreed out loud, "I'm starting to really like the idea that there are no rules here. Even if it's totally mind-bending."

Turning to her father, she found him fondly gazing back at her. "Love comes to us on the breeze," he stated affectionately. "We feel it and hear the sound of it, but we have no idea where it comes from or where it's going."

"Yeah," Amanda began. "However—"

Theo smiled inwardly at the question. *"This woman, the girl that I raised, has grown beautiful and intelligent and joyful beyond my wildest imagining. Touched by heaven, yet she remains Amanda. And* still *the most curious person I've ever known*!

"I figured there'd be a 'but' in there somewhere," he remarked, amused by his daughter's predictability.

"Well, we still haven't answered my original question: why does Jesus keep deferring to you? I realize now that we don't need to obey him. But he's still The King. Why is he so deferential?"

"It' simple, actually. Remember going to the shelter at Christmas, and passing out toys to the little kids?"

"Oh, yeah," Amanda responded eagerly. "They didn't know if they'd get anything at all for Christmas, so when we carried those presents in, their little eyes lit right up. Then wrapping paper and ribbons flew everywhere—you could hardly hold them back!"

"Gifts bring joy to the recipients, but they make the giver happy, too," Theo recalled, savoring the memory. "The Maker gave us the gift of freedom—and at great cost to himself, too. So seeing it put to good use is deeply satisfying for him. In other words, he enjoys watching us choose!

"So when he defers to us, he's just being a parent on

Christmas morning, reveling in a child's delight in opening a gift. He could make the choices for us, but it's more fun to watch us do it ourselves."

First Glimpse

"Hey Poppy," Amanda interrupted, changing the subject. "Here's a random thought. There are no rules limiting our choices here, right?"

"Yes," her dad replied. "Go on."

"Since I chose to enter heaven, can I decide to leave it?"

"How would you do that?" he answered with a shrug. "The old universe is gone, and now heaven is the only place in existence. There's literally nowhere else to go!"

"Oh, duh. I should have known that. Well, that's one less thing for my mind to wonder about."

Then Amanda spread her arms wide and laughed loudly. "Just look at this place! A stone's throw away is the River of Life, the most invigorating thing ever. It's always springtime, the temperature is perfect, it never rains, it never gets dark. You get to be with those you love, for however long you want. Every bad memory is washed away. Butterflies flit around your ankles to honor you, and the very air is filled with the harmonies of distant angels singing. You can fly, and fast travel, and see into the mind of God. And to get in, all you have to do is give up the right to choose something *worse*?!?"

She halted, turning to see the mirth dancing in her father's eyes. "Poppy, that doesn't sound like a particularly hard choice!"

He took her hands, looking at his daughter with affectionate eyes. "Standing here gazing into the heart of my darling, only child, in the country of my great lover, with the clarity of heaven—yeah, it seems like no choice at all.

"But it gets even better! C'mon, there's something just ahead I want you to see."

They ambled on in silence, soaking in the wellness that lingered in heaven's air, and reflecting on their great good fortune. Amanda had quickly grown to love walks in heaven, something she had rarely taken time for on earth.

As they strolled past a long row of dark-green trees (*Christmas trees*, Amanda thought. *Or else they just feel like Christmas*) she noticed something new. A golden gleam rose above the landscape, like a bright sun pillar dangling in the sky at dusk. But here there was no sun. An apparition of towering brightness, it stood miles upon miles away, and certainly miles high. All roads seemed to run toward it. The mind and love and longing of heaven converged there, in one focus. Beauty dwelt within, and happiness planted together with gratitude, a sober awe and gay celebration all in one.

"What is it, daddy?" Amanda asked quietly. "It looks like... I can't say how it looks. My words kind of ran out just now."

"It's your first glimpse of the Great City. The wedding place, the source of the River, the heart of heaven. The pot of gold at the end of the rainbow. It's what The Man of Light is so eager to show you."

"Wow! Even after all I have seen and experienced here, it feels like...like another dimension."

"One of the great moments the Children of Light all experience is to have The Prince of Heaven himself introduce us to his Bride."

Theo was just about to call out, 'Hey, Jesus! when The Man of Light appeared at his side. "Oh—hullo!" he stammered instead. "You gave me a bit of a start."

"Before you call to me, I will answer," Jesus chuckled. "It's fun to land on the scene two seconds before I'm expected and give everyone a little shiver. Earth could be a little frustrating in that regard: I'd be right there with you, but no one would notice til years later. I have a lot of those moments to make up for!"

"You do seem to be having a good time," Amanda smiled.

"The trick is to show up *just* as you start thinking of inviting me, but *before* you can get the words out of your mouth."

"Then your timing is perfect," Theo approved. "We just now caught sight of the Great City in the distance, and I think Amanda is ready for her personal introduction." He turned to his daughter. "I'll leave you now in the capable hands of The Great Guide." He bowed to both with an aura of ceremony, winked at Amanda, then winked out of sight.

18 Time & Justice

"I always *so* look forward to this," Jesus enthused, eyes sparkling. He pointed ahead and a bit off to the right of a cleft in a ridge. "Let's fly—the view's better from up high." Taking her arm like an English gentleman accompanying his wife on a stroll through their country garden, they waltzed upward through the crisp morning air.

The Beautiful Land spread out below as they rose. There was the coiling River of Life, glowing in its own aura, tributaries thrown out like spreading roots on all sides. Color blossomed everywhere, the lush green of the meadows speckled with butterflies and set off by rich beds of exotic blooms. Flowering trees lay basking in pools of their own light, displaying multiple new dimensions of hue. Above it all the azure sky echoed with the music of distant angels chanting wonder and awe.

Glancing sideways at the golden glory of The Man of Light, she realized they had an escort: phalanxes of what looked like great, white birds (they reminded her of swans) soared wingtip-to-wingtip overhead, forming an avian canopy. To their right and left, glowing ripples spread away like heat waves over sun-roasted asphalt, distorting the atmosphere. *Must be some of the*

Burning Ones flying along with us, she later remembered thinking. *His retinue.*

"Enjoying the view?" Jesus inquired, smiling.

"It's beyond words."

"It is for now," he whispered, a bit secretively.

"What?"

"Sorry—just sharing a joke with my Father. What I meant was that language here is always evolving. One of the Children of Light makes up a new word for a plant, a tree or some experience unique to heaven. Maybe it sticks, and maybe it spreads and becomes widely known. But eventually, you'll come up with another, better term; or one which emphasizes a different aspect of the thing."

"But The One was around for ages before humans ever got here," Amanda protested. "Didn't he already make up words for everything?"

"We Three understand each other's thought perfectly without words—we never needed them. Language was something we delegated to humanity from the beginning: 'Whatever the man called each animal, that was its name,'" he quoted.

"Well, maybe one of these days *I* will name something in heaven," Amanda imagined. Soaring through the atmosphere of heaven with The Prince at her side, anything felt possible.

"Maybe one day you will," The Man of Light responded.

"Hey," Amanda said a bit sheepishly, suddenly changing the subject. "Can I ask you a stupid question on the way?"

"Well, that depends," The Man of Light answered fondly. "Can you ask me a question? Sure—any time you want! Are you stupid for asking? Of course not! It's my delight to explain even the smallest details of my land for you." Then he smiled. "Do we even use the word 'stupid' in heaven? No—it's kind of fallen out of our vocabulary."

"Okay, thanks. What I want to ask is…well, I'm still a little concerned that I might get bored in heaven. Granted, you are totally incredible."

"Thank you."

"But on the other hand, infinity is a loooong time! And with the multiple time dimensions, this place seems like an uncountable infinity—you know, with an infinite number of moments in between each pair of an infinite string of moments—"

"Right."

"So, are we going to run out of stuff to do? How can you live for eternity without visiting the same places over and over and over again, ad nauseum? I could spend a trillion years with every single person here, and still have an infinite amount of time left over."

"That's actually a pretty good question, Amanda," The Man of Light approved. Still holding her left arm, he gave a squeeze of approval. "I never thought you were unintelligent on earth, and there is nothing you've done here makes me think any less of your smarts."

Deja Vu

"Actually, it's easier to *show* you the answer than tell it." All at once he leapt in front of her, grabbed both Amanda's hands, and with an adventurous expression cried out, "Let's go!" Then he jumped.

Amanda found herself plummeting downward through the air, the ground rushing up at a furious pace, until she tumbled onto a grassy hillside. In the process she let go of Jesus and rolled over several times. Lurching to a breathless halt (nothing hurt, of course: this was heaven), she found herself facing him on a sea of emerald turf, whose blades were soon bowing in concentric circles around him. The Prince reclined on his left arm as if at a picnic, legs stretched out beside him and a sly grin on his face.

"Okay, that was fun," Amanda admitted. "Why'd you do it?"

"To answer your question, of course! The secret has to do

with the nature of time."

Amanda was delighted. *A physics-in-heaven lesson from the one who made it all! What luck!*

"Time in the old universe was shrunk down, held within stringent boundaries by The Maker. It was necessary to restrict it to create the conditions for free choice." He plucked a single stem of grass and held it up. "Earth time moves in a single dimension, along a line, in one direction only. Imagine this blade slowly growing upward over time—making a timeline. On earth you can never jump ahead to see how it will look in the future, or go back to the seed and start over. You always, only, have one finite moment of time…and then the next, and the next."

"The arrow of time," Amanda affirmed.

"Yes! The fact that time only goes forward creates cause and effect—and that's what allows you to choose. But—what happens to cause and effect in the Beautiful Land, where time is no longer trapped in a single dimension?" he asked rhetorically. A look of joyful anticipation crossed his face. "I'll show you!"

In a blue flash she was high in the air again, the same landscape below and swans floating above, with a squadron of blazing angels flying shotgun. Jesus grabbed her hands exactly as before, and they power-dived toward an identical hillside. She landed in what looked like the same spot, rolled again, and found herself seated across from a reclining Jesus. He proceeded to pluck the same blade of grass, repeating his speech word-for-word and inflection-for-inflection, til he said, "I'll show you!" Except this time Jesus was laughing.

"Nice time trick," Amanda laughed with him. "Taking me back in time."

"Except we didn't go *back*, because time here doesn't have a forward and back. A better way to put it is that we re-visited a specific instant in the whole, multi-dimensional landscape of time. We stepped into a moment—one that on earth would be in the inaccessible past—and re-lived it. It wasn't memory: didn't you feel the wind in your hair again, and the sensation of rolling over on the grass?"

Amanda nodded. "Yeah—it was far too vivid to be simple recall!"

A golden gem appeared in his hand, hanging from a silver chain. He beckoned Amanda up close to look. She made out a small figure within…*it looks like an insect trapped in amber. Once alive, now frozen forever into a transparent gemstone.*

"You see well," Jesus affirmed. "On earth, the past is frozen in time like an insect in amber: distant and immutable. It can still be glimpsed through the gem—through memory—as a faded picture. However, the life has gone out of it, and it will never come again.

"But in *my* land, where there is no past, every moment lives forever in The Eternal Now. All times are constantly accessible. Revisit any moment, and another layer of meaning and sensation grows within it.

"For instance," he urged, "what did you experience when we dived for the second time that you didn't the first?"

"Well, I kind of lost my bearings for a moment…Oh! There was this layer of emotion like…déjà vu? Nostalgia? It was a kind of warm familiarity, like I've been here before. It felt comfortable and homey. Both times I was experiencing the moment, but the second time through was...like reminiscing with friends about a favorite old story, with the immediacy of actually being there."

Jesus chuckled, and rolled over onto his belly on the grass. "Nostalgia is another of those happy hints of heaven I stashed away on earth. The warm feeling of remembering happy times is always tinged with sadness there, because the moment is lost to the past and can never come again. But here—"

"We can relive them whenever we want?" Amanda asked hopefully.

"Yes! Heaven is not present, past and future—heaven is

NOW! All times are this time, all joys keep on happening, and no love ever passes away. Nothing gets tired or boring: the present constantly grows new layers of meaning, just as *you* constantly grow in depth and understanding the longer you are in heaven."

"Like the layers of an onion?"

"Perfect analogy," Jesus replied. "As your heavenly senses grow keener and your knowledge of the tapestry of life-threads increases, you experience the same moment more deeply. Therefore, it becomes larger than it was before. Maybe you share the story with someone else, and now it contains *their* emotions as they heard it; or it sprouts a connection to an experience in their story. Every moment in heaven's time, every layer of the onion, becomes richer and deeper and more flavorful each time you return to take another bite."

A smile spread across Amanda's face as the thought took root. "So there is always a new adventure?"

"You bet! Besides, all the billions of us are constantly creating an infinite supply of new moments to explore. Each one remains indefinitely and grows immeasurably." Jesus added proudly. "It's an uncountable infinity of adventure, learning—and fun!"

"Okay then…when I put together everything I've learned about heaven's time," Amanda mused. "First, there is more than one time dimension. A whole landscape of possible moments exist, not merely a one-dimensional line."

"Good."

"Second, time runs equally in any direction, so there is no past or future: only an Eternal Now."

"True."

"Third, the effect of it all is that every moment *stays* present in The Eternal Now, so nothing ever passes away or is relegated to memory."

"You are so perceptive! You remind me of my Father,"

Jesus exclaimed with pride.

Amanda blushed. "That's good, right?"

"It's *very* good. To be like him is the truest good. Now, Amanda," he announced, springing up from the ground while she still sat beside him. "I could unpack all the physics of living in multiple time dimensions, but let's leave it for a future when your brain is better adapted to heaven's way of thinking. We have an appointment with my city! In the meantime, I'll give you a word-picture that encapsulates all you just said.

The Great Lawn

"Imagine that time is this lawn," he began, inviting her gaze downhill. His arm swept across a great expanse of verdant grassland, gentle hills carpeted in meadow marching off into the far distance. *It almost goes on forever, this emerald ocean of living blades,* Amanda thought. *Like sand on the seashore: for all practical purposes, it's uncountable…*

"Each blade of grass, as far as you can see, is a moment in heaven's time. You are free in time here, darling—no longer bound to experience each moment in a preset order. So…"

At this he offered Amanda a hand, lifting her to her feet, and led her wading through the stalks. They swished deliciously against her ankles. "This great lawn represents all the moments in the life of Amanda, my princess. She can walk through this landscape to any blade she chooses, and experience that point in time whenever she wills.

"For instance, you could select this blade—" here he took a step to the left and knelt to point out a single green stem. "Let's say this is the moment at the cliff when you first saw me."

"A moment I'll never forget," Amanda said fondly, a far-off look in her eyes.

"Truly, you never will! All you have to do is direct your mind to it, and you will reenter that experience, re-living all its surprise and delight. In the same way that visualizing yourself in another *place* instantly transports you to that spot—"

"Fast traveling," Amanda nodded, eyes aglow. "Super cool."

"—visualizing yourself in another *moment* instantly transports you to that place in time. You might say that fast traveling works through both space *and* time. Whatever instant you visualize becomes your present—your now—whenever you desire. And with each reliving that experience will become richer, deeper and better."

"How about the time I jumped off the cliff?"

"It's right over here," he motioned, walking her to another blade. "You can take the Great Leap again, whenever you want. Or visit this blade," he said, trapesing a few paces to his right through the rippling grass, "and relive your encounter with Celeste; or this one, and watch Elanor painting on the hilltop, or this one, and run into your father's arms for the first time on heaven's field. You can even re-live your flight down into the Beautiful Land on the wings of Hope."

"I think I get it now," Amanda responded with growing excitement. "Nothing is ever over! Memories on earth fade, and all you have left afterward are little fragments of a photograph that your brain can never fully reassemble. But here…

"Hey! Is remembering something you put on earth to show us what heaven is like?"

"Good insight," Jesus approved. "It's the closest you can come to living in an Eternal Now in only one time dimension."

"Amazing. That means…if I can choose my present, then today can be anything I want it to! I could create a playlist of my all-time favorite 50 moments, and rock out on them any-time I want, right?"

"Now that's what I'm talkin' about!" The Man of Light cried, putting an arm around her shoulder and giving it a squeeze as they sauntered back up the slope. "Father and I wanted to create a universe where you never miss out, nothing is lost, and every good thing grows forever. I think we nailed it."

Amanda stopped for a moment, and quietly turned 360 degrees, taking in the entire, vast expanse of the Beautiful Land. *So many blades, in so many miles and miles of grass. Could this* really *be what time is? I'm so used to thinking of it as metronome marking one second after another, whether I want it or not, with a future I can't predict and a past I can't modify. Is it really true that time here is a* choice? *That I can order my moments according to my own desire instead?*

"Yes, it's all true," he whispered beside her. "You will no longer be mastered by time, but be its master; and the laws of nature will serve you instead of rule."

"Then you've made me into a Lord of Time, just like I used to daydream about," Amanda whispered back, leaning her head on Jesus' shoulder. "You are really something. I love how good you are."

"Well, thank you!"

Causality

They stood like that for a good while, Amanda's head on The Man of Light's shoulder, basking in love and freedom. Even though she could be in any moment she desired, right now this second was more than enough.

Which led her to a new thought. *When a great insight hits you in heaven, or you just want to bask in the peace of sitting and smelling the lilies, the moment lasts waaay longer in heaven! I guess with an endless supply of time, there's no reason to stop being in the present. So much of heaven seems to come down to just being. And there's no sense of guilt or feeling you ought to be doing something productive. No, I could just lean on his shoulder and feel this feeling forever.*

And then: *Man, I never realized how much I was driven by that sense of time passing.*

After a few moments (or was it an hour?) another question occurred to her. "Hey Jesus?" she asked, head still leaning on him. "What about causality? You know, how one action leads to another? If I can go to any moment in any order, wouldn't that create all kinds of time paradoxes? Like that old movie, 'Back to the Future,' where the teenager goes back in time to try to get his mom and dad to fall in love so he can be born…it seems as if heaven would wreak havoc on cause and effect."

"Does this place *feel* like havoc?" Jesus replied, smiling.

"Naw—I'm totally at peace here with you. I'd still like to know why, though. I like knowing why."

"Of course: I made you that way! Heaven doesn't destroy causality," Jesus answered, gazing out over his landscape with satisfaction. "It exponentially multiplies it. Instead of a single action leading to a single result like on earth, here every choice is connected to every result, and every other choice. That's another reason we never run out of new experiences."

"But—" Amanda exclaimed, raising her head from his shoulder in surprise. "Oh my *gosh*, that would be so wildly complicated! Like a computer program where every output changes the input—how would you keep it all straight?"

Jesus looked up momentarily, chuckling softly as if sharing an inside joke. "It gives The One something to do. When you have an infinite mind, you need infinite challenges to keep you occupied."

"But…okay, that raises so many questions I don't even know which one to ask!" Amanda said laughing. "But I *trust* you'll have a good explanation."

"I do! But for now, I'll give you the quick-and-dirty version," he offered, as they began ambling up the hillside again. "On the first day, when The One spoke and your universe flashed into being, time came to be with it. It ran forward from that beginning—which birthed causality. Stars coalesced, and exploded, creating the elements needed to build a planet. Mountains rose, and shaped the winds blowing around them. A drop of water fell and jiggled the leaf it landed on. A couple had sex, and birthed a child. For the first time, things occurred which The One did not directly cause.

"That was intentional. We wanted a world with other causes, so other selves could come to be who could make their own choices. We wished to create other creators, for the surprise and delight of seeing what would emerge from their own minds. We wanted beings who would *choose* relationship with us: that's the whole reason for creation!

"To make it personal, Amanda—I would not have people like you to love, and who could love me back, without a universe built on causality."

"That's sweet. You made the moon and the stars just for me?"

"Just for you!" The Man of Light said romantically. "It was a miracle, astonishing the Burning Ones: you'll really have to ask them about it sometime. Oh, the looks on their faces!" he recalled, grinning like he'd pulled off the greatest college prank of all time.

"It never came into their minds that we would create independent selves who could live in the presence the All-Consuming and still be free. That kind of freedom could only emerge in a universe where we were hidden, and they had the real independence of their own biological lives."

Their journey across the hillside slowed and meandered, as Jesus lost himself in telling the story. His eyes shone whenever he mentioned The Maker—the affection between them was obvious. *And he talks with his hands a lot, like Darren,* Amanda noted wryly.

"But the end game was not to create independence! We wanted to bring these new selves into heaven, to live with and be in Us. But to be joined to Us, they had to give up the right to choose evil—there can be no darkness in Us—and do it of their own free will. If We forced them," and here he shook his head, a look of determination on his face. "Then they'd no longer be independent selves, and would lose the capacity to love. The whole experiment would be a failure. I decided I'd die before I let that happen."

"Um…you kinda did."

"I guess so," he laughed. "That decision was made at the first moment of creation. So causality and the arrow of time were necessary, because free choice was necessary. And that meant suffering and death—including my death—were unavoidable."

Then he smiled. A satisfied, fulfilled, at-peace smile. "The great risk all turned out well in the end. The Children of Light have come home to Us, and live within love, and evil is no more. And *nothing* will ever separate us, because The One is all there is, and we are all one in him. In an earthly way of speaking, he *is* this universe."

"And you can't escape the universe you are in," Amanda breathed.

"Yup," Jesus replied, clearly pleased. "It's always fun to talk about this with the physicists."

"So, Man of Light," Amanda asked, a bit puckishly, "I'm going to be just fine without causality, right?"

"I seem to remember you agonizing at great length about the implications of your choices in the old days," Jesus laughed. "You want that back?"

"No, absolutely not! I was just teasing."

"I know you were! Amanda, you were created in the image of The One, with the ability to choose, and we love it when you exercise that ability. You will build heaven with me, and the contributions of humanity will make it more glorious than ever.

"Still, here there is only one ultimate cause, one goodness, one life, one people, one love. The saying is sure: 'In the beginning, one life. At the end, one life.'"

Mother and Child Reunion

At that moment, her ears caught a familiar sound. Looking back, Amanda saw a child of maybe five or six years approaching, chatting and laughing. A woman followed behind. The little girl kept running ahead up the hill, pigtails flying, to examine each flower, butterfly and scent along the path, beckoning her mom to come and see the latest great sight. Once that instant was shared, the girl was off again to find another adventure.

"She's so cute," Amanda said wistfully. "Who is she?"

"A little girl who died in childbirth, in a hospital mishap that was easily preventable. Another's poor choice led to her death. She lived on earth for less than a single day, and her bereaved mother felt robbed of a lifetime of what could have been. I spent many years assuaging that mother's grief and absorbing her anger at the injustice of it, before she was able to surrender her pain to me.

"Her loss, and my grief at her loss, exist because free will exists. The arrow of time creates real choices, some of which are not good. And the freedom to choose that which is not good unavoidably creates pain. We Three have endured great loss by endowing freedom to humanity in Our quest for love. Yet only by creating the arrow of time could the Children of Light find their way to heaven."

"So suffering in the world was…unavoidable?"

"The alternative is that you—and every other human—never would or could exist as free selves. And this land would never know your joy and laughter. Personally, I think you were worth it," Jesus added happily, squeezing her tightly to his side.

"So in order to be free in heaven," Amanda said slowly, carefully picking her words, "where the only choices are good ones, there had to be an Age of Choosing, where we weren't limited to only choosing the good."

"Right."

"And that meant evil and death, suffering and sadness—for us and for you. You gave up an existence where only good was possible, for the greater good of having us? Just like we have to give up the freedom to choose good or evil for the greater good of having you?"

"I love the way you said that, Amanda."

Then she continued, in a gratified tone, "Okay, I get it. The plan was to create love. Love requires independent selves. Independence requires free choice, which requires the arrow of time, which births causality. And the unavoidable, unintended consequence of love, the suffering and injustice that arises out of independence, is something heaven heals.

"A universe like ours was required, to create a people who could love God and live with him in his."

Heaven's Justice

There was silence for a few moments, as is fitting when profound truths are spoken in The Light. Jesus was beaming.

"Well, that momma sure thinks it was worth it," Amanda affirmed, watching the little girl laugh as she chased a butterfly. "And I do, too. One moment of that child's joy could soak up an ocean of sadness."

"Yes, good is incomparably greater than evil, and joy orders of magnitude larger than pain. Those two are citizens of heaven now, free to choose from amongst a plethora of good, guaranteed to receive their desire, and exempt from pain forever. Suffering is bound to the Age of Choosing, so suffering ends when that age ends."

"Then heaven can make even the untimely death of a baby as if it never happened," Amanda murmured.

"Absolutely! Her child is with her in The Eternal Now, and all that she thought was lost, is found. She can play with her child as a six-year-old, watch her grow as a teen, sit and talk with her as a grown woman, or hold her in her arms as a baby. Because infants, even aborted ones, don't remain babies in heaven, but grow up into who We created them to be. Each moment of this child's growth from toddler to teen to woman is present in the Great Lawn of Time, where mother and child can share in full every moment they missed on earth."

"But what about the injustice of it all?" Amanda questioned. Her heart was awed, seeing how death had been swallowed whole by life, but her mind still struggled. "I can see that she is perfectly happy...but don't the wrongs have to be righted?"

"Haven't they been?" Jesus asked, a curious tone in his voice. "All that was ripped away I have restored. Such an avalanche of goodness has passed into her that her sorrow is a mere dust mote next to that mountain of joy and gratitude. In her justice is fully served, without resort to punishment or retribution.

"I was pretty adamant about the necessity of forgiveness when I was on earth—"

"I noticed," Amanda interjected, under her breath.

"—because it's the closest anyone can come on earth to heaven's form of justice. Forgiveness lets victims find resolution through trusting me, instead of by taking vengeance. Forgive, and you are living on earth as if you are in heaven."

"But I always thought somebody had to be punished for there to be justice in the end," Amanda said quietly, still walking at his side. "And that you would do it in the end. Like the saying, 'Vengeance is mine, I will repay,' right?"

Jesus turned and grasped both her hands, bringing their journey to a temporary halt. His eyes held a resolute compassion, and the intensity of communicating something critical. "That statement is absolutely true: *I'm* the one who gets to decide the penalties, not you. The *right* to take vengeance is certainly mine. And I absolutely *do* repay: but with heaven's justice, not the punitive measures of earth.

"Did you notice that I forgave the soldiers who tortured and killed me? Will I then turn around and *un-forgive* them once I'm in heaven, so I can take the vengeance I refused on earth?"

"Oh. I guess that doesn't make much sense. Somehow in the grand scheme of things, I treated what you did there as a one-off and not a precedent." Amanda shook her head. "Not sure why I did it, though."

"It's okay," Jesus encouraged, smiling warmly at her. "You were on earth, so your picture of justice was from earth. Punitive justice—'an eye for an eye'—is a concession The One made for a planet soaked in evil. It was meant as a deterrent: to *prevent* crimes from happening. But the situation is different in heaven, isn't it, my darling?"

"Well, there is no evil here, for one thing," Amanda noted, gazing back in his eyes with a smile.

"There is not even the *possibility* of evil here," The Man of Light avowed. "So there is no need to deter behavior that can't happen. Punitive justice is obsolete, unnecessary, old news in heaven. Why take vengeance when the impact of evil is so fully healed that no one even remembers it happened?

"In fact, that restoration *is* my vengeance: that The Evil who tried to overthrow Us ultimately accomplished nothing, and his plan to corrupt humanity backfired spectacularly. And we had no need to stoop to evil ourselves to defeat evil."

"Okay, that's certainly a new thought. But don't you have this…anger, this wrath stored up toward those who cross you?"

"Do I *look* angry?" Jesus smiled. "Naw, I don't need that. Neither does The Maker. No, we who have willingly endured great pain for the sake of love do not enjoy inflicting it. Like this mother: after receiving heaven's justice, she has no need or even desire to punish those who killed her baby.

"Think, Amanda: do you need to get back at Caspar, now that you've heard the story of the good things I did for Theo—and you! —through his misdeeds?"

"No, no, you're right," Amanda replied immediately. "I guess when evil has been changed into good, there is no reason left to punish it."

"Well said," Jesus nodded approvingly.

Her mind quieted, Amanda stood a while longer, watching the innocence of an unwounded, unhurried child at play, and the joy of a mother in being part of the life of her offspring. *Now* that's *real justice. Everything put right, every wound healed and need filled, all without punishment, anger, revenge or regret. The justice I always longed for but could never articulate.*

No more words came to express what passed through Amanda's heart in that moment—she was too full, too awed. She simply participated vicariously in the joy of a mother and child, until finally that pair passed beyond the curve of the hill-side and were lost to sight.

"So perfect and complete," Amanda sighed wistfully. "And I'll get to return to this moment again and again, whenever I want, right?"

"Next time, go up and meet her!" Jesus encouraged. "Your joy over their good fortune will pass into them, and the story of how they taught your heart justice will become their glory. So this meeting will continue to grow in majesty and goodness, for-ever and ever."

"Wow! That was like a five-star meal of awesome," Amanda exclaimed, "that heaven can restore such great loss. It touches me deep."

"Yeah, healing people is *such* fun. I got a real kick out of it on earth, too."

19 The City

Amanda and the Man of Light finally crested a long, green-carpeted rise overlooking the valley below. On the walk upslope, Amanda had been so absorbed in talking with Jesus (let alone looking at his beaming face) that she'd barely paid any attention to what was in front of her. But now she glanced outward, and gasped with delight. A wide vale opened up in front of the hill, and the mesmerizing thread of the River lay close by, glistening like a field of diamonds as it flowed over the landscape. Yet the pillar of light she'd seen from afar still dominated the scene.

"Go ahead," Jesus urged proudly, gazing out with arms folded across his chest. "Start with the River, and describe what my country looks like through your eyes."

"Okay," Amanda replied, taking a deep breath to gather herself. "I see a dazzling stream, maybe several hundred yards wide, winding through the valley. But it's not like any river on earth. A mist is all around it, a fog, making the air glow like a halo from the River's light. And there is no river channel cutting through the landscape: it runs right on top of the green grass and flows around the trees, leaving swirling eddies in each one's wake…like the River of Life dad and I swam in."

"Yes, this is one of its main channels, winding out over the landscape from the center of heaven. But the River is much more than the glittering thread in front of you. Its water spreads out through the air, the ground, through you and me—you are standing within its outer arms at this moment. Now, what else do you see?"

"There are Children of Light everywhere, gleaming out from beneath the trees, sparkling in the River—the water makes their light more colorful. It's like laying outside on a starry night. Every rock, tree and plant in the Beautiful Land is a star, bathing its surroundings in light, yet the Children of Light shine brightest.

"I see kids of every age, laughing and playing games in the River and among the trees. With almost every child or group of children is a man—an especially bright and captivating star. The affection of the children flows toward him, and… Hey!" Amanda cried out in surprise. "It's you! There…" she pointed, "and there, and over there, and…well, everywhere. She whirled to face him, a bit flustered by the amused look on his face. "Is there more than one of you?"

"There is only The One. What you see are reflections off time's mirror. I am right here next to you—here, touch me and see for yourself."

Amanda reached over and lightly pinched his arm (it felt like warm human skin), and he grinned. "So if I am here," he asked, "Who is that down there?"

"You again," she laughed. "And again, and again, and again!"

"Yes, I am here in time, and I am there in time—I am in all places at all times," he said mysteriously, then his expression lightened and he laughed again. "It's not really that complicated: the children down by the River understand it perfectly. Each of these little ones believes he has me all to himself, and each one is right. I let the little children come to me whenever they wish, and I am fully present to each one. Dwelling in multiple time dimensions means that I can effectively be in all places at once.

It's how I hear everyone's prayers from earth at the same time.

"But enough about that for now. What else do you see?"

"There is a city."

The Bride

The source of the glittering river was a radiant city, built entirely of light. It wasn't so much perched on a mountain as it *was* its own mountain. The lower portion was immersed in a golden glow, while at the very peak (so high it would have been beyond sight on earth) its upper halls blazed a dazzling white. *Sort of like Everest, or Kilimanjaro, or Denali,* Amanda thought, *gleaming in the morning sunlight. Oh, wait! Those snow-capped peaks on earth were made to resemble* this.

And its walls! Like a sparkling rainbow, each level in different hues—or a high cliff made all of gems, shot through with twinkling light in a dozen splendid colors. "It's...it's so lovely, so inviting, so…I can't even describe it. It's like nothing I've ever seen."

"Like a bride adorned for her husband," Jesus exclaimed in admiration.

"Yes! That's a good metaphor," Amanda exclaimed (forgetting that she was talking to the one who created metaphor). "It reminds me of the patterns embroidered into the sleeves of my robe: streets twining through level upon level, upheld on columns of light, with sparkling waterfalls of life-water cascading down from the heights. The walls are like a layer cake of, of…I can't tell what they are made of."

"The foundation of the city is the first twelve of my followers. Every thread of the Great Tapestry of life goes through me, the cornerstone, and then through those twelve original lightbearers. All those who call this city home are one of their heavenly descendants. What you perceive as a foundation is their contribution—their contribution, their sacrifice, their station in the Great Tapestry—expressed as a physical reality."

"So wait—the city is made of…people?"

"It is a community of life connections, the physical reality represented in the Great Tapestry of life that I showed you. It is a city because its residents live and breathe within those connections, woven into a neighborhood by the intertwining threads of their shared life. But I call it a bride."

"Sorry," Amanda apologized. "I'm just not seeing it the way you are."

"Here," Jesus said patiently, perceiving her bewilderment. "Let me breathe on you."

She felt a gentle warmth pass over her, caressing her forehead and wafting through her hair. Understanding passed into her, and something in her consciousness shifted. It was like her heavenly senses stepped in front of her earthly ones, sat them down and took over.

"How does it look now?"

"Whoa!" Amanda blurted out. "That's different! It's like I'm seeing it in terms of…heritage is the word that comes to mind. The city is the heritage of the first twelve, and all of it rests on the legacy of…well, you. There is a foundation stone right at the corner with your name on it, and the family lines flow out from there to those first light-bearers, and up from them to every family in heaven.

"When I think about it in terms of life flow, I imagine something like a tree. You are the roots, they are the trunk, and all the leaves and branches grow out above it. But I can also perceive that entire community shares in its life equally. We are all cells in the same great tree, all members of one family. Each of us is a vital part of the tree as a whole, and there is no hierarchy of command or lesser or greater cell. The life-lines represent inheritance, not authority or rank. Every part is wanted and valued and loved fully."

God in the Neighborhood

"Well done!" The Man of Light approved. "You begin to

see my city as she truly is. What is her structure, and how is she arranged?"

"The walls and beams are made of a rich, golden light, and so are the streets. Light you can walk on—I see the Children of Light promenading down those avenues, chatting at street corners, gilded reflections on every face. And...I guess they are floating up and down from one level to another. That makes sense: you don't need stairways when gravity is optional. The city has a great many levels, with hanging gardens tumbling down from one level to the next, flowers and trees in ordered commons in some places, and riotous bursts of color in others. There seem to be parks. Children are congregating there on the grass, and many gather to talk or sing or share some good thing.

"Nothing in that whole city is dark or shadowy, because everything everywhere emits light. And I see verandas and terraces, porches and balconies—the views must be spectacular!"

"Yes—that was planned. For the Children of Light, the city is their community, house and home. The whole thing is one great insulae—that's what we called homes in my day."

"What's an insulae?"

"A courtyard house for an extended family. It had a stone wall all around it, with one door to the street. Inside, each family unit had a room nestled around the inside of the wall, with a shared courtyard in the center. Whenever a son married and brought his bride home, another room was built, and the family grew. So heaven is like an insulae—we are one big family in one big house, sharing a common life in the courtyard. Every time a new arrival joins the family, we add a new room!

"Human beings need their own space, even in heaven. So each of us has our own home within the One Great Home, their own space inside the One Great Life."

"Hey!" Amanda exclaimed. "If that's true, then I have a flat in the same building as The Maker! Now that's some prime real estate!"

"Yes, God has moved into the neighborhood, and lives on the same hallway as the Children of Light! They are his family, and he is their God. He wipes every tear from their eyes, and death is gone for good, along with pain and sorrow. The first two ages are fulfilled, and now in this third age everything is new, completely remade." As he said it, Amanda saw in his eyes the satisfaction of one whose mission in life was now complete.

"But look higher!" he cried. "At the very top of the city, dear sister—what can you make out there?"

Her neck craned as her eyes reached for the top, an apex higher than Everest and brighter than the noon-day sun, and for a moment it seemed beyond her. She looked back at The Man of Light, wondering if maybe she just hadn't adjusted sufficiently to heaven—and realized they had risen off the ground again.

"That knoll was a little low," Jesus answered her thought. "You'll get a better view from up here."

They spiraled upward, higher and higher, until at a dizzying elevation they drew level with the uppermost halls of the city. And this is what Amanda saw.

"There is a fountain," she began, looking across the miles, "at the very top. It's got layers, like—like the Step Pyramid of Djoser in Egypt. That's all I can think of. Very tall, with glorious, cascading waterfalls showering step-by-step down all sides. It comes to me that The One is seated there, in the most intense light in all of heaven—like when two powerlines cross and spark off a ball of blue plasma. I can't see his form with my eyes, only light, but the thought that he's present is like a steamroller bearing down on my mind—so heavy and tangible I don't need to see it to know for certain that it's true.

"A rainbow surrounds him. But calling that a rainbow is like calling the Mona Lisa a stick figure! Droplets of living water shoot up from the fountain for miles around, refracting The Light pouring from The One in every possible hue—I can't even describe it. Beams of light spray up into the sky like fireworks, fire tornadoes, and a laser light show all mixed together.

"The air itself shimmers, as if its molecules are ionized by all the radiation. Great bursts of energy float out across the sky far above the fountain in waves of color, like...like solar flares, maybe? Or the Aurora Borealis, if it was a thousand times more intense—that's it! The sky looks like a timelapse of the Northern Lights, where the movement is sped up so you can see the magnetic field lines pulsing through the sky. But this is bright enough to appear in daytime, and the palette of heaven's hues is so much broader than on earth. It comes to me that even the atoms in the atmosphere delight in the presence of The One, and give off these rich colors of light to celebrate him.

"My heart tells me this is center of The One—of his kingdom, life and love. I feel the same tug on my heart that I did in the hallway, but definitely much stronger here, so very close to the center of everything. Love's gravity grips my heart, pulling me into Him. Into The Fountain, The Life, The Light. All I want to do right now is climb the streets of the city, run to the fountain and stand beneath that waterfall, drinking in the presence of The One forever."

She took a deep breath and looked away momentarily, to clear her spinning head. Jesus smiled, and after a moment nodded for her to continue.

"In the midst of it all a translucent ring of light rises in mid-air over the fountain and dives down on the other side. It's a luminous, spinning cloud—a torus, a donut-shape—and light whirls into it from the fountain and sprays outward through the air in a fine mist.

"Oh, wait—it's actually a sphere, isn't it? The edges seem brighter because I'm looking through the sphere at a shallow angle, kinda like how the sky is lightest near the horizon, where you are looking through the most air, and darker straight up. Reminds me of the gilded halos around the heads of the saints in old Russian icons. Can you tell me what I'm seeing, Jesus?"

"Love is the gravity of heaven," he replied. "Next to the throne, the force of Father's love is so intense that it bends light and life into the halo you see. Sort of a like a black hole creating an event horizon in the old physical universe—another of those hints of what heaven is like. So the icons of saints with gilded haloes are quite accurate. With the eyes of trust, the artists saw them as they are in heaven."

Music

"Now, as you focus your senses on the heart of heaven, tell me what you hear."

"It's pretty far away, but…wow! These ears must be as good as my heavenly eyes, because when I tune into it, I pick up the sound right away. The water cascading from the fountain crashes like a rambunctious thunderstorm on the prairie. But it isn't noise—it's music! Down in the lowest registers there's a rumbling cadence. All the songs of heaven seem to adhere to that drumbeat: the tempo of heaven. And higher up and sideways—maybe in another dimension, I don't know what to call it—are dozens of musical phrases, intermingled and crisscrossing. Each cataract flowing down the pyramid has its own notes, but they all harmonize. Some are in the life dimension, some speak of love, or light, others exist in the physical dimensions—the music spans it all in glorious, echoing sound.

"Hey! There's Beethoven's Fifth! Da-Da-Da-Daaah!" she mimicked. "Do songs from earth make it to heaven?"

"Some do. For instance, the Israelites sing the song Moses's sister Miriam made, after they were delivered from Egypt. When you get to the city you'll hear it."

"That's cool. I hear high, tinkling notes, too. Each individual droplet makes a pitter-pattering sound when it lands. I can hear each individual drop, or just the melody, or the whole chorus at once. And, oh! That refrain is like putting on a down jacket of peace and resting under a security blanket. Another melody just oozes love There's one of approval, and another of justice and provision…my heart is melting. I'm pudding! I…I'm just going to let it touch me for a moment." Amanda stood, hands over her heart, eyes closed, feeling the music caress her soul and lay its bounty at her feet.

"Whew!" She finally said, opening her eyelids. "Oh, Jesus—that was a joy, and a four-course meal of longing fulfilled, and a thing of exquisite beauty! My heart tells me it is The Maker's song of filled desire, which is woven into every refrain of heaven."

"I'm so glad you like it!" Jesus replied, gazing fondly at his city. He seemed to be captivated, too. "All music traces its source to the fountain. Remember how the life threads of silver in the tapestry connect lives? Music is like that, too—there are threads in the music of the fountain that connect musicians, experiences and emotions. It's a tapestry forged in sound! But keep going—what else do you see?"

"Oh, I hardly want to look away! Round the fountain on every side is a mirror-like lake. You could call it a sea; it is so huge. Aah—that's what oceans on earth were copied from! It's made of life, not of water—crystal clear, the light of the fountain glowing within it. There are little stars resting in the lake; thousands of them…Children of Light. Tiny, razor-sharp points of brightness in a vast sea of glistening water coming up to their ankles, or even knees. Some stand motionless, singing the song of life. Others dance in the spray. Some lie in—or on, or under! —the water, absorbing it through their skin. Children run around between them, laughing and throwing something—rose petals maybe? —on the surface of the lake.

"And over it all is a kind of glowing mist or fog—not like on earth, where you can't see through it. It is perfectly transparent…oh—I see! The Water of Life is in the air, like water vapor. The air is alive, glowing with life. It is *so* beautiful and compelling…Jesus, can we go?"

"We will! But first, one more look. What do you see around the perimeter of the lake?"

"There is an immense garden—a paradise, a parkland surrounding the water. It would take at least a whole day to walk across it, maybe more. Between it and the lake is a colonnade—a covered walkway flanked with pillars, each pair capped by an arch. The lake is so vast it takes thousands and thousands of archways to encircle it.

"Each arch forms a doorway leading to the crystal sea, and each doorway has a name on the outside, in a beautiful script. The words look like they are fashioned from diamonds, the way they sparkle. I can read the names—vision here is, like, waaaaay better than 20/20! They're names of those who've introduced others to The One, arranged in legacies. I get it—so when you come to wade in the Crystal Sea, you come through the gateway of those who showed you the way. That's a neat touch.

"On the frieze above the arches is an inscription in beautiful letters. It repeats, running all the way around that great circle. "The Spirit and the Bride say, 'Come on in!' it reads. 'Take the Water of Life for free.' Even the words inscribed on the pediment have life in them. I can feel the nourishment enter me as I read. I'm realizing that the words in the structures are the Logos—words made physical, solid and unchanging. And the River is the Rhema—the dynamic word, the active word, constantly moving and reshaping itself."

"Very insightful! You see well, sister."

"Below the words of life on the pediment, the archways have stories incised into the walls. They are living memories you can enter into, of ordinary folks and their friendship with God. Wait—that's amazing, Jesus!" Amanda cried. "Right in the center of heaven, people are recognized simply for knowing you! Why is it such a big deal for you to be known?"

"Well," he laughed, "if you want to understand why that's dear to me, imagine living a whole life on earth with no one knowing your real name. Or walking down the streets of your hometown without a soul knowing your true identity or where you came from—even your brothers and sisters! It's a lonely feeling. Then, at the end of your life, those few who actually *did* figure it out swear that they never knew you," he added wryly."

"That's your story, isn't it?"

"Yeah. My team mostly came back in the end. Still—that doesn't mean I didn't hurt at the time. Being known touches a very deep desire of my heart. So The One—just because he loves me! —arranged it on earth so that my followers identify themselves by saying they 'know the lord.' Isn't that sweet? It's like a silly love note from him every time I hear it!

"And now, I get to live in the same house with a big bunch of friends who *do* know me, who in life were proud to claim they were my relatives. Isn't that just the best! So my deep desire to be known is filled to the brim every day in heaven."

"And to think that little me can give you something that fills your heart," Amanda confessed, feeling in that moment the pride of having stood up for the one she loved.

Jesus put an arm around her shoulder and hugged her tight. "Yep, you humans have the only thing in the universe We Three want but don't have—your hearts. Connecting with you has always been at the very center of the grand plan: to unite everyone and everything in heaven or on earth in relationship with Us. And *that* spot over there, the pinnacle of the city, is the heart of Our dream—the center of the friendship between The Maker and creation. And the center of my joy."

Twelve Trees

"Now, look once more on my city. What else do you see?"

Amanda turned back and peered into the distance. "There are shiny, golden pathways winding from the arches toward the lake. They must be paved with some kind of grass—they wave and ripple in the breeze like a wheat field at harvest. Or maybe they are gold but lie just under water, and I'm seeing real waves. Either way, it's gorgeous.

"On either side of the streets are huge, spreading trees with silver leaves, and roots going right into the water like mangroves. Or are they fountains? I can see life-water passing up through the trunk—what I first thought was bark looks like rushing foam, or the blast from an open fire hydrant. It sprays into the air at the top…but no, those look too much like leaves. I can't tell—which one are they?"

"Actually, you are seeing them as they are. Those are the Trees of Life that line the streets at the center of the city. They have branches and leaves, and so are trees in the physical. But there is so much life rushing through them that when you concentrate on the life, you see a fountain. They are really a little of both—it depends on how you look."

"Hey!" Amanda exclaimed, gesturing with the concern of someone pointing out a man jimmying a car door to a policeman. "One of the Children of Light went up to that first tree, right over there, and took something off of it. Is that allowed?"

"Everything is allowed in heaven," Jesus laughed. "The trees were placed there for that very purpose."

"Oh, okay," Amanda stated, her apprehension dissipating as quickly as it arrived. "Whatever it is glows in her hand…Oh, it's a fruit, made from the Water of Life! Now I understand. When the Children of Light come in through the archways, they first go up under the trees. Each tree casts a sumptuous pool of light from its leaves, and each one who approaches a tree picks a single fruit. The fruit is called *Therapeian*—that means 'healing' in Greek. Wait: how did I know that?" She turned to Jesus, first confused, but then smiling as she saw the pleasure on his face.

"All languages are known in heaven, because out of the *heart* the mouth speaks. Since we understand each other's thoughts here, we don't need any translators. Your heart speaks the first dialect, the language of desire that The Maker placed in it. All other human dialects descend from that mother tongue. But if you please, keep describing what you see! It is such a joy to experience what you are experiencing in your own words."

"Okay," she said, turning back to drink in more of that great sight. "From the center where The One dwells, the water reaches the lake in four main streams, one for each quarter of the city. The outer edge of the lake is kind of like a river delta: it divides the waters again and again until there are thousands of tributaries, one for each archway in the great circular colonnade. The result is that each arch vaults over a street, and each street has a stream flowing down the middle of it. When you enter any archway, you are already wading in the River.

"Outside the great circular colonnade, torrents and waterfalls of life descend to every street and alley, so no corner of the city is not awash in life. Anywhere you walk there, you're wading. Hey—that's just like Venice!"

"Yes," Jesus laughed, "you always dreamed of cities with rivers for streets. The longing for heaven was planted deep inside you, and came out in what you loved. But please, go on!"

"I see all those channels collect in pools behind the city's outer walls, far below us, so the city has a great sea in the center and a lake all around. The waters flow out through three outlets on each side—12 in all. Those gateways are round as a ball, silvery and opalescent. They must be at least 20 times as tall as I am. The gates stand wide open—there aren't even any doors to close them with. So the Children of Light can enter or leave whenever they choose."

"The gates of my city are never shut since evil is no more," The Man of Light intoned, obviously pleased. "She needs no guards or gatehouses, because there is no longer anything to defend against."

"I like it," Amanda replied, nodding in approval. "Standing tall next to each gate I can make out a gatekeeper: one of the

Burning Ones, like Kepos or Euphraino. A woman, a Child of the Light, is approaching the gate nearest us. She walks upstream through the River, her hair flowing out behind her in the current, though it doesn't seem to slow her down. She reaches the threshold and the angel bows, praises her, and calls her by her heavenly name.

"Oh—so the gatekeepers aren't there to keep anyone *out*: their job is to welcome people *in!* So that everyone who passes through the gate is honored coming in and blessed going out. She looked over at Jesus again. He seemed quite pleased at the arrangement. "That angel's got a fun job!"

"He does!" Jesus turned, put a hand on each of her shoulders and focused an intense affection toward her. "*Thank you* for allowing me to see my Bride through your eyes! I made a great sacrifice for this moment, and my heart is deeply touched by how she touches you."

He looked back to his city, took a deep breath, slowly let it out. As if he was breathing love on her. As Amanda observed The Man of Light in that moment—standing above his city in full glory, all his plans consummated, his love waiting at the door—he seemed utterly satisfied, complete, lacking in nothing.

"Centuries before I came to earth," he immediately replied to her thought, "one of the prophets said, 'He shall see the fruit of the agony of his soul and be satisfied.' He foresaw this very moment! Yes, I am fully satisfied—with my Bride, with my life, and with you, Amanda."

"Thank you, sir," Amanda bowed, then grasped his hand. "You are better than anything I ever dared to hope for in a God, and much, much more. Now—can we go in?"

"Yes, of course—we have an appointment with your father, after all!"

20 Hall of Memories

The scene went dazzling white (apparently, they were fast-traveling), then cleared. Amanda found herself standing with her father and The Man of Light inside an immense hall. Craning her neck, she tried (unsuccessfully) to take it all in: rank upon rank of bronze columns of light, crowned with capitals of stars, joined high above with lofty beams and arches. The massive cathedral walls ran arrow-straight into the distance. But the ceiling itself was an immense, transparent barrel vault made of light, its great ribs soaring across the gap above pairs of columns, so that the aisle they stood in was roofed with sky. *Oh, I see: it never rains or snows here, and the city is not afflicted with cold or scorching sun. So, no roof. Makes sense.*

The floor beneath her was a burgundy-ish stone, veined like marble. Through it twined a spiderweb of gold and silver life-threads. *Another copy of the Great Tapestry,* Amanda realized. *It's everywhere. In this version, every thread has a name. And if I focus on a particular thread I begin to see into that person's story, as if I was tracing their history in the mind of God. A person could spend days—decades, millennia—just tracing these lines!*

Glancing up, she noticed the threads converging on statues

lining the hall. The figures stood on pedestals and podiums scattered down its length, all frozen. Frozen, that is, until Amanda locked her gaze on a female figure standing just to her left. Then it came to life! There was movement in the stone: expression, words, feeling. *That's no statue!*

But the woman didn't step off the podium to greet her—didn't seem aware of her presence at all. When Amanda finally looked away, out of the corner of her eye she saw the woman solidify into stone again.

What magic is this? Some type of hologram? Most of these figures are life-size, but others quite a bit larger, more in keeping with the dimensions of the building…they must have been made to fit the room. And the walls are all hung with paintings having the same magical property: just a glance brings them to life. Amanda was so absorbed in her surroundings that she nearly missed her father's greeting.

"Are you ready for our tour?" she heard him inquire for a second time.

"What?" Oh—okay, sure!"

Both Theo and Jesus found that humorous. "A lot to take in at first, huh?" Jesus laughed. "One of the things I like about this place."

"The walls and floor around you portray the Great Tapestry, as you suspected," her father confirmed. "Or a portion of it, wrought here in living stone. If you wish you may follow the threads and learn how each life is connected to many others, and how an act of love reverberates down through the generations. But we're here to look at the exhibits."

"Exhibits? Is this a museum?"

"Yes," Theo replied, his voice echoing melodically in that vast cathedral of light. "We're in the Hall of Memories, where heaven remembers great deeds done on earth. This wing—the one I helped to create—is the Gallery of Forgiveness, where we memorialize the triumph of love over betrayal."

"You built this?" Amanda asked in astonishment.

Jesus leaned in to answer. "It is built of the sacrifices my people made for me, and the acts of service done for love. Your father had a hand in its design, with many others. His destiny in heaven is to be a Master Curator here in the Hall of Memories."

Her dad smiled; shy, grateful, proud and overjoyed all at once. Jesus nodded to him, and he continued. "I take beautiful acts of forgiveness and capture them, highlighting how grace came into each story, and displaying how each one altered history. Here, take a look!"

Monica

They walked a few paces to a sculpture of a woman in ancient dress, wrought in living color. She looked real enough that Amanda almost reached out and touched her skin to be sure. Like the others, the woman came to life as they focused on her. Breathing, her chest began to rhythmically rise and fall as she knelt in prayer on a diamond pedestal.

"This is one of my favorite creations," her dad said modestly. "It's Saint Monica. Take a minute and enter into her story!"

As they stood gazing up at the statue, light began to pour out of that face. The woman's visage softened into an expression of hope, mixed with long-fought endurance. A weariness of long struggle was there, but also steel-hard resolve. Then in the blink of an eye Amanda was inside the woman's mind, seeing as the God-who-is-with-us sees.

Monica had a son—a callous, womanizing, drunkard of a son, who rejected all her warnings and betrayed any hope and expectation she had of him as a man. Having dabbled in every available pleasure, he returned home profane, disrespectful and reckless. Amanda watched him shame his mother, and she banned him from her table. She felt the tearing in the woman's soul, her feeling of failure as a mother. Her son was lost. The One grieved with her.

But then The Man of Light walked into the room, and to

Amanda's surprise invited the woman to let go, to trust. She did the hard work of forgiveness, releasing her wounds and offenses one by one. Then she set to work, and prayed.

For 17 long years she and The One conversed each day about her son, sharing the joys of parenthood along with its sorrows. To Amanda's amazement, Monica's prayer was not a desperate plea for rescue, or a long complaint about being left alone. Just simple gratitude, that her boy was known and loved by The Maker, and thanks for what he was going to do, though she could not see what form that redemption would take or when it would come.

Then the son re-entered the scene. A prostitute on each arm, his heart lost in a zig-zagging search for meaning that led him through every philosophy and philandering cult of his age, he sat drinking morosely in the corner of a saloon. He'd scoured the earth for meaning and happiness, yet his twisted desire betrayed him. He'd found neither.

The Man of Light walked up to him there in the bar, holding a small, glass bowl in either hand, filled with glowing coals from a fire. *They're Monica's prayers of gratitude!* Amanda realized. *The answer has finally come!*

The Man of Light gently detached those girls from the son's arms, handing each a coal. They carried it away like a dearly-bought treasure, faces illuminated by the glow.

Then he turned to the son, setting the bowls under…she couldn't quite tell where. It came to her that The Man of Light placed one under his beliefs and the other under his desires. A picture came to her, of a fire under a stack of books. Only the fire was truth, and the books were ideas like little gods the son placed his hope in. His beliefs were consumed, the objects of his desire burned to smoke.

It struck Amanda in that moment that the son's futile pursuits were much like her own. Her little gods had been science and rationality, and the notoriety great discoveries might bring.

The explosion of the experiment was the fire that consumed her gods. She felt the searing separation of that moment, and understood why it was necessary, and what it had produced in her heart. Gratitude washed over her.

And still the fire of Monica's prayers burned, until the son's money was gone, and opportunity dried up, and all his fickle friends had departed. The choice before him was to leave the nothing he had to show for his life, and return home to face his shame, or to sink witless into despair and take his own life.

In the background of that scene, Monica still prayed. To Amanda's astonishment she seemed to know that her actions would lead her son to this moment, where life itself teetered on a knife's edge. Yet she pressed on. *How did she have the courage to ask for this? How could she believe so completely in The Man of Light?*

Then she saw Jesus place one hand on each of the son's shoulders, look into his eyes and speak a word of love. The son bowed his head and wept. When he raised it again, he was a different man. Then Jesus took one of the coals and placed it on his lips. Then the picture changed. That coal became a fire, and the fire swept across the Western world, and she saw it burn down through history right to her feet. Then the vision faded, and Amanda was looking at the exhibit from the outside again. Her cheeks were wet, and her heart was a flame.

"Monica must be one of the staunchest believers of all time! Who was she?"

Jesus and her father looked at one another, and she saw the pride and pleasure on Jesus's face. "Saint Monica," her dad replied, reaching over to wipe Amanda's eyes, "who lived in Tunisia 1600 years or so before you were born. She is one of the Great Ones—but I doubt you ever heard of her. See, earth remembers generals and heroes and politicians: those who shape the surface events of the world using raw power. Renown in heaven is allotted to those who shaped hearts with love. That's what Monica is famous for."

And then he was no longer a senior curator, but simply her dad. "And boy, oh boy, could that woman pray!"

Jesus laughed, and after a moment Amanda joined in, too. "Glory on earth doesn't seem to be a recipe for glory in heaven," she commented. "Monica's son isn't anyone I'd know either?"

"Actually, you would," her dad answered. "His name is Augustine, from the African city of Hippo. You'd remember him as Saint Augustine—one of the early pillars of the church. He made a fine mess of his younger life, as you saw. His mother Monica was made a saint just for praying him into the corner where he finally found life."

Then Jesus chimed in. "But Augustine didn't transform the world by ruling nations or starting wars, but through a change of heart. To give just one example, his book 'Confessions' created a new genre of biography: one that was honest about personal struggles instead of portraying the main character as an unchanging paragon of virtue. That's how all Greek and Roman biographies were written, until Augustine came along.

"The value for honesty and self-reflection that is at the heart of Western culture largely goes back to him. That's the fire that you saw, sweeping over the Western world. Every westerner today has a piece of Augustine in him, and threads from all those lives in the tapestry lead all the way back to him. And through him, they end up at Monica."

Amanda automatically looked down, and sure enough, the floor near the stature was nearly solid silver with the convergence of so many life threads.

"I'm especially proud of both of them," Jesus continued with a smile. "And your father did an excellent job of capturing the essence of how it happened."

Genealogies

Their dialog was interrupted by a woman's voice. Thinking it was another exhibit, Amanda turned to discover which statue was talking—and saw a short, pert woman in striking white cross the floor toward their little group. A real woman, not a statue. She walked with a measured, determined stride, as if she had important things to do, but that those tasks weren't her master.

"Giving another tour, Theo?" she called to them, passing from one of the many wings into the museum's main hall.

"Oh—hi, Kathryn! Yes—I'm co-leading with The Man of Light. And I have a special guest: my daughter, Amanda!"

"A biological daughter?" The woman halted a few feet away, sizing them both up. "Yes, she does look like you in the physical: the same nose, the same cheekbones. And—oh! I can see your stories are deeply intertwined! I'm so pleased to meet you!" she welcomed Amanda, reaching out to give her a hug.

"This is Kathryn," Jesus offered, face beaming, "One of my *special* favorites. She is a prayer genealogist here at the museum, where she brings hidden acts of trust to light."

"I know we are *all* your special favorites," Kathryn replied affectionately, "but my heart still flutters every time you say it to me." Then she turned to Amanda. "And we love having your father here—he has such a gift for unearthing singular stories and putting them on display."

"Thank you," Theo replied appreciatively, then turned to address his daughter. "Kathryn and I often collaborate on the exhibits. She's a rock star in her profession."

"Um, if I might ask," Amanda inquired, "What exactly *does* a prayer genealogist do?"

"Oh, I trace the effect of prayers down through the generations. Remember the welcoming committee you had when you first set foot in heaven? I help make events like that happen, by finding the connections between your prayers and their lives, and vice versa. Prayers can trickle down through a family line for generations, you know. Just look at Father Abraham! You'll see him down near the end of the hall, by the way," she pointed.

"I'm not sure what you mean by welcoming committee,

Kathryn," Amanda replied. "It was just Jesus and Poppy when I first got here."

Kathryn frowned. "*What!?* No welcoming committee?"

Jesus laughed, and put a reassuring hand on her shoulder. "That's my doing, Kathryn. Your work, as always, is perfect. Amanda is here on a special visa—kind of a technicality, really."

"Well, that sounds like a story that would be quite interesting to dig into."

"And so you shall! Since you two have already met, you can look forward to doing it yourself!"

"Ooh, wonderful!" Kathryn clapped her hands with delight. "I love an adventure!"

"So how do you learn to do prayer genealogies?" Amanda asked, still curious. "Is there like a degree or something?"

"I have my own special method of qualifying people," Jesus answered with a proud grin. "Take Kathryn: she was born in a small village in western Siberia, in the 1920's."

"It was cold!" Kathryn interjected, laughing.

"Her parents were *bednyaks*—the poorest of the poor, landless peasants," Jesus continued. "The village had one school with one teacher, and one church with the doors boarded up. As a girl, Kathryn dreamed of travel and adventure, of being part of a larger world. But the regime she grew up under had no interest in her dreams. She remained in that one small village her entire life.

"But one day she shared her secret ambition with an aunt, and that devout old woman began to pray for the little girl's dream. I took those prayers, went back in time to when Kathryn was being formed in the womb—"

"Answers to prayer are not limited by the arrow of time," Kathryn interrupted.

"—and gave her the gift of praying for others," Jesus finished. "From her aunt, she learned to talk to me. At first, we only discussed her own life, but soon she was praying for other kids in her little town. As an adult, her prayers expanded to surrounding villages, to people she read about in the newspaper—anytime she came across a name, she asked The Maker to touch that person's life. My gift of prayer took her all over the world, connecting her to the lives of thousands of others in dozens of countries. I made her dream come true, though not in a fashion she expected."

"It was years before I realized my prayers and my dream were connected," Kathryn said pensively. "We're so short-sighted on earth."

"On earth," Jesus continued," no one outside her tiny village knew her name. But after a lifetime of investing in others with no hope of recognition, I arranged it so that in heaven *everyone* recognizes her."

"It's true," she nodded vigorously. "I can barely walk down the street without someone calling out to me!"

Jesus smiled. "My pleasure, Kathryn. That's how compensation works here. And when your coronation day comes, when I lead you up on heaven's stage and tell all the Children of Light what I love about you and what you've done for me, generations of people you prayed for will shout the acclaim your life has earned."

"Now...I didn't really do all that much."

"Everyone who adds even a stitch to the Great Tapestry is rewarded with my pleasure," The Man of Light affirmed.

"He wants to make sure we all know how much he appreciates what we've done," Theo chimed in, "and that everyone in heaven knows it, too. The reward for a life well-lived isn't some ceremonial title, or crowns, baubles and trophies—it's the joy and gratitude of heaven for *who you are.* That glory becomes a literal part of you!"

In that moment Amanda caught a whiff, just the tiniest taste of the glory that this anonymous woman carried. Honor so smote on her face so that she took a step back to steady herself. It was exhilarating and exquisite, an overpowering aura of recognition and approval pouring out from within that petite frame. Her presence lit up the hall. For a brief instant she saw Kathryn as she'd seen her dad, in the glory of a child of heaven.

"Whoa," Amanda gushed, deeply impacted. "That's…I don't know what to say."

"That's because there are no earthly words for it," Jesus said matter-of-factly, smiling at Kathryn. "There is no experience on earth remotely like the honor of heaven. Fame and renown pale and fade to dust beside it. Truly, it lies beyond human comprehension. All you can do is experience it."

"Yes…well, it's quite an feeling," was all Amanda could say.

"He has another reason to reward you all out of proportion to your actual contribution," Kathryn continued after a moment. "When any two of the Children of Life share in a reward, it connects their stories, and their hearts. I see it all the time in my work."

"Like with Caspar and me," her dad added. "We are great friends in heaven because we contributed to each other's growth, and so we share in the glory of what Abba did in us."

"My pleasure!" Jesus made a motion toward Theo like tipping an invisible hat. "And since my job is to unite everyone and everything in the love of The One, I assign rewards in a way that fosters unity.

"And," he added with a grin, "when you have infinite resources, there is no reason not to be infinitely generous—especially with friends and family!"

"So…how exactly did that work out for you, Poppy?" Amanda inquired. Something deep in her soul positively celebrated at this idea of reward, and knew it was real, and solid as concrete. But to her head it still seemed impossibly disproportionate.

"Well, I get credit for the lives of all my patients—hundreds of them. And for anyone whose lawn I mowed, anyone I loaned twenty bucks to, any child I did something as small as open the car door for. And for your life, Amanda. As a parent, all that your kids accomplish—"

"Even if they are space pioneers!" Jesus laughed.

"*Especially* if they are space pioneers," Theo joined in the laughter. "I get credit for all my heavenly descendants, and all they become and accomplish for love."

"That's super amazing," Amanda finally agreed, accepting what she still didn't understand. "Just one small, tiny request—"

"That's a great question," Jesus answered, reading her thoughts. "On earth when you share something you each get less. If you and your cousin split a cookie, each of you only gets to eat half. But in heaven, give away a cookie and suddenly there are two! Heaven always multiplies whenever it divides, so no one has less than the whole. That's just another one of the ways heaven is always expanding."

"Like how earth's universe is expanding?"

"You noticed!" Jesus exclaimed, leaping over to give her a boisterous hug. "Thank you! I made it that way to give humans a picture of heaven, although it took thousands of years before science advanced to the point where you could see it."

The little party reached an intersection. Two halls branched off at right angles to theirs, two more marched off at a *different* right angle, and several more spiraled off into different time dimensions. Everything was perpendicular…but how? Amanda was momentarily confused, until her brain made the adjustment. *Oh—I'm still thinking in 3-D. A dimension is just a direction,* she remembered. *And we've got more than three dimensions, so there are more directions, all perpendicular…*

"This is where I take my leave," Kathryn stated, stopping in the crossroads and pointing to her left. "At least for now. My work takes me down this side hall."

"See you again soon!" Theo answered with a wave. "And when I do, it will be like no time passed at all!"

"True enough!" Kathryn responded. And with a bow to The Man of Light and a nod to Amanda, she turned and marched off into the distance.

Memories

The little party of three resumed their journey down the Great Hall, Amanda oohing and aahing as they passed various displays.

"Who is that?" Amanda asked, stopping in front of an exhibit that caught her attention. A young man danced in a grove of trees behind a brick-walled factory, arms raised and tears flowing down his cheeks. He was worshipping The One. The sacrifice of love he was offering burned like a fire, giving off a cloud that smelled of incense. A halo of light a few feet across surrounded the picture, blurring the trees over and around him into the background of the hall.

"This is Ethan," Jesus began. "He was reading a letter from the girl he loved on his way to work, and discovered she had gotten engaged to another guy. This was his offering— throwing himself on trust instead of giving in to bitterness and despair. He let go of the hope of finding love on earth, and entrusted his heart fully to me. This exhibit is one of the great moments of his life. Now that secret surrender is acclaimed from the rooftops, and everyone in heaven celebrates with him."

"And what happened with the girl he loved?" Amanda inquired. "How did you respond to his trust?"

"That was easy," Jesus grinned. "Ethan's act of surrender itself did most of the work. I just helped her see who she really was…and they married a few years later. When you cling to a thing you desire, you will lose it; but when you trust and let go—well, the power of heaven is released through trust. Trust is the bridge that brings heaven to earth. It's kind of fun, what I can do when people put things in my hands."

They walked on a few hundred yards, passing dozens of enticing exhibits. Amanda would have loved to stop and explore each one, but Jesus seemed to have a destination in mind. Suddenly, he halted. "Here, this is what we came for," he said, with the little head bob that connotes satisfaction. "Theo, do me the favor of show her that exhibit, the one hanging over there on the wall."

"You know its name," Theo smiled shyly.

"But the joy and surprise of discovery will make it all the better. Go ahead, lead us!"

With a nod, Amanda's father escorted them across the great aisle and under a lofty arch, to a life-sized, framed picture set into the wall. But this was no mere 2-D artwork—it was a holographic vision of a life, seen through the eyes of The One. Amanda bent over to read the plaque fastened below it.

"Daddy! This is you!"

"Yes," he replied with solemn pleasure. "I won a privileged place in this hall through the grace of my great friend Jesus, and through choosing to forgive."

"Was it forgiving Caspar?"

"No, that was my second great betrayal—the first is always the hardest. There is a lesser exhibit showing that event in a wing farther down the hall."

"It is not less to me," The Man of Light asserted, "And you receive the full honor due for your sacrifice in that favored place. But now tell us *this* story."

"Amanda," her father began kindly, facing her and taking her hands. "A lot of what you'll see here I never told you on earth. It's about your mother and me. Back then I tried to shield you from the ugliness that went on between us. But since Jesus brought you to this moment, I believe it is the right time for you to know. Step into the exhibit," he beckoned.

The step was not physical, but a decision to enter in with her mind. Peering up at her father's image, Amanda began to experience a story through his eyes.

The familiar kitchen of their bungalow on Juniper Street appeared, the one with the happy yellow wallpaper. Smaller than Amanda remembered—until she realized she was seeing it through the eyes of a six-foot man instead of a six-year-old girl. There was the tiled island with the porcelain sink, the Formica table grandma gave them when they married, the family photos plastered onto the ivory fridge door. Her mom perched on one of the bar stools in front of the island, wearing a smart dress and a jaunty hat. She was literally bouncing on the seat, smoking one of the cigarettes she denied using—Amanda recognized the manic energy that came over her during her episodes. The clock on the microwave said 11:42 p.m.

"How long have you been seeing him?" she heard her father ask, in a despondent voice.

Amanda could not hear her mother's reply, but she understood—mom was leaving. In the next scene, her suitcase rolled to a car waiting at the curb, wheels bouncing on the cracks in the sidewalk. On the way out the door, her dad handed mom the checkbook, her prescriptions and her spare pair of glasses.

"I still love you," he said. "Please come back." Then the car pulled away, and she was gone.

Her father sat down at the breakfast table and began to sob, his back rising and falling in great shuddering breaths. And The Man of Light sat across from him, handing him tissues as one of the Burning Ones collected the grief falling in his tears and stored it in a crystal flask.

Then her dad raised his head, fixed his watering eyes on Jesus. Amanda could feel his questions—*Why did this happen? Am I a failure as a husband? Will she ever come back? And what do I tell my daughter?*

Jesus looked his friend in the eyes, took his hands and cried with him. When the tears finally failed, her father and Jesus simply sat there, sharing a raw but tender silence, til Jesus rose from the table, bent down over her father, and breathed on him. And in that breath were no adages or answers; only the power of trust.

Looking through her father's eyes in that moment Amanda finally, fully understood why The Man of Light was silent. *I get it now: there is no answer on earth to the question, 'Why?' I thought if I knew I why mom left, I could get her back, or even stop it from happening in the first place. But mom herself didn't know why she did what she did, or how that chemically-imbalanced madness drove her. Those manic feelings weren't even real: they were imbalances in her neurotransmitters, and not caused by any change in her relationship with dad. Yet she was absolutely sure nothing at all was wrong with her...*

That's the blindness we walk in on earth. There is no way to protect your own heart by knowing what will be—life is beyond prediction. And even if I had known why...what answer would remove the pain from a little girl's heart when her mommy just walked out of her life?

Asking 'Why?' is a dead end. The only real answer is trust. And trust grows best by sharing the pain in silence, not with pat answers or shallow advice.

Letting Go

Amanda watched her dad rise, walk over to the window, and look out onto their darkened lawn for a very long time. While he stood there, The Man of Light leaned in behind him, with both arms around her dad's chest, holding him. Finally, her father let go of understanding why, of how it would look to his friends, his pastor and his parents, of trying to fix the unfixable. She perceived that this was the first of thousands of times he would repeat that prayer. But for that initial moment, Theo gave himself to trust, and performed a great act of faith: he went to bed.

As his eyes closed and he slept, the lens Amanda was looking through zoomed out, now above the house, then their street, their town, finally the blue ball of the earth itself. All around the globe she saw rank upon rank of the Burning Ones, standing at attention and applauding a miracle: that in his darkest hour her father trusted enough to go to sleep.

Tears were flowing freely down her cheeks as Amanda stepped out of the exhibit and turned to face her father. The Man of Light stood behind him, with his arm wrapped around Theo like she had seen in the vision.

"I never knew mom left with another man."

"She didn't want you to know," her dad answered quietly. "The temptation was there, to stab her in the back by telling you her secret. But Jesus helped me, and I honored that request."

"Pain is never healed by causing more pain," Jesus agreed. "Lashing out would only have given bitterness an opportunity to take root, and caused you to lose each other."

"You gave her the checkbook. So, she and that other guy—"

"Yeah. But I wanted her to know I still loved her, even so."

"Actually, he gave it to me," Jesus added firmly, patting where a back pocket would be if heaven's clothes actually had any pockets. "Love began with The Three in heaven, flowing from The One Cause. So every act of love originates with Us, and every gift given out of love returns to Us. Your father chose well," Jesus turned his head to smile affectionately at him, "and I am immensely proud of what he did for me."

"Daddy, how did you manage to get over what she did to you? When I saw through your eyes, I felt what you felt...I never understood how badly it hurt you."

"Well, that first night..." Theo reflected. "There was this moment of clarity while I was looking out the window into the blackness. I saw the choice. I could embrace that offense and hold onto it, and have a darn good reason for being angry. And that would justify cultivating my rage, storing it up, letting it consume me, so that one day when it was least expected...

"But no. That was the moment I knew I had to let go. Anger wouldn't lead me anywhere except into a hole I couldn't get out of. I decided I wasn't going to throw what remained of my life away for the sake of a staying mad. I had a child who needed me. And once I made that decision, it seemed like the most sensible thing to do would just be to go to bed. It was 2:00 a.m., after all."

"That was very well put!" Jesus exclaimed. "I'm impressed. You should add that thought to the exhibit."

"I think I will."

Humility

"Come! Let's walk a bit more while we talk," Jesus invited, and started down the broad hall with a sister on his left and a brother to his right.

"Amanda, today you've seen your father as he was always meant to be, fully alive within the heavenly destiny he was created for. He is a Master Curator in the Hall of Memories, telling the stories of those who paid a great price to forgive, just as their Father in heaven had forgiven them. He qualified for the job by forgiving those who hurt him on earth: creating a beautiful story out of his loss instead of getting bitter. Those choices give him the authority and insight to tell similar stories that honor the best moments of others."

"Wow, Poppy! You really are amazing."

"Thank you," he replied simply, nodding in her direction.

"I've got just one question," Amanda added after a moment.

Laughing, Jesus immediately replied, "No! You have two!" The echoes of his mirth bounced back from the far end of the hall several seconds later.

"Oh—I guess you're right. My first one is, aren't you embarrassed by all that praise, dad? You always used to deflect that sort of thing."

"Jesus, you want to take this one?" Theo answered.

"Sure! Amanda, honor causes no embarrassment in heaven. Every one of these wonderful people (he pointed to several of the living statues they were passing at that moment) is rightfully proud to be here, and we are proud with them. On earth, people try to act humble by deflecting praise, or even putting themselves down. But that's just another way to manage your own image. True humility is the willingness to be known as you are, without trying to manipulate how others see you."

"I guess 'fake it til you make it' would be kind of impossible here," Amanda remarked with a wry smile. "In a place where anyone can see right into your heart…"

"No one can pretend to be something they are not," Theo completed the sentence.

"What a pair! You two even think alike!" Jesus beamed with the satisfaction of a parent watching a child excel. "Real humility on earth is transparency. And that's practice for living in heaven, where no one wears a mask. Instead of deflecting honor in heaven, we enjoy it, together."

Damnatio Memoriae

They passed through another intersection (it took the better part of a minute to cross under that one enormous vault), dominated by an elaborate display in the center. "That's Joseph, one of my Jewish forefathers," Jesus remarked offhandedly as they circled around it. "His brothers sold him into slavery, but he trusted and let go. Years later, I restored his family by letting him save them from starvation. I was so proud of him—he was the first human to figure out that I can take the worst betrayals and make good out of them!"

"Now, as to your second question," he said gently, as they left Joseph behind and strode down the echoing hall, "I did not bring pain into your father's life so he could do a job for me in heaven. His role here grew out of his response to suffering, but my contribution was the *redemption*, not the betrayal. Divorce doesn't come from me, or sickness, or mental illness, or any other evil. But my power to redeem is so comprehensive, that when the story is over and you look back, it seems like I planned what happened from the very beginning! I can take anything you experience—*anything*—and turn it into something beautiful. In fact, The Evil himself will one day stand chained before me, and be forced to acknowledge that all it has accomplished is to make me look like the King I truly am.

"Yes, that day is coming!" Jesus announced, and then joy bubbled out of him and his laughter echoed high off the walls of the hall, and light showered down on the exhibits. "So be it! On My Day evil is annihilated once and for all, and a new age of joy begins. Hell becomes nothing, and passes utterly out of existence. It shall be *Damnatio Memoriae!* My victory is so final and absolute that my bride will forget that evil ever was."

"What's that damnation thing you're talking about?" Amanda asked plainly. She was getting over her reticence about asking dumb questions, because no one called anything dumb here.

"*Damnatio Memoriae* means to erase a person from memory," Jesus explained, as they wove in and out amongst the exhibits. "The Romans used to do it back in my day after the death of a despised leader. It happened with the Emperor Domitian, for example—not a very nice guy."

"How'd it work?"

"A decree would go out from the Roman Senate condemning a tyrant or traitor. Then people all over the empire would throw down his statues, cut his image out of reliefs and chisel his name from the monuments and buildings he erected. They even wrote him out of their histories, just like I write evil out of your life story in the Great Washing."

"Huh. Once in school, I read that Rome was an Honor/Shame culture," Amanda mused, contemplating the idea. "The single goal of any upper-class Roman was to gain honor and renown. If a rich man spent his money on anything else, he was called a fool."

"In that case, the ultimate punishment for a Roman would be to have your name obliterated," Theo mused. "To lose the fame and honor you spent your life accumulating, and finally be unremembered. Ouch."

"Damnatio Memoriae is a sign on earth of what heaven does with hell," Jesus continued, his voice firm and final. "The followers of The Evil shake in their boots when they think of it! Heaven's healing will chisel the damage they did out of every heart, and all hell's labor won't amount to a hill of beans. The names of every employee of hell—their very existence—will be lost and unrecalled. And when all trace of that evil empire is completely wiped away, The One himself will rip that page from the Book of Remembering and send it to the fire. Even *he* will forget that darkness ever entered creation. Then at last endless joy shall be all that is or was or ever will be."

"I like that evil has an end," Amanda said softly. "If it was still lurking off in the darkness somewhere while we were celebrating in heaven…no, this is much better."

"I agree," Jesus stated decisively.

Mom

"There's a little alcove over here, with a comfortable bench to sit and think," Jesus stated, after they'd traveled a short way beyond the Joseph exhibit. He walked over to that niche and held out an inviting arm. "Theo, I think this is a good moment for you two to discuss family matters. I'll take my leave until you finish talking things over. Call me when you're done!"

"Thank you," Theo answered gratefully. "Your timing, as usual, is perfect."

Jesus nodded, then turned to walk away. His body gradually became more and more transparent, until after only five or six steps he'd vanished completely.

"There he goes again," Amanda sighed romantically.

"He does go for a dramatic exit," Theo observed, smiling. "He certainly made a few on earth."

In the alcove a bench made of light stood against the wall. A beam of light curved up from the floor, then ran along the arc of the wall, forming a seat. Amanda chose a spot and curled her legs up under her torso. Father and daughter shared a few minutes of quiet contemplation in the stillness of the hall.

It wasn't the cramped silence of a stuffy back-room in a library, where dust, must and unread classics make you feel older the longer you sit. This silence was open to the sky, alive, vibrating with potential but at rest as well. After reflecting for a while (trying to quantify how much time had passed in heaven was both impossible and unnecessary), Amanda spoke up.

"All this time since Mom left…you and I had our own code of silence about her, didn't we? Sort of a mini *Damnatio Memoriae,* if you get my drift."

Theo looked up as a trio of birds flew over the hall, chirping happily. "Yeah, I know. We just stopped talking about her. At first it was too painful to bring up, and later too awkward—by then, we hadn't mentioned her for so long that the topic seemed off-limits. Which just erected another wall around our hearts. I'm glad we've put that behind us."

"Still…she was the one you chose. You loved her enough

to marry her. Does heaven put divorced couples back together again?"

"Heaven redeems what is lost on earth," Theo answered slowly, as if deep in thought. "But the redemption is always bigger than the original. The good that was lost is superseded, not merely restored. Sometimes that looks pretty different from the original. For instance, you don't get your original molecules back after you die: your new body is different, better, but still you. Caspar and I got our relationship back, but not because we went into business together in heaven. What was destroyed in that falling out was replaced with something better: now we are partners in personal transformation.

"Marriage is like that, too. Here, I'm part of the One Great Marriage with The Man of Light. I'm no longer single: I've re-married. Since I have him, I feel no sense of lack over what was on earth."

"Isn't that kind of hard on the folks who were happily married on earth?"

"Not at all! Any closeness, any depth of relationship we had on earth is multiplied in heaven, not extinguished. Remember Lelise and Abeda? A special relationship on earth is still special in heaven—just different. It's the same with us: you're still my girl here in the Beautiful Land, aren't you? And I'm still special to you, right?"

"Yeah, even if your syntax is faulty," she joked.

"Do we have *more* of a relationship now that we're in heaven, or *less*?"

"Definitely more. We see into each other's hearts, after all."

"It's the same with marriage," Theo added, leaning back against the wall. "The most intimate, lasting relationship on earth, where everything is shared, is an example of the bond that *all* relationships possess in heaven. On earth we needed the boundaries of an exclusive, romantic partnership to get even a sip of what heaven has to offer. Heaven needs no exclusive relationships to foster intimacy, because *all* relationships here go deeper than the most dear, intimate earthly marriage."

"But with mom," Amanda sighed, picking idly at a fingernail, "she got so messed up with the bi-polar thing, and didn't seem to figure any of it out before she died. At least as far as I know." Her voice grew solemn, dropping to a whisper. "Can heaven make *that* well? Or…is she even here?"

"She is not." Her father said it simply, without judgement, pain or regret. "She decided not to come, and her choice has been fully honored, even as The Maker promised her."

An Invitation Declined

"That's hard," Amanda confessed after a moment. "Even with everything she did and didn't do, she's still my mom. What kept her away?"

"Nothing—she chose not to come."

"How can that be?"

Theo smiled at his daughter kindly. "Remember when we talked about free will and the spark of life? To create us as free selves, The Maker had to disconnect us from his life, to make us independent of him. What kept us alive from that moment on was biology, not him.

"But biology comes to an end. It dies. The choice we were given is this: to hold on to control of our dying spark of life, or to sign it over in exchange for his. I let go and chose trust—so did you. We are alive now without biology, in the One Life. But your mom was too afraid of losing what she thought she had. She refused any limits on her freedom, so her life has come to an end.

"Think of it like this: the first universe, our universe, is over. Gone. God is all there is: even heaven is in God, and there is *nothing* outside of him. There is no place left in the universe for a life independent of God. Those who would rather die than be dependent on God get what they ask for. And anyone who insists on keeping the freedom to choose both good and evil cannot exist inside a God who is only good."

"She's not…in hell, is she?" Amanda whispered.

"Oh, darling," her dad turned and looked into her eyes, placing one hand tenderly on each shoulder. "This isn't the Middle Ages. When the life of her physical body ended, there was no greater life to keep her soul going. She'd been given an engraved invitation to the wedding, but she didn't want to come. So The Maker kept his promise and honored the gift of choice he'd given her. Her flame has gone out."

"So, is she going to be, like, tortured in a lake of fire forever, her skin burning off while we live here in bliss, trying to forget that we ever knew her?"

Outside of heaven, that question would have been an agonizing scream of rage and despair at an unjust universe. Here, its weight and import remained, but it no longer held the power to inflict pain.

Theo snuggled up next to Amanda and held her. "You know The Man of Light, Mandy. Does that sound like something he would do?"

The hall was silent for a long moment, waiting. Outside, joy rang in the air and peace showered down like spring rain. Finally, Amanda sighed: "No, he wouldn't."

"There is no eternal torment for those he made and loved, no punitive justice, no nine unending circles of hell like in Dante's Inferno. Dante's fears got the best of him, but you will meet him here someday—his fear has turned to laughter, and his dread to joy. Amanda, hell doesn't even exist after heaven's remodeling! There can be no eternal torment because the only place in existence is the Beautiful Land—and it certainly isn't happening here! The gates of heaven stand permanently open and unguarded because nothing exists that might come in and spoil the bliss."

"But then what is this 'lake of fire' the bible talks about?"

"It's actually the presence of God," Theo explained. "You and I could barely stand to look at the fiery brightness of The Man of Light when we first arrived, and we had *chosen* his light. The Voice was already alive and growing inside our hearts.

"To those who've said they want nothing to do with Him, the sight of his face is also a fire—but one that consumes. When God appears as he really is, in all his dimensions, all other lights are swallowed in his brightness. Every drop of rain is engulfed by his ocean. The self that resists the irresistible is annihilated in the attempt, and ceases to be. The *fire* of his presence lasts forever; but the dry grass that is burned up in it does not."

"But couldn't The Man of Light have saved her?" Amanda protested. "When I was at the cliff and saw him face to face, he said that he was irresistible. Couldn't he have shown up that way for mom?"

Theo appeared to be thinking hard for a moment, then glanced up to make a request. "Hey, Jesus? I think Mandy needs to hear this from you."

Keeping Silent

And then he was there, a warming comfort on her left side, while her father still sat with his arm around her on the right. Jesus put a hand to her cheek and gently kissed her forehead. In his beautiful eyes she saw…was it grief?

"Yes," he responded gently, "it does grieve me. I don't want any life to end. I love all that I have made, so I have done everything that could be done to save everyone."

For a long moment they sat side by side, staring across the quiet hall. Jesus gave her hand a squeeze, and she felt his love pass into her again. Love connected joy and sorrow, and she understood more deeply what it had cost this one she loved dearly to create humanity.

"Darling," he said softly, "I *have* done all. Remember what I told you on the flight down to the Beautiful Land? If your mom had seen the irresistible version of me (as I am here in heaven) against her will, it would have destroyed her. It's like putting tissue paper under a blowtorch, or flattening a ladybug with a steamroller. Without my life running through her veins, her self—her soul, intellect, and will—would be violated by my presence. She would struggle for a nanosecond to maintain her independence, but it would be like trying to mop up a tsunami with a paper towel, or quench a volcano with a thimble-full of water. To resist the unveiled face of God is annihilation."

"I guess I always thought the soul lived on after death, whether it went to heaven or hell," Amanda stated flatly, staring out into the hall with elbows on her knees and her chin in her hands. "That part of us is inherently immortal."

"No. The only immortal life is in The One, and those who share his life. Belief in the immortality of the soul comes from the ancient Greeks. That's not the story I taught, even though many of my followers bought into the Greek ideal. My own life makes the truth clear: my soul didn't live on after death. I had to be *resurrected.* Brought back to life. The Maker injected his vitality into me, and I was reborn into Our shared life." He shook his head, as if dismissing an unwanted thought. "No, the soul dies with the body, and without a transfusion of life from The Maker, there is no life at all. It is finished."

"I tried for a long time to forget her," Amanda murmured, absorbing the conversation. "I guess it was my way of protecting my heart—even of getting back at her. To forget her was to write her out of my life the way she'd written me off."

"I understand," Jesus said without recrimination.

"But sitting here with you in the Beautiful Land, it doesn't hurt any more. Your love has come into me and washed away all the rage. I am full. Even so, she did love me after a fashion, as imperfectly as all love is on earth."

Amanda looked over at Jesus, and their eyes met. In them she saw the desire of his heart, and how he had loved, and lost.

Her face was filled not with need, nor grief, but in understanding. "You really loved her, didn't you?"

"Yeah. She was my sister."

"I did, too. She was my mom."

And now Amanda held Jesus, as he held her.

"Yes, she was loved," The Man of Light breathed after a moment. "I followed her each day she walked the earth. I knew every beauty and every flaw that made her unique. I watched her grow, and flourish, and fail. But the gift of free will means that no matter how much I yearned for her, I can't make her choose life."

Jesus sighed, and they sat in silence a while longer. Waiting honored the moment.

"You know, it was true of the first woman, too," he continued. "When Eve reached for the apple, I knew exactly what her choice would lead to: wars, death, rape, disease, slavery, manipulation, pain, illness—the whole nine yards. I saw that it would end in my own death, too. Everything in me wanted to cry out, 'No Eve, *NO!*' To convince her somehow that she was making a mistake."

"But you kept silent," Theo offered quietly, sprawled in contemplation there on the bench.

"Yeah," Jesus said pensively, looking off into the distance. "I kept silent. I didn't show up in my glory and try to talk her out of it. I said nothing at all."

"And what was Father saying to you in that moment?" Theo asked.

"Oh?" The inquiry seemed startle Jesus out of his reverie. "Theo, that's a *great* question! It was beautiful. He told me he was so, so proud of me. That he was honored that I trusted in our bond, and that he felt known and understood by me. And he told me we would see this through together, for the sake of the joy ahead of us—the joy you see all around you now.

"We Three who made her gave her the gift of life and freedom *together*. The choice I faced that day was to stay loyal to Our choice, and honor Our endowment to humanity, or go my own way and take back the free gift by force. I made the only good choice: to trust."

"Now *that* gives me a whole new picture of why trust is so important to you," Amanda said with reverence. "And why you didn't try to stop Eve. At least, it makes sense to my heart. But in my head…why couldn't you find some way to save her?"

Answers

An affectionate smile crossed his lips. "The problem in the question is that your head is trying to get something that will fill the longing of your heart. And your head always misunderstands the heart, and asks the wrong question."

"What do you mean?"

"It's kinda funny, actually. I don't tell humans why because you don't really want to know why!" The Man of Light chuckled, amused by the conundrum. "You want to be *protected*. You want the pain to go away. You want your circumstances to change so you don't have to. Knowing why—even if it is a shallow, trite answer—lets your mind go on pretending you can live without trust. But it doesn't ever work. A rational answer can't fill your heart's desire."

"Amanda," he said pertly, his eyes glittering with mirth as he spoke, "it's only after you learn to trust without knowing why, that I can let you know why without the risk that you'll stop trusting!"

"But there *is* an answer out there somewhere, right? Life can't be all random?"

"There is an answer," Jesus affirmed. "Unfortunately for humanity, it only makes sense in heaven. Until you've seen the end as well as the beginning, from the author's own point of view, you'll never understand the arc of the story. It's like a good mystery novel: you can't grasp the plot until you've read the whole thing. And you can't read most of The Maker's book until you get to heaven."

"Oh, sister!" Jesus cried, standing abruptly as if to declaim a great truth. "Free will is a great mystery, bound up with the spark of life and the universe that sustains it. They are two peas in a pod, interconnected and interdependent. In fact, having life independent of The One *is* free will! Take away the freedom and you take away life with it. Or if you take away the spark of life—well, dead men have no free will, either."

"So you couldn't make mom choose life, even if you wanted?"

"I have *always* wanted her to choose life—my heart longed for that very thing! But taking away her choice would take away her life with it. My only option was to trust and let her choose."

"That's…I don't know what to say. I never thought that you had to trust like I do. I didn't realize how vulnerable it made you to give us choice."

"That's because you've never been a parent," Theo interrupted, grinning.

"Yes! We made you parents because you could never relate to Us otherwise," Jesus laughed, smiling back at Theo. "To love and let go, and trust that a teenage son or daughter's love will return to you…the story of parenting is the story of God and humanity."

"So if I understand you right," Amanda stated carefully, leaning forward on the bench. "If you had shown up to my mother as the irresistible you, to convince her to enter heaven, it would have killed her. If you took back the gift of choice, and forced her to choose the good, she would lose her humanity—it would destroy her. If you tried to bring her into heaven without the life of The One in her…since the soul is not immortal, you'd just have a corpse in heaven. And if she passes away on earth without trading in her spark for The Maker's life, you will honor her choice, and she will be truly and finally dead. So—she's gone forever?"

"Yes, my darling. And The Maker grieves, that the child who carried his image and bore his life, who he created for a great reunion with him, refused to come to the banquet. But we do not."

"Do not what?" Amanda whispered.

At this, Jesus leaned forward to look past Amanda and nod to her dad. "Theo, this question, I believe, is one you can speak to in a way that I can't."

"Thanks, Jesus. Your trust in me is a great honor."

Then turning to Amanda, he replied. "The One honored your mother—my wife! —with life and freedom. He kept his promise. Her choice of what to do with that freedom—her final request, as it were—has been fully honored as well.

"She feels no loss or regret now, because she is not. I don't grieve for myself, because grief is the emotion of loss—loss of love, of companionship, of belonging. But I have all those things in superabundance in The Maker—and you do, too. While he once supplied some of those things to me through your mom, now I get them factory-direct, straight from The One. I don't mourn because I lack nothing. Any love we had on earth I *still* have through original source."

Amanda frowned but didn't reply.

"I know it is hard to grasp with your mind. Look into your heart, Mandy. Do you feel a hole there?"

After a moment's thought she replied. "No. There is no hole in my heart. The Man of Light fills it, and my heart knows that he always will."

"And there is no hole in my heart, either. So, since you are full, and don't need to have her to be full; and she is free, and chose not to be here; can you honor her choice as The One did, and so honor The One who gave her that choice?"

"My heart can, yes," she finally stated, "and it does. I can see that everything that could be done has been, and that The

Man of Light even gave up his own spark to offer her a chance at life. And truth here is a friend, not an executioner. But my mind—maybe it is still too full of earth."

"Then let your heart lead you," her father smiled. Then Amanda realized that as they were talking, Jesus had disappeared, and it was just the two of them again. Just family.

The Question of Suffering

Amanda stood and stretched. Not because she was stiff, but because stretching somehow felt appropriate after such a heavy topic. She looked down at her father (at the top of his head actually) and could see inside him. *I can see it: he has no lack, and no regret. But still…*

"Poppy, how are people on earth ever supposed to understand this? I can accept it with heaven in my heart, with The Man of Light sitting on my one side and the person I loved best in all the world on the other. But down there…

"I agree," he replied, nodding. "It can't be understood in four dimensions. Theologians and philosophers have struggled for generations with questions like the fate of the lost, or the problem of suffering, and no one has ever come up with really satisfactory answers."

"I never did," Amanda admitted.

"Here's something funny," he added, brightening. "In all those years of searching, no one seems to have ever thought to ask the question behind the question. 'Hey, Son of Man: we've been looking for an answer to the problem of suffering for centuries without an adequate response. Could it be that you're trying to tell us something by your silence? Are you ever going to answer this question on earth?'"

"He would have said, 'no,'" Amanda laughed immediately.

"Right! Scholars and authors would have saved themselves a lot of mental anguish—and whole forests' worth of paper to boot."

"I like it," Amanda replied, still amused. "I'm picturing myself as a bible school student or apprentice nun, raising my hand while all the rest are arguing about some great theological conundrum. And I say, 'Has anybody ever thought to ask Jesus if he's going to answer this question...'"

"Imagine the frustration!" Theo giggled. "Trust: An answer so simple a child can grasp it. And it has been right there all along."

"Ah, we're back to trust!" Amanda sighed, taking a seat next to her father again. "We've talked so much about it, but my head still is mystified. I guess you can't learn it conceptually, or even vicariously—you have to take the risk yourself, and experience that The Maker can be trusted."

"Just like at the cliff," Theo stated matter-of-factly. "Instead of assigning us a textbook about God that we couldn't read and would never understand, we got a *relationship* with a fellow human we could learn to trust: The Man of Light. It was actually a pretty good plan."

22 The Center

"Now, I think it is time for you to head to the fountain and rejoin Jesus." Theo stood, with one of those pleasurable, cat-like stretches you do when you get up in the morning. "It comes to me that The Man of Light waits for you there."

"Which fountain are we talking about?"

"THE fountain. The one at the center of heaven. The source of the River."

"Oh!" Amanda exclaimed, suddenly excited. "I saw it when Jesus showed me the city—from way up high in the air. I am SO ready!"

"Very well! Take my hand, and we'll visualize landing on the steps just outside the colonnade. Ready?"

"Ready!" Amanda answered, grinning.

"And—GO!" Theo cried. And vanished. All that was left in the hall were the echoes of his voice bouncing between soaring walls and a faint violet train of light hanging in midair.

They landed at the foot of a staircase, twenty-one steps ascending to a broad plaza fronting the colonnade. Paved with what looked like veined marble, each stone was laced with the same silver threads Amanda had first noticed in the museum. *The tapestry must be a theme. You see it everywhere!* Amanda decided.

The huge, gently-curving piazza was dotted with leafy arbors, each with several chairs or benches beneath. These intimate alcoves were available for conversation, repose or contemplation of the glories ahead. Twining vines sprouting lustrous, dark-green leaves shaded the booths with light, while drooping clusters of every variety of grape kept refreshment close at hand.

Little knots, mid-sized groups and occasional large crowds of gleaming star-people were scattered over the plaza. Apparently, this was a popular gathering place. Those who had recently emerged from the inner sanctum where the fountain cascaded into the pool were easily distinguishable—they sparkled as if they'd been dipped in star-dust.

The staircase before them was arranged in a pattern: two normal steps, then a landing, then two more steps. Climbing that way put Amanda in a reflective mood. *It forces you to slow down, to move deliberately. To think about where you are and what you are doing. It's kinda reverent, in its own way.*

"You know, the Southern Steps leading up to Herod's temple in Jerusalem were the built on the same plan," Theo said, responding to her thought. "Another example of how craftsmen on earth unknowingly mimicked heaven."

Approaching the portico, the true size of its gargantuan columns became apparent. They were twice as wide at the base as she was tall, soaring upward so far that Amanda had to crane her neck to take in the spring of the great arches joining them. Above the entablature, sunbeams blazed outward through the high air, angling up from where the fountain sprayed luminance into heaven's sky.

A Burning One stood to one side of the gateway as they approached, greeting each of the Children of Light with a few words of recognition (he seemed to know every name) as they passed. While his body flickered in and out of view like a campfire in the wind, the eyes were motionless embers. Through the arch behind him Amanda espied the final roadway she'd seen from far away, paved in gold. The lush, lower branches of the Trees of Life bent over the pavement, wet with mist from the central Fountain hidden behind their silvery leaves.

When she was mere paces from the threshold, the angel stretched out an arm toward her, palm outward. He spoke a command. "Here you must halt, dearest Amanda, child of destiny. The time has not yet come for you to enter into glory."

Hearing "no" in this land of "yes" took her so aback that Amanda stopped dead, looking up at him in wordless confusion. Finally, she managed an answer: "Huh?"

The angel repeated his instruction, then turned to Theo. "You are welcome to come in, great Curator, famous in forgiveness! The Prince of Heaven comes to speak with your daughter personally."

"Very well!" Theo answered the angel, then whispered to Amanda, "You got your wish—one-on-one time with The Man of Light." Then he strode forward through the archway, turning to wave goodbye as he passed out of sight.

Your Majesty

Turning back to the angel, Amanda had just opened her mouth to ask another question when the Burning One's eyes refocused beyond her shoulder. He reverently dropped to one knee. "Your Majesty," he said, bowed his head briefly then raising it, "I have intercepted your daughter at the gate, and she awaits you."

"Thank you, faithful Uriel. The presence be with you."

"And with you." For just a fraction of a section the angel seemed to be moving in place, as if a great wind swept through a fire and stretched the flames into long, horizontal trails of sparks. Then he disappeared, leaving Amanda still gazing through the archway.

The Man of Light walked up behind and placed an affectionate hand on her shoulder. "Lovely, isn't it?"

"Beyond anything I could have imagined," she sighed, peering between the columns. Taking one last look at the source of the River, the dwelling place of The One, the Center of heaven, she turned to face The Man of Light. And realized that gazing in his eyes was seeing the same thing.

He took both of her hands in his, wearing a friendly expression. "My Amanda! You are beautiful, swift in insight, wise in the ways of trust. And you carry the light of heaven in your eyes. I see before me creation as it was always meant to be."

Amanda smiled in gratitude, yet uttered no words. It was a solemn moment, and the message of the angel told her something decisive was about to happen.

"Now we face a difficult transition," The Man of Light said earnestly. "Shall we sit and discuss it in private?"

"Certainly," she answered. Taking her arm, he led her to the nearest arbor. The foliage parted as they approached, to reveal a pair of curved, ivory benches facing a bright, golden bowl. It rested on a matching ivory table (*about the size of a nightstand,* Amanda noted) that stood waist-high. Half again as wide as the span from her elbow to her fingertips, the inside of the bowl was a perfectly-smooth half-circle, without mark or feature. A delicate, incised tracery of trees, vines and fruits decorated the outer surface.

Hanging over the far rim was a curved silver spigot, depositing a stream of living water the diameter of her little finger just inside the bowl's outer edge. But instead of flowing straight down to the bottom, the water went sideways, defying gravity. It spiraled round and round the smooth surface of the bowl until finally joining a sapphire pool at the bottom. The spiral maintained its shape without walls or channel—*like the River of Life, which needs no banks,* she thought. It wasn't until Jesus pointed her to the ceiling that she understood the bowl's allure.

Golden light poured from its inner surface. Wherever that light intersected the spiraling thread of living water, it was refracted as if with a prism, illuminating the leafy roof above with a dozen whirling rainbows, crossing and intermingling in millions of hues. The display was mesmerizing.

Before he sat, Jesus leaned over and lightly touched half-a-dozen spots on the inside of the bowl with his fingertip. Immediately the stream reconfigured itself. In some places a round bubble formed over Jesus' fingerprint and the coiled lines flowed around it (making a lobe of color on the roof like Jupiter's Great Red Spot). Others created miniature whorls and eddies within the larger spirals.

"Now watch this," he added with a grin. Grasping the rim between a thumb and forefinger, he lightly spun the bowl.

"Ooooh!" Amanda uttered in fascinated awe. The prismatic light played gaily across the leaves, creating wheels within spinning wheels of color, a glorious display. "It's looks like 'Starry Night' by Van Gogh, if all the colors were in motion. You're quite the artist, you know."

"Thanks," Jesus replied as he sat down next to her. "You're right about Starry Night, by the way: it always reminded me of this. When humans create, they function in the image of The Creator. Art often speaks truly about heaven—at least when the artist is attempting to capture beauty, and not just use paint to conjure up fame and fortune."

They sat in silence for a few moments, drinking in the light show. "Why did the angel stop me at the gateway?" Amanda finally asked.

"That's what I wanted to speak to you about," Jesus said, twisting his torso to look over at her. "You arrived here under unusual circumstances— 'on a technicality,' as your father puts it, because your experiment on earth threw you into hyperspace. It's why you've had such a singular experience—no other visitor before you has seen heaven in as many dimensions. You've beheld her with heaven's eyes, not just those of earth.

"Even so, you've not seen it all: the glory dimension is still beyond you, for example. You see heaven as it really is in some ways, and only as it looks from earth in others.

"Now, no one in human history has passed beyond these porticos and returned to earth, save for me. Father's wish is that it remains that way. That's why you were stopped: He really likes treating me like I'm special. Just like you are special to me!" At that he smiled endearingly. "So this journey must end now, while you are still able to return."

"Return where? Do I need to leave the city and go back to the countryside? Where do you want me to go?"

"Back to your old life. To earth," he said simply, looking at her compassionately with a touch of…not quite regret.

"To earth?" Amanda repeated, jerking backward involuntarily. *But…that life is over and done with. My heart has left it far behind. To return now, after all I've seen and experienced and become…* Amanda's head spun.

"Yes, my darling. 'Parting is such sweet sorrow.' I've always been fond of that line—it's from Romeo and Juliette. I will experience the sorrows of earth through your experience, and you will live with the sorrow of being distant from true reality. From your side of the mirror, I will seem hidden. Yet here in the timeless realm we will never be apart, because even when you are not consciously aware of me, I will *always* be conscious of *you.* However, this sorrowful parting is still sweet, because our next reunion will be even more wonderful."

"Oh, Jesus!" Amanda exclaimed in a trembling voice. "Back to earth means back to the crippled, four-dimensional me, the me that sees the surface of a person without seeing the heart, the me that can barely think straight. It means a head full of anxiety and fear, loneliness and depression…I don't know if I could bear it!"

"You cannot without my help. But don't fear! I've got you. You have not yet had a drought from the Fountain of Life—indeed, that would have made your stay permanent. Yet I will wash your brow with that water, which will give you the grace for what will come."

Amanda stood and paced beside the low table, prisms of light playing across her face as she moved. As the golden bowl's rotation slowed, its splashes of light coursed over her torso like rolling waves. She finally halted, looking silently down at the bowl. Still trying to absorb the implications of returning to four dimensions.

"But won't I lose half of me?" she asked, looking across at him. "I have come alive in heaven's space and time, and now I am too big to be crammed back into an earthly body. Is that even possible?"

"Normally, it's not. But, since you got here on a technicality," he said, eyes sparkling, "I'll just have to send you back on one. You were partly outside of the temporal universe when you arrived here, and your body was broken by that transition. I will put you back together again."

"But...how do you know this will work?" Amanda wasn't afraid, sitting there in the same room with The Man of Light. But she could see fear in the distant dark, lurking.

Falling

"Dearest, don't fall back on knowing to protect your heart. That would truly be going backward. Trust me and I will catch you, just like I did at the cliff."

He rose and walked to the now-stationary golden bowl on the white table, still pouring out its glorious light. Reaching out with both hands, he drew all his fingertips straight across the bowl's inner surface at once, from the far side of the rim where Amanda stood back to himself. The flowing water immediately realigned in eight parallel, sparkling streams. The Man of Light smiled, nodded to Amanda and pointed up.

Projected on the ceiling above was a river of light, a glowing bridge flowing across the leafy roof from Amanda to The Man of Light. Eight brilliant threads of enchanting light bathed his face, and she understood the picture: the bridge of trust joining heaven and earth.

"I brought you here because this arbor displays how heaven sees our relationship. You and I stand on opposite sides of the bowl: in different realities, with a great gulf fixed in between. I dwell in the dimensions of heaven, while the physical you is a scion of earth. What spans the chasm between your perception and mine is trust," he said expansively, raising his arms toward the bridge of light streaming across the ceiling. "I trusted my Father enough to put aside heaven and fall to earth, just as you trusted me enough to hurdle off the cliff and fall into heaven."

"And you caught me," Amanda stated, focusing on his eyes. They seemed to anchor her heart in that moment when everything around her was shaking.

"Yes, I caught you. That Great Leap of trust has given you what you need to do as I once did and fall to earth, trusting that I'll catch you once more. Armed with trust, I know that you'll make it, and make me proud. Because I trust *you*, Amanda. Even as The One trusted me when I walked the hard road from heaven down to earth."

"What was it like?" Amanda wondered.

Jesus looked away, lost in thought, as the majestic procession of light continued its march across the living canopy above.

"I had to strip myself of heaven's dimensions," he remembered, speaking quietly, "and undergo the Great Disrobing. With the guidance of The One I took off my glory, and wore the plain and the physical. I detached myself from the River, and accepted a tiny spark of biological life in its place. And I who made the earth and designed every molecule submitted myself to its laws of nature. I made gravity my master, and crops my sustenance, and even obeyed the rule of death."

"Oh…" was all Amanda could manage. She saw it in her mind, saw him start to descend…

"I had the privilege of being a defenseless infant, dependent on others to feed me, change my diaper, burp me. I, who held the stars in their courses, became reliant on what I'd made to nurture me."

Still looking in his eyes, Amanda was surprised to see that his face shone not with grief or loss but with…fulfillment? Satisfaction?

He smiled. "You see correctly. The Plan worked: the whole darned thing."

In his eyes Amanda began to see images, like a movie playing memories of majesty and humility. In the glorious light of heaven, a being of still-greater light came down the steps of the Fountain of Life, taking his stand on the shores of the shining lake. He was resplendent, clothed in searing white and burning gold. He wore love and authority on his sleeve, his visage the very definition of honor. Heaven was his kingdom, and every denizen of that land delighted in being his subjects. The fountain rumbled his praise. The Trees of Life sang, branches bowing to their Maker. Ten thousand, thousand Burning Ones stood at attention atop the great portico around the epicenter of heaven, saluting their commander.

Then, to the astonishment of the angels, The Prince knelt by the crystal sea and began setting aside his honor and stature. A gasp went up from the throng, and then they were silent, as the stars surrounding his head like a crown fell into the lake. The song of the grass and the trees ceased, and all heaven was silent but for the roaring water. The Man of Light appeared smaller now. The majesty on his brow dimmed as he let his right to exercise omnipotent power slip into the sapphire pool; then his birthright of omniscient wisdom, and then his timelessness. As he removed each of heaven's dimensions, the water buoyed them up, lifting it back up the steps of the fountain and into The One. Kept in trust, where his Father and partner awaited his return.

Watching, Amanda could feel the stripping. A tearing, rending sensation, as if a part of you that had always been there was surgically removed, without anesthesia. And after it was over, only a numbness, a memory of the good that once was living reality. Like a phantom limb for an amputee.

Then the man reached into himself and removed a golden bowl—Amanda couldn't see quite how—brimming over with a radiant liquid that shone like the sun. The overwhelming luminosity lit up the sky and danced on the spray from the fountain as The Son of God raised his bowl to The One in a gesture of honor and submission. Then he slowly poured his life into the lake. As he did, the light in him dimmed and almost went out…

Amanda turned away, covering her eyes, and nearly wept. It was almost too much to bear, even in heaven.

Then she felt a hand on her shoulder, and with it a rush of peace entered her, spreading from that shoulder through her whole body. Looking up, she saw him smile.

"That was a hard day and a beautiful day, when The Son of God took the form of a son of man, and stood naked before the brightness of heaven." He reached over and gently wiped a tear from Amanda's eyes. "It was all worth it, though—every bit of it. In the end, The One gave it all back to me."

"Gave what back?" Amanda sniffled.

"Every ability, attribute and dimension I laid down that day was entrusted to his keeping. When I died and returned to his side, he restored all that I'd removed in order to fit within earth's orbit—with interest! The acclaim I walked in before is but a shadow of what I bear now, because the sacrifice I made to unite all things in Us is transformed into glory in heaven."

"Like the Mona Lisa and the fire hydrant," Amanda

remembered.

"A new dimension of glory," Jesus laughed. "It will be the same with you."

"But you're still the same person, right? I…I guess what I'm really asking is, will I still be me when I take heaven off and go back to earth?"

"You will be you. It's the soul that makes you who you are, not the body. Same with me: it's not the attributes of God that make me one with him, but the heart. Knowing everything does not make me God, or being everywhere, or even being all-powerful. I am God because I am one heart with my Father, and he with me. I am The Son no matter what form I choose to take, because my relationship with him remains.

"It's just like on earth, really—you are your father's daughter whether you live at home or go off to college. I was The Son before I took off those attributes, I was The Son when I was a newborn on earth, and I am still very much The Son now. And you will always be my Sister no matter where you are, in that exact same way."

She took a deep breath, steadying herself, then let it out with a whoosh. "Alright. I believe you. I will do it," Amanda said plainly. Then she stepped over and knelt in front of him beside the golden bowl. "You are my King, The Prince of Heaven, and I trust you for…well, everything. I owe you my life, my love, and everything I have and am." And then she looked up in his face and saw him smiling at her. "But I'd really, really like a hug right now."

And standing there under the light-bridge of trust pouring from the golden bowl, their embrace was long and deep.

Last Words

"Um, if it's not too much to ask…" Amanda began haltingly.

"Actually, it is far too little to ask," Jesus chuckled, "when everything here is yours. Yes, we will say goodbye to your dad before you go! He is wading in the crystal sea under the Trees of Life, but he's already heard my call and is coming to the gate to meet us. Just like on earth," Jesus added with a smile. "'Before you call to me, I will answer.'"

"Thanks. I appreciate that—a lot."

Taking her hand, Jesus led her to the arbor's entrance. As they passed the table, Jesus spoke a word to the golden bowl, and the water immediately returned to its original course, spiraling down the inside to the pool at the bottom. With one last upward glance at the marvelous, wheeling luminosity playing on the canopy of leaves, Amanda stepped out onto the plaza, arm-in-arm with her Prince.

The scene appeared much as it did before—the rank of gateways looming over the piazza curved off into the distance, with light pouring through each opening. Knots of moving stars crossed the pavement on every side—the Children of Light, come to soak in the presence of The One. Jesus began picking his way through the crowd toward the nearest entrance, nodding and smiling to others as they passed. Meanwhile. Amanda was mustering up the courage to pose the question pinballing around in her brain.

"It's okay," Jesus replied, still focused on navigating the crowd. "You can ask."

"So, um, did taking all that off hurt?" she finally asked. "It felt like that when I watched it—there was this terrible tearing sensation."

"Yes," Jesus stated matter-of-factly. "Humanity has grasped, at least in part, what it cost me to be tortured to death on a Roman stake. But few have pondered what I endured for the sake of love by becoming human." Then he shrugged, grinning across at her as if remembering a joke. "But then, giving up the life of heaven was good preparation for yielding my spark of biological life on earth."

"Will it hurt like that when I go back?" Amanda asked.

"Oh, child!" Jesus suddenly turned to face her. "Do not fear! When I put your spirit back into your body, you will be unconscious, both physically and spiritually. You will not feel the stripping as it happens. But your leg is broken pretty badly, in several places, and so are your ribs. One of your lungs has collapsed, too," he stated matter-of-factly. "All that is going to hurt for a good while. When you recall the unmarred joy of heaven, you'll miss it fiercely—and that's also a wound. But I've got a little secret that will help you."

"And that is?"

"Heaven is not a place—it is a person. Heaven is Us! And because you have chosen Us, we have already come and started building ourselves a room in the house of your spirit. You literally carry piece of heaven around with you wherever you go!

"So when you miss the Beautiful Land, call to me, and I'll answer. It works the same on earth as it does here. Yes, the mirror of time stands between us, but trust can bridge the gap. We'll get through this together, just like Father and I did when I landed on earth."

Glory

They'd come to the very threshold of the gate, and Amanda rested a hand on the giant column towering up right next to them. The dark green vines winding up it were similar to those covering the arbor. Great, golden grapes in huge clusters (*as big as Christmas ornaments,* Amanda thought idly) drooped from every branch.

"They call it the golden vine," Jesus explained, reaching up to pick a pair of succulent fruits. Popping the first in his open mouth, he handed the other to Amanda. It positively melted on her tongue.

"A copy of this vine hung over the gateway of my temple in Jerusalem, wrought in pure gold out of donations to the treasury. I saw it there at Passover.

"Oh, Jerusalem, Jerusalem!" he sighed. "Most of those who contributed golden grapes did it for the acclaim of their peers. What a cheap substitute for the glory of heaven! We have far better rewards here. When you come back to me, and I initiate you into the glory dimension…in some ways, you'll hardly recognize yourself."

The sensation of that magnificent grape still lingered on Amanda's palate, a fading remnant of the eruption of flavor that hit her taste buds when she first bit into it. "Tell me more about glory."

"Okay," Jesus replied. "On earth, it's mere words. Real glory—the kind given in heaven—is part of your heavenly body. You have a lifetime of love and service ahead of you; so when you return, your heavenly body will be changed by it. Remember when I showed you a little bit of your dad's glory? You'll look like that."

Amanda sat down on the low base of the column, a square section about knee-high that jutted out from its round bulk. "And what about her?" Amanda asked, pointing to a stately woman just passing outward through the gates, cheeks aglow from standing in the spray of the fountain. Her long hair flew like strands of fire behind her head. "What glory did her life earn?"

"Since you haven't entered the glory dimension, you can't see it—yet! I gave you a taste when I glorified your dad, but it was *only* a taste. Because your eyes were not alive to that dimension, what you saw were the human analogues of glory, not the thing itself. Your memory recorded words of praise from me, a royal robe, a crown, a sense of awe—that kind of thing. Right?"

"Yes," Amanda mouthed, feeling a bit chastened.

"It's okay, darling," Jesus replied, taking her chin in hand and raising it to look into her eyes. "The picture you saw was real, and it was true. And yet, still merely a human portrait of heaven, seen from earth's side of the mirror. If you saw your father as he truly is in the glory dimension, as I see him now—well, any human would collapse at his feet and worship. He'd have to tell you not to! That's what usually happens when glory is revealed on earth."

Goodbyes

"Darn! I haven't seen it all, and now I have to go back," Amanda concluded, with resignation. "Bummer."

"A better way to say it is that even with all the beauty and goodness you've experienced, there are still whole dimensions of heaven to explore! Even this will turn out for your good."

Amanda perked up. "Okay—I like putting it that way. But… I do have one little practical question."

"You wouldn't be Amanda without another question!" he laughed.

"So why me? I mean, you're telling me I got to experience things that no one else on earth has. But the experiment that brought me here was motivated by pride and hubris, not love! I'd have thought garnishing my pay would be a more appropriate response than a promotion. Why did you choose me?"

"Well, I was aware of the pride thing from the very beginning," Jesus answered, an amused look on his face. "I work *all* things for good, not just what comes from pure motives. If that was the criteria for helping you humans, I'd never help anyone!

"But as to why you were chosen," he continued gently, "you are looking for an answer that makes sense on earth. Earth arranges people in hierarchies, to determine who is most important, or most worthy of love, or most beautiful. It's the curse of twisted desire at work: trying to get your needs met by thinking you are better than someone else.

"Heaven makes no such comparisons. You are extra-special to me, in the same way Kathryn is, or your dad, or every other child of heaven. You were chosen because it pleased Father to choose you, that's all. His choice does not make you better or worse, or mean you are more or less deserving than others. You were chosen just as all are chosen."

At that moment one of the Children of Light strode out under the archway. He moved with the easy grace of a man who had a purpose to his step but was free of all hurry or anxiety. Stopping, he glanced around, as if seeking a loved one. Brown hair, dark eyes, and a white linen robe. Tall and straight in his integrity, clothed in love, perfect, pure and utterly secure in the acceptance of his Maker. The Light of life pouring out from him watered everyone for yards around.

The man's gaze met Amanda's, and he smiled in recognition. It was her dad. In a moment he stood beside her.

"Um, daddy…" When thc moment came, she didn't know what to say

"I know, pumpkin. The Voice told me you have to go. And you will miss me!" Then the laugh lines crossed his face. "But I will not miss you! Do you know why?"

"Um…because The Man of Light fills you?"

"That's true, but there is another, more satisfying reason. It's about time."

"Here we go again—what *about* time?"

"Don't you see? How much time has passed since you came to heaven?"

"Hmm," Amanda thought, noticing Jesus grinning next to her, like a prof who already knows the answer but is looking forward to watching you figure it out for yourself. "Well, I've kind of stopped thinking in terms of hours and minutes and seconds…"

"And why is that?" Theo coaxed.

"Because heaven is an Eternal Now—it's always the same day in heaven." Then she got it. Jesus smiled broadly at the exact, same instant. "Oh—you all live in the Now! Therefore, no matter how much time passes for me on earth, for you it will always be—"

"The same day!" Theo finished.

"The same day," Amanda echoed. "You'll never experience a day without me."

"Neither will I," Jesus added, beaming.

Then he spread his arms wide, and the three of them joined in a joyful, sober, intimate group hug, where their thoughts and emotions and stories mingled like the grapes of the City of God in heaven's wine.

Looking over the shoulder of The Man of Light, Amanda's gaze passed through the great archway, beyond the Trees of Life, and up the roaring cataract cascading endlessly down from the high seat of The One. Then, as if a door opened in the glowing air, she saw a throne, and One seated on the throne. He was the source of The Light, the River, and the Love which is the gravity of heaven. The fragrance of eternity touched her nostrils, and she drew in a breath of it in surprise and delight. There within the throne she saw a girl, all clothed in happiness, freedom and life, dancing across the sky with The Man of Light.

The girl turned, looking back through the cloud of glory. Amanda understood that she was seeing her true self, as The Man of Light had always beheld her: in the center of his love, joined forever to Jesus in the heart of The One. And she felt full, and content, and desired, and all was beauty and music and laughter.

Then everything went white.

23 Awake

There was a light. That was first. Watery and indistinct, it gradually sharpened into a cold, square glow. She was there and not there, her mind floating in and out of the light. The place was somehow familiar, and yet…

Her vision swam, blurring as she tried to focus on The Light above her. Blinking rapidly (it was strong enough to hurt her eyes) Amanda finally closed her eyelids. Things unexpectedly became dark, enough so that the ache in her eyes went away. Thinking about what she'd seen in those few seconds, she concluded she was lying down, inside some kind of box. *But why do my eyes hurt?*

She tried to open them again, but the bright rectangle above was too intense. *The Light never hurt me before when I gazed at him, even at his brightest. Why is he so hard to look at? And why does darkness overshadow the light when I close my eyes?*

She tried to tune into her other senses. There was a distasteful smell, a sort of alcohol-ish odor pervading the room. And such a dull, ordinary scent! It was so flat and one-dimensional that she wondered how such an odor ever found its way into heaven. It didn't belong. Amanda drew in a long breath (which seemed to make a lot of noise), but noted no delicious, laughing aroma of flowers or the green, springtime smell of the grass. No hint of the mist from the River of Life pouring excitement and energy into her. Only that one flat, boring, antiseptic smell.

It was only after a few more moments that she missed it. *Where was the music?*

The song of life always whispered in the background wherever one went. She strained to hear that comforting refrain, but instead of growing louder as she focused on it, the only sound was a faint humming noise, toneless and monotonous, with no melody at all. *It sounds like machinery—but there's no machinery in heaven, is there? At least none I ever saw. Heaven is all music and melody, but for some reason I can't hear it. And why am I in a box?*

Then she became aware of her leg. Pain. It hovered in the background, a deep, dull ache that ran from her toes to her hip. And instead of molding to her body, what she lay on created spots of discomfort that seemed to penetrate her bones.

How can I be in pain? There is no pain here! Instinctively she focused on her leg, assuming that by doing so her body would tell her the story of where this pain came from. She heard nothing. No story, no insight—just the ache.

A feeling welled up from her gut—an agitated tension that contracted her stomach muscles, making the leg hurt even more. Her heart began to pound. Fear. She was afraid.

How can this be happening? her racing mind protested. *There is no fear in heaven—I left that behind at the edge of the cliff! But I feel it all the same. There is nothing in the Beautiful Land that can hurt me, but I feel pain. Why won't my body tell me its story? Why does the light hurt my eyes? Where are the amazing, multi-dimensional scents from the garden of God? Why don't I feel life flowing into me every time I take a breath?*

Sharp, new sounds—a click, a creak, and a rush of air—interrupted her thoughts. She heard a voice. But it didn't sound or feel at all like The Voice she knew so well. Instead of overflowing with peace, joy and acceptance, this voice was clipped, businesslike, clinical.

"Okay, honey, time to check your IVs."

She heard footsteps, then a shadow passed in front of the light. Amanda flinched involuntarily. She hadn't seen a shadow in forever. Immediately the voice spoke again, seeming surprised.

"Ohmygosh! You're awake! Honey, can you hear me?"

The light was still dimmed by some obstruction, so Amanda tentatively opened her eyes. A woman in a blue smock and a sort of matching blue skull-cap leaned over the bed, looking directly at her. She had a rectangle of plain, white fabric—it paled next to anything she'd seen in the Beautiful Land—across the lower part of her face, covering her nose and mouth.

Amanda didn't know her: didn't know her name, couldn't hear her story, knew nothing about who she was. All that was visible was the outer, impersonal, physical shell. A body, with graying hair, dark eyebrows and green eyes. That was all. She began to cry.

"It's okay, dear..." the woman looked at her clipboard. "Amanda. Amanda, you're okay, you're safe. Can you nod if you hear me?"

Amanda nodded.

"Are you in pain?"

You have no idea, Amanda thought darkly through her tears. It came to her that the woman in blue was a nurse—but not like the insight of heaven. It was just a memory connecting the present to a past event. Plain, dead, untouchable memory.

I'm in a hospital. A hospital on earth. *Oh, God, I'm back on earth!* She cried harder, increasing the pain in her leg.

"I'm going to go get the doctor, okay honey? I'll be back in just a minute."

A minute. There are no minutes in heaven. I'm trapped again in earth time, doomed to just one moment after another after another. Unable to go back and relive the joys of my past. Only ever in one place, missing out on everything else because there is only one dimension of time. Vulnerable to aging. And to pain, fear, disappointment, rejection…

"Jesus!" she cried out in anguish. But The Man of Light didn't appear at her side, with his comforting smile and electric touch. No life-light poured from his being to make a circle of honor in the grass at his feet. There was only pain, fear—and now a touch of despair. Because she was still crying, it took her a moment to recognize the little voice inside her head.

"I'm still here."

The Voice was faint and muffled, but it sounded familiar.

"Sorry I can't be there in the flesh. Just remember—I can be with you whenever I want, even when you aren't even thinking of me. And I always *want to be with you."*

Her heart began to quiet down as it ingested those words, just as it did on the cliff at the edge of heaven. Now she knew for sure: The Voice *was* speaking inside her, there but not visible.

Jesus, I don't know if I can do this! I feel dis-membered, like parts of me are missing.

"I know what you mean. I felt just like that when I came to earth."

How can I ever face existing in this barren world after being in heaven? Coming back feels like dying all over again! No tree here will ever look green, no flower will seem beautiful ever again. To live with the fear and pain and grief I left behind—how will I keep from drowning in despair?

Then she felt something. An object in her hand, cool to the touch, smooth, weighty. With a great effort she lifted it above her torso *(what happened to my poor arm?)* and turned her neck slowly until her hand came into view. She could no longer see through her fingers—she had to open them to glimpse the polished black stone cradled in her palm. Flipping it over with her thumb, she read the word carved into the other side: 'despair.'

"Step off the edge; and I will catch you."

Then she remembered. After a few last sniffles she began breathing normally again, and the corners of her mouth turned up. At that moment a doctor bustled into the room, the nurse in tow. Taking a deep breath, Amanda whispered, "Okay. I will trust you." Her hand was extended out over the side of the bed, away from the door and the doctor. Dropping it back behind her torso, she opened her fingers and let go of the black stone. It vanished before it hit the floor.

Epilogue

"What happened to the stone?" I asked, genuinely curious.

"After I got well enough to get out of bed, I took a quick glance underneath," Amanda answered matter-of-factly. "But there was nothing there. I guess I kinda expected that."

"Okay," I replied with finality, closing my laptop and standing to stretch my arms (it's a weird affliction, but typing for too long at once hurts my shoulders). "That's all the questions I have for the moment. I should have the first draft done in a week or so."

Amanda drained her coffee mug and rose as well, a hint of stiffness still showing in her leg. The sunlight streaming through the window highlighted the scar on her forehead, faded a bit more since we last spoke but still visible.

"Thanks Jamarcus. It means a lot to me that you were willing to do this."

"My pleasure," I replied, and that was the genuine truth.

"You know, I do have one more question," I added. "This probably won't make it into the book, but—how has this whole experience changed the way you live now?"

A distant look came into Amanda's eyes. She lowered herself back into the armchair and kept silent for a long moment, as shadows from the venetian blinds slanted across her face. I got the distinct impression that all of her wasn't there in the room. Maybe a piece of Amanda still walked the Beautiful Land.

"I'm not afraid anymore," she finally stated. "That's a big thing. Not of death, or of life, or of trust. I've mostly stopped second-guessing myself and waiting for the other shoe to drop. And I don't obsess about the future and getting every decision right like I used to. He likes it when I choose."

Swiveling to look me in the eye, she spoke with conviction. "And I quit being bitter about the past. How could I, when everything I thought I'd lost was found in the Beautiful Land? My daddy is there, basking inside love. Someday when I die again, I'll rejoin him at the exact, same moment I left. I have no fear of missing out, since he'll never experience a day without me! Yup, every desire and every good thing I long for is waiting for me there in the lopsided grin of The Man of Light. Oh, I just remembered: his nose is crooked! You should put that in someplace."

I nodded, waiting for her to continue.

"Actually," she added, "probably the biggest difference is I lost my ambition."

"Your inhibitions?" I repeated, mishearing.

"No, no!" she laughed. "My *ambition.* My need to accomplish—to justify my existence by what I produce. Our whole culture simply *marinates* in the desire to be someone and to do something to prove our value. We dress it up in words like 'following your destiny,' or 'pursuing your life purpose'—as if we need to change God's world for him. What will satisfy our hearts isn't changing the world, but being his."

"But aren't we Christians *supposed* to change the world?" I asked incredulously, unable to get my head around the idea of following God without busying myself doing God's work.

Amanda thought for half a moment before answering. "Hmm…I can't recall Jesus ever saying that when I was with him in heaven. Or reading it anywhere in the bible. No, it's his world to change. When we take over and try to do his job for him, we just make a mess!"

"So then," I replied, admittedly a bit exasperated. "What *are* we supposed to do with our lives?"

"Oh Jamarcus— 'supposed to' is such a restrictive phrase for what is freedom itself in the Beautiful Land!"

She looked away for a few seconds. "I sure wish we had

better words for this on earth," she muttered to herself with a shake of her head, then looked back at me.

"What he asks of me is simple: to love my neighbors. That little circle of people who are dear to me or who come across my path. That's all," she ended with a smile. "Not to change the world, but to love the ones in *my* world: people like you."

At that, it seemed we were finished for the day. I watched idly as she rose out of the chair, reaching down for her sweater.

Suddenly, for the tiniest instant, it seemed the very air in the room was rent in two. A flash of color and light and music burst in, bathing the walls and blowing off the ceiling. For that one nanosecond I was on the other side, and glimpsed the Amanda of heaven. Laughing as she danced with The Man of Light. Swallowed in bliss. Clothed in purity. Free in the presence of The One, in love with the Prince of Heaven and he with her. Inside love, forever found and never to be lost.

Then The Voice entered my mind. *Love is everything, Jamarcus. It's the only thing. Great exploits don't make you great in heaven, but loving what We love. Loving people like you.*

And the vision was gone.

It took maybe ten seconds for me to regain my wits after that. When the room finally settled back into focus, the first thing I noticed was Amanda staring down at me, a curious expression on her face. She must have seen something in my eyes, because a broad smile erupted on her face.

"Aah—he gave you a little taste of eternity, didn't he?"

"Yeah," I answered, gulping like a fish.

"Excellent! And what did he tell you?"

"That love is everything. And he loves people like me."

She laughed loudly. "Yup—that sounds like him!"

Start a Book Club

Meet with friends and enjoy The Heaven Experience together! Leading a group is easy and fun with our free book club outlines. They include discussion questions, imagination exercises to help your group envision heaven, schedules, and more. Get them at: www.HeavenExperience.net/bookclub

Converse with The Man of Light

Deepen your connection with these resources:

- The free *Questions for Jesus Mobile App* offers dozens of questions to ask The Man of Light, instrumental music to play while you listen, and a journal to record what you hear. Available for iPhone on the Apple App Store, or Android on the Google Play store.
- The *Questions for Jesus* book features 52 meditations with five questions each that ask The Man of Light to speak to your deepest desires. Find it on Amazon or our store at www.Store.Meta-Formation.com
- Join an on-line *Questions for Jesus Course* to jump-start your conversation with God, overcome obstacles to hearing or learn to help others on the journey. Courses feature small cohorts, high-interaction, trained facilitators, and lots of practice time. Visit www.meta-formation.com/how-to-confidently-hear-god/

Pay it Forward

We gift thousands of copies of this book to people who need the hope of heaven—and you can join in the fun! You can donate books to send to spiritual seekers and those who've suffered grief and loss, or even support a translation to another language. Visit www.HeavenExperience.net/donate

Become a Partner
We donate books through partners, where there is a personal connection. If you loved the book and have contacts among the suffering and the seekers, you can sign up to give free books away. Visit: www.HeavenExperience.com/partner

Get Heaven's Perspective on YOUR Life

- Get a Personal Heaven Story
  Our team takes the most difficult experiences in life and rewrites them from Heaven's Perspective. If you've ever wanted to know what God was doing in your adversity, here's your chance! Visit: www.HeavensPerspcctive.com
- Get the *Heaven's Perspective* Book
  Learn how God redeemed betrayal, grief, abuse, and more in sixteen real-life heaven-stories created by our team. On Amazon or www.Store.Meta-Formation.com

Heaven in the Bible
These free, bite-size videos highlight key concepts in the book and show you where they are grounded in scripture. Find them at www.HeavenExperience.net/videos

Get to Know the Human Jesus
How to Read the Bible Like a Human Being is an innovative way to study the story of Jesus in the New Testament, letting scripture renew your emotional brain instead of only your head. It really brings the bible to life! Learn more or join an on-line study at www.LikeaHumanBeing.com. Or get the book on Amazon.

Made in the USA
Las Vegas, NV
18 December 2025